8-16(15)
12-18(17)

W9-BCD-209

THE MURDER MAN

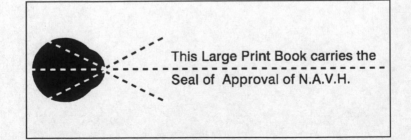

This Large Print Book carries the Seal of Approval of N.A.V.H.

THE MURDER MAN

TONY PARSONS

THORNDIKE PRESS

A part of Gale, Cengage Learning

GALE
CENGAGE Learning·

Farmington Hills, Mich • San Francisco • New York • Waterville, Maine
Meriden, Conn • Mason, Ohio • Chicago

GALE
CENGAGE Learning

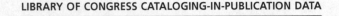

LIBRARY OF CONGRESS CATALOGING-IN-PUBLICATION DATA

Parsons, Tony, 1953–
    The murder man / by Tony Parsons. — Large print edition.
      pages ; cm. — (Thorndike Press large print crime scene)
      ISBN 978-1-4104-7537-4 (hardcover) — ISBN 1-4104-7537-9 (hardcover)
      1. Serial murder investigation—England—London—Fiction. 2. Large type
books. I. Title.
PR6066.A725M87 2014b
823'.914—dc23   2014036020

Published in 2015 by arrangement with St. Martin's Press, LLC

Printed in Mexico
1 2 3 4 5 6 7 19 18 17 16 15

*For David Morrison, Barry Hoy
and Kevin Steel.
Somewhere East of Suez.*

Crimes as serious as murder should have strong emotions behind them.

George Orwell,
The Decline of the English Murder

And nothing in life shall sever
The chain that is round us now.

Eton Boating Song

PROLOGUE

1988

When they had finished with her they left her face down on the mattress and it was as if she was already dead.

The pack of boys in the basement room, boys with the strength of men and the cruelty of children. They had taken all they wanted, and now it was as if there was nothing left.

Their voices were no longer in her face, leering above her, pressed hard against her ear. Now they were coming from the long dining table where they smoked and laughed and congratulated each other on what they had done.

There was her T-shirt. If she could only get her T-shirt. Somehow she found the strength to reach it, pull it on and roll from the mattress. She was not meant to stay in this room. She began to crawl towards the basement stairs.

The voices at the table fell silent. The pipe, she thought. The pipe makes them slow and stupid and sleepy. God bless the pipe.

There was blood in her mouth and her face hurt. Everything hurt. The blood was coming from her nose and it caught in her throat and made her choke back the sickness.

She stopped, gagged, then began to move again.

The muscles in her legs were heavy slabs of pain. Nothing worked as it should. Nothing felt like it would ever work again.

Everything was ruined.

She could have wept with frustration. But she bit back the tears and gritted her teeth and kept edging to the door, an inch at a time, no more than that, feeling the torn skin on her elbows and knees as she dragged them across the basement floor, doing it again and again and again.

There was evil in this room.

But she was not meant to die tonight.

She was not meant to die in this room.

At first she thought they hadn't noticed. Because of what the pipe did to them. Because of the way the pipe made them slow and stupid. God bless the pipe. Then she stopped to rest at the foot of the stairs and she heard their laughter.

And when she looked, she saw they were all watching her, and that they had been watching all along.

Some of them gave her a round of mocking applause.

Then the one who had been the worst, the fat one who had talked to her all the time, and called her names, and taken pleasure in hearing her cry out, and left his marks on her from tooth and nail — the worst bastard in that bunch of rotten bastards — he yawned widely, revealing a mouth full of expensive orthodontic work, and said, 'We can't just let her go, man.'

She took a deep breath and placed the palms of her hands on the bottom step.

There was something wrong with her breathing. Because of her nose.

A single bead of livid red blood fell on to the back of her hand.

She ran her fingers across her top lip and with great effort struggled from her hands and knees on to her feet, leaning against the wall, closing her eyes and longing for sleep.

The pain revived her.

And the fear.

And the presence of the boy.

One of them was standing right next to her, a look of wicked amusement on his face. The one who had spoken to her first, and stopped her with a smile, and pretended to be nice, and brought her to this place.

Now he took a fistful of her hair and pulled her head to one side. Then, tightening his grip as he turned away, he began to drag her from the stairs and back into the room, that underground room where she was not meant to die.

Without the prompting of conscious thought, her hands flew to his face and she pressed her thumbs into his eye sockets as hard as she could.

Deep and deep and deep.

His turn to feel the pain.

Rotten bastards. Rotten bastards the lot of them.

The two of them stood there, locked together in the intimacy of dance partners, his fist still in her hair while she summoned all her remaining strength to push into the mocking blue eyes, her fingers with their nails cracked and bloody and suddenly stinging as she scrabbled for purchase in his thick black hair, gripping his ears, losing the grip, finding it again, pushing the thumbs deeper, then her left hand falling away as he reeled backwards with a rising shriek of agony, lashing out at her, and missing, but her right thumb still there, still pushed into his left eye socket as he tried to shove her away, her thumb pressing against his eyeball for a few more crucial seconds until she suddenly felt it give with a soft wet squelch and sink towards the back of his head.

He screamed.

His scream filled the basement, filled her head, filled the night. They were on their feet at the table but paralysed by the screams of the boy who had just lost an eye.

Then she ran.

How she ran.

Flying up the stairs.

The door locked from the inside but with the key mercifully still in the lock — *thank God for the key* — fumbling with it, the cries behind her, and then she was out into the air, stunned to find the night had almost gone.

How long had they kept her there?

In the distance was the road, on the far side of playing fields with a misty shroud hanging over the great white H-shapes of the rugby posts.

She began to run across the playing fields, the fog wet on her face, her bare feet sliding on grass slick with the dawn, and the beautiful buildings of the famous old school rising up black and timeless behind her.

She ran without looking back, expecting to hear their voices at any moment, waiting for the pack to come and run her down and rip her to pieces.

But they did not come.

On the far side of the playing fields there was a tiny stone cottage, as unlikely as a woodman's house in a fairy tale, but its lights were out and she made no attempt to run towards it. Instead she headed for the road. If she could make it to the road then she would not die tonight.

Halfway to the road, she rested against a rugby goalpost and dared to look back. They had not followed her.

A leather strap slapped against her side, and she remembered that at some point they had put a dog collar and lead around her neck. She tore them off and threw them aside.

A solitary car had stopped by the road, headlights on, engine running.

Someone had seen her.

She stumbled towards it, waving, calling, crying out for the car to please wait for her, don't-go-don't-go, running alongside a wire mesh fence, looking for a gap, the wet grass of the playing fields no longer under her bare feet, asphalt now, then through a hole in the fence and running on the road's rough tarmac, crying oh please don't go; and then the passenger door opened and the fat one got out, the one who had been the worst, his face not laughing now, but clenched with absolute murderous fury, and for the first time she knew with total certainty that she would die in this place tonight.

More of them were getting out of the car.

The fat one flipped open the boot and the black hole waited for her like an open grave.

Some part of her mind registered that someone was screaming in the back of the car, screaming about his eye.

The one she had hurt. The one she had blinded.

She wished she could have hurt them all. She wished she could have blinded them all. God knows they deserved it.

But it was too late. She was done now. She felt the weakness and exhaustion flood her body, overwhelming her. They had won.

Angry hands on her, touching her, squeezing the last juice out of her, and then the hands lifting her off the ground and forcing her into the boot of the car.

The lid slammed down on her and she was lost in darkness as the car drove slowly back to the grand old school where she would die on the mattress in the basement where she was never meant to die.

In her last moments she saw the family who would never see her again, and — beyond them, like a road briefly glimpsed but never taken — she saw quite clearly the husband she would never meet, and the children who would never be born, and the good life full of love that had been taken away.

And as her soul passed over, her last breath was a silent cry of rage and grief for everything they had stolen on the night she died.

OCTOBER
#KILLALLPIGS

1

I was waiting for a man who was planning to die.

I had parked the old BMW X5 just up the road from the entrance to the railway station and I drank a triple espresso as I watched the commuters rushing off to work. I drank quickly.

He would be here soon.

I placed three photographs on the dashboard. One of my wife and daughter. The other two of the man who was planning to die. A passport photo from the Home Office and what we called a snatch shot taken from some CCTV footage.

I slipped the photo of my family inside my wallet and put the wallet inside my leather jacket. Then I taped the two photos of the man who was planning to die to the dashboard.

And I watched the street.

I was parked with my back to the station

19

so I could face the busy main road. It was washed in thin autumn sunshine that was like a fading memory of summer days. One hundred metres away there was a young woman who was dressed for the gym looking in the window of the newsagent's, a large German Shepherd sitting patiently by her side, its lead loose, its intelligent face carefully watching her, the dog totally at ease among the rush hour crowds.

'Now that's a beautiful dog,' I said.

The woman smiled and scratched the back of the dog's ears in response, and then there was a man's voice in my ear, although he was not addressing me.

'Reception's good for Delta 1.'

Then there were more voices in my ear as they checked transmission for the other radio call signs and all over the surveillance chatter I could hear the studied calm that the police use at moments of extreme tension, like a pilot talking to his passengers when all his engines are on fire. Nothing at all to worry about, folks.

I scanned the street for the spotter vans and unmarked cars and plainclothes officers on foot. But they were good at their job. All I could see was the woman with the beautiful German Shepherd.

'Delta 1?' the surveillance officer said to

me. 'We see you and we hear you, Max. You're running point. We're waiting on your positive visual ID when Bravo 1 is in the grab zone. Stay in the car.'

Bravo 1 was the man who was planning to die.

'Copy that,' I said.

And then a voice I knew: 'DC Wolfe, it's the chief super.'

Detective Chief Superintendent Elizabeth Swire. My boss.

'Ma'am,' I said.

'Good luck, Wolfe,' she said. Then there was a little smile in her voice as she played to the gallery: 'And you heard the man. Stay in the car. Let the big boys do the heavy lifting.'

I stared at the street. It would not be long now.

'Ma'am,' I said, as nice and calm as the German Shepherd.

If I tilted my rear-view mirror I could look up at the grand Victorian façade of the station hotel. It was like a castle in a fairy story, the turrets and spires rising up to a blue sky full of billowy white clouds. The kind of place where you blink your eye and a hundred years go by. I could not see any of the big boys. But inside the railway station hotel there were enough of them to start a small war.

Somewhere beyond the net curtains and drapes, SCO19 were waiting, the firearms unit of the Metropolitan Police. Every one of them would be armed with a Heckler & Koch G36 assault rifle and two Glock SLP 9mm pistols. But no matter how hard I stared I still couldn't see them.

There would also be bomb disposal squads seconded from the RAF in there. Negotiators. Chemical and biological warfare specialists. And someone to order pizza. We also had maybe twenty people around the station but I could still only see the woman and the dog. The surveillance chatter continued.

'All units report. Echo 1?'

'No sign.'

'Victor 1?'

'Nothing.'

'Tango 1?'

'Contact,' said a woman's voice.

For the first time the piece of plastic stuffed in my ear was totally silent.

'I have visual with Bravo 1,' said the same voice. 'Contact.' And then a terrible pause. 'Possible,' she said. 'Repeat — possible contact.'

'Possible,' the surveillance officer said. 'Checking. Stand by.' His voice was winding tighter now.

And then the woman's voice again, and all the doubt creeping in: 'Possible. Red backpack. Just passing the British Library. Proceeding on foot in an easterly direction towards the station. Approaching the grab zone.'

'Delta 1?'

'Copy that,' I said.

'And I'm off,' Tango 1 said, meaning she had lost visual contact with the target.

I glanced quickly at the two photographs taped to my dashboard. I didn't really need to because I knew exactly what he looked like. But I looked one last time anyway. Then back at the crowds.

'I don't see him,' I said.

Then a more urgent voice in my ear. Another woman. The officer with the dog. It watched her intently as her mouth moved.

'This is Whisky 1, Whisky 1. I have possible visual contact. Bravo 1 coming now. Two hundred metres. Far side of the road. Easterly direction. Red backpack. Possible contact.'

A babble of voices and a sharp call for silence.

'Possible. Checking. Checking. Stand by, all units. Stand by, Delta 1.'

Then there was just the silence, crackling

with static. Waiting for me now.

At first I stared straight through him.

Because he was different.

I looked quickly at the two photographs on the dashboard and he was nothing like them. The black hair was light brown. The wispy beard had gone. But it was far more than that. His face had changed. It was filled out, puffed up, almost the face of someone else.

But one thing was the same.

'Delta 1?'

'Contact,' I said.

The red backpack was exactly the same as the one in the CCTV snatch shot on the day he bought hydrogen peroxide in a chemist's wholesale warehouse.

He was wearing that red backpack when he wheeled out the 440 litres of hair bleach to the cash desk. Wearing it when he counted out the £550 in fifty-pound notes. Wearing it when he unloaded his van at the lock-up garage where we had put our cameras.

You couldn't miss that red backpack. It looked like the kind of bag you would use to climb Everest. Big and bright — safety red, they called that colour.

But his face was not the same. That threw me. It was meant to. The face had been pumped full of something. He was planning to go to his death with the face of another man.

But I could see it now.

There was no doubt.

'That's him,' I said. 'Contact. He's had something done. I don't know. Some work to his face. But that's him. Contact. Confirming visual identification. Contact.'

'Sniper 1 in range,' said a voice, and across the street I saw the shooters for the first time, three figures moving on the rooftops above a shabby strip of shops and restaurants, their weapons winking in the sunlight. Police marksmen, settling into position.

Our last resort, if it all went wrong. And it was already starting to go wrong.

'Sniper 2 in range. But I don't have a trigger. No clear shot. It's crowded down there.'

The man with the red backpack had paused on the far side of the road, waiting for the lights to change. Traffic thundered by, and in the gaps there were flashes of safety red. I touched my earpiece. Suddenly nobody was talking to me any more.

'That's our boy,' I said. 'Positive ID. Contact. Contact. Over.'

The lights changed and the traffic reluctantly stopped. The commuters began to shuffle across the road. The man with the red backpack went with them.

I spoke slowly and clearly: 'This is Delta 1 confirming contact. The target is about to enter the grab zone. Do you copy me? Over.'

And nothing but the white noise in response.

And then: 'Possible. Checking. Stand by.'

I shook my head and was about to speak again when the calm voice of DCS Swire said, 'It's a negative, Wolfe. That's not him. Negative. Cancel.'

And then the voice of the surveillance officer: 'Negative. Cancel. Stand down all stations.'

The lights changed again.

The man with the red backpack had crossed the road.

He was heading for the railway station.

'Do you expect him to wear a burka?' I said. 'That's Bravo 1. That's the target. That's our boy. His face —'

'We do not have visual confirmation,' the surveillance officer said. 'We do not have positive ID, Delta 1.'

And then Swire. 'That's not him,' she repeated. 'Stop talking, Wolfe.' A note of steel now. 'You had one task. It is concluded. No further action necessary. We're standing down all units. Negative. Cancel. Thank you everyone.'

The crowd slowed outside the station as it merged with the flow of commuters coming over from King's Cross. I figured that I had one minute to stop him before he disappeared inside the station. Once on a mainline train or down on the tube or on the concourse of the station itself, the man with the red backpack would simply touch his hands together and the world would blow apart.

The battery he probably already held in one hand would create an electric current connecting it to a simple terminal held in the other. The current would then pass down two wires and into that red backpack — a discreet slit would have been cut in the side — where a modified light bulb would trip a detonator stored inside a small tube. This would trigger the main charge — the hydrogen peroxide I had watched him buy with eleven £50 notes on CCTV.

At the same time he had bought a bulk supply of six-inch steel nails. Sacks of them. They would be taped to the outside of the main charge to inflict enough misery to last for several hundred lifetimes.

If it detonated.

If he was that smart.

If he hadn't messed up the cook.

I choked down a lump of hot bitter nausea

as it rose in my throat.

'You're wrong,' I said. 'That's him. Contact.'

I had been inside his lock-up. I had seen the hundreds of empty bottles of hair bleach. I had watched the CCTV footage of the day he bought them until my eyes were burning with the sight of him.

I didn't need the photographs taped to the dash. I knew him. He was in my head.

He could not hide from me.

'Stand down all units,' a self-consciously calm voice was saying. 'Do you copy me, Delta 1?'

'No,' I said. 'You're breaking up.'

Thirty seconds now.

And among all those crowds, and surrounded by all those firearms, I was on my own with the man who was planning to die.

I once attended a lecture at the police academy in Bramshill, Hampshire — the Oxford and Cambridge of police higher education.

An FBI agent had been flown over to help us combat terrorism. I had been impressed by the whiteness of the agent's teeth. They were a fine set of teeth. Very American teeth. But what impressed me more was that the man knew his business.

His teeth shining, he told us that the FBI had identified twenty-five threat areas for terrorist activity. It wasn't quite an A to Z, but it was close — it was an A to T, from airports to tattoo parlours.

Everywhere, basically.

The Fed also suggested what possible terrorists might look like.

Everyone, basically.

The students at Bramshill, the brightest and the best, all these fast-tracked cops, the next generation of CID, young and tough and smart, had almost wet themselves with laughter. But unlike the rest of them, I did not find the talk useless. Just the opposite. Because I remembered the FBI man's number one point of potential indicators.

The suspect significantly alters his appearance.

Although my colleagues had smirked and rolled their eyes, I thought that was a point well worth making. Never overlook the obvious. Don't expect him to look like the photographs and the CCTV images. Be ready for him to look like someone else.

And here was another thing the FBI agent could have mentioned. The target who significantly alters his appearance will probably not bother to get a new bag.

'The same backpack,' I said, opening the car door. 'In the CCTV. Red backpack. When he bought the gear. Red backpack. All the way through. That's the red backpack. And that's him.'

'You can't park here, mate,' an Afro-Cockney voice said through my window, and I jumped to hear a voice that did not come from somewhere inside my head.

A traffic warden was writing me a parking ticket. I got out of the car. He was a tall man with West African tribal scars on his cheeks, and he reared back slightly, expecting trouble. I looked past him and could see the man with the red backpack.

The crowds had thinned now.

He was about to enter the station.

Fifteen seconds.

Then a voice inside my head: 'This is DCS Swire. Get back in the bloody car, Wolfe.'

All pretence at calm now gone.

I hesitated for a moment.

Then I got back into the car.

The traffic warden was tucking a ticket under my windscreen wiper. I shook my head and looked in the rear-view mirror.

The man with the red backpack was directly behind me now, standing right outside the main entrance to the station. The crowds were melting away. There was nothing stopping him entering. But he had paused directly outside the station.

He was talking to himself.

No.

He was praying.

Ten seconds.

The man with the red backpack moved forward.

Nine seconds.

I stuck the car into reverse.

Eight seconds.

I twisted in my seat and slammed my foot to the ground.

The car shot backwards and I stared at the man with the red backpack as I hurtled towards him. I had one arm braced across the passenger seat for the shock of impact and the hand on the wheel pressed down hard on the horn, keeping it there, scattering the stray commuters.

He did not move.

But he looked into my eyes as the old X5 shot towards him, his mouth no longer praying.

Five seconds.

The car ploughed into him, striking him

31

just above the kneecaps, shattering the thigh bones of both legs as it whipped his torso forward against the back of the car. His face shattered the rear window and the rear window did the same to his face.

Then the impact threw him backwards into a wall of red Victorian brick where the back of his head erupted like a soft-boiled egg being hit with a sledgehammer.

Three seconds.

I stuck the car in drive and tore back across the forecourt to where the traffic warden was staring at me, motionless, open-mouthed, his ticket machine still in his hand.

I put the car into reverse, ready to go again.

But there was no need to go again.

Zero.

I slowly got out of the car.

People were screaming. Some of them were commuters. Some of them were the voices in my head. A dog, getting closer every second, was barking wildly.

One voice in my ear was shouting about gross misconduct and manslaughter. Another was shouting about murder.

'Wolfe!'

Swire.

I tore out the earpiece and threw it away.

The man with the red backpack was sitting up against the brick wall, staring straight at me with a baffled expression on his ruined face. One hand still twitched with the surprise of sudden death. Both of his hands were empty.

I was not expecting his hands to be empty.

Suddenly there were armed men in balaclavas. Guns were trained on the dead man. Glock SLP 9mm pistols. Heckler & Koch submachine guns. Then I saw that some of them were pointing at me.

'He was the target,' I said.

Armed officers from SCO19 were everywhere. Commuters were running and crawling for cover. A lot of people were screaming and crying because these men with guns did not look remotely like police officers. They wore Kevlar body armour. They had metal carabiners on their shoulders so they could more easily be dragged away if they were down. The black balaclavas they wore had the eyes and mouths cut out. They looked like paramilitary bank robbers.

People thought it was to protect their identity but I knew it was to spread terror.

And it worked.

They were shouting into the radios attached just above their hearts. The masked faces were bawling at me to get down and stay down and lie on my face.

Now. Now. Now. Do it now!

Slowly I took my warrant card out of my jeans, showed it, and tossed it at them. Then I held up my hands. But I wasn't getting on my knees for them. I wasn't getting down on my face. I kept walking towards the man on the ground.

Because I had to know if I was right.

Last chance! Do it now!

Crouching above the dead man on the ground, I saw that the impact had not cracked the back of his skull. It had removed it.

A huge slick of fresh blood was already spreading across the pavement.

All around there were the screams of terror and fury. The dog was so close now that I could smell it, so close now that I could feel its breath.

I could see the strange flat-nosed Glocks in the corner of my vision, aimed at the dead man on the ground and also at my face. The safety catches were released.

But this was our boy, wasn't it?

I looked at my hands with wonder.

They were covered in the dead man's blood.

But they were not shaking as I tore open the red backpack and looked inside.

2

'Sorry,' I said, my body clenched tight inside the suit I had not worn since my wedding day.

The office was crowded with the full cast of a murder investigation. A SOCO was standing directly in front of me, trying to get past, all in white apart from the blue facemask that covered everything but the irritation in her eyes. I was in a big corner room near the top of a shining glass tower, but I flashed briefly on the many school playgrounds of my childhood, and how you can feel both invisible and in the way just because you are new.

And then there was a spark of recognition in the SOCO's eyes.

'I know you,' she said.

'I'm the new man,' I said.

'No,' she said. 'You're the hero. At the railway station. When did you start working Homicide?'

'Today.'

Now she was smiling behind her blue facemask.

'Cool. What did they call you in court?'

'Officer A.'

'You kill anybody this week, Officer A?'

'Not yet,' I said. 'But it's only Monday morning.'

She laughed and left me standing by the dead man's desk. There wasn't much on it. Just fresh blood and an old photograph.

In the photograph, seven young men in military uniform smiled for the camera as if they were looking at their unbreakable future. Blood had splattered across one corner of the glass. But it did nothing to hide their cocky faces.

It was a strange photograph to have on an office desk. No wife, no kids, no dog. Just seven young soldiers, defaced now with a bright spurt of blood.

Travel blood. Fresh from an artery.

I looked closer and saw the photograph was taken in the eighties, judging by the washed-out colours and the mullet haircuts of the cocky lads. Their hair was from another decade and their uniforms were from another century. They looked like Duran Duran at Waterloo.

And I saw that they were not men. These

were boys who would be boys for perhaps one more summer. And despite the military uniforms, they were not real soldiers. Just students dressed as soldiers. Two of them looked like twins. One of them was the dead man on the far side of the desk. He had grown up to be a banker. He had grown up to be murdered.

I stood aside as a forensic photographer started taking pictures of the desk's bloody mess.

'Who would want to kill a banker?' the photographer said.

It got a laugh. Mostly among the SOCOs, chuckling away behind their facemasks. Spend your life collecting microscopic samples of blood, semen and dirt and you are grateful for any laugh you can get. But the senior detective standing on the far side of the desk did not smile, although I could not tell if he had not heard the remark, or if he was preoccupied with the corpse before him, or if he disapproved of levity in the presence of death.

He was waiting patiently while a small man with a briefcase — the divisional surgeon, here to pronounce death — knelt over the body.

The detective's large head was shaved so clean it shined, and despite his extravagantly broken nose — and it had been broken so often that it looked like a wonky ski run — he had enough vanity to keep his pale goatee beard neatly trimmed.

He turned his piercing blue eyes on me and I thought that he looked like a Viking. I could imagine that pale, fierce face coming up the beach for a spot of pillaging and monk bothering. But Vikings didn't wear glasses and the detective's were round and rimless, John Lennon Imagine specs; they softened his ferocious appearance and gave his hard face a kindly, slightly perplexed expression.

My new boss.

'DC Wolfe, sir,' I said.

'Ah, our new man,' he said, the quiet voice precise and clipped with the vowels of the distant north, Aberdeen or beyond, the kind of Highlands accent that sounds as if every word is carved from granite. 'I'm DCI Mallory.'

I already knew his name. I had never met him before but I had heard of him enough. Detective Chief Inspector Victor Mallory was one of the reasons I wanted the transfer to Homicide and Serious Crime Command.

We were both wearing thin blue gloves and made no attempt to reach across the desk and shake hands. But we smiled, and took a second to size each other up.

DCI Mallory looked very fit, not just for a man in his early fifties but for a man of any age, and it looked like the kind of fitness that comes from natural athleticism rather than hours in the gym. He watched me with his blue eyes as the divisional surgeon fussed briskly over the corpse.

'You're just in time,' Mallory said. 'We're about to begin. Welcome to Homicide.'

Friendly, but skipping all small talk.

The divisional surgeon was standing up.

'He's dead all right,' he said, snapping his bag shut.

Mallory thanked him and gave me the nod. I stepped forward. 'Come and have a look at our body, Wolfe,' he said, 'and tell me if you've ever seen anything like it.'

I joined DCI Mallory on the far side of the desk and we stood above the dead man. At first all I saw was the blood. Lavish arterial sprays with a man in a shirt and tie somewhere beneath it all.

'The deceased is Hugo Buck,' Mallory said. 'Thirty-five years old. Investment banker with ChinaCorps. Body discovered by cleaning staff at six a.m. He gets in early. Works with the Asian markets. While he was having his first coffee, somebody cut his throat.' Mallory looked at me keenly. 'Ever seen one of these?'

I did not know how to respond.

The banker's throat had been more than cut. It had been ripped wide open. The front half of his neck was cleaved away, sliced out with clean precision. He was flat on his back but it felt like only a bit of bony gristle was keeping his head attached to his body. The blood had erupted from his neck in great spurts; his shirt and tie looked like some monstrous red bib. I could smell it now, the copper stink of freshly spilt blood. I shut my mind to it.

Hugo Buck's jacket was still on the back of his chair. Somehow the fountains of blood had not touched it.

I looked quickly at Mallory and then back at the dead man.

'I've seen three cut throats, sir,' I said.

I hesitated and he nodded once, telling me to carry on.

'First week in uniform, there was a husband who saw a text message on his wife's phone from his best friend and reached for a carving knife. Maybe a year later I attended a robbery in a jewellery shop where a gun failed to discharge and the thief produced an axe and went for the man who pushed the security button. And then there was a wedding reception where the father

40

of the bride objected to the best man's speech and shoved a champagne flute into his neck. Three cut throats.'

'Did any of them look anything like this?'

'No, sir.'

'This is almost a decapitation,' Mallory said.

I looked around.

'Somebody must have heard something,' I said.

'Nobody heard a thing,' Mallory said. 'There are people around in a building like this even at that time of day. But nobody hears a thing when a man almost gets his head chopped off.'

He considered me with his pale blue eyes. But I didn't get it.

'Because the victim's windpipe was cut,' he said. 'The trachea. There was no air. And you need air to scream. Nobody heard anything because there was nothing to hear.'

We contemplated the body in silence while all over the large office the SOCOs moved in slow motion like scientists examining the aftermath of a biological catastrophe. They were identical in their masks and gloves and white suits, patiently hunting for prints, placing tiny fibres in evidence bags and taking samples of blood from the desk, the carpet and the glass walls. There was a lot of blood to choose from. One SOCO was drawing a sketch. The photographer who had wondered why anyone would want to kill a banker had stopped taking stills and was now filming the room. Small numbered yellow plastic markers were blooming all over the lush carpet as SOCOs harvested footprints for forensics to match against SI-CAR, the Shoeprint Image Capture and Retrieval database.

Mallory watched them. 'Most professional hits are very amateur, Wolfe. Is that an irony or a paradox? They're carried out by thugs hired in the pub. Morons who will kill anyone for some cash in hand. Most professional hits come with a guarantee — they guarantee to do it badly. But not this one. You see how clean that cut is? Most people, cutting someone's throat, they slash and chop and saw. They make a mess, don't they? You saw that with your three. About as big a mess as an enraged human being can make to flesh and blood with something sharp. But this looks like just one cut. It almost took his head off, but it's just one cut. Now who cuts a throat like that?'

'Someone who knew what they were doing.' I thought about it. 'A butcher. A surgeon. A soldier.'

'You think we've got Rambo running

around out there?'

'I don't know if he's running around, sir. Maybe he's sleeping on the streets.'

Mallory nodded beyond the glass walls to the city thirty floors below, spangled with autumn sunshine around the old grey serpent of a river.

'How many ex-servicemen are sleeping on those streets?' he asked.

'Too many,' I said. I tried to imagine it. 'He comes in here during the night. To find somewhere warm to sleep. To find something worth stealing. Gets disturbed.' I couldn't make it work. 'But he has to get past security.'

'Butcher, surgeon, soldier,' Mallory said. 'Or perhaps it was someone who had no idea what they were doing. One of Mr Buck's fellow bankers. One of the cleaning staff. Perhaps it was just beginner's luck. Or perhaps it was his wife. Apparently she didn't like him much. Officers were called out to a domestic dispute between Mr and Mrs Buck three nights ago. There was some violence. Did you see the marital bed?'

A mattress was leaning against one of the glass walls, a king-sized bed still wrapped in courier's cellophane and bearing the purple and orange FedEx markings.

'That's their bed?' I said. 'His wife sent

their bed to his office?'

'Mrs Buck returned home early from a business trip and discovered Mr Buck with the housekeeper.' Mallory frowned with embarrassed disapproval. 'And he wasn't helping her to unload the dishwasher. So Mrs Buck went for Mr Buck with an oyster knife.'

'An oyster knife?'

'Yes, an oyster knife. It has a short, broad blade. These are affluent people. They like oysters. Anyway, she threatened to cut his testicles off and shove them up his back passage. Responding to sounds of a violent struggle, the neighbours call 999. Officers restrain both of them. Mr Buck hasn't slept at home since.'

We looked at the marital bed in its FedEx wrapping.

'You think the wife did this, sir?' I said.

Mallory shrugged. 'Right now she's all we've got. She's on record as making a threat to remove her husband's testicles.' He looked down at the banker's mutilated throat. 'Although nobody's aim is that bad.'

'She may have delegated,' I said. 'She has the money to hire someone good.'

'That was my thought,' Mallory agreed. 'But then there would be glove prints. And we can't find any glove prints. And unless she hired someone who didn't have any idea what they were doing, there should certainly be glove prints in this room. As you know, glove prints can be as distinctive as finger-prints. If the gloves are thin enough, finger-prints can pass through the material. Finger-prints can also be present inside the gloves. Few villains take their gloves home, prefer-ring to ditch them close to the crime scene. So we're looking for a pair of gloves as well as glove prints.'

'And what happens if we can't find glove prints?'

'Then we have to eliminate every print in the room.'

I looked again at the photograph on the desk. And I could see it now — the boy the man had been. Hugo Buck was standing on the far right of the photograph and one tiny spot from the spray of blood had flecked his image. Twenty years had gone by but the smooth good looks of the future banker were there, buried under a shallow layer of puppy fat. The boys become the men, I thought, and the living become the dead.

'Did you see his hands?' Mallory said.

Buck's hands had fallen by his side but still gripped the vial of pills he had been holding in the last moment of his life. It was another thing I was seeing for the first time.

'Cadaveric spasm,' Mallory said. Smiling now, perhaps happy to show me that I hadn't seen everything yet. That I hadn't seen anything yet. 'Instant rigor, caused by shock of sudden death, locking the body in its final second of life. That Pompeii moment. Can you make the pills out?'

I crouched by the corpse and peered at the label, trying to shut out the copper stink of his blood.

'Zestoretic,' I read. 'Take one daily as directed. Prescription only. Made out to Mr Hugo Randolph Buck. Zestoretic?'

'For hypertension,' Mallory replied. 'Blood pressure pills.'

'He was a bit young to be taking blood pressure pills, wasn't he?' I said, standing up. 'Must be a lot of stress working in banking.'

'And more stress at home,' Mallory added.

We stared at the dead man in silence.

'Why didn't they just shoot him?' Mallory asked suddenly.

I looked at him. 'The banker?'

'The bomber,' Mallory said. 'Your bomber. The chief super panics. The surveillance officer freezes. Nobody's sure if it's the man they want. I understand all of that.

Nobody wants Jean Charles de Menezes on their CV. Everyone's jumpy because any fatal shooting has to go before an IPCC inquiry now. You've got the Crown Prosecution Service waiting in the wings. The human rights lawyers.' Mallory smiled shyly, blue eyes twinkling. 'But you confirmed a positive ID. You overruled the surveillance officer. It was your call. You had seen the man. Watched him. Followed him. Studied him. It was your career on the line. Your liberty. Why didn't they shoot him?'

'They can only shoot him in the head, sir,' I said. 'New rules of engagement. Everything else is too risky. Can't shoot him in the torso because he could be wearing a vest. Can't shoot him in the arms or legs because then he still has a chance to detonate whatever he's carrying.' I shrugged. 'Maybe they didn't feel confident they could get a clean head shot. Maybe they believed the SO and the chief super and not me. All I can say is, there was a genuine element of doubt. And maybe shooting a man in the head when there was an element of doubt seemed . . . rash.'

Mallory nodded. 'And maybe we're becoming afraid to do our job. How do you like this for a robbery?'

'This wasn't robbery,' I said. 'The Rolex

on Mr Buck's wrist has to be worth fifteen grand.'

'Unless it was a robbery that was disturbed,' Mallory said.

I looked beyond the banker's door to the vast open-plan office.

'This place must take some cleaning,' I said.

'All authorised personnel,' Mallory said. 'You can't take a leak in this building without a laminated card and photo ID. We're waiting for a translator so we can interview the cleaner who found Mr Buck. He's fresh from Vilnius.'

'I thought everyone spoke English now.'

'He can't speak it today. Just Lithuanian. Finding the body shook him up. The rest of the cleaning staff are down in the under-ground car park. We can't let them go until we've had a word. My two DIs are down there — Detective Inspector Gane and Detective Inspector Whitestone. If you can give them a hand . . .'

'Yes, sir,' I said.

At the door of the banker's office two uniformed officers had established an entry and exit corridor where they logged every-one who came and went from the crime scene. Two PCs, one male and one female, both young, both of them with dark red hair. They could have been brother and sister despite the fact that the woman was small and whippet-thin, and the man tall and gangly. From the state of them they had to be the officers who had answered the call.

The man — a boy, I thought, although he was in his mid-twenties and only a few years younger than me — looked on the verge of passing out. As I approached he leaned against the wall and choked back the urge to be sick. The woman — and she looked like a girl, despite the Metropolitan Police uniform — placed one small hand on her colleague's shoulder.

She looked up at me as I signed out of the crime scene.

'His first body, sir,' she explained, almost apologetic. She hesitated for a moment. 'Mine, too.'

She was dealing with it better than the boy. But both of their startled faces were wide open and frozen with shock, like children who had just come downstairs and found their pet dead in its cage, or seen through Santa's disguise, and got their first real glimpse of this wicked world.

'Breathe,' I told him. I inhaled deeply through my nose, released it through my mouth with a controlled sigh. Showing him how to do it.

'Sir,' he said.

There were six lifts for the office workers and one, much larger and much dirtier, for the help. I took the stairs, thinking I might find gloves. Thirty flights. By the time I was halfway down I was starting to sweat but my breathing was still even.

I stopped at a sound in the stairwell, a hundred metres below.

Looking down, I glimpsed a blur of movement. There was the hint of a shadow and then a distant door slammed shut. I called out but there was no response and I took the final flights more slowly, stopping when I saw something written on the wall.

One word in black.

The shade of black that blood dries to.

PIG

Not taking my eyes from the three letters, I took out my phone and photographed the black word on the filthy wall. Then I went down the rest of the stairs, hearing a babble of voices now, rising up from below ground, the sound getting louder every second.

On the basement floor I shoved open the door and looked out at an underground car park that was full of cleaning staff. They had been invisible from the street. Men and women, young and old, talking in twenty different languages, the unseen people who came every day to clean the floors and the windows and the toilets in the shining glass tower.

And I saw that they were beyond number. The armies of the poor.

3

When I arrived home that night I knew something was wrong even before I got through the front door.

We lived in a big top-floor loft and the stench filled every corner of it. I knew immediately where the stink came from because the clues were everywhere. A single shoe in the hallway, studded with teeth marks. Wooden floorboards that had been scrubbed clean to conceal evidence. A rubbish bin stuffed with stained kitchen roll. And everywhere there was that smell, meaty and musty and peaty. The smell of animal.

The dog had been bad again.

On the far side of the loft an elderly woman with white hair was sitting at one end of a sofa with a little red dog on her lap. At the other end of the sofa was a fresh wet stain that would now be there for ever.

Mrs Murphy was watching TV with the sound turned off, which was always her custom when my daughter Scout was sleeping.

Without moving his tennis ball-sized head from his front paws, the red dog — Stan was his name — rolled his huge round eyes up to look at me. You could see the whites of his bulging eyes around the blackness, as though the sockets were too small to contain such a pair of headlamps.

He caught my eye and quickly looked away.

'Mrs Murphy,' I said, 'you've had so much work again.'

'Don't worry none,' she said, scratching the dog behind his ears, her soft accent sounding as if she had never left County Cork a lifetime ago. 'Stan's still little. And the good news is that Scout ate her dinner. Some of it, anyway. She doesn't eat much, does she? There's nothing of her.'

I nodded and went off to look in on my daughter.

Scout was five years old and still slept in the baby fashion with her hands held up in loose fists by the side of her head, like a tiny weightlifter. The light was on in her room, although she must have been sleeping for hours.

She had slept with the light on ever since we lost her mother.

I picked up a school sweater from the floor, folded it and placed it on the back of a chair where Mrs Murphy had tomorrow's school uniform all neatly folded and waiting. I hesitated, wanting to turn off her light. She couldn't keep it on for ever. But in the end, I didn't have the nerve.

Mrs Murphy was putting on her coat.

'It will get better,' she told me.

I woke before dawn.

I always woke before dawn.

In the dreaming period of sleep, the lightest phase of sleep, REM sleep, I surfaced, waking on my side of the double bed, the left side, chased from my rest by yesterday's coffee and my dreams of the dead.

I was always right there waiting for the day before the day ever had a chance to begin.

Turning off my alarm before it had the chance to ring, I slipped out of bed without making a sound. I brushed my teeth and went back into the bedroom, got down on my hands and knees and quickly pumped out twenty-five press-ups. Then I sipped the water by my bedside, looking out of the window at the October sky — six in the morning and still black over the nearby dome of St Paul's Cathedral.

I got down and did twenty-five more press-ups, slower and more deliberate this time, thinking about technique. I gave myself a minute's break then did twenty-five more, starting to feel it now, my arms shaking with the build-up of lactic acid in the muscles. I stayed on the ground, found my breath and forced out the final twenty-five — an act of will, not strength.

I padded quietly to the kitchen, anxious not to wake daughter or dog, but hearing Stan breathing in the dark, a snorting, snuffling sound coming out of a nose that did not really resemble anything up to the difficult task of breathing. I stood there listening to him, enjoying the sound. He was wiped out after another busy night destroying our home. Then he stirred at my presence, the large ears falling across his face like silky curtains, the soulful eyes blinking open and glittering behind his lavish ears. And then he was awake too, staring at me through the bars of his cage, hopeful of an early release.

I got him out. Held him against my chest. Stan pressing a nose like a squashed prune against my fingers, sniffing them with interest.

Stan had been with us for a month (it felt much longer) — my present to Scout on her fifth birthday. I had found the breeder online, collected Stan on the day he turned eight weeks old, and carried him into the loft with a blanket over his head like a guilty man heading for the high court.

Every time I thought I had made a mistake, that the dog was my pitiful attempt to give Scout a proper family life, I remembered the first time she had seen Stan. Her smile was like the sun coming up. That's how I knew the dog was not a mistake.

In the kitchen I drank a triple espresso with him on my lap, the only light coming from my laptop as I searched medical sites for information on how to cut a windpipe.

Stan went back to sleep as I learned that either side of the windpipe are the carotid arteries, bringing blood from the heart to the brain, and that severing them is one of the most fatal head injuries known to man.

But no matter how many surgical websites I looked at, and no matter how many times I typed 'cut throat' into the search engine, I could find no weapon that looked remotely capable of doing the job.

In the end the search engine gave up on me, directing me to shaving websites where they sold foam, balm, gel and a variety of old-fashioned straight razors. They were interesting-looking blades, vicious enough to put a smile on Sweeney Todd's face. But I couldn't see how any of them could have cut deep enough to remove most of Hugo Buck's throat.

At seven the sky finally started to lighten. I snapped shut the laptop as Scout appeared, padding into the kitchen still in her pyjamas and puffy with sleep.

Stan struggled down from my lap and flew at her. Our loft was huge. Far too big for a man, child and dog. Our family had grown smaller while the loft seemed to get bigger. Now we rattled around in all that empty space under the exposed wooden beams and brickwork, the dog's paws skidding on the polished wooden floorboards as he chased towards Scout, sniffing and licking and nuzzling, clambering up her leg, crazy with love.

'Stan was bad,' she said, absent-mindedly scratching the top of his small head.

'I know.'

'On the sofa.'

'I saw.'

'And in the kitchen. And by the door.' She thought about it. 'Everywhere really.'

'Mrs Murphy took care of it.'

'I helped her.'

'Thank you for that.'

A pause.

'Do we have to give him back?' she said.

I squatted down to be level with her head. Her light brown hair, her dark brown eyes, the sweeping curve of her face — they all came straight from her mother. Even her name was from a character in a book that my wife loved. My wife was gone, but every time I looked at my daughter, I saw her face.

'This is our dog,' I said, and found myself quoting Mrs Murphy. 'It will all get better, OK?'

'OK.'

We slipped into our breakfast routine. Toast for Scout. Porridge for me. Nature's Menu dog food for Stan. After carrying her plate to the sink, Scout went off to brush her teeth. That had been one of her mother's rules — teeth are brushed after the meal, not before, and we really did our best to stick to her rules.

We lived opposite the great old meat market of Smithfield. At this time of the morning, the men were ending their long night shift. The butchers and porters were finishing the last of their loading and making their way to cafés and pubs that had opened long before dawn. A few were already outside the early morning pubs with pints of lager in their red fists, big men wilting in the daylight and blurry with exhaustion, white aprons smeared with blood and gore. As we walked through their world, some called out a greeting to Stan, and Scout and I smiled with pride.

He was a striking dog. In the pale daylight you could see the beauty of his colour — a rich chestnut somewhere between rusty red and old gold. His fur was wavy, and on the tips of those oversized ears there were ringlets of extravagant curls, as though he'd spent the previous evening with a fancy hairdresser rather than urinating on our furniture. Held in check by Scout, who had his leather lead wrapped twice around the wrist of her right hand, Stan trotted happily by her side, his small head up and alert, his tail stiff with anticipation and then whipping like a windscreen wiper in a thunderstorm when something caught his eye.

And Stan was amazed by everything. He stared with awe at a porter across the street having a cigarette outside the market. A jogger went by and Stan stood stock still, his head tilted to one side, as if witnessing an alien landing. Scout and I laughed. Most of our laughs came from the dog. He looked at a piece of chewing gum, or a discarded cup, or a shard of broken glass, and instantly lurched towards it, dragging Scout with him.

The sun was up now and making me

squint: fresh autumn light can be more crystal clear than summer's haze. I felt the rawness of the day and the bad sleeper's burden — the knowledge that every hour would have its own weight and no amount of coffee would ever take the place of lost sleep. Yet I still needed more coffee, immediately.

There was an all-night stall near the market, serving mostly black cab drivers and meat porters, and I got in line while men with shaved heads and fierce faces fussed over the chestnut-coloured dog at my daughter's feet. Stan leapt like a salmon, overcome with excitement, and they laughed, all the hard men of the London night, and I was happy then, knowing that our dog had yet to learn fear.

As we neared the school gates Scout fell into step with another little girl. The girl's mother turned away to talk to another mother and I waited at the gates with Stan and soothed him as he whimpered to see Scout leave. We waited in case she turned round to wave but she was with her friend now and she had forgotten all about us.

Before she disappeared into her own world I reflected that her school uniform was too big and it would be too big for a long time.

Mrs Murphy was right. There was almost nothing of my daughter.

There was almost nothing of her, and she was my everything.

Hugo Buck's home was in a portered apartment overlooking Regent's Park.

The porter must have been on his tea break when I got there because the double glass doors were locked. I stood outside, leaning on the bell and watching the dogs in the park. They were all off lead. Big, good-looking dogs, Labradors and Retrievers and Airedales, and some small fry, Beagles and Westies, all of them panting and confident as they sniffed piles of leaves and each other, coming back when their owner called. I could not imagine a time when Stan would come when I called.

'Detective?'

A young woman and man in their twenties were walking towards me. I had clocked the pair of them when I was parking, taken them for a couple of local rich kids. A pair of good-looking scruffs, carefully unkempt, passing a single cigarette between them as they sat on a low wall by the manicured gardens. Only the children of the wealthy can afford to be that laid back at that age.

On the driveway there was a chauffeur

lounging in a big black Merc, squeezed in tight between a couple of Porsche 911s, and he eyed up the girl as he played with his peaked cap. I saw now the young guy had a camera slung around his neck. Press, then, I thought. It was the girl who did the talking.

'You're here to speak to Mrs Buck? Is she a suspect? Do you expect to make an arrest soon?'

I pressed my thumb on the buzzer and left it there.

'Is this a hate crime, detective?'

I looked at her.

'Every murder is a hate crime,' I said. 'Who did you say you write for?'

'I didn't,' she said.

She dug a card out of her bag, and when she gave it to me I saw that there was a tiny digital voice recorder in her other hand. A red light was shining. *Scarlet Bush,* I read. *The Daily Post.* Then her mobile phone number, email address and four or five social network accounts. That seemed like a lot to me.

'Scarlet Bush,' she laughed. 'Sounds like a porn star, right?'

When I looked up she nodded at the photographer and, almost lazily, he swung his camera towards me and pulled the trigger. It took photographs like a machine gun.

'Hey,' I said, raising a hand to protect myself.

'Have you seen what the online community are saying?' The little voice recorder was in my face. 'They're calling Bob the Butcher a hero.'

I stared at her. 'Bob the Butcher?'

'He's all over the social networks. He's been trending for twenty-four hours.' Scarlet Bush had a disbelieving little smile on her face. 'You genuinely weren't aware of that?'

The porter was finally opening the door. I pressed my warrant card against the glass and said my name and rank. So she knew my name, too.

'And how does that feel for you, DC Wolfe?' she asked. 'When the social networks are calling the murderer a hero and the victim a scumbag?'

'Sorry, sorry,' the porter said, finally opening up.

I paused in the open doorway.

'Murderers are never heroes,' I said.

Scarlet Bush smiled at me, more broadly now, as if we both knew that wasn't quite true.

Mrs Natasha Buck, widow of the dead banker, was in dark glasses and wet from the shower. Tall, early thirties, still in her bathrobe.

The strange combination of robe and shades made her look as though she was on holiday, heading for the pool. Her damp hair was blonde — very blonde, the white-gold you see on black-and-white film stars. She looked like a natural blonde, but maybe not that natural. She had the worked-on thinness that you see with a lot of wealthy women, and the same sense of entitlement.

Towelling her long blonde hair, she frowned at my warrant card as if it was junk mail from Pepe's Pizza Parlour.

'I'm very sorry for your loss, Mrs Buck. I know this must be a very distressing time.'

'I already told the police what I know,' she said. 'A young black man and an older white woman.' She had the carefully clipped enunciation of a foreigner who has spent ten years around serious English money.

'DI Gane and DI Whitestone,' I said. 'I know.'

'They even swabbed my mouth.'

'They do that for your DNA. To rule you out. We just need to double-check some details, if that's convenient.'

'Not *really.*' She glanced at her watch, shining like a diamond-encrusted bauble on her thin wrist. 'Actually I'm about to go out.'

She was strikingly attractive, with the kind

of face that you would not look away from until you found yourself staring. And perhaps not even then. But it felt like a lot of men had told her she was beautiful.

'We do have an appointment, Mrs Buck. If it's inconvenient now we can do it at some later date.' A pause. 'At the station.'

She looked at me properly for the first time. Then she laughed.

The more money they have, I thought, the less they fear the police.

'Should I call my lawyer?' she said.

'We're just talking, Mrs Buck.'

Her hair fell across her face. She looked at me through the damp veil as she lazily pulled it back.

'Am I a suspect?'

Her voice had become lower and slower. I liked it more.

'Not yet,' I said.

We stared at each other.

'Oh, let's get it over with,' she said. 'Coffee? I'll have to make it myself. I had to let our housekeeper go when I found her with my late husband's penis in her mouth.' She stood up with a sigh. 'It's so hard to get good help.'

It was a lovely apartment. Clean, expensive, uncluttered. Big budget, good taste, no children. I thought of the office with all the blood and tried to feel her husband's presence in this place. But if his spirit was near, I couldn't sense him. It felt like the home of a woman who had been living alone for a long time.

There were two paintings on the wall, clearly by the same artist. City scenes with a kind of Sunday morning stillness about them. One was of deserted railway lines, the other some kind of tunnel, and they were both misty and dream-like, bathed in the soft light of dawn or twilight. There were no people in them and that gave them a strange kind of peace. I felt like I almost recognised these places.

I leaned in close to the painting of the tunnel, looking for the artist's name, but there were just two lower-case initials.

j s

A miniature dog came into the room while Mrs Buck was making the coffee. Looked like a Pekingese-Chihuahua cross. I let her sniff my hand and then picked her up and placed her on my thigh. She stood there shivering, as weightless as an insect.

When I tried to stroke her she ambled off to the far end of the sofa and stared at me defiantly as she emptied her bladder.

Mrs Buck came back into the room with a cafetière on a silver tray.

'Susan, you bad girl,' she said. 'You know you're meant to do that on the carpet.'

Mrs Buck dropped a silk cushion over the stain, pushed the dog on to the floor and then sat opposite me, leaning back, crossing her long legs, and sighing as her robe slid open. She pulled it shut as an iPhone on the coffee table between us began to vibrate. The dog barked at it, quaking with rage as Mrs Buck picked it up and began reading a message. She made me feel like I wasn't there at all.

I cleared my throat.

'Who would want to kill your husband?' I said.

Her pretty face was frowning at the iPhone.

'Apart from you,' I added.

Now she looked at me.

'Mrs Buck,' I said. 'Please try to concentrate on me for the next little while.'

She took a final look at her phone and turned it off, her face tight with anger.

'Do you really think I wanted my husband dead?' she said. 'You stupid little man!'

I took a breath.

'Officers were called to this address three days before he died.'

'That? A lover's tiff.'

'You made threats on your husband's life.'

'What do you expect me to say when I find the help blowing him? You say all sorts of things in the heat of the moment.'

'You FedExed your bed to his office.'

'I wanted to embarrass him. I wanted to humiliate him. I wanted him to know what it feels like.'

'And then someone cut his throat.'

She exhaled as she poured out coffee.

'I can see it looks bad. Sugar? Milk?'

'Black, please.'

'I didn't want him to die. I just wanted him to *stop*. To stop . . . what's the nice way of saying it? Sleeping around.'

It was good coffee.

'Did your husband have many friends?'

'You know what the English are like. Or at least that kind of upper-class Englishman. Hugo came from a family where they let their dogs get in their beds and send their children to kennels. He was shipped off to boarding school at the age of seven, made friends there and kept them for ever. He didn't have much use for the rest of the world. Including his wife.'

I thought about the photograph on his desk.

'Where did he go to school?'

'Trinity College Cambridge. Prince Charles went there.'

She was smiling with wistful pride.

'Before that,' I said.

'Potter's Field,' she said. 'His father went there. And his grandfather. Hugo called it the Eton for athletes, musicians and thugs. He meant it as a compliment.'

'Which one was he?'

'An athlete. My husband was good at games, detective.'

'Did he enjoy his years at Potter's Field?'

'Sadistic masters. Stodgy food. Cold showers. That constant obsession with sport. Casual bullying. A lot of homosexual sex. He always said they were the best days of his life.'

'Did your husband have lovers?'

She snorted.

'Apart from your housekeeper,' I said.

'Plenty.'

'And did the lovers have husbands?'

'Some of them. You think a jealous husband might have killed him? Possible, I suppose. But Hugo was fond of the help. He stayed away from my friends, I'll give him that. Although I don't think he did it out of any sense of morality. He just preferred his entertainment below stairs.'

'I'll need the name and contact details of

the housekeeper. You told my colleagues you didn't have them.'

The anger flared. 'Because the bitch caught a plane back to Kiev. I *told* them. Do I have to say everything twice?'

'Did he fall out with any business partners? Did he receive any threatening phone calls, emails, letters?'

She shook her head. She had had enough. She took out her phone.

'Where were you between the hours of five and seven a.m. yesterday? I am going to need your credit card records, mobile phone bills, computers and their passwords. Laptops, desktops, tablets, the lot. Are you listening to me, Mrs Buck?'

She stood up.

'Do you really want to know about my husband?'

We stared at each other.

'Yes.'

'Then let me tell you about my husband,' she said.

With a shrug she let the robe fall from her shoulders and to the floor.

I saw the bruises on her arms and legs. On her long limbs there were fresh, livid marks and there were old and fading marks. All the signs of systematic and regular beatings that carefully avoided the face.

'This was my husband.'

'Mrs Buck —'

'*He* was the violent one, not me. When I picked up that little oyster knife he laughed in my face. He laughed at me, detective. But I didn't want him dead, no matter what I told him.' The tears finally came and they seemed real enough to me. 'I wanted him to be *kind,*' she continued. 'I wanted him to stop running around. I wanted him to stop humiliating me with women too poor and too stupid to tell him no. I wanted him to *stop.*'

I was on my feet. 'Please, Mrs Buck —'

'Natasha.'

I picked up her robe and draped it around her shoulders. She put her arms around my waist. I think she just wanted to be held for a while. I think she was sick of all the questions. I think she was just lonely. Our faces were next to each other. I could feel her breath. And I felt the blood flood into me unbidden.

Because I was lonely too.

After a long moment I pulled myself away, cracking my shin against the coffee table and waking up the dog.

Natasha Buck smiled sadly as she slipped the robe back on and tied the belt around her slim waist.

'Ah, that rare breed,' she said, nodding towards my left hand. My wedding ring had caught the soft light as I picked up my cup. 'A married man who loves his wife!'

'Drink your coffee,' I said.

The porter was nowhere to be seen when I left. The journalist and the photographer had disappeared. The chauffeur was dozing at the wheel of the Mercedes, his peaked cap pulled over his eyes. The dogs in the park had all gone home and the day was dark far too soon.

I was walking to the car, kicking through the piles of autumn leaves and thinking of Natasha Buck's long naked limbs, when DCI Mallory called.

'It wasn't beginner's luck,' he said. 'We've got another one.'

4

A blacked-out mortuary van waited at the mouth of the alley as the swirling blue lights of a dozen response cars lit up the Soho night. Uniformed officers were still unreeling spools of blue and white crime scene tape across Shaftesbury Avenue and shoving back crowds hopeful of glimpsing fresh corpse.

I ducked under the tape.

The Airwave digital radios chattered and clacked. The SOCOs were putting on their head-to-toe white body suits while Mallory's two detective inspectors, Gane and Whitestone, were already ripping off their protective gear. They were excited.

'It's a good body,' Gane said to me. He was young and black, his head shaved fashionably clean, and under his protective clothes he was far better dressed than he needed to be.

I pulled on thin blue latex gloves. 'A good body?'

'A bad body is one that's found by the public,' Whitestone said. 'Some drunk who needs a pee or a puke. A dog walker clomping through the gore before it's had a chance to get cold. Destroying evidence, tampering with the scene before we've even confirmed death.' Whitestone was in her middle thirties, a thoughtful-looking blonde woman with black-rimmed glasses. You might not have guessed she had more than ten years on murder investigation teams. 'A good body is one that's found by the police when it's definitely dead. A good body keeps things simple. Saves us work.'

'And this is a good body,' Gane said. And then, 'We read about you. You're famous, Wolfe. What did they call you in court?'

'Officer A,' I said.

'Officer A. You were in SO15?'

I nodded. 'Surveillance officer, Counter Terrorism Command.'

'You were a surveillance officer?' he said, clearly underwhelmed.

I could see how a Homicide detective like Gane would think surveillance was life in the slow lane. It's true there was a lot of hanging around, following people on foot and in cars and watching endless hours of

CCTV footage, whereas Homicide and Serious Crime's work is carried out by Murder Investigation Teams, the Metropolitan Police's specialised murder squads, and is one of the Met's elite units, investigating nothing but murder, manslaughter and the threat of murder. But Gane made it sound like I had spent my time asking people if they wanted fries with that shake.

'I heard that it would never have detonated,' he said with a grin. 'Because the bomber ruined the cook.'

'I heard that too,' I said, flexing my fingers inside the latex gloves. 'In court the tech guy said the perp didn't distil the hydrogen peroxide to the correct concentration. Simmered when he should have stirred. Forgot to whisk his egg white. Maybe it's true. Maybe they're just trying to cheer us up. Anyone who makes a bomb in their old mum's kitchen can't be that bright, can they?'

'And what did they give you?' Gane asked.

'The Queen's Police Medal.'

He almost whistled. 'A QPM? Was it for exceptional courage, skill, exhibiting conspicuous devotion to duty, or all three?' He laughed. 'Lucky he had a bomb in his bag. Or they would have given you twenty years to life.'

'It's good to have you, Wolfe,' Whitestone told me, ending the chat. 'The boss is waiting for you.'

SOCOs were putting up arc lights at the end of the alley where Mallory stood next to a black shape lying on the ground by giant recycling bins, his long lean figure stock still in the blazing white glare as the scene was carefully prepared, looking like an actor waiting for his cue to step on stage. The filthy alley felt like it was light years away from the shining tower where we had found Hugo Buck.

'I thought we had another one,' I said.

'We do,' Mallory said.

There's a look that you see in all boxers and in certain breeds of dog — German Shepherds have it. It is a look that reveals knowledge of how serious the world is. Mallory had that look now.

'Different postcode, same killer,' he said. 'Look.'

The dead man wore the sad rags of homelessness. And someone had cut his throat out.

All of it.

The fierce white lights revealed a neck that had been ripped open, torn out, the front half of the victim's neck cleaved clean away. Again. It felt like only the spine was keeping

76

the head attached to the body. Again. Mallory was right. The homeless man in the stinking alley was a world away from the banker in his glass tower.

But he was another one.

Even under the arc lights the alley was cold, and through the thin rubber gloves I could feel the sweat tingle on my palms.

I turned on my torch to look beyond the reach of the lights' glare, and let the thin beam trace slowly across the great spurts of arterial blood covering the walls and the recycling bins. I turned the torch off as I looked at the blood that soaked and stained the top half of the body.

The blood stank with that distinctive metallic odour that is also sickeningly human, and the smell mixed with the fuel and food and alcohol scents of the West End.

I tried to look beyond the blood and the horror. I tried to look at what had once been a man.

His hair was long and matted, the clothes rags, blackened by the grinding toll of living on the streets. It was hard to estimate his age because he looked all used up, as though he had lived an entire lifetime long before this brutal death.

'There will be needle marks on his arms,' I said, 'and perhaps on the legs, and even between the toes.'

Mallory said, 'But why kill a man who was so busy killing himself?'

There were a few pitiful belongings by the dead man's side. A black rubbish bag secured by an elastic band holding his worldly goods. A woollen cap still full of coins. And a musical instrument. A thin piece of black wood with a complicated tangle of silver metal buttons and keys.

'A clarinet?' I said.

'Not a clarinet,' Mallory said. 'Too small. An oboe.'

'Nobody's busking is that bad,' said one of the SOCOs.

Nobody laughed.

Mallory's gaze took in the bloodied body, the untouched money, and the musical instrument. He shook his head with what looked like real sadness.

'Looks like he was on the streets for a while,' I said. 'Plenty of addicts and former addicts around Soho. But the homeless don't often kill each other.'

'No,' Mallory agreed. 'It's the people with homes to go to who are the problem.'

I looked back at the street. The SOCOs moved in slow motion now, plodding white ghosts, falling into their routine of photo-graphing footprints, gathering cigarette butts, collecting fibres, prints, and samples of blood. One of them was drawing a sketch. The photographer stopped taking stills and started filming the scene. The usual crop of small numbered yellow markers were blooming on the ragged ground and the SOCOs trod carefully between them, like scientists tiptoeing through the aftermath of nuclear Armageddon. Beyond them, in the festive swirl of the blue lights of our cars, uniformed officers were pushing back the crowds recording the drama on their phones.

'They think we're putting on *Les Misérables* down here,' Mallory sighed. 'This is a strange space, isn't it?'

I lifted my head. Mallory was right. It was not really an alley at all, more of a crevice between two of the grand old theatres of Shaftesbury Avenue. At the end of the alley, above the heads of the gawping crowd, I could see the bright lights of the very heart of the city. The white neon of the theatre marquees, the reds and golds of Chinatown.

'And nobody heard a thing,' Mallory said, reading my mind.

'Because his trachea had been cut,' I said. 'No windpipe, no scream.'

As the crowds were moved to the far side of the street their voices rose in protest.

They craned their necks for a better view and held their little phones even higher above their heads.

'God spare us from stupid people with smartphones,' Mallory muttered.

The SOCOs began to erect a tent over the dead man to shield the scene from the public and to protect the thousand tiny scraps of evidence from the weather. Mallory's gaze settled on the beanie cap full of coins, then moved on to the musical instrument.

'What kind of heroin addict busks with an oboe?' he said.

I thought about it. 'One who comes from money. One who had all the chances. One who comes from privilege. The music teacher coming round once a week to practise the oboe. The lessons going on for years. Money never a problem.'

Mallory ran the palm of one large hand over his bald head and then pushed his John Lennon glasses a bit further up his broken nose. 'Or maybe he just stole it.' A beat. 'But I don't think so. I think you're right. I think there was all kind of care lavished on him. A long time ago now.'

The flash from a SOCO's camera lit up a part of the alley wall that the arc lights had not reached. Among the fresh spurts of travel blood there was a tangle of graffiti I had missed. One word shouted at me and I stepped closer to see, although I already knew what it said.

PIG

On the far side of the street I could see perhaps a hundred mobile phones, held above the shoulders of the uniformed officers who stood on the far side of the PO-LICE DO NOT CROSS tape. The crowds had been pushed right back now but the numbers were growing, stretching our officers, and as their excitement mounted the white lights on their phones glowed like the eyes of wolves in winter.

A SOCO came down the alley, carrying a laptop in one hand and pulling off her face-mask with the other.

'Good body, sir,' she said to Mallory.

'No witness, no weapon, no CCTV, no ID and no glove prints,' he said. 'I've seen better.'

In the morning I took care of my daughter and my dog and then I drove to work — 27 Savile Row, London W1. The Met call it West End Central.

27 Savile Row is a modern block of of-

fices with one of those ancient blue police lamps outside — the kind of blue lamp that makes you think of Sherlock Holmes hunting Jack the Ripper through the London fog. But although Savile Row is famous for two things, West End Central isn't one of them.

For hundreds of years Savile Row has been home to the most exclusive men's tailors in the world. The short Mayfair street is also where, on the rooftop high above number 3, the Beatles played their final gig, attracting the attention of the local police. The attending officers from West End Central let the Beatles finish their last ever set because they were all music fans. That's what they tell you in West End Central.

Carrying the triple espresso I had bought at Bar Italia in Soho, I went up to the Major Incident Room, MIR-1, on the top floor. MIR-1 would be the centre of Homicide's murder investigation. It was a large suite of connecting rooms with a computer station at every desk and it was now completely empty apart from DCI Mallory, who stood cradling a carton of takeaway tea as he stared at a blank whiteboard.

'You're early,' he said. 'Morning briefing's not for an hour.'

'I thought I'd be the first to arrive, sir,' I said. 'Look keen and all that.'

He laughed. 'I like to spend a bit of time figuring before I start opening my mouth,' he said. 'What could possibly connect a wealthy investment banker and a homeless heroin addict?' He shook his head. 'I don't know. I have no idea. And I need to know. At least I need to have a theory.' He sipped his tea. 'Have you heard of the Golden Hour principle?'

I nodded. 'It means early action can secure material that would otherwise be lost. Witnesses remember things more clearly. Offenders can still be nearby. CCTV footage hasn't been deleted. The longer we leave it, the harder it all gets.'

'I believe in the Golden Hour principle as much as the next man,' Mallory said. 'But I also believe in what the old SIOs call "creating slow time". Meaning you need to put your foot on the ball and have a figure; meaning you have to leave time for figuring as well as action.'

He was such a soft-spoken man that it took me a moment to realise that by coming in early I had intruded upon his private time — his figuring time. He must have seen the alarm on my face.

'Why don't you go down to the basement?' he suggested kindly. 'See if you can find our weapon.' He held out an A4 file. 'Take this with you.'

'Sir.'

I bolted my coffee and went down to the basement. The lift doors opened on to a low-ceilinged room where row upon row of canteen dining tables were covered with knives.

A young uniformed officer was filming them and making notes on a clipboard. He looked like a tourist in some exotic market-place.

'Help you, sir?' he said.

'I'm looking for a knife,' I said.

'What kind of knife, sir?'

'A knife that can do this.'

There were four photographs inside the file. Two of Hugo Buck's corpse and the other two of the homeless man. They were all graphic close-ups of the fatal wounds. I held them up for the constable and saw the blood drain from his face.

'Go ahead, sir,' he said. 'We've got all sorts here.'

It was true. There were hundreds, perhaps thousands, of knives glinting under the harsh strip lighting. Knives that had been seized, found, dumped, bagged as evidence or surrendered during an amnesty. So many knives that I didn't see how I could fail to find a suitable candidate for the one that had cut the throats of the banker and the unknown man.

The uniformed officer had fallen into step beside me. He cleared his throat nervously.

'It's PC Greene, sir,' he said. 'PC Billy Greene? From that morning at the bank? You told me to breathe. When I came over all funny.'

I looked at him properly and remembered the young officer who was good for nothing after finding the body.

'PC Greene,' I said. 'You don't call me *sir* just because I'm in plain clothes.' I was wearing my black Paul Smith wedding suit. Savile Row being still a bit beyond my pay grade. 'I'm a detective constable — DC Wolfe. Exactly the same rank as you. You can call me Wolfe. You can call me Max. You can call me pretty much whatever you like. But if you call me *sir* then you make both of us look stupid. You do know that a DC has exactly the same powers and authority as a uniformed PC, don't you?'

He looked embarrassed. 'Of course, sir — Max, er, DC Wolfe. But anyway, I didn't thank you. A lot of them were laughing at me for wimping out that day. You helped. It definitely helps. The breathing.'

'You're not on the street any more?'

His white face flushed red. 'They've put

me on desk duties. Reassigned. A canteen cowboy.' He laughed miserably. 'They think I fell to bits.'

I grimaced. 'That's a bit hard.'

Greene gestured at the knives, changing the subject. 'See what you're looking for?'

'Not yet.'

I walked between the tables, looking at the knives in their careful lines. Throwing knives. Hunting knives. Bowie knives. Knives so small and thin they could fit into a credit card holder. Samurai swords. Carpet cutters. Gurkha kukris. Rust-dappled Stanley knives. And the height of knife fashion — compact semi-automatic folding knives, with titanium handles and stainless steel blades, knives that whipped out like a gunslinger drawing his Colt 45.

I picked one up and looked at it in my hand.

'We're getting a lot of those,' Greene said. 'Gang members like them. You think it might be something like that?'

'I don't see how it can be,' I said, replacing the knife. 'It's not long enough. I figure what I'm looking for is about twelve inches long. Most of it blade. It has to be a blade that's long and thin and I guess double-edged. Something that's made to cut throats.'

He swallowed hard. 'This is about Bob the Butcher, isn't it?'

'Who *is* Bob the Butcher?'

He fetched his laptop and found the page. A newspaper's website.

BOB THE BUTCHER STALKS SCARED CITY BOYS
by Scarlet Bush
Crime correspondent

Champagne-swilling City boys are living in mortal terror after a senior detective revealed that the death of investment banker Hugo Buck was a hate crime.

'Yes, Bob the Butcher murdering that innocent young banker was a hate crime,' confirmed Detective Constable Max Wolfe. 'But then all murder is a hate crime.'

In the bars all over the financial district, high-flying young City boys busy blowing their bonuses are now living in abject terror of Bob the Butcher.

'It's terrible to think that Bob the Butcher is targeting bankers,' said Bruno Mancini in fashionable Cheapside watering hole The Lucky Cripple. 'What's wrong with being rich? We work hard for our success.'

I cursed under my breath. 'I didn't say

any of that,' I said, then glanced at the piece again. 'Well, maybe just a bit of it.'

There was a small photograph next to the article. It was the young woman outside the flat in Regent's Park. I wasn't sure what this meant, but I knew it wasn't good. The one good thing was that she had not connected the murder of Hugo Buck with the unknown man in the alley. But it was the only good thing.

I carried on walking between the tables, somehow knowing that the knife I was looking for would not be found here.

'Thanks for your help, Billy. I'm sorry they took you off the street.'

He brightened. 'It's actually not so bad. I like the nights. And you get a sense of the history down here. Have you got a minute? Have a look at this.'

Greene opened the door to a storage room. It was as small and cluttered as an attic that had been abandoned around the time the Beatles were playing on a rooftop at the other end of Savile Row.

'It's full of stuff that nobody knows what to do with,' Greene said. 'It's not evidence so they can't bag it. It's not junk so they can't chuck it out. And it's not important enough to be in a museum. I think they've all just forgotten about it. Have a look, DC Wolfe.'

We stepped into the dusty room and I looked around in disbelief. There was a stovepipe hat, half eaten away by moths and mould. Cardboard boxes overflowing with old-fashioned rubber truncheons. A collapsed stack of elderly riot shields. Metropolitan Police baseball caps that had never quite caught on. A rack of heavyweight Kevlar jackets, nothing like the wafer-thin stab-proof numbers that we had these days. And there were other bits and pieces of uniform — helmets with the badge gone, jackets with their brass buttons missing, abandoned kit that had to be twenty, fifty, a hundred years old. Police junk that nobody quite had the heart or the energy or the permission to chuck away.

So they stuck it in here.

'Have you heard of the Black Museum?' Greene said. 'It's in New Scotland Yard. It's closed to the public. This is just like the Black Museum.'

I smiled. 'This is a bit more of a mess than the Black Museum. It's true that the Black Museum has a lot of old kit. Guns. Knives. Walking sticks that turn into swords. Umbrellas that turn into guns. They've got a sword that turns into a knife called a Cop

Killer. But the Black Museum is not really a museum at all. It's more of a classroom. A training aid.'

Greene's eyes were wide. 'You've seen it?'

I nodded. 'Part of my training. They've got a display about Met officers killed in the line of duty. They show you around the Black Museum so that it doesn't happen to you.'

Greene took a deep breath and let it out slowly as he turned to point at a dusty shelf in the darkest corner of that strange little room.

'Look,' he said.

'I can't see anything,' I said, taking a step closer to where he was indicating.

And then I saw it.

It was an ancient leather bag sitting all by itself on a shelf tangled with cobwebs. The dark brown cowhide was worn and cracked. The brass hardware and locks were blackened with rust. Greene lifted it up for my inspection and at the back of the shelf a spider scuttled away as if late for an urgent appointment.

'It looks like an old doctor's bag,' I said.

'It's a Gladstone bag,' Greene said. 'What makes this one special is that it's a Murder Bag. I think it's one of the originals. Did you ever hear of Murder Bags?'

I shook my head.

'Murder Bags were where modern detective work began,' he explained. 'They had two of them in the Yard from 1925. Always packed and ready to go. They contained rubber gloves, magnifying glasses, containers for holding blood, test tubes for fingerprinting, all sorts of gear. The Murder Bags came in when Sir Bernard Spilsbury saw a detective handling a dismembered body with his bare hands. They were the start of modern homicide investigation.' He looked at me shyly. 'What you do.'

He gently replaced the ruined old bag as if it was priceless. 'The history,' he said. 'I love all the history.'

'One thing I don't understand,' I said.

Greene looked at me.

'Your colleague — the woman PC — told me that the dead banker was your first dead body.'

'PC Wren,' he said. 'Edie. Yes.'

'But that can't be true,' I said. 'How long have you been in uniform, Greene?'

'Six years.'

'You must have seen more dead bodies than me,' I said. 'You must have averaged a dead person every day. Motorists who went through their windscreens while sending a text. Cyclists who got hit by a bus. Pedestrians who got hit by the cyclists and the motorists.' I shook my head. 'I can't believe that Hugo Buck was your first dead body.'

Greene thought about it.

'It's true,' he said. 'I've seen a lot of dead people. But what Edie — what PC Wren and I found that morning, on the floor of that man's office, it wasn't rotten luck or fate or stupidity. It didn't happen because somebody was drunk or stoned or sending a text message. What happened to that man, that banker, was the most deliberate thing in the world. It felt like a violation of everything. It's not like the daily slaughter on the roads. I don't know how to explain it. It's just *different,* isn't it?'

I nodded. 'You're right. Murder's different.'

I wake too soon.

It is the sharp point of the night — too late to go back to sleep, too early to get up.

I slip out of bed and go to the window. The lights are blazing in the meat market. I come back and sit on the bed and I still haven't looked at the alarm clock. It feels like catching the eye of a mad man.

And then I look.

03:50

I walk across to the big cupboard built into the wall and push the double doors. They spring open, and the collection of belts and necklaces hanging on the back of the door jangle softly in the dark.

There are shoes on the left-hand side. All kinds of women's shoes. Strappy sandals and spike heels. On the right are stacks of drawers. Knitwear. Carefully folded jeans that will never be worn again.

And directly in front of me there are all the hangers with her dresses and skirts and shirts and jackets and tops. Lots of white cotton but splashes of colour too, although you can't see it in this light. But there are orange silks and blue batik and gauzy things spangled with silver. Soft as a feather, light as a sigh.

I spread my arms wide and sort of gently fall against it, pressing my face into her clothes, her essence, the old life.

I breathe her in.

And then I sleep.

5

The children had painted their families. An entire wall in the classroom was covered with pictures of brightly coloured stick figures. At five they were starting to make sense of the world and their place in it.

The stick-figure mothers had long flowing hair, squiggly lines of black, brown and yellow, and some of them held a sausage-shaped package with a circle for its head — a baby brother or sister. The fathers were mostly bigger stick-insect figures, and nearly all of them carried brown squares and rectangles — briefcases. All of the pictures seemed to be full of life, crowded with parents, siblings, stick figures of assorted shapes and sizes.

Apart from Scout's.

'Look, that's my one,' she said.

How could I miss it?

In Scout's picture there was just an unsmiling stick-figure daddy with no briefcase, a little stick-figure girl with huge brown eyes, and at our feet a small red four-legged daub — Stan.

We had left the dog at home that morning, to his high-pitched howls of rage and despair, because once a month the parents were allowed into the classroom to look at the children's work. It was meant to be a happy time. But I looked at her picture as parents and children jostled around us and I did not know what to say.

Most of the dads were dressed in suits and ties and carrying briefcases, while the mothers were either dressed for the office or for exercise, and some of the ones who were dressed for the gym were carrying babies or shepherding toddlers. So there was definitely a social realism about the pictures.

A young teacher, a blonde New Zealander, Miss Davies, watched us all with a kindly smile.

'Do you like it?' Scout said, disturbed by my silence.

'I love it,' I said.

The truth was it tore at my heart. The surrounding whiteness in Scout's picture seemed to overwhelm the three little figures. And I felt it again, as I knew I would feel it for ever. The completeness of other families, and the shattered nature of what was left of ours.

I placed my hand on Scout's shoulder and she looked up at me with her mother's eyes.

'Good work, Scout,' I said.

'Miss Davies said just family,' she said and, suddenly losing interest, wandered off to her desk to prepare for the first lesson.

It was time to go. Mothers and fathers were kissing their children goodbye and exchanging a few smiley words with the teacher.

But I stood there until the bell went, looking up at Scout's picture of our family, surrounded by all that empty white space.

Stan didn't like being left at home. He had upended his water dish, torn the puppy pad in his cage to shreds, and for an encore climbed on to the coffee table and contemptuously batted away the mouse of my laptop, so it dangled just above the floorboards like a hanging man.

We stared at each other.

A Cavalier would not have been my first choice for a dog. Or even my fifth or sixth choice. I would have gone for something larger. A Labrador or a Golden Retriever. A German Shepherd. Stan considered me with his bulging eyes, absent-mindedly gnawing on a TV cable as I cleaned up his mess. Something larger and smarter, I thought.

But Scout had done her research and she knew what she wanted. Stan was her dog.

And even if he had burned the place down, I couldn't be angry with him today. Without Stan in our lives all the white space around us might have swallowed us alive.

It was still early as Stan and I cut through Charterhouse Square on our way home from our walk. Mallory would be alone up in MIR-1, drinking his tea and figuring. Stan and I still had some time together before I put him in the custody of Mrs Murphy and went to work.

He was squatting for his wet when I became aware of the men on a bench. Three of them. Still up from last night. We got a lot of committed drinkers round our way, drawn by the all-night pubs surrounding Smithfield meat market. Two pasty-faced white boys in cheap grey sports gear, and an Asian man, older and larger, wearing a T-shirt despite the early morning chill. A weightlifter. He was the one who made a kissing noise at my dog.

I smiled.

The three men stared back.

It wasn't a good moment.

Then Stan was scampering happily to-wards them, mad with excitement, pulling me, incredulous at the coincidence that they happened to be here at exactly the same time as him.

I dropped the lead to allow him to greet them.

And that was my mistake.

The weightlifter picked Stan up — and picked him up all wrong, with both hands wrapped around the dog's chest, not sup-porting his weight with one hand under his butt — and recoiled with disgust when Stan attempted to lick his face.

As his milky-faced mates laughed, the weightlifter dropped Stan heavily. He twisted as he fell, landing hard and yelping. Stan was whimpering now, his tail rigid between his legs, ears flattened — all the hallmarks of dog terror.

He came back to me and I picked him up, one hand around his chest and the other under his bottom, the way you should hold a dog, and I held him to me, feeling the frantic drumbeat of his heart.

Because now he had learned fear.

'That's not a dog,' the weightlifter said, 'that's a rat.'

'Man, you freaked it out because you

wouldn't give it a kiss!' said one of his mates.

'It's a dog!' the other said. 'But it's a gay dog!'

They all laughed.

I put Stan down and he prostrated himself on the ground, his tail tucked up, his ears flattened, big eyes bulging. I placed a reassuring hand on his flank, feeling the fragile ribs under the silky chestnut fur, the small heart still pounding wildly. I held the lead loosely in my hand.

The three men were still laughing on the bench. Tough guys, I thought. Tough guys who are only having a laugh.

I tried to walk away as they chuckled and chatted among themselves but Stan stopped for a sniff of a bin. Then he squatted on his hind legs, looking shyly at me as he emptied his bowels. I scooped the three little droppings up in a bag, tied a knot, and placed the bag in the bin. They turned their attention back to my dog, pointing and leering. They had decided that Stan was here for their amusement.

And that was their big mistake.

'Walk on,' I said.

Stan's melancholy eyes rolled up to look at me. He made no attempt to move.

The men roared.

'Walk on!' the weightlifter said. 'Do you

hear him? Walk on, he says! Hey, mate, does he bite? Or does he just suck your cock?'

I was looking down at Stan. He had never taken his eyes off me, and he seemed to flatten himself even lower now, his tail stiff and quivering between his legs, the paws either side of his head, the giant ears hanging down like shoulder-length hair, his chin pressed against the concrete.

It had to happen one day.

He had to learn fear sooner or later.

We all have to learn fear.

But it seemed a crying shame that it was today when I felt so grateful to him, genuinely grateful, for joining me and Scout in our family portrait on her classroom wall.

'Walk on,' I said.

Still Stan did not move.

'Not very obedient, is he, man?' the weightlifter said.

There was a confusion of cities in his accent. London and Los Angeles and Islamabad. And the very worst of all of those places.

I wrapped the old leather dog lead around an empty bench in a loose knot and turned to the men.

'I wasn't talking to the dog,' I said, walking towards them.

The weightlifter stood up, his smile fading, and he opened his mouth to say something just as I punched him in the heart.

One punch.

Right hand.

Full force.

They don't do it in the movies. But the heart is the very worst place to be hit hard. You really don't want to get hit in the heart.

It was a punch that began in the pivoting sole of my left boot and travelled up the muscles in my left leg, gaining full momentum with my twisting torso and then racing down my right arm into the first two knuckles on my right fist.

Less than a second after it had begun its journey, the punch slammed with enormous force against the man's sternum, right on the flat bone at the front of the chest where the upper ribs are attached by cartilage just in front of the heart.

I can never understand why nobody ever punches the heart. Drunks in a bar fight would not think of punching their opponent's heart. Street fighters at closing time would never dream of hitting a man in his heart. The average yob, like these three very average yobs in Charterhouse Square, know nothing about a blow to the heart.

But I knew.

The heart is everything.

101

The weightlifter staggered backwards, his hands on his heart, reeling from the trauma of chest compression. He sat back down on the bench, between his dumb friends, the fight all out of him. The punch had collapsed his sternum maybe an inch, no more, but it was devastating enough to shock the heart.

I looked at the other two, their faces already frozen. They didn't know what to do now. I didn't expect them to. And I looked at the weightlifter, clutching his chest, pawing at his collapsed sternum, and I could see that he lacked the will to get back up.

It was more than just the shock of being punched in the heart. The punch had induced tachycardia — an abrupt and terrifying increase in the heart rate.

He felt like his heart was about to explode.

He felt like he was dying.

I walked back to my dog and rubbed his neck.

'This is Stan,' I told them. 'Stan is a Cavalier King Charles Spaniel. Cavs are the most peace-loving dogs in the world. They are famous for being mild-mannered and polite. Great with children. They were the favourite dog of the Tudor and Stuart kings because of their gentle nature — the gentle nature that you can still see with Stan.'

'We don't want any trouble, man,' one of them said.

I looked at him sharply. 'Can you see Stan's gentle nature or not?'

'Yes,' he said.

I needed coffee immediately. A triple espresso that you could stand your spoon up in. Stan gazed at me with bashful love. He would sit on my lap outside the café and I would drink the short black coffee while I fed him Nature's Menu chicken treats until it was time to go to work.

I nodded at the men, glad that they understood at last.

'He's not the one who bites,' I said.

'Let's visit the dead,' Mallory said at the morning briefing.

If you cut across St James's Park it is a brisk ten-minute walk from 27 Savile Row to the Westminster Public Mortuary on Horseferry Road, and the Iain West Forensic Suite.

'Iain West was the Elvis of forensic pathologists,' Mallory told me as Gane, Whitestone and I struggled to keep pace with him. 'A genius who changed everything. Proved WPC Yvonne Fletcher was shot from the Libyan Embassy. Located exactly where the Brighton bomb was placed in the Grand Hotel by interpreting the injuries of the victims. Examined the victims of the IRA atrocities at Harrods and Hyde Park. Single-handedly improved rail safety with his autopsies of the King's Cross fire. And taught us all an invaluable lesson before dying while he was still a young man.'

'What's that, sir?'

'The dead can't lie.'

Deep inside the Iain West Forensic Suite we waited patiently in our blue scrubs and hairnets as Elsa Olsen, forensic pathologist, smiled and spoke with all the polite good grace of a hostess of a dinner party who was about to make the introductions.

Elsa had a lovely smile, I thought, as she turned her friendly gaze from our faces to the two naked corpses on the stainless steel tables before us.

'Our mystery man,' she said, indicating the drug-withered body of the homeless man. 'Adam Jones. Born New Year's Day, 1973. Died tenth of October 2008.' She indicated his neighbour, the over-fed body of the banker. 'And Hugo Buck, who I think you know already. Born on the seventh of January 1973, died ninth of October 2008.'

Elsa let the dates sink in. Mallory and I stared hard at the bodies. Born within seven days of each other. And died within twenty-four hours of each other. But what else connected them? Apart from the livid wounds that had opened up their throats, now gaping black slits, they looked as though they were from different planets.

Even in death, Hugo Buck's body looked like that of a good amateur sportsman who was only just starting to run to expense-account fat. It was the body of a man who had serious gym sessions a few times a week, probably a personal trainer screaming at him for fifty quid an hour, no matter how busy he got at work; but the years were passing and there were plenty of meals at good restaurants during the working day, and a steady social drinking habit.

You wife-beating bastard.

In comparison, the shell of Adam Jones looked totally depleted, a pathetic sack of bones blotted with bad tattoos and veins scarred by damaged tissue — the squalid souvenirs of a thousand needles. He already looked on the cusp of old age, as if he had shot not just opiates into his veins but all his future years.

I shuddered.

The temperature was kept just above zero in here. Beyond an impatience to get started, I felt nothing when I looked at the bodies. Their spirits had flown. Now there were just the living in this freezing room, and two brutalised empty husks.

'The four questions of death,' Elsa Olsen continued. 'Cause? Mechanism? Manner? Time?' She smiled pleasantly. 'Death's fifth and final question — who? — I leave to you gentlemen.' A smile for DI Whitestone. 'And lady.'

Elsa stepped between the two steel tables.

'Cause of death for both men was suffocation,' she said.

Mallory said, 'They didn't bleed to death?'

Elsa shook her head. 'The single wound to the neck caused a massive haemorrhage. Death would have been quick, quiet and messy. An initial spray, perhaps several, as the artery was cut and then massive bleeding. As you noted, DCI Mallory, the trachea was severed, so screaming was a physical impossibility — there was nothing left to scream with. But it wasn't just the trachea that was cut. The carotid artery was also severed along with the internal jugular vein. Death would have been almost immediate, but neither man had the chance to bleed to death. They suffocated before they had the chance to bleed out.'

Elsa spoke the effortlessly perfect English of the Scandinavian abroad. She was fortyish, Norwegian, tall and slim and dark, one of those black-haired, blue-eyed Norwegians who defied the Nordic stereotype. Mallory had told me that she was his favourite pathologist because she talked about the dead as if they had once been among the living. He said they did not all do that.

'We don't have a weapon,' Mallory said. 'We don't even have an idea of a weapon. What kind of blade can cut a throat like that, Elsa?'

'The mechanism would need to be long and thin and razor-sharp,' Elsa answered. She peered at the gaping black letterbox in Hugo Buck's neck which extended from ear to ear. 'The assailant was standing behind the victim, as we can see from the classic long sweep of the wound. The mechanism would be something like a short double-edged sword, a long scalpel, something similar. Something with a sharp stabbing point and good cutting edges. These are remarkably clean cuts. A torn artery tends to contract and stem the bleeding. But a cleanly cut artery starts bleeding and it doesn't stop.' And then, almost as an after-thought, she said, 'Manner of death was murder.'

'Time of death?' Whitestone said.

'Hugo Buck had an algor mortis or temperature of death of ninety-seven degrees Fahrenheit,' Elsa said. 'Not far below normal body temperature of 98.6. Adam Jones was ninety-five degrees. But Mr Jones died on the street and Mr Buck died in a climate-controlled office.'

'And bodies lose temperature more quickly in the open air,' Whitestone said, looking at Gane.

'Adam Jones was found just after seven p.m.,' Elsa said. 'I would estimate the time of death was between five and seven p.m. Hugo Buck was found at six a.m. and I would estimate time of death between four a.m. and six.'

Mallory smiled. 'Two-hour windows, Elsa? Not taking many chances, are you?' He looked at his detectives. 'I think we just missed them — both of them. I think they both died just before we got there.'

The pathologist raised her hands — the perfect hostess trying to avoid an unpleasant scene. 'Time of death is only ever a best guess,' she said. 'You know that as well as I do.'

'We have to cut Elsa some slack,' Mallory said, still smiling. 'Time of death can eliminate subjects or damn them. So time of death is where our forensic colleagues are at their most cagey, and least willing to speculate.'

'And where the investigating detectives are most desperate for accuracy,' Elsa added.

'Defensive wounds?' Gane said. 'I can't see anything obvious.'

'Nothing,' the pathologist said. 'Neither of them had the will or the chance to put up a fight. There are no defensive wounds on the hands, arms, wrists, legs or feet.' She peered at the body of Adam Jones. 'Although on the body of Mr Jones I did discover some old cuts, bruises and abrasions from minor, earlier incidents.'

'Life on the streets,' I said. 'Takes its toll. No sign of recent substance abuse? He wasn't using at the time of death?'

Elsa shook her head. 'Surprisingly not.' There was a note of pity in her voice. 'Mr Jones was drug free. He was trying to change his ways, despite what you can see.'

What we could see were the exhausted veins on the man's arms — track marks, the miniature railway lines of heroin abuse. They were fading now.

'I think he was trying to kick the habit,' Elsa continued. 'I think he had tried more than once.' She smiled apologetically. 'Do stop me if I start doing your job.'

Mallory said, 'Star sign?'

Elsa stared at him. 'Taurus,' she said. 'The oboe you mention in your notes gave it away. Taureans are lovers of music and song.' Then she smiled. 'Oh bugger off, Mallory!'

We all laughed.

I leaned close to the dead men, looking at the neck of first Adam Jones and then Hugo Buck. In length, depth and darkness, the wounds were absolutely identical.

'One cut,' I said, shaking my head. 'Just one cut in the right place.'

'Sometimes one cut is all it takes,' Mallory said. 'The assassination squad stabbed Julius Caesar twenty-three times. But the Roman physician who examined him concluded that Caesar would have survived the assault if not for the wound to his heart.'

Elsa pointed at the wounds where she had cut open, examined and then closed up their stomachs.

'As you noted from his locked fists, Mr Buck had a cadaveric spasm in the moment of his death — instant rigor,' she said. 'What you like to call that Pompeii moment, Mallory. But Mr Jones is different. There was rigor in his legs but only in the legs. As you know, rigor mortis usually takes two hours to kick in unless there's a cadaveric spasm — as in the case of Mr Buck — or a loss of energy in a part of the body. That causes a chemical reaction, a loss of adenosine triphosphate — ATP — that makes the muscles stiffen and contract. So rigor in the legs means one thing: there was strenuous muscular activity in the legs prior to death.'

We considered the corpse of Adam Jones.

'So Jones was running,' Mallory said.

'He was being chased,' I said.

Elsa Olsen smiled at me, like a teacher looking at her star student. She held out her hand, as if I had won a prize.

'And this belonged to Mr Buck,' she said, and dropped something into my palm.

A small blue thing, round and hard and staring at me from beyond the grave.

'Hugo Buck had a glass eye,' she announced.

6

It was late afternoon with the day's light already fading when I parked outside the block of flats in Regent's Park. The trees in the park were at their most beautiful now, a riot of red and gold leaves that had not yet become serious about falling. But it wouldn't be long, I thought as I walked to the glass doors, wishing I had a coat. You could feel the world turning.

The porter let me in. Natasha Buck opened her door in her robe again. I couldn't decide if it was a bit early to be in a robe, or very late. But this time her hair wasn't wet. And this time she wasn't alone.

A man moved across the living room, glaring at me, with a frosted champagne flute in one hand and a cigarette in the other. I recognised the chauffeur who had been lounging in the big black Merc. I recognised him even in his underpants. It must have been all my training.

'You're too late,' Mrs Buck said.

'This will only take a minute,' I said.

The chauffeur came to the door, sipping his drink. He had come up in the world.

'Is there a problem?' he said.

'Not yet,' I said. 'Would you like one?'

'I'll be in the other room,' he said.

Smart chauffeur.

He went away and took his iced champagne flute with him.

'Tell me about your husband's eye,' I said. 'The one he lost.'

'What do you want to know?'

'How it happened.'

'At school,' she said. 'At Potter's Field. He told me he was kicked in the eye when scoring a try. Hugo was a natural athlete.' She sounded proud of him. 'All those sports the English invented. Rugby. Cricket. Tennis. Football. They came easy to him.'

'So it's something that happened when he was a boy?'

Natasha Buck nodded. 'He was very good at games.'

The next morning I left West End Central after our morning briefing and one hour later I was parking the X5 on a sweeping gravel drive and looking up at a large detached house. It felt like the countryside.

Adam Jones had fallen a long way, I thought, as a Filipina housekeeper let me in. She left me in the hall and I stared through glass doors at the back garden while I waited for the dead man's mother.

There was a neglected swimming pool out there, the surface coated with dead leaves, and the huge garden was wild and over-grown. A fox dozed undisturbed on the far side of the pool, as if he knew that no gardener was coming round any time soon. The house felt abandoned. But there had been money here once. Maybe the money was still here. Maybe it wasn't the money that had run out.

There was one painting on the wall. A shaft of dying sunlight striking the side of a skyscraper. It was a city street but the people had all gone home. It was clearly by the same artist as the one on the wall in Hugo Buck's apartment. And there in the corner I found the same two lower-case initials:

j s

'Thank you so much for coming,' Mrs Jones said, coming down the stairs with her hands outstretched as if I was paying a social call.

I tried not to look shocked but I recognised the function of the colourful scarf she had tied around her head, and the pale, puffy look that comes with long months of intensive chemotherapy.

This lady was dying.

And yet there was an undeniable youthful beauty about her appearance. Under the headscarf, beyond the cancer and the chemo, there was an unlined face, preserved in time like some enchanted creature from a magic land.

'Mrs Jones,' I said. 'I'm DC Wolfe. We spoke briefly on the phone.' I offered my warrant card and she smiled at it politely. 'Mrs Jones, I'm so sorry for the loss of your son.'

She flexed her mouth with a spasm of pain, nodded once and composed herself. She was a proud woman and determined not to show her heart to a man she would probably never see again.

'Please,' she said, gesturing towards the living room.

I followed her. She moved with the careful deliberation of someone whose body has betrayed them. I waited until she had sunk into an armchair, and then took my place on the sofa opposite. An ancient black Labrador padded silently into the room, sniffed the hand that I offered and then ambled over to settle on its owner's feet.

The Filipina housekeeper appeared.

'Tea, please, Rosalita,' said Mrs Jones. Then she looked at me with her shining eyes, bright blue behind her spectacles, intelligent eyes that were still shocked with grief. 'I do appreciate you coming,' she said. 'And how are your enquiries progressing? Have you arrested anyone yet?'

'No, ma'am,' I said. 'But if you could answer some questions, that would be an enormous help to our investigation.'

She nodded, her hand absent-mindedly stroking the back of the black Lab's neck. The dog grunted with contentment.

'Your son,' I said, 'Adam. It would be helpful if you could tell me about Adam.' I hesitated. 'He had no fixed abode at the time of his death?'

His mother smiled, remembering an earlier time.

'He was a very gifted boy,' she said. 'Enormously talented. Sensitive. A wonderful musician. Wonderful!'

She looked around the room, and now I saw that it was a shrine to her dead son. On the bookshelves were trophies, prizes, and small white busts of men having bad hair days. Beethoven and the boys. Between the shelves the walls were covered with framed certificates. And massed on top of a small piano was an array of silver-framed photographs.

'My son was at the Royal Academy of Music,' Mrs Jones told me. 'For one term. Before they asked him to leave.'

Rosalita brought our tea. Mrs Jones lifted a hand and the housekeeper understood that we would serve ourselves. I waited until she had left the room.

'Why did they ask Adam to leave?'

Mrs Jones ruffled the dog between the ears, her face clenched with tension, and I saw that she was in what must have been constant pain.

'Because,' she said, 'there was a darkness in him.' She smiled with an old sadness. 'I don't know how else to explain it. There was a darkness in my son, and that led him to the drugs. And then the drugs took away everything.'

'I think he was trying to stop,' I said. 'The autopsy showed there were no drugs in Adam's body at the time of his death.'

'Yes, he was trying to stop. He was trying very hard.' She looked at me. 'Thank you,' she said.

I wasn't sure what she was thanking me for, and I didn't know how to respond.

Mrs Jones poured our tea. I looked out of the windows. The fox had gone.

'When was the last time you saw your son?'

'A month ago. He came to borrow some money.' She laughed. 'Borrow — that's a good one! His father died two years ago and it was easier for my son to come home and ask for money — to borrow money — after that. When his father was alive, it was difficult. Arguments. Refusals. Raised voices. Tearful promises to change his ways. You can imagine. And things disappeared. A watch left by a bedside. Money in a wallet. That made relations with his father very difficult. But he never stole from me. Not from me. And some do, I know. Some heroin addicts — and my son was certainly a heroin addict — do steal from the people who love them most.'

I sipped my tea. Already Adam Jones had become more than a homeless junkie found dead in an alley, more than a naked corpse on a freezing bed of stainless steel. He had become somebody's son.

'And I saw him last night,' Mrs Jones said. 'My son. Adam. In my dreams. Or in my sleep. But it didn't *feel* like a dream. He was very sad. Have you ever heard of such a thing?' She laughed again. The dog sat up, and then settled. 'Am I going dotty in my old age?'

'I think it happens all the time,' I said. 'A loved one appearing in a dream. Especially at the start. Especially when you have just lost them. I think it takes a while before the dead rest easy.'

She looked at me. 'I get so tired,' she said. She gestured impatiently at her headscarf. 'All this business.'

I nodded.

'Perhaps you're not eating as you should, Mrs Jones,' I said. I hesitated for a moment. 'Chemotherapy makes food taste awful.'

'Yes, it does,' she said. 'They tell you about the hair loss and the nausea. Everyone knows about that. But they don't warn you about what it does to your sense of taste.' She looked at me levelly. 'You seem to know something about the subject.'

'Not really. My grandmother went through the same thing. But it was a long time ago.'

'You must have been close to your grandmother.'

'She brought me up,' I said. 'She raised me. After my parents died. She was more like my mother.'

'I see. Your grandmother sounds like a wonderful woman.'

'She was the kindest person I've ever met,' I said.

'And then she died.'

'Yes. Please tell me some more about Adam. Did he have enemies?'

She raised her eyebrows. 'Somebody killed him. Somebody did *that* to him. But he was a gentle boy. Everyone loved him. Everyone who ever met him. As far as I know.'

'Mrs Jones, most murder victims know their killer. Can you think of anyone who would want to harm Adam? When he came home, did he talk about his money problems? Money that he owed? Outstanding debts?'

'Money problems were a way of life for my son,' she replied. 'But there was no malice in him. He was one of those people who make the world a better place. Then he lost his way and he never found his way back. And it didn't do any good — however much we loved him, however much it hurt us, however much we wanted him to be well. However much he wanted it for himself. None of it mattered. But under it all he was a good boy. A happy boy. There wasn't always that sadness in him. There wasn't always that darkness.'

She suddenly seemed very tired. She nodded towards the piano and the silver-framed

120

photographs. 'Look for yourself. Look at my son. Go on.' It was more than an invitation. 'Look,' she said.

I went across to the piano where there were dozens of photographs. But they were all of a baby and a boy. It was as if Adam Jones had never made it beyond his middle teens. There were shots of a bonny baby, in his cot and in the arms of Mrs Jones, when she was young and pretty and healthy, in love with life and her newborn son, laughing with delight at the miracle of this baby; and then Adam as a chubby-legged toddler, holding hands with his father, both of them smiling on some sunny English beach; and Adam a bit older, six or seven, long-haired and grinning to reveal the gaps in his front teeth, holding a child's violin. The boy grew before my eyes. But he did not grow to manhood. Not in these photographs.

I looked across at Mrs Jones. Her eyes were closed. The dog had seized the opportunity to climb on to the sofa and snuggle up to her. Her head was dropping forward.

'I get so very tired,' she said, looking up at me sharply. 'Did your grandmother experience that tiredness?'

'Yes, ma'am.'

I picked up a photograph of Adam at the

age of about ten, on stage in an evening suit standing before an audience of adults and children who were on their feet and clapping. He held a child-sized oboe in his hands.

I put it back down.

'Chemotherapy makes you exhausted,' I said.

I looked at her, and she was sleeping. I turned back to the piano, my eyes ranging over the photographs, waiting for them to tell me something. No brothers, no sisters. Adam as a little boy in his Superman pyjamas. A posed picture of a youth orchestra. And another, a year or two later. And sitting in front of his mother on a carousel, both of them grinning and waving as their horse rode past the camera.

Goodbye, Daddy, goodbye.

I was holding the photograph in my hands before I knew it. The silver frame was flecked with the first signs of age. And I held it for a long moment before I realised that the Filipina housekeeper, Rosalita, was standing in the doorway, watching me. She came into the room and began to clear away the tea things. I looked back at the photograph in my hands.

Soldiers, I saw.

Young men in uniform, I saw.

This was the same photograph I had seen in the shining tower, sitting all alone on the desk of Hugo Buck, splashed with his fresh blood. The same seven with the same unbreakable smiles.

And again I saw that it was only at first glance that it looked like a photograph of soldiers. Despite the old-fashioned military uniforms, these were boys, not men. Schoolboys dressed as warriors. No, not men, but boys who would not be boys for much longer.

One of them was the young unspoilt Adam Jones and the other, on the far side of the photograph, was the teenage Hugo Buck.

I had only known them a couple of decades later, as dead men, murder victims, drowned in their own blood. I had only ever seen them as corpses on stainless steel slabs in the cold room of the Iain West Forensic Suite.

But when you looked, when you really looked, they were both unmistakable.

'I must have nodded off,' Mrs Jones said, suddenly standing next to me, and so close and so unexpected that I almost gasped out loud.

She took the frame from me, looked at the photograph as if she had not seen it for a while, then replaced it exactly where it had been, in its little groove of dust on the black lacquer of the piano.

She'd wanted me to see, and she'd wanted me to understand, but I saw now that this courteous, kind and dying woman would really prefer it if I did not actually touch her photographs.

'Did you ever meet Hugo Buck, Mrs Jones?'

'Hugo? I haven't seen him for, what, must be nearly twenty years. He went into the City. I understand he's doing very well.'

'And your son knew Hugo Buck,' I said. 'They were friends, weren't they?'

She nodded. 'At Potter's Field. They were at school together.'

7

I drove back to 27 Savile Row and for the rest of that day and for most of the next our team never left Major Incident Room One.

The discovery of the second photograph changed everything. It gave us our MLOE — main line of enquiry — and focused all of the double homicide investigation on seven schoolboys in military uniform, grinning at a camera twenty years ago.

'Work out from the photograph applying the ABC principle at all times,' DCI Mallory warned us, moving between the workstations where we hunted, our phones on permanent charge and HOLMES2 — the Home Office Large Major Enquiry System, the mainframe police computer — flickering on the screens in front of us. 'Assume nothing. Believe nothing. Challenge and check everything.'

The sky was flat and white above the rooftops of Mayfair when Mallory faced us for his afternoon briefing. He ran a hand across his scalp and took a joyless gulp of cold takeaway tea.

'Right,' he said. 'What are we looking at?'

We were looking at the large flat plasma screen on the wall of MIR-1, and on the screen was the photograph that had been in the home of Adam Jones's mother, and also on Hugo Buck's desk.

DI Whitestone, the MIT's deputy SIO, cleared her throat and said, 'Sir, this photograph was taken at Potter's Field College in the spring of 1988. Potter's Field College is a boarding school for boys aged thirteen to eighteen on the border of Berkshire and Buckinghamshire. The seven boys in the photograph are all wearing the uniform of the school's Combined Cadet Force. On the far left of the picture is Adam Jones. And on the far right is Hugo Buck.'

Next to the screen was Mallory's wall — a massive whiteboard with the physical photograph of the seven smiling boys, eight inches by ten inches out of its frame, looking tiny tacked up there, and next to it a selection of pictures of Jones and Buck taken at the scenes of their murder and again at their autopsy at the Iain West.

'The Combined Cadet Force is the Potter's Field version of the Officer Training

Corps,' Whitestone continued, 'which they still go in for at a lot of these old public schools.'

'And Potter's Field is one of the oldest,' Mallory said. 'Five hundred years old? It has to be as old as Harrow, St Paul's, Westminster, Winchester, Rugby and Marlborough. And of course Slough Comprehensive.' He glanced at our blank faces. 'Eton,' he explained. 'They call themselves Slough Comprehensive. It's their little joke. What's our source for the photograph?'

I said, 'Sir, this is the copy I obtained from the mother of Adam Jones.'

'And we're absolutely certain it's the same one that was on the desk of Hugo Buck?'

DI Gane looked up from his laptop. 'The one at the bank had some superficial damage, sir. There was a blood trace that had seeped under the glass. But it's the same photograph all right.'

'And were Jones and Buck in contact after leaving school?' Mallory asked.

'Looks like they went their separate ways, sir,' I replied. 'Jones's mother hadn't seen Hugo Buck in nearly twenty years. She wasn't aware of his death.'

Gane said, 'Doesn't she read the papers?'

'She's in the last stage of terminal cancer,'

I said. 'I think she has other things on her mind.'

'Because the mother wasn't aware of contact doesn't mean there wasn't any,' Gane reasoned.

'Natasha Buck, Hugo Buck's widow, has no recollection of ever meeting Adam Jones,' I said. 'She would have remembered a homeless heroin addict turning up at their door or their wedding.'

'Jones tried to make contact with Buck at his office,' Whitestone said. 'I spoke to the PA at ChinaCorps and she can remember a man claiming to be an old friend of Buck's turning up at the office wanting to see him. This is two or three years back. She described the man as looking like a tramp. Sounds like Jones. But Buck wouldn't see him and security had to escort the unknown visitor from the building. Apparently it was an ugly little scene.'

'The junkie tapping his rich mate for money and getting a knockback,' Gane said.

'That's a reasonable assumption,' Mallory said.

'So we're definitely treating this as a double homicide, sir?' Gane asked. 'We're working on the theory that it's the same perp? Even without contact since — what's the school? — Potter's Field?'

'Yes,' Mallory confirmed. 'The killer's MO. The manner of death. The school connection. It's enough. It's more than enough. How are we doing with prints?'

'We've identified and eliminated all the prints found in the ChinaCorps office,' Gane said. 'The alley where Jones was found is a forensic nightmare. Full of prints that we can't identify and never will.'

'Glove prints?' Mallory said.

'No, boss. Sorry, boss.'

Mallory shook his bald head. 'There should be glove prints.' He stared up at the photograph. 'Who are the other five boys?'

'We're chasing that down, sir,' Whitestone said. 'Should have names by the end of play today. DC Wolfe's going to talk to Adam Jones's mother again and I've sounded out the school. The Head Master's calling me.'

'And I want the photographer, please,' Mallory said. 'Find out who took the photograph, will you, DI Whitestone? And give us a close-up, would you, DI Gane?'

Gane tapped some keys and the camera seemed to move in for a better look. Seven faces swam out of the past and into vivid close-up.

We looked at them in silence.

The boys had all looked the same to me at first. Seven smiling sons of privilege, cocky and smug in their military uniforms and their mullet haircuts, certain that tomorrow belonged to them. But now they were starting to look like individuals.

Adam Jones on the left — a skinny kid with an open, guileless face, looking far younger than the rest. The only one who still looked like a child.

Hugo Buck on the right — dark and mannish, already looking like he needed to shave every day, confident in his looks and his strength and his place in the world.

I was looking harder at the photo, really seeing it for the first time. They were not all the same.

They were not even all smiling.

In the middle of the group was a serious, delicate-looking boy in dark glasses, his fringe swept back off a high forehead.

He was flanked by the twins — identical, I could now see. Tall, good-looking and cold. One of them had a jumble of jagged scars running down one side of his face.

Next to the twin with the scars, between him and Adam Jones, there was a chubby, leering adolescent, the tip of his tongue exploring a corner of his mouth.

And on the other side, next to Buck, there was a grinning dark-skinned youth, possibly Indian, far taller than the rest.

Only their uniforms were the same.

'So what exactly is this Combined Cadet Force?' Gane said. 'Posh rich kids playing soldiers?'

'They take it seriously,' Mallory said. 'A significant number of boys take up commissions in these schools. I bet the British Army is still the biggest employer of Old Potter's Field Boys. Even now. They say that Old Etonians go into the army, politics and acting while Old Potters go into the army, banking and jail.'

I wondered how Mallory knew so much about it.

'But what's the point of them?' Gane persisted. 'The Officer Training Corps. The Combined Cadet Force. Why do a bunch of public schoolboys need to dress up as soldiers?'

Whitestone looked at her notes. 'It's been around for quite a while. The Potter's Field Combined Cadet Force was founded in 1805 as the Potter's Field Rifles.'

Mallory smiled with affection at Gane, his round John Lennon glasses glinting in the overhead lights. 'That year ring any bells, DI Gane? No? The country thought that Napoleon was about to invade. He had an army of two hundred thousand men on the coast of France. These grand old schools were preparing a home guard. A youth movement to repel the invaders.'

'And did Napoleon bottle it, sir?' Gane asked. 'Excuse my ignorance.'

'Yes, Gane, Napoleon seriously bottled it.' Mallory looked at the screen. 'But whether they called them an Officer Training Corps or a Combined Cadet Force or something else, the public schools all kept their Rifles.'

'They join at fifteen,' Whitestone said, 'around the age of the boys in the photograph. And they're taught by regular serving army officers. Leadership skills, signals. And how to shoot. They have a range weekend where they use live ammunition.'

'Any other business?' Mallory said.

'Bob the Butcher, sir,' Gane said.

And then he turned on me.

'You don't talk to the press, OK? You just never do it. We have people to do that for us. The media liaison officers — leave it to them, all right? Because as soon as you start talking to journalists, as soon as you start mouthing off with your little theories, then every mummy's boy with an iMac and a grudge against society starts crawling out of the woodwork, boasting on all the social network sites about how antisocial they've been. And once they do — once they start claiming to be Bob the Butcher — then we

132

have to follow it up, chase down their IP addresses, go round to their house and tell them they've been very, very naughty. So we don't talk to the press, the MLOs do. OK?'

'Fair enough,' I said.

He saw that I wasn't going to argue with him, and he softened.

'Especially to this Scarlet Bush,' he continued. 'She's poison. They say she's got a tabloid brain and a broadsheet mouth. Or is it the other way round?'

I hesitated. 'But you're taking Bob the Butcher seriously?'

'We have no choice,' Gane said. 'If someone claims to have committed murder, then we have to take them seriously. And run them down. It's sort of our job.'

Mallory said, 'You've got the IP address for this Bob the Butcher?'

'Not yet, sir,' Gane replied. 'He's running his messages through some kind of anonymiser or anonymous proxy. Probably Tor or 12P. It's an intermediary that's meant to act as a wall between the user and the rest of the digital world. Most of the child pornography online is run through anonymisers. It's the deep web, designed to bury an IP address. Bob's been in touch again, if anybody's interested.'

Gane hit a couple of keys. On the big TV screen a social network site replaced the photograph of the seven boys. A black-and-white photograph the size of a postage stamp featuring a thin-faced man in a suit, tie and hat, an insolent cigarette dangling from one corner of his mouth. A face from history.

Mallory read the message aloud: 'I am become Death, the destroyer of worlds. Behold the dark angel of the people, righteous avenger of the dispossessed. Bob the Butcher is coming. Kill all bankers. Kill all pigs. #killallpigs.'

Gane laughed. 'Now there's someone who has played one too many computer games.'

Mallory wasn't laughing. 'The first part is from Robert Oppenheimer, the father of the atomic bomb,' he said. ' "I am become Death, the destroyer of worlds". The photograph is of Oppenheimer. He was quoting a Hindu scripture, the Bhagavad-Gita. He said it after they tested the first nuclear weapon. After the world changed for ever.'

'I'll find him,' Gane said, stabbing some keys.

The photograph of the seven boys returned to the screen.

'The school is the key,' Mallory said. 'Potter's Field.'

134

'Potter's Field,' Whitestone said. 'The school was founded by King Henry VIII in 1509, the first year of his reign. The name is taken from the Bible. A potter's field is a piece of land that's good for nothing but burial. The priests bought the potter's field with Judas's blood money. Matthew 27:3–8. "And the chief priests took the silver pieces and said; It is not lawful to put them into the treasury, because it is the price of blood. And they took counsel and bought with them the potter's field, to bury strangers in. Wherefore that field was called — The Field of Blood. Unto this day." '

She smiled modestly.

'Sunday school?' Gane said.

'Google,' Whitestone replied.

'They're more of a mixed bunch than I thought they would be,' I said. 'Hugo Buck comes from an old banking family. Adam Jones was at Potter's Field on a music scholarship. They didn't just die in different worlds. They came from different worlds.'

Mallory nodded. 'Old money. New money. And no money. But who hates them?'

We stared at the photograph of the Potter's Field Combined Cadet Force, class of 1988. The only sound was the traffic crawling along Savile Row five floors below. And I saw how Mallory used the silence, how it created a space for the truth to seep in.

'Maybe they hate each other,' I said.

I was late. Horribly late.

Scout had an extra class after school. Fashion illustration, whatever that was. Something for kids who loved to draw and whose parents were stuck in an office. But I was still late.

Scout was waiting with her teacher, Miss Davies, just inside the school gates. Everyone else had gone home long ago. The pair of them were chatting happily — or Scout was talking and the blonde young New Zealander was listening, smiling and nodding and unable to get a word in edgeways. Scout really loved Miss Davies.

I parked the car as close as I could get to the school gates and ran to them.

'Sorry,' I said. 'The traffic.'

Miss Davies was all smiles and Kiwi cool and very understanding. Scout was poker-faced, revealing nothing.

In the car on the way home I looked at her in my rear-view mirror, watching her watching the street.

'Scout,' I said.

She looked at my eyes in the mirror. 'Yes?'

'I'm sorry.'

'It was one of your days to pick me up.

Not one of Mrs Murphy's days. One of your days.'

'I'll work it out better,' I said. 'Maybe Mrs Murphy can do more days. But I'll never be late again.'

She wasn't looking at me any more.

'Scout?'

'What?'

'Forgive me?'

She looked back at the street.

'I always forgive you,' she said.

And I thought about that all the way home.

Scout rolled on the floor with the dog.

'He cries in the night sometimes,' she said. 'Stan does. I hear him.'

I nodded. 'I hear him too,' I said.

'I think he misses his old home.'

'No,' I said. 'He misses his mother's heartbeat. But there's a trick for young dogs that miss their mothers. I'll show you.'

I found an old alarm clock and slipped it under the blanket in the dog's basket.

'He'll think it's his old mum dog,' I said. 'He'll hear the tick-tock of the clock and he'll think it's her heartbeat.'

Scout looked so doubtful that the idea suddenly seemed ridiculous to me.

But it worked.

That night I lay awake until just before dawn, turning my pillow over until the meat market fell silent and the light in the room was milky grey. Stan did not whimper once.

8

The Black Museum of Scotland Yard is not a museum at all. It is not open to the public and its contents are guarded behind heavily locked doors. Officially, it is not even called the Black Museum. After complaints from officers working in areas with large ethnic minorities, it was renamed the Metropolitan Police Crime Museum, an enforced change that ensured we would always and forever call it the Black Museum.

As I had told PC Greene, the Black Museum is a teaching aide. That was why it was established in the Victorian era, that was why it still existed — to save the lives of policemen by educating them in the criminal's tools of the trade.

And that was why DCI Mallory and I went to the Black Museum. I had spent a full day on HOLMES2, slogging through just one item on the MLOE checklist — identifying modus operandi suspects, murderers who killed by cutting throats and who were neither dead nor in prison. It was a long, frustrating day of too many dead ends and too much caffeine.

So when the day's light was fading, we went looking for a murder weapon.

DCI Mallory and I stood outside Room 101 in New Scotland Yard. He was grinning broadly.

'Room 101,' he chuckled. 'It's almost too perfect, isn't it?'

I must have looked baffled.

'Room 101,' he repeated, frowning with mild disappointment. 'The torture chamber in the Ministry of Love. George Orwell? *1984?*'

My brain scrambled to catch up. I had read *1984* when I was a kid. Somebody made me. 'Where the rats are,' I said. 'The rats in the cage that get strapped to Winston's face.'

'Room 101 is the place of your worst nightmare,' Mallory said. 'It's the room that contains the worst thing in the world. O'Brien tells Winston that we all know what is waiting for us inside.'

Mallory knocked on the door and a voice told us to come in.

Even for a detective chief inspector in

Homicide and Serious Crime, visits to the Black Museum were meant to be by appointment only. But the curator in Room 101 — a Sergeant John Caine with thirty years' service on his face and not a gram of flab on his body — greeted Mallory like an old friend.

'What can we do you for, sir?' the keeper of the Black Museum said as they shook hands.

'We're looking for a knife, John,' Mallory said. 'Or at least some kind of double-edged blade.' He was opening his briefcase. 'I figure it has to be less than a sword but more than a knife.' He removed a file containing a sheaf of photographs and spread them on the curator's desk. 'Something that could have done this.'

Sergeant Caine calmly studied half a dozen photographs, copies of the same murder scene and autopsy pictures that were on Mallory's wall in the Major Incident Room, while I looked around me. The walls were covered with bookshelves and badges from police forces around the world, presumably showing their gratitude for a glimpse inside the Black Museum. I picked up an elderly hardback book from Caine's desk. There was no dust jacket. *Forty Years of Scotland Yard,* it said. *The Record of a*

Lifetime's Service in the Criminal Investigation Department by Frederick Porter Wensley.

'Don't touch that,' Sergeant Caine said, not even looking at me.

I put the book down.

To Mallory he said, 'These are the Bob the Butcher killings.'

'We've yet to make that connection,' Mallory said.

'But you're treating it as a double homicide, sir?'

Mallory nodded. 'Same killer, same MO. But I'm not convinced it's Bob.'

Sergeant Caine looked at me without warmth or welcome. Mallory had warned me that he was wary of strangers. Although wary didn't quite cover his cold, gimlet-eyed hostility.

'This is DC Wolfe, the newest member of my MIT.'

I held out my hand but Caine didn't seem to see it. Happy to remind me that, as a sergeant, even one in uniform, he outranked me.

'Right,' he said. 'Ground rules. No photographs. No touching, unless I say so for the purpose of demonstration. And absolutely nothing I say is for the record. Got it?'

'Got it, sergeant,' I said.

'Good. Then let's go.'

There was a locked door inside Room 101. Sergeant Caine unlocked it and we went inside. It was a living room from the distant past. There was a fireplace, a bay window, gaslights. It took me a moment to register that although these were false, there were weapons everywhere, and these were very real. A glass case full of firearms. A desk covered with what looked like the results of a sword armistice. A hangman's noose dangled from the ceiling, which I thought was overdoing it a bit.

'What was the name of the detective who founded the museum?' Mallory asked.

'Inspector Neame, sir,' Caine said. 'In 1874. Do you want to have a wander round in here? There are plenty of blades.'

Mallory was peering at what looked like a pirate's cutlass. 'Please,' he said. 'You go ahead with DC Wolfe.'

I followed the curator through a doorway with no door.

'I heard they might open this place up,' I said, filling the silence.

He stopped to look at me sharply. 'Open it up?'

'To the public,' I said. 'To raise money.'

'The public?' he said with some distaste, as if it was the public who were largely responsible for the human misery on display in Room 101. 'Who wants to open it up to the public?'

'The council,' I said, wishing I had kept my cakehole shut.

'Over their dead bodies,' said Sergeant Caine.

'Don't you mean —'

'I know whose bodies I mean,' he said. Then he clapped his hands, his mood brightening as he gave me an evil grin. 'Not one of those queasy types, are you? Let me know if you're going to bring up your Weetabix.'

'I've been here before,' I said. 'A Crime Academy visit.'

'Ah, an expert. An old hand. Let's see how much of an expert you are, sonny.' He picked up a walking stick. 'What does this look like?'

'A sword,' I guessed. 'A sword disguised as a walking stick.'

Sergeant Caine smiled. 'Clever boy.' He pulled apart the walking stick to reveal twelve inches of gleaming Sheffield steel. Then closed it up again.

'So if I came at you . . .'

He swung the stick towards my face. I caught it with both hands.

'I would grab it before you had a chance to use it as a sword,' I said, twisting my grip and pulling the walking stick from his hand.

I allowed myself a small smile that immediately faded when I saw that he was still holding the handle. It was a handgun.

'Which would leave me with nothing but my firearm,' he said, pointing it at my face. 'Bang, bang, you're dead.'

'Does it work?' I asked, handing him the walking stick.

'Oh, they all work,' Caine said. He carefully attached the walking stick to the handle. 'That's the point.'

Mallory came into the room.

'See anything you fancy, sir?' Caine asked.

Mallory shook his head.

'Probably here somewhere,' the curator said cheerfully.

You would think so. The Black Museum contains every murder weapon you can imagine and plenty more that you can't. More than a hundred years' worth of explosives, firearms and poison. And every item in there has seen active service.

On the counter in front of me was a cutlass used by the Kray brothers. Next door was a rocket launcher used by the IRA. At first I thought Caine had a mini-kitchen in here, but it turned out to be the cooking pot where serial killer Dennis Nilsen boiled the meat off his victims before pouring it down the drains. And there were more knives than I had seen in the basement of West End Central.

The Black Museum was spread over several large, neat rooms full of glass display cases and exhibits and shelves with the face-masks of men who stole lives. Blank, ordinary, banal-looking men who shot, poisoned, stabbed, chopped up, boiled and ate their victims. All these pathetic little men who had abruptly aborted the happiness of countless lifetimes, all these savage creeps who had built a mountain of human misery.

Yes, I had been here before.

But this time was different.

Now I was not with my peers.

There was no hiding in a crowd, and no easy laughter to relieve the tension. This did not feel like a school trip. This time the Black Museum confronted me with all its horror, and its collection of human cruelty, and it was just too much for me.

Or perhaps it was something else. The first time I had been here, on that visit with the Crime Academy, I was a cocky unmarried kid who knew nothing about loss. And now I knew.

First came the sweat, and then suddenly I was crouching over a wastepaper basket, quietly being sick. Mallory and Sergeant

Caine came into the room. If they saw my discomfort then they gave no sign.

'Your weapon could be custom-made,' Caine was saying. 'Some kind of knife that's made to cut a man's throat — and only that. Something that's made for that purpose and that purpose alone.'

Outside, Big Ben was chiming six. Mrs Murphy would have picked up Scout and would be making their dinner while my daughter and our dog chased each other across the great open space of our loft.

I stood up, looking with embarrassment and disgust at the yellow bile I had brought up. Mallory lightly patted my shoulder.

I couldn't look at him just yet.

'Nice cup of tea?' he said.

Mallory took me to his home.

His wife appeared at the door as we pulled up outside a terraced house on a quiet street in Pimlico. A tall, slim, grey-haired woman with an amused twinkle in her eye and carpet slippers on her feet. A West Highland White Terrier stood watch between them as Mr and Mrs Mallory communicated in the shorthand of the long-term married.

'Done for the day then?' she said, folding her arms.

'Not quite, hen,' he said, pecking her cheek.

'Going out again then.'

'Spruce up a bit first.'

'Something to eat?'

'Tea would be lovely.'

She had the same Aberdeen accent as her husband. They could have been born in the same street.

'Who's this?'

'New man. DC Wolfe.'

'Hello, hen,' Mrs Mallory said, her face breaking into a broad smile. 'Come on in.'

She brought us tea and biscuits, and I began to feel better with sugar and caffeine inside me. Mallory bolted his tea quickly and disappeared, shoving in a ginger nut.

'Five minutes,' he told me.

The Westie followed him, panting with pleasure.

Their home was a small, neat maisonette. The photographs on the mantelpiece and bookshelves, their colours fading now, showed the Mallorys' old life under some tropical sun. The pair of them, fifteen, twenty, twenty-five years younger, raising glasses and smiling shyly at some café table. And Mallory, his hair already gone at thirty, grinning in shorts, short-sleeve shirt and a black peaked cap, two Asian men in the same uniform grinning either side of him. And the Mallorys smiling again for the camera with a city built by a harbour behind and far below them.

'Hong Kong,' Mrs Mallory said. 'My husband was in the Royal Hong Kong Police Force for fifteen years. "We serve with pride and care". Maybe he told you.'

'No, ma'am.'

She laughed. 'You can call me Margaret.'

'DCI Mallory hasn't told me anything, ma'am — Margaret.'

'We came back in 1997. After the changeover. When it lost the royal bit. The British went home and so did we. Bit of a shock to the system. We miss it. Although of course that old Hong Kong is not there any more.'

The photographs ran the course of two lifetimes. But I could see no pictures of children.

'And do you have a family?' Mrs Mallory asked me.

'I have a little girl,' I said. 'My parents are long gone. No brothers, no sisters.' A beat. 'I lost my wife.'

She waited for more, but there wasn't any more.

'I see,' she said.

'I have my daughter. Scout. She's five.' I

stirred my tea. 'But there's just me and her.'

Mrs Mallory nodded. 'Then you have a family,' she said, and she had me for life.

We crossed the river as the sun set, the groups of tourists on the bridge taking photographs of the Palace of Westminster, Big Ben and Westminster Abbey, all majestic in the dying light, as the London commuters hurried home, not even noticing the everyday magic of this place.

'And now you've met my wife,' Mallory said. 'Take the Lambeth Road on the far side of the bridge.'

'Sir.'

I drove south until two giant cannon reared out of the twilight. They sat before a domed building flying the Union Jack.

'We're going to the Imperial War Museum?'

'It was once the Bethlem Royal Hospital,' Mallory said. 'Bedlam. The lunatic asylum. Did you know that? You can park round the back in St George's Road. We're not going through the front door.'

A security guard emerged as we were coming through the gardens. He stared at us with suspicion until a woman's voice called out to him: 'It's all right, Charlie, they're with me.'

The security guard stepped back, and there was a young woman in a wheelchair. She smiled when she saw Mallory.

'Sir,' she said, and her smile grew bigger as she saluted.

'Hello, Carol,' he said, leaning forward to kiss her on each cheek.

He introduced me and we waited while she turned her wheelchair in a tight space. I went to help but she stopped me with a curt, 'I've got it'.

We followed her down a narrow corridor that led to the main hall. The lights were off. In the darkness Spitfires and Messerschmitts and Hurricanes and V2 flying bombs hung above us, frozen in mid-flight, frozen in time.

'How can I help you, sir?' Carol said.

Mallory was opening his briefcase. 'We're looking for a murder weapon, Carol.' He handed her the file.

She slowly leafed through it.

'Our conjecture is that the weapon was designed for cutting a man's throat,' Mallory said.

'Your conjecture is right, sir,' she said, smiling again. 'I know just the thing. We should have one in storage. Please follow me.'

■ ■ ■ ■

The knife was just under twelve inches long, most of it blade, a blade that was long and thin and double-edged, designed to slip easily into human flesh and then cut through it without fuss. Mallory handed it to me, and I was surprised to find that it weighed next to nothing. The handle had a comforting ring grip, sitting easy in my closed right fist, and the thing conveyed a sense of terrible power.

'The Fairbairn-Sykes fighting knife,' Carol said. 'Developed by William Ewart Fairbairn and Eric Anthony Sykes when they were policing in Shanghai before the war.'

'The commando knife,' Mallory said. 'Of course.'

I could not get used to how light it felt in my hand. It was so easy to hold. A sharp stabbing point, a good cutting edge. The double-edged blade glinted in the half-light of the storage room.

'This was invented by two policemen?' I said.

Carol nodded. 'W. E. Fairbairn was an expert in close-combat fighting. This was designed to be the perfect fighting knife but it turned out to be the perfect killing knife.

Standard-issue sidearm for all World War Two commandos. If the Nazis caught you with one of these, you were shot on the spot as a spy. Most knives are not specifically designed to kill — apart from the Fairbairn-Sykes. It looks easy to use, but it's not. You have to know which arteries are closest to the surface and unprotected by clothing. Give it here, will you?'

The young woman in the wheelchair gave us a demonstration. With the fingers on her left hand spread wide she mimed pulling a man's head to one side. With the knife in her right hand she stabbed the point sideways and then quickly pushed it forward.

'Punch and pull,' she said. 'Punch the tip of the knife through the side of the neck and then pull the blade out of the front. You can't patch that up with a couple of stitches and some Nurofen Plus. Most people who want to cut a throat start on the outside. They hack and saw and chop.'

She mimed hacking and sawing and chopping.

'That's all right if you want to hurt their feelings,' she said. 'That's all right if you want to put a crimp in their day. But not if you want to be certain of killing them.'

'The punch and pull,' Mallory said. 'It cuts the windpipe and then you have a good chance of cutting the carotid arteries.'

'More than a good chance,' Carol said. 'That move is called the carotid thrust. Cutting the carotid arteries is the whole point, sir. If the shock doesn't immediately kill them, then they die because the carotids have been severed and there's no blood being pumped from the heart to the brain.'

'How long?' I asked.

'Brain-dead immediately,' she said. 'Unconscious in five seconds and dead in twelve seconds.'

'And when did they stop making these knives?'

'They've never stopped making these knives. It's been evolving for almost a hundred years. There's a contemporary version used by the Special Forces — the UK-SFK. It's the greatest combat knife ever invented.' She looked at Mallory, and I wondered how they knew each other. 'And now Bob the Butcher's got one.'

Mallory smiled. 'We don't know if it's Bob,' he said. 'What we do know is that it's someone with training who has access to specialist weapons.' He looked at me. 'Presumably you can get a Fairbairn-Sykes online?'

'You can buy anything online,' I said.

'Apart from training and knowledge and

the expertise you would need to execute the carotid thrust,' Carol said. 'That takes years to accumulate. And there's something else.'

We watched her feel the weight of the Fairbairn-Sykes fighting knife.

'To kill someone with one of these — to stick the stabbing point in the side of their neck and then pull it clean out the front . . .' She paused and looked up at Mallory from her wheelchair. 'You would have to really hate their guts, sir.'

I was in the ring and my legs were gone.

We were only a minute into the third round of sparring but already I was weak with exhaustion, flat-footed and breathing through my mouth, sagging against the ropes, my elbows pressed protectively against my lower ribcage, my hands raised to protect my head, the black leather of the fourteen-ounce Lonsdale gloves slick with sweat against my face.

The punches kept coming.

They were being thrown by a small man with long silver hair poking out of his old Everlast headguard. He grinned broadly at my exhaustion, revealing both a mean streak and a blue mouthguard. Hunched behind his tight, high guard, risking nothing, he moved in for the finish.

With my face buried deep into my gloves, I felt his body shots rip into my side with blinding speed. The small man was both skinny and muscle-packed, and hit very hard. Left ribs, right ribs. Left ribs, right ribs. I dug my elbows in deeper, but I could still feel their whiplash sting.

We were face to face now. At six feet, I towered above my opponent — Fred was his name — but probably the first thing I had ever learned in a boxing ring is that speed beats power. The bigger you are, the more there is to hit.

A left hook came through my ragged defence and made me gasp as it struck the lowest rib. I dug my elbows in deeper, really not wanting another one, and the moment I lowered my gloves a few inches Fred smacked me in my poorly guarded head.

Upstairs downstairs, I thought, cursing my basic mistake — leaving one area undefended while another is being attacked. I rolled against the ropes, willing my legs to work, trying to get back up on the balls of my feet.

But a left hook cracked against the right side of my headguard, and then a right hook cracked harder against the left side, making my ears ring despite the thick protective leather of my headguard.

I must have instinctively lifted my gloves a fraction to protect my head because Fred whipped in a wicked left hook, digging me low in the right ribs.

He was flagging too. Hitting someone non-stop takes it out of you. His combinations were slowing down, but a body shot is the hardest punch to recover from and I felt my dead legs sagging. Everything was telling me to go down. But I didn't go down. I stayed on my feet, kept up by nothing but the ropes behind me and the will inside.

Fred grinned at me, revealing that old blue mouthguard. I watched him lift the elbow of his left arm, preparing for a left hook. But such is the beautiful balance of boxing that if your opponent can hit you then you are in a position to hit them back.

I saw my chance and took it.

Before Fred could slam a short hard left hook into my aching body, or my ringing head, I whipped a short left uppercut on to the point of his chin, jerking back his head just as the buzzer went to end the third and final round.

We fell into each other's arms, totally spent, both laughing.

When we broke from the embrace, I stood there bent double, fighting for breath. I could hear the sound of skipping ropes, the business news on the TV by the treadmills, and a trainer chanting yoga instructions. When I looked up, Fred was taking off his battered headguard and his long silver hair was tumbling down — the hair of a veteran pirate. He pulled out his mouthguard.

'You're so lucky to be training,' he said.

He lifted a glove in salute and I touched it with my own glove.

'Good,' he told me. 'But keep those elbows tucked in and don't be a statue. When you've thrown your punches, get out of there. Don't stand around taking pictures. Even when you're knackered. Especially when you're knackered.'

My breath was slowly returning. 'It's hard,' I managed.

Fred laughed. 'It's supposed to be hard. If it was easy, then everyone would do it.' He patted my back. 'Warm down with thirty minutes on the bike and don't forget your stretching.'

Fred climbed out of the ring. He wandered over to the sound system and put on The Jam. This was Smithfield Amateur Boxing Club, and Fred ran the place, so he got to choose the music. 'Going Underground' began to belt out.

I was feeling better already. My ribs might be sore in the morning but the ringing in my head had already calmed down and nothing else had sustained serious damage. It was not the pain itself that wore you out so much as the shock of being hit. Yet I was always surprised how little being punched in the face actually hurt. It was those body shots that killed you.

Then I was aware of someone watching me.

He was by the free weights, and had gloves on, those fingerless gloves for lifting weights, and his meaty shoulders looked as though he had lifted a lot of them. You don't see many Asians that heavily into their weights. But I guess you see more than you used to.

He held my gaze for a long moment, then removed his gloves and walked to the cupboards where Fred stored the boxing kit. He took out a black headguard and a pair of bright yellow gloves. Then he walked back across the gym and climbed into the ring. And by now I knew him. Just poking out of the top of his training vest I could see the bruise where I had punched him in the heart because he'd laughed at my dog.

'I'll fight you,' he said, pulling on the gloves.

'We call it sparring,' I said, 'not fighting.'

'But it's full contact, right?' he said. 'You're trying to punch each other's lights out, right?'

I shrugged. 'Of course.'

I saw no point explaining that there was an etiquette involved in sparring, an unwritten and unspoken code of honour, and a deep degree of trust. He didn't look as though he would be very interested in any of that stuff. I had been sparring with Fred for five years, but neither of us had ever been hit with a low blow, neither of us had ever left the ring feeling angry. Our friendship had been forged in the rough intimacy of sparring. But it was true what the weightlifter said: when we sparred, we didn't hold anything back.

'You sucker-punched me,' the weightlifter said, the anger flaring.

'You were rude to my dog.'

'I wasn't ready then. But I'm ready now.'

'I just did three rounds,' I said.

'I want to see how tough you really are,' he said. 'Unless you're chicken.'

I was looking at his yellow gloves — a pair of ten-ounce Cleto Reyes gloves, the best boxing gloves in the world, handmade in Mexico, but far too light for hard sparring. But that wasn't what bothered me.

'I'm not sparring with you,' I said, taking my gloves off.

When I moved to get out of the ring, he

blocked my path.

'Why not?'

'Because you don't have a mouthguard.'

'I don't need a mouthguard.'

'Yes you do,' I said. 'Everybody needs a mouthguard. Because I could catch you with my elbow. Or I could bang you with my forehead. And there's even an outside chance that I might actually punch you in the mouth.'

Then Fred was there. He took the weight-lifter by the elbow and easily turned the far bigger man around. Fred had worked the doors at some point.

'See that sign?'

On the walls of Smithfield ABC gym there were framed photographs of boxers. They were a certain kind of boxer — natural-born fighters, all grit and glory, the kind of boxers Fred loved. Jack Dempsey. Jake La Motta. Joe Frazier. Marvin Hagler. The hard men of the sport. And there were other framed photographs — pictures of kids boxing in Cuba, a dozen of them in the ring at a time, shirtless and skinny and sparring with gloves that looked as though they had just been dug up. And above them all there was a sign.

NO SPARRING WITHOUT PERMISSION

'You don't have permission,' Fred said.

Fred was the smallest man in the gym. But in that place of assorted hard nuts — where policemen came to keep fit, and rough boys from sink estates came to learn the sweet science of bruising, and young women came to learn self-defence, and white-collar City types came to push themselves to the limit — nobody argued with him.

The weightlifter got out of the ring.

'There are many bad things about steroid abuse,' observed Fred, who was the kind of boxer who is also a philosopher. 'Shrunken balls. Acne. Hair loss. But the worst thing is that it wipes out the part of the brain that inhibits aggression. In the end they want to kill someone.'

There was a heavy bag near the exit door. Just before the weightlifter walked out of Smithfield ABC, he hit the bag as hard as he could.

Fred laughed with contempt.

'It's not about how hard you can hit,' he said.

9

Stan knew something was up.

The dog was the only member of the family who had eaten breakfast, but Scout was standing at the window with her palms pressed against the glass, watching the street, occasionally flinching with anticipation at the sight of a car pulling up, while I kept checking the clock, my watch, my mobile.

She should have been here by now.

Stan lay Sphinx-like in the middle of the loft, his front paws demurely crossed, his huge round eyes watching us with suspicion.

Something you want to tell me?

'Oh — oh — oh!' Scout said, and when I went to the window I saw a white van that was stuffed full of dogs.

An Irish Wolfhound occupied the passenger seat, staring with interest at a white-coated porter emerging from the meat market, arms stained red up to the elbow. A pair of Pugs pressed their flat faces against the rear windows, while behind them a forest of tails were erect and wagging as small faces sniffed large bottoms and large faces sniffed small bottoms.

A young woman in muddy combat fatigues got out of the driver's seat. A Labradoodle got out with her. She placed it back in the van and closed the door.

'Stan,' I said, 'it's your ride.'

She was a cheerful young Czech called Jana, and Stan welcomed her like an old friend. It was nothing personal. Stan welcomed everyone like an old friend.

Scout was saying goodbye when without further ceremony the dog walker snapped a lead on Stan's collar and headed for the door.

We returned to the window. A Bichon Frise had somehow squeezed through the van's half-open window and was sniffing the pavement as the Irish Wolfhound considered it with lofty disdain. Stan and Jana appeared on the street. The dog walker put the runaway Bichon Frise under one arm and Stan under the other and delivered them both to the back of the van. Then they were off. We stood at the window until the tail lights had disappeared.

'I hope Stan's all right,' Scout said.

'Are you kidding?' I said. 'He'll have the time of his life with the rest of the pack.'

We went down to Smiths of Smithfield for our breakfast. I was just getting the bill when Stan walked past the window, his lead trailing behind him. Scout went outside to collect him as I got Jana on the phone. I could hear furious barking, sounds of terror and fear, human and canine howls of protest.

'How's Stan doing?' I said.

'Ah,' Jana said. 'Ah, yes. Sam is very fine.'

Scout came into SOS with Stan. He was wild-eyed and panting with thirst and exhaustion. A kindly SOS waiter brought him a large silver bowl of water. Scout set him down and he began to lap it up, very loudly.

'You're sure Stan's fine?' I said.

At the sound of his name, Stan looked up at me, his huge eyes bulging with outrage. Then he went back to his water, Scout's small hands fussing over him.

'Ah,' said Jana. 'Yes, Sam — lovely little Sam — is very fine. Sam is — ah — enjoying the beautiful park with his friends. There he goes now! Ha ha! Into the trees! Good boy, Sam!'

I looked at Scout and Stan, down on the floor and delighted to see each other, and I knew that from now on we would be walking our own dog.

At the morning briefing in MIR-1, DI Whitestone stood with her back to Mallory's wall. A blown-up photograph of the seven boy soldiers was visible just behind her. She had a list of names in her hand.

'Then there were four,' she said.

She turned to face the wall and carefully drew a red cross over the face of the boy on the extreme left.

'Adam Jones — deceased.'

She drew another red cross over the face of the boy on the extreme right.

'Hugo Buck — deceased.'

And finally she drew a red cross over the boy in the dead centre. The one in dark glasses. The one who wasn't smiling.

'This is the Honourable James Sutcliffe,' Whitestone said. 'Younger son of the Earl of Broughton. Or rather, this *was* the Honourable James Sutcliffe. Two years after this photograph was taken he committed suicide. Walked into the sea off the Amalfi coast where his parents were renting a villa.'

We were all silent.

'The summer he turned eighteen,' Whitestone added.

Mallory said, 'He has a daughter, doesn't

he? The boy's father, I mean. The Earl of Broughton.'

Whitestone nodded. 'The Honourable Cressida. She was a bit of a wild young thing in the eighties. Took a pee on the Cenotaph during an anti-capitalism riot.'

'That's the one,' Mallory said.

'Ran off with some German artist thirty years her senior. Reconciled with her parents now, all forgiven.'

'When the boy killed himself, did the carabinieri find a suicide note?' Mallory asked.

'No, sir,' Whitestone said. 'They didn't even find a body. Just his clothes folded on the beach and a half-finished sketch. He was an artist. Apparently the most brilliant of the bunch.'

'Why was there an assumption of suicide if no note was found?'

'James Sutcliffe suffered from clinical depression. He was on quite a cocktail of medication.' DI Whitestone read from her notes. 'Prozac. Luvox. Lustral. Cipralex. He had a history of self-harm.'

Gane said, 'What does a rich kid like that have to be depressed about?'

'Perhaps we need to ask his friends,' Mallory said.

There were four of them left alive.

The twins — identical apart from the starburst of facial scarring on one of them.

The tall, dark, whippet-thin, foreign-looking youth.

And the leering fat boy with the stub of his tongue poking out.

The three red crosses did something to the old photograph. Whitestone picked up a sheaf of eight-by-ten photographs. Photographs of the living. She tapped the image of the unscarred twin standing between James Sutcliffe and the dark-skinned boy.

'Ben King,' she said. 'He's famous.'

She pinned a head-and-shoulders shot to Mallory's wall. A serious, well-groomed man in a suit and tie smiling for some kind of official photograph. It was recognisably the boy in the picture, twenty years on. His face looked vaguely familiar from late-night news shows glimpsed and turned over.

'I know him,' Mallory said. 'Ben King. He's a politician, isn't he?'

'Yes,' Whitestone said. 'His late father was the libel lawyer Quentin King. Ben King is MP for Hillingdon North. Educated at Potter's Field and Balliol, Oxford. PPE first class. On his party's fast track.'

Gane said, 'Which party?'

'Have a guess.'

Gane guessed the wrong one. I would have got it wrong, too.

'There's talk of him as a future Prime Minister,' Whitestone said.

'Independently wealthy, privately educated, slick on TV,' Mallory said. 'Never employed anyone, never run a business, never done a real job.' He thought about it for a moment. 'He'd be perfect. What about his brother? The one with the scars.'

'Ned King,' Whitestone replied, pinning a photograph of a soldier to the wall. 'Serving officer in the British Army. Captain in the Royal Gurkha Rifles. Two tours of Helmand Province. Decorations for valour. He also has a conviction for assault, fifteen years ago.'

The scar tissue on the left side of Ned King's face looked like the price of the medals on his dress uniform.

Next to him Whitestone put up a photograph of a thin balding man in a tuxedo, his bow tie hanging around his scrawny neck like something that had died. He had lost so much weight since his teenage years that he was almost unrecognisable from the fat boy he had been at school.

'Guy "Piggy" Philips,' Whitestone said. 'Known the King brothers since prep school. Father made a fortune in the property market. Played tennis at a high level — junior Wimbledon semi-finals. Then his knee blew up. Teaches sport at his alma mater — Potter's Field.'

'What sports?' Gane asked.

'Tennis. Fencing. Cricket. Skiing. Posh sports, Gane, OK? And distance running.'

'That's how he dropped the weight,' Mallory said.

There was one left. Whitestone pinned a portrait of an intense, unsmiling man to Mallory's wall. He was posing for some kind of company photograph and he considered the camera with eyes that looked black.

'Salman Khan,' Whitestone said. 'From a wealthy Anglo-Indian family. Builders, funnily enough, defying all the racial stereotypes. His father made a pile building estates in the sixties and seventies. Khan has also known the King brothers and Philips since prep school. Works as a human rights lawyer in the London offices of Butterfield, Hunt and West. Considered one of the rising stars of the legal profession. Successfully sued the Ministry of Defence on behalf of disabled servicemen.'

'You mentioned a conviction of assault for Ned King,' Mallory said. 'Anything else on their records?'

'Adam Jones had multiple convictions for drug offences and vagrancy. Six months after the school picture was taken, he was expelled for selling controlled substances behind the tuck shop. Pills. Dope. And plenty of it.'

'The upper class are always a greater mix than they are given credit for,' Mallory noted. 'What was he doing? Supplementing his personal use with some dealing?'

'Looks like it, sir. Adam went off the rails early. He was getting into heroin when the others were getting into Oxford, Sandhurst and Goldman Sachs.'

'DC Wolfe, was Jones expelled from the Royal Academy of Music for dealing?'

'No, sir,' I said. 'Not for dealing. He was smacked out of his brain during an Albinoni concert in Duke Hall. Nodded off during the adagio.'

'Don't you hate it when that happens?' said Gane.

'Our two victims,' Mallory said. 'They were both living dangerously, weren't they? One had a long-term commitment to opiates. The other was a violent, serial philanderer. Either one of those lifestyles would shorten life expectancy.'

He left the rest unsaid, but it hung in the air: their lifestyle choices did nothing to explain their identically butchered throats.

I looked down at a slim red volume I had before me. *Get Tough! How to Win in Hand-*

to-Hand Fighting — *As Taught to the British Commandos and the U.S. Armed Forces.* The author was Captain W. E. Fairbairn, co-inventor of the commando knife. On its front was a drawing of two grappling soldiers. It looked like some old-fashioned *Boy's Own*-style comic. But inside was a manifesto for murder. I had placed a yellow Post-it note on the page I wanted, the one where they taught you how to execute the carotid thrust.

Artery #3. Knife in right hand, edges parallel to the ground, seize opponent around the neck from behind with your left arm, pulling his head to the left. Thrust point well in; then cut sideways. See Fig. C.

'Piggy Philips has three convictions for criminal damage in an eighteen-month period in the late eighties,' Whitestone continued. 'As far as I can tell, the boys enjoyed smashing up the odd restaurant. Seems they couldn't always buy their way out.'

'Boys will be boys,' Gane said. 'Especially when Daddy's picking up the bill.' He snorted with contempt. 'My dog could get five A levels at Potter's Field. While licking his bollocks.'

'Piggy Philips seemed happy to always take the rap,' Whitestone said. 'According to the local rag, he nearly went down for contempt of court one time. "Disorderly, contemptuous and insolent behaviour towards the magistrate".'

We stared at the photographs, at the boys they had been, and then at the men they had become.

'So they were a gang?' Gane said.

'It's more than that, isn't it?' I said. 'Most of them had known each other pretty much all their lives. One of them sounds as if he was happy to take the rap for the rest of them. It sounds like they were — I don't know — almost brothers.'

'But did that relationship end with their school days or did it endure?' Mallory said. 'That's the next question. And we can start answering it by going to a funeral.'

He stepped closer to the wall.

'What does it say on their jackets? The Latin just above the crest. I can't make it out.'

Whitestone closed her notebook. 'Aut vincere aut mori,' she said. 'Their school motto.'

'Conquer or die,' Mallory said. 'Good motto.'

173

I found my eyes drifting to the boy in the centre. James Sutcliffe. The one without a smile, the one with the hidden eyes. The boy with the marks of self-harm on his arms who folded his clothes neatly and walked into the sea off the Amalfi coast. He was the only one not represented on the wall by a photograph of the man he had become. Dead by his own hand at eighteen. Even more than the pictures of the two murdered men, Sutcliffe's unsmiling presence made the old school photograph seem heavy with mortality.

These boys are not growing up, I thought. They are rushing to their graves.

The late afternoon light was dying over Highgate Cemetery when the soldier rose from his place on the front row of the crowded chapel, immaculate in the black dress uniform of an officer of the Royal Gurkha Rifles.

Captain Ned King was a big man and he moved slowly to the pulpit, glancing at the large black-and-white photograph of the late Hugo Buck that was placed before his coffin. As Captain King stood in the pulpit, looking at his notes, a bar of the waning light came through the high stained-glass windows and caught him, glinting on the medals he wore on his black jacket and highlighting the white starburst of scar tissue on the left side of his face.

Someone in the packed congregation cleared their throat. Captain King began to speak.

'Death is nothing at all,' he said, reading with the clipped, careful delivery of a man accustomed to public speaking. 'I have only slipped away into the next room. I am I, and you are you.'

My eyes drifted to where he had been sitting. The other three were all there.

Ben King.

Salman Khan.

Guy Philips.

The dead man's oldest friends, in their places of honour, in the front row with the parents of Hugo Buck and his widow, Natasha, her face hidden by a long black veil. Buck's parents were in their late sixties but tanned, attractive, looking as though nothing bad had ever happened to them in their lives before now.

Natasha turned her head and stared at me. Behind the veil her face was impassive and showed absolutely no sign of recognition. I had seen her chauffeur when Mallory and I had arrived at the cemetery, sneaking a cigarette out on the street as he waited with the other drivers. Even now he had seemed like her driver rather than her date. I wondered why the hell that even mattered to me.

'Whatever we were to each other, that we still are,' Captain King said, his voice rising in the high vaulted chapel. 'Call me by my old familiar name. Speak to me in the easy way which you always used. Put no difference in your tone. Wear no forced air of solemnity.'

Mallory leaned his head towards me and his one word was less than a whisper: 'Look.'

Salman Khan was crying. I could not see his face, but the man's shoulders were clearly juddering with sobs, and his hands were over his face to hide his grief. I watched as Ben King slowly turned his head, muttered something consoling in Khan's ear, then turned back to watch his brother. Guy Philips watched the exchange with a kind of cool indifference.

Khan swabbed his face with the palm of one hand. His crying seemed to stop.

'Life means all that it ever meant,' said Captain King, and I saw the shadow of a smile flit across his handsome, ruined face. 'It is the same as it ever was — there is unbroken continuity. Why should I be out of mind because I am out of sight?' He paused. 'I am waiting for you — for an interval — somewhere very near — just round the corner.' King folded his notes. 'All is well,' he said.

I looked at the mourners. Almost all of them were young. Men and women in their thirties, some of them carrying new babies or trying to control toddlers, all of their faces white with shock at the early and brutal death of one of their own generation.

Captain King had returned to his seat. The vicar was talking.

'Come, ye blessed children of my Father, receive the kingdom prepared for you from the beginning of the world.'

Hugo Buck had friends. Many friends. But it was the four men in the front row who flanked his coffin at the end of the service. And now, for the first time, I saw the other three faces clearly.

Salman Khan — a fit, prosperous businessman, in control now but clearly carrying a sadness that pressed on him like a physical weight.

Guy Philips — the top button of his shirt undone, sleepy-eyed, perhaps slightly bored, his face criss-crossed with the broken veins of the hardened drinker. He looked like a sports master from central casting — there was exactly that kind of hearty cruelty about him.

And Ben King — calm, self-contained, an impressive man, his smooth, unmarked face making his brother's image look like a defaced mirror.

At Ben King's word, the four men — the brothers at the front, Philips and Khan behind — crouched, linked arms, and stood up as one with the coffin on their shoulders. They began to walk slowly down the aisle, Buck's parents and his widow behind them.

Music was playing. People were crying. One of them was Salman Khan. With the weight of his dead friend on his left shoulder, grief seemed suddenly to overwhelm him. This time his friends let him weep. All over the chapel, men and women were doing the same. For their friend and for themselves. But Hugo Buck's widow looked straight ahead, passing by without looking left or right, her green eyes dry and unflinching behind that long black veil.

A youngish blonde woman who looked as though she knew her way around a horse was giving out single red roses at the door to the chapel. Mallory and I held back, letting the crowd go, and by the time we left the chapel the woman and the roses were gone, and the congregation were making their way to the grave.

By special request from the family, Hugo Buck was being buried in the West Cemetery, and it looked like a graveyard in a dream. As we followed the mourners up a steep winding path, we walked between row upon row of massive vaults, giant granite crosses and a host of stone angels whose faces were worn away by the years. A colossal stone dog slept for ever by the resting place of his master. An angel carried a sleeping child to heaven. All of it seemed consumed by nature. Ancient trees had grown between the graves and blotted out the dying sun. Ivy clung to tombs, as if claiming ownership. Everywhere wild flowers bloomed among the dead.

I shuddered as the committal prayer drifted through the trees. You could feel winter coming.

'Behold, I show you a mystery,' said the vicar.

'Corinthians,' Mallory said, with some approval. 'The resurrection of the dead. Let's see if we can get a little closer.'

'We shall not all sleep — but we shall all be changed. In a moment — in the twinkling of an eye — at the last trumpet.'

We skirted the back of the crowd. The sound of crying was louder now, in the open

179

air at the edge of the freshly dug grave. Small children had joined in the wailing, upset at seeing grown-ups cry for the first time. The red roses were splashes of colour in a sea of black.

'For the trumpet shall sound — and the dead shall be raised incorruptible — and we shall be changed. For this corruptible must put on incorruption — and this mortal must put on immortality.'

We stopped when we were behind the vicar and directly opposite the mourners at the graveside. I could see the faces of the principal mourners over the shoulders of the crowd. Hugo Buck's parents were unravelling at the task of burying a child. Ben King stood with his arm around them. The politician had a consoling thought for everyone. Only Natasha Buck seemed drained of all emotion, numbed by the rituals of grief.

'Death is swallowed up in victory. Oh death, where is thy sting? Oh grave, where is thy victory?'

There was an electronic buzz as the coffin was automatically lowered.

When the sound stopped, Ned King casually dropped his red rose into the grave. Then they were all dropping their roses. Something inside the parents of the dead man seemed to break as they let go of theirs. They threw them in the grave and turned away, their legs uncertain. Guy Philips was next. Then Salman Khan, composed now. But Ben King paused, and with a gentle smile motioned Natasha to come forward.

'He stands in the presence of the Lord, the same Jesus who said to the dying man on a cross — Today you shall be with me in Paradise.'

Natasha took a step towards him. I saw her lift her veil, stay a moment with her memories, and then very carefully spit into her husband's grave.

Almost as an afterthought, she tossed in the rose.

There was a sudden burst of activity at the graveside. I saw Natasha's head twist towards the red features of Guy Philips, her face suddenly contorted with anger and pain as he expertly did something to her arm and marched her away. Erect and unresisting, Natasha came through the crowd with her hand held by Philips in a grotesque parody of caring, as if she might fall or run away or return once more to the grave of his dead friend.

'My hand,' she said. 'You're fucking hurting me, Piggy.'

I started forward but was stopped by Mallory's hand on my arm. I looked at him and he shook his head once. I felt a stab of shame for doing nothing. But we were here to observe. That was all. I nodded briefly, showing Mallory that I understood, and we followed Natasha and Philips down the path to the cemetery gate.

Out on the street, drivers were springing to attention. Philips opened the back door of Natasha's car. I thought of her as a strong woman, perhaps a hard woman, and it shocked me to see her so passive as he herded her inside.

Philips leaned into the driver's window and gave some instructions, and I saw the chauffeur's face torn between alarm and anger, but he nodded with mute obedience and drove her away. Philips watched them go.

Mallory and I walked back to the graveside. Most of the congregation seemed oblivious to what had happened. Heads had turned briefly to watch the overcome widow being helped away by her husband's friend, but soon they had returned to see the flowers falling on the coffin. Only one mourner had kept his eyes on the ugly little scene — a freakishly tall man in his sixties who had the hooked, unblinking face of a bird of prey. Now he too stared at the open grave, a single rose in his hand.

Mallory and I watched as Guy Philips returned expressionless, and I knew Mallory had seen it too — how efficiently Philips had dispensed with the problem of the woman.

The crowd was forming a queue to offer their condolences to Buck's parents. Ben King was still by their side, every inch the politician, dispensing handshakes and soft words.

'No, Natasha's fine,' he said. 'She's not herself today. Yes, thank you so much.'

He caught my eye and smiled.

Then suddenly it was over. The prayers were all said, the coffin lowered, the roses in the grave. The living mopped their eyes and returned to their cars and their lives, even the mother and father who had buried their son.

But as Mallory and I walked away, I caught a glimpse through the trees of four men still standing at the open grave, wiping dirt from their hands, bound by something so strong that death could not touch it.

Scout cried out in the deep of the night.

Although I believed that I never really slept, I was aware of the sensation of waking, and surprised by it, the abrupt surfacing from a dream I would never remember.

I glanced at the numbers on the clock — 03:10 — and stumbled to her bedroom. She was sitting up in bed, her face wet with wailing, shielding her eyes with the sleeve of her pyjamas.

I put my arms around her, held her for a bit, then placed the back of my hand on her forehead. She felt a little warm.

'Monsters,' she said.

'Angel,' I said. 'There are no monsters.'

Stan was awake now, whimpering in the darkness. I let him out of his cage and he padded after me as I returned to Scout's bedroom. He was up on her bed with one silent bound and she automatically reached out to scratch behind his ears. The dog stemmed her crying in a way I could not. But it didn't stop completely and I felt the flutter of panic that her tears always made me feel. I was afraid that if she started crying then she would never stop.

'Why are you crying, Scout?'

'I don't know. I don't know.'

We both knew but neither of us had the words, neither of us knew where to begin. There was a hole in my daughter's life and no matter how much I loved her, no matter how hard I tried, I would never be able to fill it. The thought clawed at my heart and made me feel like weeping too.

'Don't go,' she said.

I smiled in the darkness.

'I'm not going anywhere.'

Neither was Stan, who had curled up by her side, seeking the warmth, and I decided to leave him there. Soon they were both sleeping, Scout grasping the dog like a hot-water bottle, the dog letting her.

I looked at Scout's alarm clock. It was far too early to get up and far too late to go back to bed.

I knew that I would not sleep now. So I sat on the side of Scout's bed, watching my child and her dog, and I let the night crawl by as I had done so many nights before. But watching my daughter sleep made the small dark hours seem very different tonight. They did not feel wasted.

10

Bob the Butcher had aged thirty years over-night.

His new photograph showed a much older man, the cockiness of youth and the rakish hat both gone, a black pipe stuck into his set mouth in place of the cigarette. In the new photograph Robert Oppenheimer stared straight at the camera, his hair thinning now, his eyes huge and full of a terrible knowledge that had not been there before.

The destroyer of worlds.

The large screen on Mallory's wall showed Bob the Butcher's timeline but we stared at our laptops as Gane read the new message.

'The rich have known sin,' he said. 'And this is a knowledge which they cannot lose.' He sat back in his chair. 'Kill all pigs. #killallpigs.'

I had already chased down the quote.

'What Oppenheimer actually said was "the

physicists have known sin; and this is a knowledge which they cannot lose".' I looked over at Gane. 'Not the rich, the physicists.'

He nodded briefly. Then cursed.

'This should be simple. We sent a search warrant to the social network and received an IP audit within twenty-four hours. As I expected, Bob's got an anonymiser. It's a proxy server that acts as a privacy shield between the user and the rest of the digital world. Unless he's a complete idiot — always a possibility — he was bound to have one. He might even have multiple anonymisers. I can usually work around them once I have the IP audit.' He shook his head. 'Usually. But Bob's using some kind of enhanced security architecture. Onion routing, they call it. Tor or something similar, some beefed-up anonymity network that I've never seen. It routes data through multiple relays, encrypting and re-encrypting every time. It's designed to make the web safe for whistleblowers — users reporting corporate or government corruption, and people living in dictatorships. Not serial killers.'

'What are you telling us?' Mallory said.

'He's gone deeper,' Gane said. 'Bob's digital footprints are exactly like his finger-prints or glove prints.' He shook his head. 'Invisible.'

'Turn it off,' Whitestone said. 'I'm sick of these idiots treating him like some kind of hero.'

The Bob the Butcher timeline had exploded with activity as the social network reacted to his message. The screen on Mallory's wall unrolled a constant stream of fan mail, marriage proposals and slavish compliments. Gane stabbed a key and it was instantly gone from the screen, replaced with the still photograph of the seven boys at Potter's Field.

'I don't know how they can make a hero of him,' Whitestone said. 'Someone who kills school friends.'

Mallory almost smiled.

'But they don't think he's killing school friends,' he said. 'They think he's killing the rich.'

After the morning briefing, Mallory and I walked from Savile Row to Hanover Square, where tall thin young women stood smoking in glamorous packs outside Vogue House.

We were expected at the law firm of Butterfield, Hunt and West, who had their offices on the north side of the great green expanse of Hanover Square. Salman Khan's PA showed us into his office, then offered us coffee, tea or mineral water, sparkling or still. We were spoilt for choice. But before we could reply, Khan was rising up from behind his desk and telling us how to do our job.

'But you must do more!' Khan said, his upper-class English laced with just a trace of India. 'This is simply not good enough! Two men murdered and no arrest? It's appalling! I intend to take the matter up with Detective Chief Superintendent Swire, who is a friend of my father. Do I make myself absolutely clear?'

Mallory turned politely to the PA, who was still waiting in the doorway. 'Tea, please, miss. A dash of milk and two sugars.'

He glanced at me.

'Coffee, please,' I said. 'Short and black.'

She closed the door without making a sound and we turned to look at Salman Khan. He was staring at us with open belligerence. You see that kind of aggression in poorly socialised dogs, I thought. They don't bark because they are angry. They bark because they are afraid.

He ranted for a minute or so. We let him get it out of his system. A big part of our job was talking to people who were scared.

Scared of getting in trouble. Scared of getting hurt. Scared of getting more hurt than they were already. But I had never seen a man quite as scared as Salman Khan. He looked like a man who was scared of having his throat cut.

When Khan paused to catch his breath, Mallory introduced us in his mild-mannered way, and we both showed our warrant cards. Khan slumped back down in his big leather swivel chair as we took a seat opposite him, Mallory making reassuring noises about various leads being pursued while I watched Khan fiddle with an unlit cigarette in his hand. The offices of the law firm Butterfield, Hunt and West were non-smoking, but there was a silver cigarette case on Khan's desk. He worried the cigarette in his fingers like a set of rosary beads.

'We realise this is a traumatic time, Mr Khan,' Mallory said.

'You shouldn't be talking to me,' Khan said, placing the cigarette in its silver coffin. 'You should be out there finding the killer.'

'Why do you think someone wanted to kill Hugo Buck and Adam Jones, Mr Khan?'

'Because they were addicts,' Khan said. 'One of them was a sex addict and the other was a drug addict. Hugo was a dear friend. Adam — I hadn't seen Adam since leaving school. But they were both, in their own way, hopeless addicts. And that's what killed them.'

It was a credible theory on the surface. One man was a sexual adventurer and the other was a junkie. They were the victims of random murders, acts as senseless and irrational as most murders. Very sad and all that, but they were living dangerously and they died because they had it coming.

But the theory did not explain Khan's naked terror.

'You knew both men for many years,' Mallory prompted. 'Since you were at school.'

'I remember the first time I met Adam,' Khan said, shaking his head. 'Thirteen years old. We were coming in from the playing fields. All of us. The six of us. Ben and Ned. Piggy Philips and Jimmy Sutcliffe. Hugo and me. The First Fifteen rugby trials. Covered in mud and blood. And there was Adam in his nice new uniform carrying his bloody oboe in its case. Waiting for some music tutorial. And somebody — probably the Pig — said, come on, give us a tune, new boy. Give us a tune, will you? Making fun of him, of course. But Adam took his instrument out of its case and he gave us the sweetest smile — and he played Bach. "Sheep May Safely Graze". And it was the most beautiful thing I had ever heard.'

There were photographs on the walls of Khan's office. I stood up to get a closer look. It is always worth studying a man's shrine to himself.

Khan smiling in a dinner jacket receiving an award from another man in a dinner jacket.

Khan making a speech at a podium that bore the words 'Aut vincere aut mori' — the Potter's Field school motto: Conquer or die.

The teenage Khan on a cricket field flanked by the King brothers, and Piggy Philips grinning behind them, all of them in immaculate whites, Philips resting his bat on his shoulder like a caveman with his club.

I did not see the photograph of the seven boys in their Combined Cadet Force uniforms.

'Can I help you?' Khan said sharply.

'Do you get back to your old school much, sir?' I said, smiling at him.

He was immune to my charms. 'I speak to the boys. There are various events. I still have friends at the school. Among the masters, I mean. There are various military charities the school helps this firm support. Look, what's your point?'

'Best days of your life, eh, sir?'

'Indeed.'

There was one lone painting on the wall. A hidden corner of the city, a canyon of office blocks glazed with a shining haze, like a city seen in a dream, or remembered far from home. There were no people. I already knew what the initials would be in the right-hand corner.

j s

'James Sutcliffe,' I said. 'James Sutcliffe painted this picture.'

'James was a genius,' Khan said. 'He could have achieved more than any of us.'

'Why did he kill himself?'

'James was troubled. His parents thought that having those Harley Street doctors stuff him with happy pills would make everything all right. But it pushed him over the edge.'

'You made some close friends at Potter's Field,' Mallory said.

Khan picked up an unlit cigarette, put it into his mouth, then took it out. He shivered with undisguised contempt.

'That's what school's *for,*' he said.

For a moment I thought he was going to ask us where we had gone, but he decided against it. He knew we hadn't gone anywhere. And suddenly he was furious.

'Resentment killed them,' he said. 'Jealousy — this country reeks of it now.' He put the unlit cigarette back between his lips. 'Isn't it bloody obvious? Envy killed them.'

The Officers' Mess at RAF Brize Norton overlooks the airfield, and from the window I could see a huge fat-bellied aircraft waiting on the runway, its four turboprop engines idle as all around its great bulk men in sleeveless yellow tabards made the last of their checks.

A wide ramp was open under the tail of the aircraft — a Lockheed C-130 Hercules — but the troops in their camouflage fatigues stood patiently on the tarmac, as though waiting was one of the things they were trained for, and good at. The Royal Gurkha Rifles were shipping out tonight.

I watched the faces of the men, all those small golden-faced warriors who somehow looked both gentle and fierce, and far off in the darkness I could see the distant lights of Oxford glinting and glittering in the night. It had only taken us ninety minutes to drive from Savile Row to Brize Norton after the afternoon briefing, but London felt far away.

I turned at the sound of a man's harsh laughter.

Captain Ned King and DCI Mallory sat

facing each other on red leather sofas in the red-carpeted room. Mallory was leaning forward, his face impassive, unsmiling, letting the other man fill the silence. Like the men on the runway, Captain King was dressed in camouflage fatigues.

'Forgive me,' he said, grinning broadly, 'but there's no great mystery here. Adam, who I hadn't seen in many years, was a drug addict. And Hugo was a sex addict. These are high-risk hobbies, detective.'

'But who would want to kill them?' Mallory said.

'Off the top of my head? Try Adam's fellow drug addicts. Try Hugo's Russian wife — or possibly some of her Russian friends.'

Mallory nodded, as if giving the matter some thought.

'You really think Hugo Buck's wife is capable of killing someone?' I said.

King turned his scarred face towards me. He was not smiling now.

'I think that anyone in the world is capable of killing someone else,' he said.

'But your friends died in exactly the same way,' I said. 'All the evidence suggests the same killer. Do you really think that's just coincidence?'

Captain King shrugged. 'What I think is that death is random. That's what I think.

And that's what I know.'

From the back of the mess came the sound of snooker balls kissing. Two officers were laughing easily together.

'Helmand is the only place I've ever seen a man eat his lunch and defecate his breakfast at the same time,' one of them was saying.

'Yes, they're four hours and thirty minutes ahead of us,' said the other. 'And a thousand years behind.'

Outside on the runway, the engines of the Hercules air transport started up. King suddenly had to raise his voice.

'I would very much like all those men out there to come back,' he said. 'I don't want them crippled. I don't want them killed. I don't want to see them repatriated — in the hideous modern parlance.' His broken face twisted with disgust, as if the word physically sickened him. 'I don't want those good brave men brought back to face the pity of the Darrens and the Sharons who stand outside Tesco.' He smiled without mirth. ' "You smug-faced crowds with kindling eye who cheer when soldier lads march by —" '

' "Sneak home and pray you'll never know," ' Mallory said, ' "the hell where youth and laughter go." '

King chuckled. 'Very good, detective.

Where did you go?'

'Where did I go?'

'Your school.'

Mallory smiled. 'I didn't go anywhere. I went to a state school in Banff. In the Highlands. Get to Aberdeen and keep going. But we liked our First World War poets.'

'Siegfried Sassoon, of course,' King said. 'Lived to a ripe old age. Died in 1967. But his great friend Wilfred Owen was killed just one week before the Armistice. The fate of our two greatest war poets perfectly illustrates the random nature of death. I want all those men out there to come home. That will not happen. We arrive in Afghanistan at night so they can't kill us immediately. But they always get around to it eventually. The really unlucky ones will be wounded and live. Single amputees, double amputees, triple amputees and — full house — both arms and both legs gone. Or no balls, no cock, no face. Phallic reconstruction is a growth industry, I'm told. And no cheering crowds for those lads. There will be roadside bombs. There will be friendly fire from our American chums and our Afghan allies. There will be the local policeman who decides that his god wants him to blow up as many of my men as possible. My men will be killed by IEDs. They will step on

197

bombs left behind by the Russians as well as the Taliban. Some of those men out there will come home in wheelchairs, and some will come home in a coffin. Death is the price we pay for life, gentlemen, and sometimes the bill arrives early. And it will not be fair. It will not be rational. You both know that as policemen. Death doesn't play the game, does it?'

He stood up. Outside, the soldiers were preparing to board the plane.

'We arrive on Sunday, and Sundays are the most dangerous. They pray on Friday, plan on Saturday and attack on Sunday. Holy Shit Sundays, we call them. But, you know, people are polite there. People are decent. There is no litter at Camp Bastion. Now, if you will excuse me, gentlemen.'

'Thank you for your time, Captain King,' Mallory said.

We followed him to the door of the mess.

As King stepped outside into the chill of the October night, every one of his men turned to look at him. Some of them smiled shyly, and I was struck by their youth, the jumble of equipment they all carried, and their obvious love for their commanding officer.

'Why did James Sutcliffe kill himself?'

King winced at Mallory's question.

'Well,' he said. 'That was all a long time ago.'

'But you must have some thoughts.'

'Why does anyone kill himself? Because he was weak.'

'I thought he was your friend.'

'James Sutcliffe was more than my friend. Far more. And I think about him every day of my life. But James was weak.'

Mallory nodded thoughtfully. 'My apologies for detaining you, Captain King.'

He shook our hands. 'I wish I could have been more helpful.'

'Just one final thing,' Mallory said.

King waited.

'What happened to your face?'

King laughed out loud.

'Ben did it,' he said. 'When we were boys. Threw a glass at my head at the breakfast table. Must have said something that annoyed him. Nobody ever asks me that,' he added cheerfully, his spirits rising now that he was joining his men. 'They all assume I copped it in the line of duty.'

Mallory shook his head. 'No, those marks are too old. I know what scars look like.'

11

Scout was silent over breakfast.

I knew there was a time coming, maybe not that long from now, when she would be able to hide her feelings from me. But at five years old we were not there yet.

I sat down opposite her, moved aside a cereal packet with grinning monkeys on the side, and looked into her eyes.

'Something's wrong, Scout,' I said. 'What's wrong, angel?'

Scout glanced down at the milky brown gloop in her bowl, then back at me.

'You have to make me a costume,' she said.

I leaned back in my chair, trying to take it in.

'Why do I have to do that?'

'A costume for our play. Our Christmas play.'

'A Nativity play?'

She nodded. 'The mummies all have to make the costumes for the children.' A moment of doubt. 'And the daddies. Miss Davies said so.'

If Miss Davies said something then it was burned into tablets of stone and carried down from the mountain in the trembling hands of Moses.

'What's the play?'

'*The Grumpy Sheep.* It's about the sheep that doesn't want to go to see the baby Jesus getting born in the manger. Everybody goes to see the baby Jesus. The wise men, and the angels, and all the other sheep. But he doesn't want to go, the grumpy sheep. Do you know that story?'

'No.'

'He's grumpy, the sheep. Then he's sad. Then he's sorry. He's very, very sorry in the end. He sees the mistake he made.'

A costume, I thought. How do you make a costume? What stuff do you need?

'What part do you play, Scout?'

'The grumpy sheep.'

I was impressed. 'You've got the lead — the big part?'

A flicker of pride. 'Miss Davies chose me for the grumpy sheep,' she confirmed.

'That's a good part, Scout. That's the best.'

She refused to be distracted by flattery.

'I need my costume,' she said. 'You're going to have to make it.'

'I will,' I promised, not knowing how to do it, not even knowing where to start.

Instead of going to the morning briefing I drove off the edge of the *A to Z*, the BMW X5 alone on the road north as massed ranks of commuter traffic crawled into town in the other direction. It felt like nobody in the world was going where I was going.

It felt the same way when I sat in the back row of the crematorium waiting for the crowd to come.

And they never did.

Finally a handful of lost souls wandered slowly in. Tattooed faces, missing teeth and the pallid flesh of addiction. So few of them that everybody had their own row. They sat well back, avoiding close proximity to the simple coffin awaiting the flames.

When Guy Philips arrived, ruddy-faced from double games or a hard night on the tiles, he sat across the aisle from me in the other back row. I got up and sat next to him.

'Morning, Piggy.'

He reared back in his seat.

'I know you,' he said. 'You were at Hugo's funeral. The two plods. Spot you a mile off. Big feet, small dicks.'

'Have you been drinking, sir?'

'Not nearly enough.'

'And I saw you. You were a bit rough with the girl, Piggy. I think you hurt her.'

He smirked. 'Natasha? She was tired and emotional, that's all. Took her in hand. For the best.' He took a better look at me. 'You were up at Pak's office, weren't you?'

'Pak?'

'Paki Khan.'

'I understood Mr Khan was Anglo-Indian.'

'I don't want to split hairs, constable, but that's a kind of Paki, isn't it? Not that I'm racist. It's just an old school name. An affectionate nickname. I *adore* Indians.' He surveyed his fellow mourners and sighed. 'Christ, this place looks like a convention of *Big Issue* sellers.' And then to himself, shaking his large red head: 'What happened to you, Adam?'

'Why aren't the others here? The old gang.'

'Well, Ned must be in Helmand by now. Ben's a public figure, of course. Might not look good in the *Daily Mail* hanging out at the AGM of Junkies Anonymous. And I believe the Pak's in court, probably defending some gyppo's human rights.'

'Excuses, excuses.'

'I know. Dreadful, isn't it? But as you can

see from his new chums, Adam was always a bit different.'

'Because he was a heroin addict? Cut him off, did you, Piggy?'

Philips chuckled. 'Do you think we care about that? Some of the best families have drug *issues*. Dreadful word. No, Adam was always an outsider. Adam was always different. Even more than Paki Khan — who was, lest we forget, a Paki. Thing about old Pak — bloody good cricketer, the Pak. *Bloody* good. Opened the first eleven's batting three years in a row. Hitting sixes gets you accepted, see. But Adam was a different creature entirely. Not because of the drugs. Because he was a scholarship boy. The rest of us, our parents paid for us to be there. Poor little Adam had to get there on merit. Strumming his banjo. Blowing his flute. Oh, I've offended you now. You think I'm a snob.'

'When did you last see him, Piggy?'

'Could you please stop calling me that? It was mildly amusing the first three or four times. But it's what we call unearned intimacy, constable.'

'Detective.'

'Of course. Sorry, constable.'

'Piggy is just an old school name,' I said. 'An affectionate nickname.'

'I don't remember you at school,' he said. 'Were you cleaning the lavatories?'

'Come on, Piggy. When did you last see Adam Jones?'

'Not for years. He came to me, begging for money. Boo hoo hoo. Poor little me. Look what a mess I've made of my veins. Don't know where my next fix is coming from. All of that. I gave him what I had. And he went away.'

'It didn't concern you that he would spend the money on heroin?'

'Not really. I wasn't expecting him to spend it on low fat yoghurt.'

'But why would anyone want to kill him? Hugo Buck I can understand. The woman-beating bastard.'

Philips gave me a sly look. 'Not soft on our Natasha, are you? Bit rich for your blood, I reckon. Out of your pay grade.'

I gently touched his arm. 'I'll ask you again. Very politely. Why would anyone want to kill a homeless heroin addict, Piggy?'

He shot me a furious look. 'Look, you've not earned the right to call me that name. It's a stupid name. A childish name. Give me *your* name. Give me your warrant card number. What exactly are you doing here?'

'I'm trying to understand. You must have some thoughts. And don't give me the line about Hugo Buck banging the help. Don't tell me that Adam Jones had it coming. Your friend Captain King told us that the deaths are unrelated. Mr Khan told us the same thing. But I don't think they believe it. And I don't think you do, Piggy.'

But he wasn't listening to me. Mrs Jones had entered the crematorium with Rosalita. They sat down in the front row directly in front of the coffin. I thought that Philips was shocked by the sight of Adam's mother. I had seen her far more recently and she shocked me. Her face was swollen with chemotherapy and twisted with grief. The coffin she stood before could have been her own.

But Guy Philips wasn't looking at Mrs Jones. He was looking at Rosalita.

'Christ,' he said, 'it's the same house-keeper. She's aged a bit.'

The minister was talking: 'Man that is born of a woman hath but a short time to live, and is full of misery.'

When the coffin had slid into the flames and the curtains had primly swished across the mouth of the furnace, I stood up.

'Are you off?' Philips said. 'Very pleasant talking to you, constable.'

'We haven't talked yet, Piggy,' I said.

As I walked down the aisle to the front

the few mourners coming in the opposite direction eased out of my path with the instinctive cringe of people who are used to getting out of the way.

I found Mrs Jones contemplating the empty spaces.

'We should have waited before starting the service,' she said. 'More people might have come.'

'Ma'am,' Rosalita said. 'We had our time slot, ma'am. Forty-five minutes, ma'am. We had to begin, didn't we?'

Mrs Jones smiled weakly when she saw me. 'You came,' she said. 'How thoughtful.' She took my hands. 'I enjoyed our talk.'

'I'd like to talk to you again,' I said. 'About the old days. When Adam was a boy.'

She was suddenly distressed. 'It's all so long ago,' she said, pulling her hands away, turning to the woman by her side. 'I don't remember. Rosalita, tell him, will you?'

Rosalita put her arm around Mrs Jones, and glared at me.

'You upset her now.'

'I just don't remember,' Mrs Jones said.

'Of course not, ma'am, why should you?' Rosalita said. 'That's all right.'

They disappeared into a side room to collect the sad little pot containing the final remains of Adam Jones. I looked back for

Guy Philips, but he had gone. Everyone had gone. I sat in the front row for a long time, feeling my face burning with the heat of the flames.

The crematorium's car park was almost empty by the time I drove away. But at the end of a quiet green lane I saw Rosalita waiting at a bus stop.

I stopped, rolled down my window.

'I remember,' she said.

I took her to a small café in Golders Green and bought her tea. She said she had to send a text message.

'My son,' she explained. 'He pick me up.'

I sipped a triple espresso as she typed and sent it. Then I watched her staring at her tea. I thought she was already regretting speaking to me.

'What do you remember, Rosalita?'

She nodded, relieved to begin.

'Adam's friends. The brothers. The Indian one. I remember all of them. And the one who died. And the one who was there today. I saw him. A man now. I saw him sitting at the back with you. And I remember.'

'But what do you remember?'

She nodded again.

'They would come in the summer. The boys. All the boys would come. When Mr and Mrs Jones were away.'

'When Adam's parents were on holiday, his friends would come? They stayed at the house when his parents were away?'

'Yes.'

'What did they do?'

Silence. Then she shook her head.

'They were not good boys.' How old was she? Mid forties. Two decades ago she would have been in her twenties. Two decades ago she would have been young herself.

'Adam was a good boy. When he was little. A sweet boy. But he was not good when he was with them.'

'What happened? Did something happen?'

She stared at her tea.

She wouldn't look at me.

'Did they — did they do something to *you*?'

She looked up as a young man walked into the café. Early twenties, the blue overalls of a garage mechanic. He spoke to his mother in Tagalog.

'We don't want no trouble,' he said, taking his mother's arm, lifting her from her seat.

'Wait,' I said. 'Where are you going? What's wrong?'

'We don't want to talk to the police,' he

said. 'We don't want any trouble.'

'What are you worried about?' I said to him. 'You don't have anything to worry about.'

But they were not listening to me now. They were arguing in their own language. Rosalita's son still had her by the arm.

'Are you worried about your visa status?' I tried. 'You don't have to worry about that. I don't care about that stuff. I can help you with all that.'

But they were leaving.

'Rosalita,' I said, 'what happened at that school?'

She turned at the door of the small café.

'It all went to hell,' she said.

12

PC Billy Greene lifted the twelve-ounce gloves in front of his face and marched slowly across the ring in a totally straight line. Fred was waiting for him. My heart sank as I watched from ringside.

It was the Charge of the Light Brigade in there.

Fred stuck out a jab and Greene, looking heavier after long days on desk duty, blocked it high on his gloves. There wasn't much force behind the blow but it was hard enough to slap Greene's gloves back against his face.

Above the gloves and inside the thick leather headguard, I saw Greene's eyes blink with surprise, the bridge of his nose grazed red. Fred danced sideways, light and springy as a dancer on the balls of his feet, arms dangling loosely by his side. Greene plodded after him.

Fred fired a flurry of jabs. They all detonated harmlessly on Greene's tight, high guard. Emboldened, he stuck out a shy jab of his own. Fred's head seemed to whip sideways as if on a string and the punch sailed harmlessly over his shoulder.

Now Fred was in the corner. He waved Greene forward, grinning, the blue mouth-guard showing. Flat-footed, Greene accepted the invitation. He threw another jab. When he wanted to, Fred had a guard as cosy as a nuclear bunker — hands held high and close together, elbows tucked into his ribcage, chin down. He bounced against the ropes, inviting Greene to hit him. And he did. Jab. Hook. Jab. All of it unanswered by Fred.

Greene's confidence visibly rose.

He unloaded a right, as slow as a fat man leaving a buffet. Fred slipped the punch and, more from instinct than malice, dug a short left hook into Greene's ribcage. The air came out of him with a whoosh and he sank to one knee, his head hanging down, his elbow tucked into his side, as if trying to understand the source of this sudden and terrible pain.

Fred was immediately kneeling by the bigger man's side, a protective arm around his shoulder.

'I know I should be able to hit a bit

harder,' Greene said, his face contorted with pain. 'Sorry.'

'It's not about how hard you can hit,' Fred said. 'It's about how hard you can *get* hit and then keep going.'

At this hour the gym was almost empty. They went on the pads, Fred holding up the worn leather mitts for Greene to hit, all the while giving him instructions.

'Get that jab out faster. Don't let the punch fade away. Harder, faster, sharper. Keep your guard up. You're so lucky to be training!'

And behind it all, there was the secret knowledge that boxing gives you. *There is good stuff inside you. You are better than you know.*

Outside Fred's gym, I shuddered in the cold night air, and hunched my shoulders inside my leather jacket. On the far side of Charterhouse Street the men of Smithfield had begun their night's work, and as they laughed and shouted at each other, their breath came out as steam. Winter was no longer coming. Winter was here. The full yellow moon of October hung low over the dome of St Paul's. You only see that moon once a year. A hunter's moon, they call it.

I turned up my collar and hurried home to take over from Mrs Murphy.

■ ■ ■ ■

The next day I left Savile Row in plenty of time to make my two p.m. appointment with the Right Honourable Ben King, MP.

The address I had was just the other side of Piccadilly on St James's Street and it should not have taken me more than a few minutes to get there. But I walked up and down the street staring at windows and doors and the address in my hand, feeling like a fool.

Because Ben King's club was behind one of the many unmarked doors on St James's Street and if you did not know it was there then you were never meant to find it.

Through one window I glimpsed silver heads, all men, dipped behind newspapers. I took a chance, and this was the place. Inside there was a counter where a uniformed porter took my coat. He had hung it up on what looked like a row of old school pegs before he noticed I was still waiting.

'Anything else, sir?' he said.

'Ticket?' I said, already sensing that I had made some stupid mistake.

'Sir?'

'Don't I need some sort of ticket for my coat?'

There was another porter behind the front desk and I saw him smiling to himself. The porter who had hung up my coat grinned with hideous good humour.

'Oh, no tickets in here, sir,' he said. 'Your coat is quite safe with us.'

I was escorted into the dining area with my face burning. It was more like a room in a private house than a restaurant. Solitary diners muttered to themselves behind broadsheets. An elderly man in a three-piece pinstripe suit sipped a glass of red wine. Another dozed peacefully, a bowl of rhubarb and custard cooling before him.

And Ben King, the youngest man in the room, Member of Parliament for Hillingdon North, was rising with a smile to greet me.

He was alone at the table but the waiter was clearing away two places. Because of the timing, I had assumed I was going to be offered lunch. Apparently not. The clean-picked bones of a grilled fish were on one plate, a scrap of bloody steak on the other.

'DC Wolfe,' he said. 'I'm sorry this was so difficult to schedule. My apologies. Please.'

We ordered coffee, black for both of us — I couldn't risk asking for my favourite, a triple espresso, fearing more blank stares followed by suppressed laughter — and

King fixed me with a frank but friendly gaze, leaning forward, giving me his full attention.

'My office is here to help your investigation in any way it can,' he said. 'As, of course, am I.'

He had a smooth, clean-cut, untouched version of his brother's face. He was a reassuring presence. I could understand why someone would vote for him.

'This must be a very traumatic time for you,' I said, 'losing two close friends in a short space of time.'

He smiled sadly. 'We lost Adam many years ago.'

There was a pause as the coffee was placed before us.

'I had been dreading that phone call for years — the one telling me he had gone. But Hugo — that was a blow, yes.'

'So you were not in contact with Adam Jones?'

'A few years ago he approached me for money — or rather my office. I didn't see him.'

'And you didn't give him any money?'

'I would have given him money for rehabilitation. I would have given him money for treatment. I wasn't giving him money for heroin. I think he approached a number of old friends. Guy saw him.'

'He told me,' I said, and the thought rushed in — *but you knew that already.* 'It's a tragedy that he couldn't get help. What a waste.'

Ben King looked at me. And I saw that he had a way of looking at someone as if he was suddenly seeing them clearly for the first time. He cocked his head to one side, as if readjusting his gaze, as if I had just said something unique, or momentous, or true. As if I were suddenly a man of substance in his eyes, coming out with things that had never been said before. He looked at me as if I were the last man left alive. That was the way he looked at me. But perhaps all politicians do that.

'That's three of your old school friends who have died before their time,' I pointed out.

He thought about it for a moment.

'You mean James? That was a tragedy. As I get older, I find myself thinking of James constantly.' For the first time he seemed genuinely moved, the eighteen-year-old suicide somehow a wound that was more raw than the two recent murders. 'Hugo and Adam,' he said. 'Are their deaths connected?'

'That's our conjecture,' I said, echoing

Mallory. 'We're going to be visiting Potter's Field in due course.'

He sipped his coffee before speaking again. 'But why would you go to our old school?' His voice was calm and quiet.

'It's just one of the leads we're pursuing. As far as we know there's only one thing that links Mr Buck and Mr Jones — the past. Did anything happen during your school days that —'

'Might make someone want to kill them?' King said. The practised smile drew some of the sting from his words. He was trying not to laugh at me. 'You're talking as if their murders were somehow justified, detective.'

'I didn't mean to give that impression.'

'I'm sure you didn't,' he said, forgiving me. He let his eyes drift away, as if remembering. 'We were just ordinary boys,' he said. And then back at me. 'But if anything occurs, then of course I will immediately get in touch. I want what you want. Could I possibly have your card?'

I gave it to him, and realised that I was being very politely dismissed. And that there was someone else being brought in to see him. A dishevelled, overweight man blinking with awe behind his greasy specs, some kind of journalist, there for an interview, looking like a tourist. All hot and flustered, as if it had not been easy to find the un-marked door of a gentlemen's club on St James's Street. And then I was standing up and shaking Ben King's hand and thanking him for his time and the coffee.

I collected my coat from the smirking porters and I was back on St James's Street before it sank in that the MP for Hillingdon North had scheduled a meeting for every course of his lunch.

I was dessert.

'That little gang,' I said back at the incident room. 'It was all about the King brothers, Ben and Ned. They were the alpha males. Ben looks like the pack leader.'

'Why do you think that?' Mallory said.

'The mess he made of his brother's face. Guy Philips was their pit bull. Salman Khan was their poodle. Hugo Buck was their jock, their star athlete. Adam Jones — I think he just tagged along. Let them run wild at his house when his parents were away. Adam was their mascot. Their lapdog.'

'And what about the one who killed himself? James Sutcliffe.'

'They all seem to love him,' I said. 'Died young. Good-looking corpse and all that. I doubt if it was so different when he was alive. And he was the one genuine aristocrat among them. The Honourable James Sutcliffe, younger son of the Earl of Broughton. These boys — these men — they all come from money. Even Adam, with his music scholarship, grew up with money. But Sutcliffe was the only true toff, the only one of them that came from a family where the money had been there for generations. He was their hero.'

We looked up at the photograph of the seven soldiers, and at the boy dead centre, dark glasses, unsmiling, hair swept back off that high forehead. I pictured him folding his clothes on the beach at Amalfi and walking into the sea.

'If they don't hate each other,' I said, 'then who does?'

Mallory said, 'Oh, everyone hates them.'

'Sir?'

'It's that very British hatred with class resentment at its core. We pity the small boys packed off to their boarding schools where they wet the beds and cry for their mothers but we end up wanting to be them, because they have something that the rest of us will never have.'

Mallory considered the big screen and the grinning boys in their uniforms.

'It's more than confidence,' he continued. 'It's more than the sense of entitlement. It's the total and unequivocal certainty that tomorrow belongs to them.' He smiled at me. 'Who wouldn't want to feel like that?'

The next day I drove us to Potter's Field.

13

'Now get down on the ground,' Guy Philips said.

Fifty boys, shivering in their running shorts and vests, stared at their sports master. They grinned foolishly at each other, still hoping that he might be joking. A bitter wind whipped across the school playing fields. Three in the afternoon and it already seemed to be getting dark.

'Now!' he screamed.

And they saw he wasn't joking.

Slowly they got down on all fours. The rugby pitch had been churned to mud by ten thousand studmarks and their hands and knees made squelching sounds as they tested the ground. Philips walked between them in his pristine white tracksuit, a grin spreading across his red face. He was enjoying himself.

'Not doggy style, toads. On your bellies. On your backs. Roll around in it. That's good. Now on your back, Knowles. Give it a good old wriggle, Jenkins. Come on, Patel, you big girl, rub it a bit harder than that!'

Soon their running gear — white shorts and vests trimmed with the purple and green of Potter's Field — was rank with mud and damp. But Philips left them down there as he strode across to where we were watching.

'A five-miler through the woods and I'll be with you after a shower,' he said to Mallory. 'Should be an hour plus another thirty minutes or so for the retards. That all right?'

Mallory nodded, and Philips jogged back to his boys. The sports master was in a good mood.

'Get up, get up!' he barked, as if it had been their idea to roll around in the mud. 'Now you don't have to worry about getting your knees dirty, do you?'

'Sir, no, sir,' they chorused.

'Then let's get cracking. Across the fields, through the woods to the Old Mill and back in time for evensong.'

They took off across the playing fields, Philips pristine in his tracksuit among the small muddy figures. By the time they reached the woods he was flanked only by the fastest runners while the bespectacled, the fat and the surly trailed behind.

We started back to the school.

Potter's Field was mostly a great jumble of redbrick Victorian buildings but there were also more modern blocks that were clearly residential, and some more ancient buildings, black and crumbling, that looked like something from the Middle Ages. You blinked your eye and a hundred years went by.

Flocks of boys drifted past. They wore straw boaters — the hats on the older boys threadbare and falling to pieces — green blazers trimmed with purple and light grey trousers. All of them lugged books or sports gear or both.

'It hasn't changed since Hugo Buck and Adam Jones were here in the eighties,' Mallory said. 'A thousand pupils. All boys. All boarding. Three resident staff in every boarding house — House Master, house tutor and matron.'

We paused to look at the statue of the school's founder in the courtyard of the main building. Not Henry VIII as a fat, bearded king, but as a long-haired scholar and athlete, a lean young man clutching a book, two stone spaniels at his feet — the King Henry VIII who wouldn't hurt a fly.

'And it probably hasn't changed very

much since he founded the place,' Mallory added. 'Did you know he buried his greatest love here in the school grounds?'

'What wife was that, sir?'

'Not a wife. His dogs.' Mallory indicated the spaniels. 'Henry buried his favourite dogs at Potter's Field. We should have a look at their grave. I wouldn't want to miss it.'

Five hundred years. I couldn't imagine anything lasting for five hundred years. I was always happy to make it to the weekend.

There was a small graveyard behind the church chapel. Crumbling tombstones, many of the inscriptions wiped clean by time and weather. But the grave of the dogs was easy to find. It was a large square tomb in the very centre of the graveyard with a short epitaph.

Brothers and sisters,
I bid you beware
Of giving your heart
To a dog to tear.

As we walked back to the main buildings a coach was unloading visitors from a local state school's rugby team. The state school kids grinned with bewildered amusement at the boys from Potter's Field in their boaters and their green and purple blazers. But the

225

Potter's Field boys gave no indication that they had noticed, which made the smiles on the faces of the state school kids look like some kind of defensive wound.

A towering man in a gown moved among the visitors, nodding and smiling at nobody in particular with his hands behind his back, like royalty inspecting Third World troops. I had seen him before — the impossibly tall man at the funeral of Hugo Buck.

'That's the Head Master,' Mallory said. 'He's expecting us.'

Peregrine Waugh, Head Master of Potter's Field College, stood at the window of his study and stared across the playing fields.

'Three Prime Ministers, twelve Victoria Crosses and four Nobel Prizes,' he said. 'Two in physiology and two in physics. Fifteen Olympic medallists, forty-four Members of Parliament and six BAFTAs. Our drama department has always been very active. The boys were treading the boards, as it were, long before the first Old Etonian was admitted to RADA.'

'And two murders,' I said.

He stared at me over his rimless glasses.

'What's that?' he barked.

'Hugo Buck and Adam Jones,' Mallory said. 'They were Potter's Field old boys too.'

'Yes, yes. A terrible tragedy. Both of them. Did you arrest anyone yet?'

'Not yet,' Mallory said.

Waugh returned to his desk with a release of breath that might have been a sigh.

'Although Jones left the school under a cloud,' he said. 'And they are not the first old boys to be murdered, sadly. Persian chap in the seventies. Filthy rich. Oil money. Mistress clobbered him with an empty bottle of Bollinger on The Bishops Avenue.' He offered us a thin smile. 'Privilege is no guarantee of a happy life, or even a long one. And we do know we're privileged at Potter's Field, gentlemen. But we give something back, you know — it's part of the Potter's Field tradition. Part of our ethos. Always has been. Remembrance Day service. A carol concert for the people of the town. We pay for a street cleaner. Potter's Field Lawn Tennis Club uses our courts. And the school's facilities — the playing fields, the swimming pool — are used extensively by local schools and various charities.'

He rose from his chair and returned to the window.

'In fact, I think — ah yes.' He looked at us with a delighted smile. 'Look.'

We joined him at the window, the great

green playing fields of Potter's Field spread out before us. They were deserted apart from three figures who hovered by the touchline of the nearest rugby field. There was a man in a wheelchair, another with a walking stick, and a third, their physiotherapist, was demonstrating a stretching exercise. They all wore T-shirts. The physio's face looked somehow unnatural, as if he were wearing some kind of mask.

The man in the wheelchair had no legs. Where his legs should have been there was simply nothing. What looked like two white bowls were attached just below his waist. One of his arms was a far lighter colour than his black skin and it was only the weak sun glinting on a curved piece of metal where a hand had once been that made me understand he was wearing a prosthesis.

The man with a walking stick had also lost his legs. Or most of his legs. Two thin black poles stuck out of his long baggy blue shorts. What remained of his right leg had some kind of white bandage around the knee area. He appeared to need the stick to stand up but his upper body was incredibly muscular.

They were all laughing.

'The British Army is still the biggest employer of Potter's Field old boys,' Waugh said. 'Despite what the general public may think, not all the old boys go into investment banking in the City and the RSC in Stratford. We never forget our debt to our country.'

We watched the three men perform a few gentle exercises, the man in the wheelchair and the one with the stick taking their directions from the physio, the man who looked as though he was wearing a mask.

'Splendid, splendid,' Waugh said, turning away when he decided we had seen enough.

'You knew them,' Mallory said. It wasn't a question. 'You knew Hugo Buck and Adam Jones. When they were at Potter's Field. You were here too, were you not? Twenty years ago. In fact, you were their House Master.'

'Yes, yes,' Waugh said. 'Did I not mention that?'

Mallory let him fill the silence.

'Buck and Jones were both in The Abbey. It's the oldest and smallest house at Potter's Field. Not the most obvious of friendships — the athlete and the musician. But sharing a house throws boys together.'

'Could you explain the role of a House Master at Potter's Field?' I said.

Waugh sniffed.

'A boarding school is really just a day school with hotels attached,' he said. 'The

House Master is in charge of the hotel where the boys live. He assumes a parental role — encouraging, supporting and making sure they participate fully in the life of the school. Disciplining when necessary.' The thin smile. 'Although of course there's not so much of that these days. Boys don't get flogged and they don't learn so much. So what they gain at one end they lose at the other.'

There were bird-like noises from the far side of the playing fields.

'Hark,' said Waugh. 'I believe Mr Philips and the boys are coming home.'

The soldiers saw it first.

Mallory and I had left the Head Master's office and were standing on the touchline of the main rugby pitch, watching the state school boys getting thrashed by their hosts, not really noticing the boys as they poured out of the tree line, covered in mud, their thin limbs flying.

But the soldiers had stopped their gentle exercise regime and were staring. And then we saw it too.

The boys were crying.

They ran past us, some of them locked in silence as tears streamed down their faces, some of them making the animal noises of shocked grief.

I grabbed one of them by the arm.

'What's happened?' I said.

'Please, sir,' he sobbed. 'It's Mr Philips, sir. Please, sir, someone's killing him.'

Then Guy Philips came out of the tree line with his hands around his neck and his white tracksuit livid with fresh blood. He stumbled across the playing fields, his legs on the edge of going, his eyes telling us that he was drowning.

We ran to meet him, and as he collapsed in Mallory's arms, the blood began pumping out of his wound.

Mallory tore off his tie, already covered in blood, and I saw the wound, a far deeper red than the blood that was flowing. Then Mallory was winding the tie around the sports master's ravaged throat, pressing it against the wound, trying to staunch the terrible flood, crouching beside him in the mud. Mallory had his phone in one hand but it slithered away from him, slick with blood.

And I heard him call my name as I began running towards the woods.

I was alone in the woods. I kept running until I came to an open field, as barren as the surface of the moon. There I stopped, finding my breath, uncertain if I should turn back to the woods or cross the ploughed field. There was a farm on the far side.

I saw the tree I was standing next to had a perfect bloody handprint on its trunk.

I looked across at the farm. There was nothing moving. And then something seemed to stir inside. There was a glimpse of a shadow. I didn't know if it was my imagination or a man or a trick of the dying light. But I began jogging towards it.

There was some kind of square brick pen, crumbling with age, and as I paused by it I saw that the windows of the farmhouse had all been joyfully smashed. Nobody had lived here for years.

I leaned against the low brick wall and jolted when I heard the noise. Like a baby's cry. I looked into the pen and I saw the pig. Its hind legs had been tied with some kind of twine, as if in preparation for slaughter, and fearing for its life it had crawled on its belly across the dirt of the pen. I stepped over some broken brickwork and crouched down beside the pig. It squealed with terror as I pulled at the twine with my bare hands until I had set it free. It scampered away, wild-eyed with panic.

And as I made to stand up there was a

sudden explosion of pain at the back of my skull.

And then, following each other so closely that it felt like one blow, the inner edge of a forearm smashed into my throat and a fist hammered into the small of my back.

Now strong arms were around me, and he was right behind me, forcing my head back. He was near enough for me to kick him in the shins but I was suddenly not strong enough to do it, and he was close enough for me to rip his balls off, but suddenly I was too drained by shock and pain to even try.

Then he had me.

The palm of his left hand pulled hard against my right cheek, his fingertips pressing through the flesh and into my teeth as he twisted my face to one side. I looked down and glimpsed the knife.

The Fairbairn-Sykes commando dagger. The only knife ever designed to sever the carotid arteries of a man's neck.

The long thin blade moved a fraction and the steel tip pressed into the side of my neck, found a muscle it didn't like, edged forward, prodded the Adam's apple for a moment and then slipped back to the fleshy, resistant part of my neck and settled there, pressing harder.

The knife broke my skin with a sharp prick of pain.

I could feel his steady breath on the back of my throbbing head.

The wet warmth of fresh blood slid down my neck.

I tried to drop my centre of gravity. Terrified now, I lashed out with the heels of my shoes. I fought him and I fought my exhaustion, I bit and I cursed, refusing to let either overwhelm me.

But he held me tighter, and I was weak with pain, and the tip of his knife went in deeper, and the blade was buried in my flesh now.

I felt myself sag in his arms.

'Please,' I said. 'I have a daughter.'

He stopped.

The stump of metal at the knife handle's base banged once against my right temple. And then once against my left temple. It must have put me out for a few seconds because the next thing I knew I was down on my knees, dizzy and sick.

'Please,' I said, and when I looked up I saw the bag.

A worn-leather Gladstone bag.

A Murder Bag.

Waiting for him on a dry patch of ground inside the pigpen.

A boot's steel toecap slammed with full force into the base of my spine. The pain was blinding. I saw yellow light and exploding stars. I felt my back go into spasms of agony.

I realised I was screaming.

There were noises and lights but they were all inside my head. I dragged myself away on my hands and knees. I could not stand. I kept crawling. My muscles were paralysed slabs of pain and only my fear kept me moving. Time meant nothing but I knew it was passing because the ground changed beneath me, from the hard churned mud of the ploughed field to the carpet of dead leaves that covered the woods. And finally I was on grass. Now I heard voices that were not inside my head.

Then there was hot breath on the side of my face and I reared away in mortal panic.

'Please,' I said.

And I stared into the terrified face of the pig.

■ ■ ■ ■

November
Dreams of
the Dead

■ ■ ■ ■

14

I lay on my bed in the darkness and the sound of my daughter playing with the dog in the main room edged me closer to sleep. It was a soothing sound, their play — Scout's laughter like temple bells, and the soft padding of the dog as he chased after whatever chewed-up old toy she was trailing. But then another spasm of pain would grip my back and I would jolt awake.

When they found me at the edge of the playing fields they had taken me to the nearest A&E to Potter's Field. The doctor wanted to keep me in overnight but that was impossible. I had to get home to Scout. So, after the usual routine — lights in the eyes, questions about being sick, checking for broken bones — the doctor reluctantly let a uniformed officer drive me home where Mrs Murphy took one look at me and packed me off to bed, saying she would call her family, take care of Scout and sleep on

239

our sofa. For a night and a day I stayed in my bed, true rest always just out of reach, the pain never far away.

The tremors began at the bottom of my spine and rolled all the way to the base of my skull, and it was like every muscle in my back, shoulders and neck was clenching at once. At first the pain had an exact centre — the spot in my back where he had kicked me. But as the hours dragged by in that exhausting place between sleeping and waking, that centre point seemed to migrate, up to a shoulder, across to my ribs, to my neck, to the very middle of my back, as if it was seeking a happier home. I never knew where it would be next.

But the muscle spasms were the worst. They made me arch my back whenever another wave of blinding pain rolled through me. I almost cried out loud with the latest one.

'Daddy?'

Scout was in the doorway. I thought I had frightened her. But she was holding the phone.

'It's some lady,' she said.

I waited until she was in the other room and I could hear Mrs Murphy quietly talking to her, telling her they needed to fix her hair.

'Wolfe,' I said.

'Scarlet Bush.' I could hear the excitement in the reporter's voice. 'You met him. You met Bob the Butcher.'

'I don't know who I met.'

'It has to be Bob.'

'How did you get this number?'

'We want to help you find him,' she said. 'My editor has spoken to our proprietor. We have his full backing to help you bring Bob the Butcher to justice.'

'You stitched me up. Your bloody story put words in my mouth that I never said.'

She remained completely calm. 'E. L. Doctorow said, "I am led to the proposition that there is no fiction or non-fiction as we commonly understand the distinction, there is only narrative." '

'You mean you make stuff up?'

'Not quite. I mean there are facts and then there's the truth.' She paused. 'Was that your little girl who answered the phone? Was that Scout?'

I struggled to contain my anger. 'Never call my home again.'

'Did you see his face?'

'Never speak to my daughter.'

'Did he talk to you?'

'Stay right away from her.'

'Did you say something to him?'

A spasm of pain clenched my back. I bit down against it, my mouth tight shut, and ragged breath came from my nose. It made the reporter feel like she was on to something.

'You did, didn't you?'

Please. I have a daughter.

Begging him.

Begging a murderer for my life.

Sick with the fear. Unmanned by the terror.

Please.

'What did you say to him, detective? Did you reason with him? Did you threaten him? How did you feel? We are hearing reports about the murder weapon. Some kind of Special Forces knife? Old school.' I could hear her tapping a keyboard. 'A Fairbairn-Sykes commando dagger. Is that what you saw?'

I cursed under my breath. Where did they get this from?

'One final question,' she said. 'Technical point. A third murder is the game changer, isn't it?' Her tone was lighter now. She was happy. 'Because when we have three murders, it's official: we have a serial killer. That's true, isn't it?'

I hung up.

Stan padded into the room and watched

with interest as I tried to get dressed. He cocked his head to one side as I struggled to get my socks on. There was no longer enough give in my back for me to bend forward.

'You're not allowed in this room,' I said. 'Go on, Stan, get out.'

He lay down, still watching me. Sitting on the bed, I pulled my shirt on. Stan rested his chin on his front paws. I buttoned up the shirt and had another go at my socks. But it was no good. The muscles in my back were petrified.

Apparently bored with my pathetic efforts, the dog got up and yawned. Then he stretched, first lifting his tailbone in the air, his chest almost touching the ground, and then rocking forward on to his front legs, his hind legs and back almost a straight line.

Then he looked at me.

You try it.

But I knew if I got down on the floor I would need the fire brigade to get me up. So I stood with my forearms resting on the bed and pushed back with my tailbone, feeling the stretch in my lower back. Then I rocked forward, and there it was in my hamstrings — that sweet feeling of muscles that had been sleeping suddenly waking up.

I kept doing it — rocking back, rocking

forward, a modest approximation of my dog's stretches — until I was sweating and breathless but finally loose enough to sit on the bed and pull on my socks.

Stan watched me.

Yeah, he seemed to say. *You got it.*

Scarlet Bush was right — three deaths and we were no longer hunting a murderer. We were hunting a serial killer.

But we were not there yet.

Piggy Philips was lying in a hospital bed, breathing through a ventilator because of the puncture wound in his windpipe, uniformed officers outside his door twenty-four hours a day as he stubbornly clung to life.

15

There is a canteen in 27 Savile Row, but just the other side of Regent Street all of Soho is waiting for you with every kind of food in the world. So if you work out of West End Central, the backstreets of Soho are your real canteen.

I found Elsa Olsen in a Korean restaurant at the top of Glasshouse Street. The forensic pathologist was just polishing off a bowl of dak bulgogi and steamed rice.

'You look like death warmed up, Max.'

I eased myself into the chair opposite her.

'Coming from someone in your job, Elsa, I'm going to consider that a compliment.'

She waved her chopsticks. 'You want something to eat?'

I shook my head.

'If you don't want lunch then you're here to ask me about a man with a knife wound in his windpipe,' she said.

I smiled at her. 'You know me so well.'

'You want to know if he's going to live.'

'It had crossed my mind.'

'That depends entirely on the severity of the penetrating trauma.'

'It's a puncture wound, Elsa. A knife was stuck in Guy Philips' throat but his throat was not cut open. I'm giving you the edited highlights, you understand.'

'I understand. But *you* have to understand that there are puncture wounds and there are puncture wounds, Max. Tracheal perforation ranges from a small wound to complete avulsion. He's survived for, what, forty-eight hours?'

'Yes.'

'Then I would think he has every chance. But not even his doctors will know for certain. If you don't like dak bulgogi, you'd be far better off talking to them.'

'There's something more, Elsa.'

She placed her chopsticks across her rice bowl and waited.

I leaned forward. My back throbbed in protest.

'Would he have lost consciousness?' I said. 'He had a knife stuck in his throat — the assailant was disturbed, we don't know why — and the victim somehow stemmed the blood for long enough to save his life, long enough to get up and get away. Was he awake through all of that? I got a couple of taps on the head and there were whole seconds when I was out for the count. This man had his throat cut. Would he have blacked out?'

She thought about it.

'I don't know.'

'Please, Elsa. Have a guess.'

'I doubt it. Because if he had blacked out then he would have bled to death. But, like you, there may have been moments when he was not fully conscious.'

'What's the timetable?'

'There is no timetable! There are only a series of approximations.'

'But we know that Hugo Buck and Adam Jones died almost instantly.'

'Yes, because if you cut the carotid artery then loss of consciousness is within five seconds. But even that's an approximation. And the killer didn't get the chance to cut the carotid artery this time, did he?'

'Because he was disturbed. Or he panicked. There were fifty kids in those woods. Or maybe he was spooked by a bird. Whatever happened, he didn't finish the job. So did Guy Philips lose consciousness?'

'What I'm telling you is that severing any artery will eventually result in loss of consciousness. *Eventually*. Suicides who cut their radial arteries — slash their wrists, in plain English — have approximately thirty seconds to regret it before they black out and then another two minutes before they die. But it is entirely dependent on the severity of the trauma. Or, more specifically, the loss of blood plasma.'

'So how about a punctured windpipe, Elsa? My guess is that the victim was awake all the time. Even with an open wound in his windpipe. He was always awake. That's what I think. What do you think, Elsa?'

'I know exactly what you're asking, Max, and I'm not going to give you an answer. Because I just don't know! And there's no way I could possibly know for certain.'

A waiter brought a bowl of kim chi and placed it in front of Elsa. She did not look at the waiter, the kim chi or me. She stared out at Glasshouse Street, which is really little more than a glorified alley that runs parallel to Regent Street, and she sighed, shaking her head.

I did what I had seen Mallory do. I let the silence between us grow and waited for her to fill it. And eventually she did.

'A body only has to lose approximately a fifth of its normal blood volume to produce hypovolemic shock. Lose that amount of blood and the heart stops pumping. Veins

dilate, blood pressure drops, and eventually
—'

'You flake out.'

'Yes. If we're going to use the medical term, you flake out.'

'But that didn't happen to Piggy because he didn't lose enough blood. He lost a lot of blood — a hell of a lot of blood — but not enough to put him out.'

'That's a reasonable supposition.'

'So the killer sticks the blade in his neck, cuts through the windpipe, but doesn't finish the job — something spooks him — and he lets the man slide from his arms. But Philips doesn't black out. Just so we're clear, he doesn't black out, right?'

Elsa reluctantly nodded.

And then finally she gave me what I had come to Soho to find.

'I know what you are asking, and the answer is yes,' she said. She picked up her chopsticks and selected a slice of kim chi. The chilli soaking the napa cabbage was as bright as fresh blood. 'There's a good chance Guy Philips saw his assailant's face.'

A uniformed sergeant was outside the main entrance to the hospital, red-faced and stamping his boots.

'He's still alive,' I said.

It wasn't a question.

The PS gave me a grin, indicating the deserted street outside the private hospital. 'You'll know soon enough when he's snuffed it,' he said. 'They'll all come running.'

I nodded. The death of Guy Philips would swamp the street with cameras and microphones because then we would have a serial killer.

There was another uniformed officer outside the lifts. I didn't recognise him and I had my warrant card in my hand before I reached him.

'All quiet?' I said.

'These nurses keep bothering me, sir,' he said. 'They love a man in uniform.'

I stepped into the lift. 'You'll just have to try to be strong,' I said, thinking that they should teach mindless banter at Hendon, the Training School of the Metropolitan Police.

The gangly figure of PC Billy Greene was waiting outside the Intensive Care Unit. He looked half asleep but snapped to attention when he saw me coming.

'Back on the beat,' I said.

He grinned. 'Yes, DC Wolfe.'

'Visitors?'

'The same gentleman,' Greene said. 'His friend. The politician. Mr King. It's still restricted visitors but Mr King must have had a word.'

The door to the ICU opened and a doctor emerged.

'Doctor,' I said, 'DC Wolfe. When can I talk to your patient?'

'Detective,' he said. 'Mr Philips has a severe tracheal rupture. Someone, as you know, stuck a knife through his windpipe. Thirty per cent of patients with tracheal tears die, most of them within one hour.'

'I get it,' I said. 'I understand the severity of the injury.'

'I'm not convinced you do. Mr Philips is currently sedated and breathing through a ventilator. If he survives, he will need extensive surgery to repair the severed windpipe. If he has surgery, even surgery that is successful, he will have breathing difficulties for the rest of his life, due to a narrowing of the airways in his throat.' He looked up from his notes. 'And you're seriously asking me when you can talk to him?'

'Because we believe he may have seen his assailant's face,' I said. 'He wouldn't have to speak. He could write something down.'

The doctor looked at me with open hostility. 'He's not well enough for visitors,' he said. 'And I'll let you know when you can talk to him.'

He walked off.

I gave Greene my card.

'If he wakes, you call me. If his condition changes, you call me. And if there are any problems, what do you do?'

'I call you.'

'Good.'

Then I entered the Intensive Care Unit. PC Greene followed me inside, concern flitting across his face as he watched me scrub my hands in one of those big deep sinks you only find in ICUs.

'Don't worry,' I said, 'I'm not going to operate on him. And I'll be quick.'

I went inside Philips' room. In the gloom I could see a figure propped up in bed. I could not recognise him as the man I had last seen emerging from the woods at Potter's Field with blood pouring through hands around his neck. Guy Philips looked like the sole survivor of some catastrophic disaster. He looked like someone I had never met.

Three tubes, two fat and corrugated and one thin and smooth, snaked over the side of the bed like tentacles, and were connected to another tube, which in turn was connected to his nose and throat. The doctor had told me that the puncture in his trachea meant that he could only breathe through a ventilator. And the doctor was right — I didn't really understand what that meant until I saw him and heard him. The ventilator made every single breath Piggy took sound like a small war.

His neck was swathed in bandages which made him look like a relic from an Egyptian tomb, or as if someone had tried to decapitate him. There was no blood.

'Detective Wolfe,' a voice said, and only now did I see Ben King sitting on the far side of the room, hunched up in the solitary chair. 'I want to thank you for saving Guy's life.'

His voice was very soft, and although there was no chance of us waking the man in the bed, I responded in the same hushed tones.

'I don't deserve any credit for that,' I said. 'Thank DCI Mallory. He stopped him bleeding to death.'

'Of course. And I will thank him personally. Have you any leads?'

'No.' I hesitated for a moment. 'But we think he saw a face. We think he can identify whoever attacked him. And we believe he will. When he wakes.'

'When he wakes,' Ben King said. 'Then let's hope he wakes soon.'

He stood up in the darkness and I thought he was leaving. But he just wanted to shake my hand. There were tears in his eyes as he held my gaze.

'This has to end,' he said. 'These senseless murders. This unspeakable violence.'

'I want to end it,' I said.

His eyes blazed at me in the twilight of the hospital room, and that was when I felt the full force of his personality, and I understood exactly why he had climbed so far so fast.

'And I want what you want,' he told me.

16

I recognised her as soon as I walked into MIR-1 the next morning.

She was alone in the room, having arrived even before Mallory, sitting on a desk, looking at a laptop that was open on a PDF of the Murder Investigation Manual.

She turned to look at me with the cool, steady gaze that I remembered from my first day in Homicide, up at the bank, Hugo Buck on the shag carpet with his throat opened up. It was the rebellious red hair that really gave her away. Everything else seemed different, because this time she was not in uniform.

'DC Wolfe?' she said. 'I don't know if you remember me. From the one-oh-one at ChinaCorps. TDC Edie Wren?'

'I remember. You're a trainee detective constable now? How did that happen?'

'The usual way. I passed my National Investigations Exam. I'm working towards

my PIP Level 2 Portfolio. You know —
demonstrating competence, all of that?'

'What you doing here?'

'I'm the bagman on the double homicide.'

'Our bagman? The bagman's usually a
detective sergeant or detective constable.'

'Cuts,' she said.

The bagman was the lowest rank of the
investigation, answering directly to the
senior investigating officer, DCI Mallory,
and giving assistance wherever it was
needed. I remembered how calm Wren had
been on the day she and Greene found
Buck's body and I had no doubt she could
do the job.

'So this is where it all happens,' she said.

'This is where some of it happens,' I said.
'There's plenty of legwork outside. I've
learned that murder is labour intensive. In
the Yorkshire Ripper case, the law checked
over five million car registration numbers.'

'Yes, and they still cocked it up,' she said.
'Did you see the new Bob the Butcher post?'

She stabbed a few buttons on her laptop.
The social network site came up. It was
nothing I hadn't seen before. The later
photograph of Robert Oppenheimer. The
same apocalyptic boasting: 'I am become
Death, the destroyer of worlds. Kill the
protectors of the rich. Kill all pigs.'

'Seen it,' I said.

'But did you see the link?' Wren said. 'That's new. And you're in it.'

She clicked on the link. And there I was on my hands and knees, a thin trickle of blood running down the side of my face from a wound in my temple. Another sliding down the side of my neck. My mouth was open and my eyes were fixed on nothing.

And I was crawling.

There was only a few seconds of footage, but it kept repeating, and looping back on itself, so it looked like I was crawling forward, and then reversing, as if doing some comic jig. In one corner of the screen the pig edged towards me, its eyes bulging with terror. Our faces would almost touch and then we would back away from each other. And then the mad dance would begin again.

There was music, I realised. Not really music at all. Just mad laughter, on and on, hysterical screams of laughter over an oompah-oompah beat as the pig and I crawled towards each other and then backed away. And did it again. Laughter in the dark, laughter from the grave.

'Who filmed you out there?' Wren said.

'I don't know.'

'Did he film you, the killer? Did Bob make this film?'

'I doubt it,' I said. 'Not his style.'

'I would have thought it was exactly his style,' Wren said. 'I Shazamed it. That song. It's some old music-hall number. "The Laughing Policeman" by Charles Jolly.'

As if on cue, Charles Jolly stopped laughing and started singing.

He said, 'I must arrest you.'
He didn't know what for.
And then he started laughing
Until he cracked his jaw!
Ah ha ha ha ha ha ha ha ha ha ha ha ha
    ha!

'It's gone viral,' Wren said. 'You see how many hits you've got?'

My phone went.

It was the chief super.

I pictured her in one of those top-floor offices at New Scotland Yard where they either have a view of the river or a view of the park. And I knew from the ice-cold ferocity in her voice that she was looking at neither. Detective Chief Superintendent Swire was looking at my little film. I was no longer flavour of the month. I was a flavour that had been discontinued.

'I think you've been promoted beyond your ability and experience,' she said. 'That day at the railway station — you were right and I was wrong. You got your medal and your pay rise and your transfer to Mallory's outfit. But here's the thing: I think nothing could have stopped you running that man down. I think that is who you are, Wolfe. I think you would have run him down if he'd had a bag full of onion bhajis. I think because of your personal history — don't be surprised, it's all in your file — you are completely out of control. Do you know why we don't have guns, detective?'

I knew the answers off by heart.

'Because we don't need them, ma'am. Because we have trained firearms officers. Because the public do not want their police to be armed. And because if every officer had a firearm, then standards would slip from their current high level.'

'No,' she said. 'The real reason we don't have guns is because of reckless bastards like you. In a war of smart bombs, you're an unexploded device. You're not even a loose cannon, Wolfe.'

She hung up, and I saw that Mallory was standing in the doorway of MIR-1, holding his takeaway tea and staring at me.

I couldn't look at him.

Not because the world was laughing at me.

Please. I have a daughter.

But because the world had seen me crawl.

I did not feel like going to the gym. But I knew I needed to. I knew I had to. I knew I must exhaust my body tonight, that muscle and blood and bone must be so weary by the time I got into bed that a few hours of sleep was at least a possibility. And I had to fill my head with something other than my humiliating new career as an internet sensation.

There was a sign in Fred's, and as the gym emptied near closing time I stood looking up at it. It was placed between a posed black-and-white photograph of Sonny Liston and a picture of a dozen Cuban kids sparring in a ring with ropes like snapped elastic.

PAIN IS JUST WEAKNESS LEAVING THE BODY

It was a good message, and there had been times when I'd believed in it, and it had helped me. But not today. Today I did not feel that the thick burning knot of pain in my lower back was just weakness leaving the body.

Today, pain was just pain.

Fred walked in. He went over to the music system and fiddled about with it until he found some early Clash. The gym was filled with the crashing guitar chords of Mick Jones and Joe Strummer's machine-gun bark. Fred picked up a towel that somebody had dropped on the floor and went off to put it in the laundry. When he came back I was leaning against the ropes and staring at the square that we call a ring. My back was stiff with pain, and I reflected on the fact that the things that hurt me the most were a source of entertainment for others.

Fred and I leaned on the ropes, the sweet stink of a boxing gym all around us, The Clash at full volume, and the silence between us was not awkward.

And then he spoke.

'It's not about how hard you can hit,' he said. 'It's about how hard you can get hit and then keep going — for just long enough to hit the bastards back.'

17

'Let him go!'

On the far side of a field that glittered with early morning frost, Scout released the dog and he began tearing towards me.

Hampstead Heath, early Sunday morning. The forest at the top of London. We were in a meadow high on the Heath and my daughter and my dog seemed giddy with all the sunlight, fresh air and freedom. All around us were trees that still clung to the last of the red and gold leaves of autumn. Beyond them you could see the city from Canary Wharf to the BT Tower. It felt like it all belonged to us.

We should do this more often, I thought. We should do this all the time.

The field we were in looked perfectly flat until Stan began racing across it. With him in top gear I suddenly became aware of all the dips and bumps and rabbit holes. As he came to one sudden drop in the ground he extended his front legs before him and his hind legs behind to dramatically bound across. He looked like he was flying.

Scout shouted with delight. 'Superdog!'

Stan raced towards me, his large ears streaming behind him, bright eyes shining and mouth open, panting, going flat out. It was his first time off lead and he was almost hysterical with excitement. And so were we.

I got down on my knees, my back moaning in protest, and held my arms wide to greet him.

Then he was on me, breathing hard and snuffling for the chicken treats I held in my fists. I fed him the treats, his nose a wet button in my palm, and I kept hold of his harness until Scout gave me the signal.

And he flew back to her side.

Hampstead Heath was dog heaven. Dogs of all sizes passed through this meadow on their walks, some of them coming over to give Stan an investigative sniff, others lost in their own world of smells, uninterested in the little red squirt off lead for the first time.

Dogs paced along the perimeter of the meadow where the trees began, noses pressed to the ground on the trail of some long-gone rabbit or fox. But Scout and I stayed on the meadow with Stan running between us, until he was gasping with exhaustion and our bags of chicken treats were almost empty.

We were both grinning with happy relief. Stan had gone off lead and he hadn't been lost. I took out his dog lead. It was time to go home.

And then he saw the birds.

Two fat crows, pecking the ground just beyond the tree line, and they took flight as Stan hurtled towards them. Scout and I chased after him, calling his name, but the birds had touched some ancient nerve and suddenly he was not interested in chicken treats or us.

The elm trees were old and huge on that part of the Heath, and their spreading boughs formed a thick canopy that made it impossible for the birds to take to the sky. So they flew low, flapping wildly, unable to break free.

And Stan went after them.

Within seconds we had lost sight of him. We staggered among the trees, calling his name, and within minutes we too had completely lost our bearings. The Heath was dense and wild up here, although we could hear the distant buzz of traffic on Hampstead Lane and could easily imagine our dog under their wheels. Scout began to cry.

Silently, hopelessly. I put my arm around her and called Stan's name again, though it felt useless. The traffic was closer now. There was a tight knot of fear and grief in my stomach.

And then we saw them.

The woman coming through the trees with a little red dog in her arms and another dog scampering off lead by her side. A Pekingese-Chihuahua cross. I recognised the dog before I recognised Natasha Buck in her flat cap, green Hunter boots and black waterproofs, a city girl dressed for the country.

Scout and I choked out our thanks for Stan's safe return.

'Don't thank me,' she said. She pointed at the Pekingese-Chihuahua cross daintily snacking on rabbit droppings by her boots. 'Thank Susan.'

We thanked Susan.

I clipped on Stan's lead and we walked back to the meadow, while Natasha told us how they had been walking back from Kenwood House when they came across a young Cavalier King Charles Spaniel shivering alone under the elms. Then she asked us if we wanted a cup of hot chocolate.

I looked at Scout, and Scout looked at me.

'Yes, please,' we said.

We walked back to our cars with our dogs on their leads, and I thought that we looked like one of the families who take their dogs on the Heath at the weekend, one of those lucky families. Not perfect, but intact.

At first I thought she was moving out. There were boxes in the hallway of Natasha's flat, some of them sealed and some of them open, piled high with clothes and sports equipment, and shoeboxes overflowing with old photos. But she was only shipping out her husband's things.

She brought us our hot chocolate.

'First time off lead?' she asked.

'Yes,' Scout said. 'I don't like it. Off lead is scary. I don't like it when he can just run away.'

Natasha laughed. It was the first time I had seen her laugh properly, without anything behind it.

'But you have to let him go,' she said. 'You have to give him that freedom. He's a dog.'

'I know he's a dog,' Scout said. 'But I don't like it.'

Stan roamed the perimeter of the flat, sniffing the skirting board. Susan followed him, sniffing his backside. Natasha and Scout followed the pair of them, laughing together.

Some people who don't have children themselves try too hard. But Natasha wasn't like that. She was easy and friendly, and I thought I saw her for the first time. This wild girl who wanted to settle down but picked the wrong man. She looked back at me and smiled. They paused at the window, looking across Regent's Park. Natasha slipped her arm around Scout's shoulder. My daughter lifted her face to say something.

I sipped my hot chocolate. Hugo Buck had owned a lot of stuff, I thought, looking at the boxes. The two paintings of the empty city were no longer on the wall. I could see them sitting alone in an old champagne box.

I went over and picked one of them up. The style was very familiar to me now. The secret corners of the city, empty of people, changed by twilight. I'd seen it here, I had seen it on the wall of the Jones family home, and I had seen it again in Salman Khan's office. The abandoned city in soft half-light; London — I took it to be London — as a place of loneliness and shadows and sadness, full of the Sunday morning stillness that James Sutcliffe saw in the world.

The one I'd picked up featured the deserted railway lines. I looked in the corner for his initials.

But they were not there.

Instead there was a name I did not recognise.

Edward Duncan

I stared at the unknown signature, and then I picked up the other painting, the tunnel in the soft light of dawn or twilight.

j s

James Sutcliffe. Then who was Edward Duncan?

I placed the paintings side by side. And I saw what I had not seen before. The style was similar — so alike that it was easy to assume they were by the same artist. But the painting by Edward Duncan was different. It was different from the painting that had 'j s' in the corner, it was different from the painting on the wall of the Jones family home, and it was different from the painting on the wall of Khan's office. It was something to do with the artist's use of light.

Natasha was saying something to me. The dogs were at my feet and Scout tugged at my sleeve. But I could not tear my eyes from the painting.

Edward Duncan's world was darker than the one James Sutcliffe knew. The light was not fading in his painting of an abandoned city.

It was dying.

18

First thing Monday morning I found TDC
Edie Wren alone in MIR-1 reading a new
post from Bob the Butcher on her laptop.

' "If the radiance of a thousand suns were
to burst at once into the sky, that would be
like the splendour of The Mighty One.
#killallpigs." A shy, unassuming fellow, isn't
he? You seen how many followers he's got
now?'

Wren had her laptop plugged into a workstation and on the desk screen I could see
that she was logged into HOLMES. Every
scrap of evidence produced during the
investigation — Operation Fat Boy, they
were calling it, after the attack on Guy
'Piggy' Philips — had been entered into
HOLMES: witness statements, forensic
reports, crime scene photographs, autopsy
records, every bit of it tagged with a number, a security level and a priority status.
Wren had HOLMES open at the Action

Management page, a yellow document that would allocate the day's work schedule for our team. But it was the social network site on her laptop that she was focused on.

'Just sending Bob a message telling him how much I love him,' she said. 'Not much chance of getting a response, I know. But if he replies I can find his IP address in sixty seconds.'

I watched her sending Bob the Butcher some fan mail.

'You're good at this stuff,' I said. 'The whole digital thing.'

She shrugged with false modesty. 'Good enough.'

'Do you think we've done all we can to find him?' I said.

'Bob or the perp?'

'I was thinking of Bob.'

'Everyone in here talks as if they're one and the same. But you don't think so.'

I shrugged. 'It comes down to this. If Jack the Ripper was around today, would he Tweet? Would the Boston Strangler be updating his single status on Facebook? I don't think so.'

Wren laughed. 'You're dead wrong. I think that's *exactly* what they'd be doing. Are you kidding? Jack the Ripper would have *loved* social media. The Boston Strangler, the

Yorkshire Ripper — they would have got a big bang out of the digital community. Taunting the law, puffing out their little chests, revelling in the horror, the horror. The digital world is made for sociopaths. As long as you don't get caught.'

'Then you don't think we've done enough to find Bob.'

She pushed a strand of red hair from her face. 'Clearly not, because we haven't found him, have we? But it's not necessarily DI Gane's fault, and I'm not being diplomatic. Bob's hiding behind multiple firewalls, and IDS — intrusion detection systems, like a burglar alarm for computers — and Tor, the onion router, where every message is en-crypted and re-encrypted multiple times through countless servers. So it will prob-ably take more than a love letter to flush him out.'

Wren pushed back her chair and picked up what looked like a thick exercise book — the Action Book, which logs the tasks that have been done and the tasks that are yet to be done, and who should do them. It was the real-world equivalent of the Action Management page on HOLMES. Mallory still liked to have a paper record of every-thing.

'I see you're going back to Potter's Field

today with a Specialist Search Unit, and taking more statements from the boys who were out running with Philips,' Wren observed.

I nodded.

As well as monitoring the Action Book, Wren was responsible for all the statements coming in, logging them into HOLMES, and for maintaining the integrity of the chain of evidence, the paper trail leading from the crime scenes to MIR-1 and all the way to court.

It was a big job, and I could see that it bored the hell out of her.

I indicated the laptop.

'Is it true what they say?' I asked. 'Does everyone leave a digital footprint?'

'Now I wouldn't go that far,' she said. 'Everybody leaves a digital *shadow*. We all live two lives — our physical life, and our digital life. All of us. And the finest minds of my generation are currently working out how to sell you stuff you've already bought. So there's pixel tracking, page tagging, tracking codes — it's why all these ads seem to follow you around, to magically know it's *you*.' She laughed. 'At its hollow heart, the internet doesn't really *want* anyone to be anonymous. Because it wants to sell you stuff.'

'So everyone leaves a shadow.'

'Yes.'

'Good,' I said. 'Because there's someone I want you to find.'

'Bob the Butcher,' she said. 'Because he broke your back. Because he made you the laughing stock of millions. And because he could have killed you if he wanted to.'

'Not Bob,' I said. 'I don't think Bob has anything to do with these murders. But the man I want to find just might. He would be somewhere in his mid thirties. Name of Edward Duncan.'

She found herself a pen. 'Edward Duncan,' she said as she wrote. 'Do we have a date of birth?'

'I can get you a possible one but I don't want you to treat it like gospel.'

'OK. What does he do, this Edward Duncan?'

'He paints.'

'Houses?'

'Cities.'

'Should I put it in the Action Book?'

I smiled at her. She wasn't bored now.

'This one's off the book,' I said.

As the afternoon grew colder and darker I stood on the edge of the ploughed field, watching twelve uniformed officers from the

Specialist Search Unit inching across it on their hands and knees, fingertip-searching for evidence, the manual labour of police work.

A photographer was standing in the middle of the field staring at something on the ground. I walked over to him and we both looked at a dip in the field containing a single perfect footprint. On one side of it the photographer had placed a yellow marker with the number 1, and on the other side a plastic ruler. He hummed to himself, as cheerful as a wedding photographer, as he began setting up his tripod, lights and ladder.

'Not you, is it?' he grinned, nodding at the footprint.

'I don't think so,' I said.

'Well,' he said, adjusting his tripod. 'Maybe it's the farmer's wife. And maybe it's our man. You never know your luck, do you?'

I agreed that you never knew your luck and headed towards the woods, my back aching in protest at being forced to cross a ploughed field.

The SSU van was parked just beyond the tree line and another dozen officers were sitting around it gulping down tea and bars of chocolate, their clothes filthy from the fingertip search, their exhausted faces as black with sweat-streaked dirt as coal miners'.

I came out of the trees and on to the playing fields of Potter's Field. In the distance the wind whipped the flag of St George that flew above the main building. I'd just started towards it when I was caught by the smell of burning leaves. Smoke was drifting up from behind a tiny stone cottage at the edge of the rugby pitch. I walked round the back of it and found an old man unloading a wheelbarrow piled with dead leaves on to a small bonfire.

'Excuse me, sir?'

I showed him my warrant card. He peered at it and nodded. Then carried on with what he was doing. Whatever you do, get their name and address, they tell you at Hendon. It's the very first thing they tell you.

'May I ask your name, sir?'

'I'm nobody. I'm just the groundsman.'

A strange accent that contained both Eastern Europe and the West Country. I watched him unload the wheelbarrow. There was something wrong with his hands. He glanced at me and saw that I was still waiting for an answer.

'Len Zukov,' he said.

'Where you from, Len?'

He gave me a sharp look. 'I'm from here. How about you? Where you from?'

The accent was Russian, maybe.

'I'm from here, too,' I said.

'Then we're both from here.'

'Worked here long, Len?'

He was silent for a moment, as if adding it up.

'Thirty years,' he said.

'Do you remember these boys?'

I was holding out a photograph of the seven boys in their Combined Cadet Force uniforms.

He shook his head. Too quickly?

'Many boys come and go,' he said.

'This was taken in 1988. In your time. You don't remember them? Have a closer look. The King twins? You don't remember identical twins?'

'No.'

The worst thing about being a policeman? People lie to you. They lie all the time. They lie because they are afraid of getting into trouble, they lie because they are afraid of getting into deeper trouble, and most of all they lie so that you will go away.

But maybe he was telling the truth. It was a long time ago, and boys had come and gone in their thousands.

'But you know Mr Philips,' I said. 'The

sports master. And you know that someone tried to kill him.'

The old man looked at me as if I was some kind of idiot.

'Everybody knows,' he said.

I watched him load more leaves on the fire and then saw what was wrong with his hands. The fingers did not open. He was building his fire with two fists closed by what looked like the advanced stages of rheumatoid arthritis.

'It was in the woods,' he said. 'Far from here.'

When the last of the leaves were on the fire he brushed his closed fists on his trousers and we walked to the front of the cottage. There was a figure standing in the doorway — the physiotherapist Mallory and I had seen on the playing fields with the disabled men. Now I saw that he was not wearing a mask. Most of his face had been lost to burns.

I held out my hand.

'Sergeant Tom Monk,' he said. 'Formerly of the Royal Green Jackets.'

His shockingly burned face split with a wide white grin. He looked like a member of some lost race; I could not believe there would be a time when his face would not shock me. He clicked the heels of his Asics trainers, and Zukov smiled for the first time. He seemed much more relaxed in the presence of Monk.

'You do rehab here?' I asked Monk.

'One afternoon a week,' he said. 'I'm mostly down the road. I'm the senior physio at Barrington Court. Or the senior physio's assistant. Yeah, that's more like it.'

I had heard of Barrington Court. It was a rehabilitation centre for severely wounded veterans, most of them victims of IED blasts in Afghanistan.

'Mr Waugh lets us use the running track on Thursday afternoons,' Monk said. 'Quite funny really, lending us a running track when most of us don't have any legs.'

I automatically looked down at his faded jeans. Monk laughed.

'Oh, not me,' he said. 'I've still got all my parts. Some of them are just a bit overcooked.'

I smiled weakly.

'How's he doing?' Monk said, suddenly serious. 'Mr Philips.'

I shook my head. 'You know what? I really don't know, Tom.'

Because on the other side of the playing fields I could see the flag of St George being lowered, and stopping when it reached half-mast. The phone in my jacket began to vibrate.

I pulled it out and saw that it was PC Greene, and that he had already tried to call me five times.

Peregrine Waugh was crossing the playing fields towards me, his gown flowing behind him.

But I already knew.

Piggy Philips was dead.

19

I was waiting for Ben King in the central lobby of the Palace of Westminster, the most beautiful space in London — a high-vaulted octagonal hall with a giant central chandelier and an intricately tiled floor, lit by natural light that pours through massive windows.

The central lobby bustled with life. Constituents waited to talk to their MP. Political journalists gossiped and snickered and fawned. MPs and peers came and went from the corridors that led to their chambers — the Lords to the south, the MPs to the north.

With its statues of kings and queens and a national saint over each of the four exits — St George for England, St David for Wales, St Andrew for Scotland, St Patrick for Northern Ireland — the central lobby felt like more than the core of Parliament, more than the place where all the corridors of power converged.

It felt like the ultimate seat of British power.

I watched Ben King emerge from the corridor that led to the House of Commons. He was in a group of men surrounding the Prime Minister. King saw me and peeled away from the crowd.

We shook hands and walked out to the Terrace Pavilion, where there were white tables and chairs and people drinking tea. We stood with our backs to them all, the Palace of Westminster rising above us, and the Thames flowing far below.

'My condolences,' I said.

'Thank you.'

'You were with Guy Philips when he died.'

'Yes. I spent the last night in his room.'

'Did he say anything? I'm sorry but I have to ask you.'

Ben King stared at the river without seeing it.

'It was four in the morning. He was sleeping. I was sleeping. I awoke because the machine that monitored his heart rate was making a different sound. I called the nurse. She was sleeping too. When she came to the room she immediately called the doctor. But it was too late.' At last he looked at me. 'Guy died in his sleep. I know what you're asking. But he never woke, he never said anything about who attacked him and he passed away peacefully. And I am profoundly grateful for that small mercy, detective.'

'And you were with him every night he was in the hospital?'

'Yes. Guy never married. His parents were dead. My brother and I — all of his friends — were what he had instead of family.'

'I think he saw his killer's face. I'm certain of it.'

'He didn't say a word.'

A young blonde woman was standing in the entrance to the Terrace Pavilion, trying to attract King's attention. He raised his hand to show that he understood. But his manners were too good to rush me.

'There's something else,' I said. 'You — and your brother, and Mr Khan — you're all going to be issued with Osman Warnings.'

'Osman Warnings?'

'If the police have reason to believe that someone is at risk of being murdered or seriously injured we issue an Osman Warning — it's both an official warning and an offer of police protection.'

King almost smiled. 'It sounds rather like a way of the police trying to protect themselves from future accusations of negligence.'

'There's an element of that,' I agreed. 'My superiors will be writing to you to offer protection and to give advice on the steps you can take to ensure your safety.'

'Is that really necessary? Perhaps for Salman — who, I understand, is now too afraid to leave his house. But I'm surrounded by high security in the House. And Ned is out of the country and has the entire British Army watching over him. I think he's more at risk from the Taliban.'

'We have a duty of care to warn people when they are in mortal danger,' I said. 'On Hugo Buck's desk there was a photograph of seven boys at Potter's Field. You probably know the photograph.'

'Yes, I know it.'

'Now only four of you are still alive.'

He was watching the river again.

'Three,' he said. 'James Sutcliffe killed himself in Italy.'

'Of course. My apologies. Three of you.'

Then he looked at me. 'I want to put an end to this,' he said. 'I want to help you in any way I can. I want to assist you in apprehending this murderer.' He gripped my hand and he held my eyes.

'I know,' I said. 'I know you do.'

We walked back inside and said goodbye.

As he crossed the central lobby, people approached him — lobby journalists, other MPs, women and men, all of them with the half-smile of the truly smitten — and he had a word for each of them. But he kept walking, he never broke that long easy stride, eventually disappearing into the northern corridor that leads to the House of Commons; and for the first time I appreciated his true power, and how much he had to lose.

It's a five-minute walk from the Palace of Westminster to New Scotland Yard, and even though I did not have an appointment in Room 101, I thought it would be all right. They don't get many visitors in the Black Museum.

'I saw your film,' said Sergeant John Caine, the keeper of the gate. He looked at me with his hard eyes, but there was no mockery in them. 'Everybody saw your film, didn't they?'

'Will you watch it with me again?'

He was startled. 'Why?'

'It only lasts a minute. I want to ask your advice about something. I know you've seen it already, but will you watch it with me?'

There was an old computer on his desk.

He pressed some keys and it wheezed into life.

'My one might be quicker,' I said.

He snorted. 'All mod cons at West End Central, eh?'

I took out my Mac and we waited in silence as it powered up. We remained silent as I went to the social network site and found the profile page of Bob the Butcher. I began scrolling down all his postings about killing pigs and destroying worlds.

'This one,' I said.

I clicked on the link, and there it was, the mirth with no mercy of 'The Laughing Policeman' as the camera watched me crawl. Just as the pig appeared, I hit pause.

'You see that?' I asked Sergeant Caine. 'By my right hand?'

He leaned closer. 'A white line.'

'A straight white line painted on grass,' I said. 'It's a touchline. It's the edge of a rugby field. The rugby field that's closest to the trees at Potter's Field.'

We stared at the image together. Then he shrugged.

'So what?' he said.

'Doesn't it prove that Bob the Butcher isn't the killer?'

'Why does it prove that?'

'That film wasn't shot when I got a good

hiding. Whatever Bob tells his devoted followers, he had nothing to do with it.'

Sergeant Caine had a think.

Then he said, 'You reckon that whoever
had a knife to your throat is not the same
person who stuck a camera in your face.'

'He can't be, can he?' I said. 'Whoever
put me down wouldn't have followed me
across a ploughed field and through some
woods just to shoot this funny little film,
would he?'

'How far did you crawl?'

'I was running through those woods for
perhaps five minutes. It would have taken a
lot longer to crawl back. But that film wasn't
taken anywhere near where I was attacked.
It wasn't taken at the pigpen at the farm. It
wasn't taken in the ploughed field. It was
filmed when I was back at Potter's Field. It
was filmed on the edge of the playing fields.'

'So who put it on the internet? Where did
Bob get it from?'

'I don't know. It doesn't matter. That
school has a thousand boys and they all
have phones with cameras. There are reporters crawling all over the place. The staff.
Everybody's walking around with a camera
crew in their back pocket. What it proves —
what I *think* it proves — is that Bob the
Butcher is full of bullshit. Whoever took that

film didn't kill anyone. And neither did he.'

I closed my laptop and we looked at each other. Sergeant Caine folded his heavy arms. Then he nodded once.

'Yes,' he said, 'I think you're probably right.'

'Thank you.'

'You're welcome. What's the problem?'

'The problem is they're chucking everything they've got at Bob,' I said. 'All of our resources are being poured into looking for Bob the Butcher, serial killer of the year. Operation Fat Boy is being led up a dead end.'

A spasm of pain travelled up my spine and I ground my teeth together, arching my back until it passed.

'You want to find whoever messed up your back,' Sergeant Caine said.

'I want to find the killer.' I took a breath and let it go. 'And you can help me.'

'How can I do that?'

'I want to see the From Hell letter,' I said.

He looked away, then looked back at me. Suddenly he was angry.

'The From Hell letter? Do you know what you're asking? The From Hell letter was lost.'

'I don't think so,' I said. 'I think it's here. I think it's somewhere in this room. I think it's in your possession.'

'What do you know about the From Hell letter, detective?'

'I know that it was also known as the Lusk letter,' I replied. 'It was a letter posted in 1888 by a person unknown who claimed to be Jack the Ripper. What made the police think it was the one genuine correspondence from Jack the Ripper was that it arrived with part of an internal organ from a human body.'

'Where do you think you are,' Sergeant Caine said, shaking his head with disbelief, 'Madame Tussaud's? This is a training facility for officers who put themselves in harm's way. Not a freak show.'

'I just want to see the letter.'

'What makes you think it's here?'

'I just don't believe it was lost. I can't believe that. The only letter from Jack the Ripper? Come on. I think it would have been filed, saved, preserved.'

'Why lie about it?'

'Don't want the public getting too excited about some unholy relic, do we? Don't need them turning a serial killer into a bigger cult hero than he is already. But I think we would have saved it.'

'We?'

'The law. The Met. The good guys. And I

think that if it is anywhere in London, then it will be in some secret corner of the Black Museum.'

He laughed. 'I suppose you might just make a detective one day. But why do you want to see it — assuming it's in my power to show it to you?'

'I want to see what the real thing looks like.'

He moved towards the door and I thought he was going to call for some help and have me kicked out. But Sergeant Caine wouldn't have needed any help to kick me out.

I watched him lock Room 101.

'There were hundreds of letters claiming to be from Jack the Ripper,' he said. 'The Dear Boss letter. The Saucy Jacky postcard. The Openshaw letter. What made the From Hell letter different was that, as you say, it came with a small box containing half a human kidney.'

I watched him remove a calendar from the wall that said MERRY CHRISTMAS AND A HAPPY NEW YEAR FROM THE METROPOLITAN POLICE.

There was a safe in the wall.

'Turn away, detective,' he said, and I turned my head as he tapped some numbered keys. 'It was addressed to George Lusk, the head of the Whitechapel Vigilance

Committee. You can turn back now.'

There was a dark green folder on his desk.

He opened it. Inside the folder was a plastic envelope. Inside the envelope was a single sheet of paper, rust-coloured with age, as brittle as something scorched, like something pulled from the fire at the very last moment.

Large red letters, a dozen lines, words written quickly, words written in a fever.

'Somebody slung out the kidney,' Sergeant Caine said. 'Sorry about that.'

From hell
Mr Lusk
Sor
I send you half the
Kidne I took from one women
Prasarved it for you tother piece
I fried and ate it was very nice, I may send you the bloody knif that took it out if you only wate a whil longer.

Signed
Catch me when
You Can
Mishter Lusk

'It's real, isn't it?' I said. 'You can tell. It's from him. It's from Jack the Ripper.'

Caine nodded. 'It's at a much lower

literacy level than the other letters they received, but back in the day they thought that was deliberate. What's fake about it is the pretence of illiteracy. Look. He apparently can't spell to save his life but he manages to observe the silent "k" in knife and the silent "h" in while. Unlike all the other letters, he doesn't sign it "Jack the Ripper". And I'll say this for him — he did include a human kidney.'

'He was sick of the fakes,' I said. 'He was tired of all the nutcases claiming credit for crimes they didn't have the skill and the madness to commit. And it's going to be the same this time. Sooner or later, the real killer will show himself.'

Sergeant Caine watched me staring at the letter.

'Bob the Butcher is not real,' I said. 'But this is real. May I touch it?'

The keeper of the Black Museum stared at me.

'Be careful,' he said.

20

'One murder is a tragedy,' said Detective Chief Superintendent Elizabeth Swire. 'Two murders are a tragic coincidence. And three murders are prime-time entertainment.'

The call from the chief super had come just as Mallory was about to start the morning briefing at West End Central. Fifteen minutes later we were in a conference room on the top floor of New Scotland Yard. This high up the brass had a picture-postcard view of either St James's Park or the Thames. This room overlooked the park. But nobody noticed the view.

The death of Guy Philips had put Operation Fat Boy on all the front pages. Bob the Butcher was being called a serial killer and treated like a national celebrity. The popular press were going wild, but with a sneaking regard for Bob's dysfunctional social conscience. BOB THE BUTCHER — FEARED BY THE RICH, LOVED BY

THE POOR? asked the *Sun*. The unpopular press saw Bob as the embodiment of the seething resentments at the rotten core of an unfair society. BUTCHER BOB — IS HE A ONE MAN RIOT? pondered the *Guardian,* as if all Bob was doing was kicking in store windows and stealing plasma TVs.

The chief super was not happy. And DCS Swire had a genius for registering her displeasure. She was a fifty-year-old woman with a ferocious blonde haircut, hair sprayed as stiff as a Spartan helmet. Swire looked like Mrs Thatcher's recently exhumed corpse, but with slightly less human warmth.

She considered DCI Mallory with dead eyes.

'You initially expressed doubts that Bob the Butcher was the perpetrator,' she said.

'That's correct, ma'am.'

'So have you eliminated him from your enquiries?'

'Not yet, ma'am,' Mallory said.

'Not yet, ma'am,' she said, her tone so caustic you could have used it to strip paint.

DI Gane spoke up, his voice shaking just a little. He talked about anonymity networks, onion routers and layers of encryption.

Swire cut him off with a short jerk of her head.

'Let's skip the tech talk, shall we?' she said. 'But tell me this: how likely is it that the average social network psycho would have security architecture that elaborate?'

'It would be . . . unusual,' Gane answered.

Swire may not have cocked a disbelieving eyebrow. But that was the impression she gave.

'Only unusual?' she said quietly. 'Really? No more than that?'

'It would be unprecedented, ma'am.'

Swire nodded, as if we were at last getting somewhere.

'What's the latest on prints?' she said. 'Are we working the prints?'

Mallory's fingertips brushed his SIO policy book. He cleared his throat.

'The situation is unchanged, ma'am. We have no prints at any of the crime scenes.'

Swire stared hard at him.

'You mean you have smooth glove prints?'

'No prints, ma'am. No smooth glove prints, no partials — no prints at all. The absence of prints remains . . . unexplained.'

Swire let this sink in.

'So he's a ghost?' she said.

The base of my spine pulsed with pain.

'He's no ghost,' I said. 'Ma'am.'

She nodded, as if she had only just decided something.

'We're rebooting Operation Fat Boy,' she said. 'I'm bringing in three new bodies.'

Swire was flanked by two men who had remained silent throughout the meeting, avoiding eye contact with the incompetent Murder Investigation Team from West End Central: a young East Asian in glasses with digital geek written all over him, and a much older man, about sixty, with soft white hair who couldn't possibly have been a part of the Met because he was wearing a suit but no tie.

Now they stirred.

Swire nodded curtly at Mallory and told him, 'You will remain as SIO for the time being. But I'll be sitting in at the morning briefings and you will be reporting directly to me.'

Gane and Whitestone exchanged a look. Mallory's time was passing. He was still senior investigating officer but this no longer felt like his investigation. Operation Fat Boy now felt like it was being run from Broadway, SW1 — New Scotland Yard — not 27 Savile Row.

Mallory was a good man, but the world was beating him down. Suddenly his authority felt like a fragile thing that could be taken away by one gesture from the woman at the top of the conference table. I saw that Gane and Whitestone could not look at him.

Swire gestured to the digital geek on her left. 'This is Colin Cho of the Police Central e-crime Unit. As you know, the PCeU is jointly funded by the Home Office and the Met to provide a national response to the most serious incidents of cyber-crime. Bob the Butcher comes under their remit.'

'Hopefully we might be able to show you a few new tricks,' Cho said to Gane, his accent somewhere between Hong Kong and London.

Gane said nothing.

'I want Bob flushed out,' Swire said. 'I want him dragged out from behind his firewall. I want him taken *seriously*. We're becoming a laughing stock.' She nodded sharply at me. Her hair did not move. 'Especially after DC Wolfe's recent stroll in the country.'

'We *have* taken Bob seriously, ma'am,' Mallory insisted.

She did not slap the table. She did not need to. She fixed Mallory with a look cold enough to give a snowman hypothermia.

'Not seriously enough,' she said. 'The MP for Hillingdon North is highly thought of in Whitehall and Westminster.' She inhaled deeply, exhaled slowly. 'I am receiving phone calls.'

So that was it, I thought. The murders were too close to Ben King, and Swire had the full weight of Downing Street and Whitehall pressing on her back.

She turned to the older man on her right. 'And this is Dr Joe Stephen of King's College London. Introduce yourself, Dr Stephen?'

'I'm a forensic psychologist and I'm here to give assistance in any way I can,' Dr Stephen said. He had the smooth sing-song vowels of a Californian who had lived in London for twenty years. The Hollywood Hills meets Muswell Hill.

'What can you tell us so far?' Swire asked.

'Well,' he said. 'Forensic psychology is more art than science. All I can do is look at the evidence, and estimate what kind of individual would commit these crimes.' There was a file before him and he glanced down at it without, I sensed, really needing to. 'To apprehend the unsub — sorry, the unknown subject — you need to understand that he is re-ordering the world. When women kill, they almost always kill someone they know. When men kill more than once, it's almost always strangers. Serial killers are invariably male.'

Gane folded his arms. 'So we're looking for a man?' he said. He smirked at Whitestone but she wouldn't return his look, or his smile. 'That narrows it down,' he muttered.

Dr Stephen stared at him. 'A white man,' he added.

'And why's that?' said the black DI.

'Because the dead men are all white,' Dr Stephen said, 'and serial killers almost always kill within their own race. That's not universal, but close enough to be considered a given.'

He looked a little rattled. He had come in wanting to be our friend and he was being forced to defend himself.

'What kind of white man, Dr Stephen?' Whitestone said, far friendlier than Gane. 'Any guess as to age, motive, social group?'

'A white man who is trying to right some perceived wrong,' Dr Stephen said. 'A man who is punishing his victims. These are all planned attacks. Very carefully planned attacks. These are not confrontational homicides, these are revenge homicides. The unsub is trying to right a wrong by the only means at his disposal — extreme violence. He is the product of a place where violence is the means of achieving your aims.'

The resentment was coming off Gane like

steam, but to me Dr Stephen was making sense. I thought of the terrible neatness of those carotid thrusts and the ease with which they opened arteries that could never be closed again. It was the work of a man who was remaking the world.

'Maybe he's just a nutter,' Gane said.

Dr Stephen smiled at him with a kind of embarrassed pity. 'Then he is a nutter — your term, detective, not mine — who is restoring control over what he perceives to be a mad world. Honour. Power. Control. That's what matters to him. And when you find him, as you no doubt will, you will find a man who needs to control other men, a man who needs that more than anything in the world.'

'So you don't really know anything about him at all?' Gane persisted.

'Look, the reason I'm in this room is because these are stranger killings,' Dr Stephen said. 'Most of the homicides you attend, the killer and the victim are known to each other. The husband who murders his wife because of her infidelity, the mother who murders her child, the drug dealer who murders his business associate.' He paused. 'That link does not exist with a serial killer. He is not known to the victim. He is not a husband, a business associate, a friend. But the unknown sub leaves evidence. Psychiatric evidence. Behavioural evidence. Ritualistic evidence. The remnants of fantasy and madness.'

On the other side of the glass walls I saw Scarlet Bush being escorted to the conference room.

'Ah, this is Ms Bush,' Swire said when she entered the room, 'who some of you will know already as crime correspondent for the *Daily Post.*'

The reporter circled the table, shaking hands and making smiling eye contact with everyone, including me. She played it as if we had never met. Then she took her place at the top of the conference table, next to Dr Stephen.

'This is the plan,' Swire said.

The shock of these words jolted Mallory upright and made the pain at the base of my spine pulse with alarm. Whitestone and Gane exchanged a startled look.

What plan?

'Dr Stephen is going to provide a detailed profile of Bob the Butcher,' the chief super continued. 'Then, based on this profile, Ms Bush is going to write a comment piece in the *Post* designed to tempt Bob into explaining himself in an online interview. And Mr Cho will be waiting to drive a very large hole through his firewall.'

'Press his buttons,' said Scarlet Bush. 'Make Bob stop hiding behind the grandiose Robert Oppenheimer sound bites and raise his head above the parapet.'

Mallory shifted uncomfortably in his seat. 'You really think he'll respond if you — what? — insult him in print?'

'If I do it in the right way,' Bush said. 'Bob wouldn't be preening on a social network site if he wasn't vain, and if he didn't want attention, and if he wasn't a narcissist, and if he didn't want to justify himself to the world. Not necessarily insults — we have agreed that Dr Stephen will have copy approval — more observations. Just enough that Bob will feel the need to explain himself. Just a little. Just enough.'

A look of disbelief must have passed across my face. Bush stared at me, not smiling now.

'He'll talk to me for the same reason that, in the end, they all talk to me,' she continued. 'Not because it would be great to hear his side of the story. But because I'm going to tell his story anyway. So he can either have his say or stay quiet and let the world have its say.'

'That's the way it works, is it?' I said.

'That's exactly the way it works, detective.'

I turned to Swire.

'Ma'am, we're throwing everything we've got at this Bob the Butcher and —'

'And that's what we're going to keep throwing until we bury him,' the chief super responded, cutting me off. She turned to Cho. 'Colin?'

'I'm confident that PCeU have the kit to find cracks in whatever encryption systems, anonymisers and onion routers he's using.'

Swire's eyes swept across the subdued MIT from West End Central.

'And then you're going to bring me his head on a spike,' she told us.

Mallory was staring bleakly at his SIO policy book. The strength seemed to be visibly draining from him. The chief super had made it sound easy, so it felt like a betrayal when I looked out over St James's Park and thought — *why shouldn't it work?* Trace, interview, eliminate — the TIE process was standard police procedure in any major investigation. Maybe Swire's plan was for the best. Flush the preening little bastard out from under his digital rock.

Scarlet Bush leaned back in her chair.

'So, Dr Stephen, what kind of guy is Bob the Butcher?' she said.

'I can tell you about the unsub,' the American said. 'I can — I believe — also tell you something about Bob the Butcher. What I can't tell you is that they are one and the same.'

Swire and Bush glanced at each other. And I saw just how desperately they both wanted Bob to be the same man — our killer.

'Society struggles to understand the repeat serious offender,' Dr Stephen continued. 'The serial rapist and the serial killer. Often they are the same thing but at different stages on the road to madness.'

'But there's no sexual element to Bob's crimes,' Swire said.

'My point is that the serial rapist and the serial killer tend to share the same basic characteristics. Because transgression is a way of life, they tend to be charming, manipulative, vain, ruthless, morally numb and devoid of even a shred of human empathy. The unsub will have a rich fantasy life — a fantasy life so rewarding that it will have come to have more substance than the real world. The unsub is likely to be a liar of near genius. As you know, serial killers often sail through lie detector tests. Trauma in his background is a given. Frequently, but not always, they come from backgrounds of mental and sexual abuse.'

Scarlet Bush perked up. 'You think Bob

the Butcher was the victim of child abuse?'

'It's possible. The rational mind struggles to understand the psychopathology of the irrational. These murders are an expression of the killer's masculinity. As I said, these homicides are displays of honour, power and control. Their sole purpose is punishment — for some perceived wrong done against the killer himself or a third party. The killer almost certainly doesn't know his victims. He is simply righting a wrong — or a series of wrongs.'

Scarlet Bush was jotting down notes.

'So you're saying that Bob the Butcher has a fragile masculinity?' she said.

'Not necessarily. But the unsub has a limited means of expressing his masculinity. He can't do it, for example, in the business world. So he does it with violence. He does it with murder.'

'What if I — I mean *we* — implied that there was, for example, a gay element to the crimes?'

Dr Stephen looked at her levelly. 'I doubt you will endear yourself to him. Look, he's seeking to gain control of a situation that is totally *beyond* his control. Unlike the overwhelming majority of murderers, he fully intends his victims to die. What's unusual is that most homicides, as you know far better than me, are simply a by-product of extreme violence. Most murder victims are just unlucky.'

'I'll say,' said Gane.

Dr Stephen had become good at ignoring him.

'Medical help is delayed,' he continued. 'A vital organ is accidentally severed. A fatal injury is sustained when a head hits the pavement.'

A sharp point of pain in my neck began to throb. *Please.* The cut beneath the scab where I had felt his knife. *Please.* I slowed my breathing before it was out of control.

Please. I have a daughter.

'Our unsub sets out with the intention to kill,' said Dr Stephen. 'Honour. Power. Control. If I can tell you anything at all, it is that: honour, power, control. There's your motive. These murders are an expression of affronted masculinity.'

Bob and the killer no longer sounded to me like people who were just different. They sounded like polar opposites.

Dr Stephen smiled pleasantly.

'And I can tell you one more thing for nothing,' he said.

We all looked at him.

'He won't stop.'

21

The fox had the playing fields to himself.

I had driven out to Potter's Field for Guy Philips&' memorial service, and with an hour to kill I had wandered out to the playing fields, remembering when Piggy had come running from the woods with the life draining out of him.

The rugby and football pitches were all empty now. There was just the lone fox, which I'd watched come out of the trees and mooch along the touchline of the far rugby field, heading towards the little stone cottage.

There was no sign of Len Zukov, the groundsman, but the fox moved more warily near this sign of civilisation, slowing his pace and raising his head to sniff the air. My phone began to vibrate as I saw the fox veer away from the cottage and move into the great muddy green expanse of the playing fields.

Wren was calling. She wasn't in MIR-1. I could hear street noises, voices I didn't know.

'Edward Duncan,' she said.

'Yes?'

'He doesn't have a criminal record. He doesn't have a driving licence. He doesn't have a national insurance number. He doesn't have a passport. And he doesn't have a credit card, a bank account or a wife.'

She was pleased with herself. I could almost see her grinning with pleasure, brushing a strand of red hair from her pale face.

'What does he have?' I said.

'Edward Duncan has an art dealer.'

I let it sink in. 'Well done, Wren.'

'Nereus Fine Art. Small place. North London, right at the top of Heath Street, Hampstead way. I drove past it.'

'I didn't ask you to do that, did I?'

'Relax, detective, I didn't go in. It was closed anyway. It's tiny.'

'Nereus Fine Art,' I said.

'It's a Greek myth,' Wren explained. 'Nereus was a god of the sea. He was kind and just and he had a special power.'

'Go on.'

'He had the power to change his shape.'

The fox was trotting towards me, taking

his time.

'Thank you,' I said.

'See? Everyone leaves a shadow.'

I took down the details of Nereus Fine Art.

'When are you going to check it out?' she said.

'When I get back to town,' I said. 'Tonight.'

'Pick me up at West End Central?'

'Why would I do that?'

'Because I'm coming with you.'

I almost laughed. 'You're not coming with me. This is off the book.'

'And that's exactly why I'm coming with you,' she said. 'It's off the book and I found him and I'm coming with you.'

I figured we could argue about it later.

'Who is he?' she said. 'Who's Edward Duncan?'

The fox had paused in the centre circle of the football pitch.

He sniffed the air, then pointed his face at the dirt and began to dig furiously.

'Edward Duncan is a dead man,' I said.

It was a shock to see Captain Ned King again.

He wore the immaculate black dress uniform of an officer in the Royal Gurkha

Rifles, but he was unshaven and red-eyed, as if he had come to the Potter's Field College Chapel straight from Brize Norton, as if he had spent last night on a Hercules transport plane. But what shocked me was how alike Ned King was to his brother, yet how totally different. They sat side by side in the ancient chapel, as Peregrine Waugh glared out from the lectern. Ben King with his smooth politician's face, Captain King with his scarred soldier's face. Although I remembered it wasn't soldiering that had scarred his face.

Salman Khan was by Ben King's side, and he was looking up at the stupendously tall Head Master, as if he might be asked questions later.

'We gather today to remember Mr Philips,' Waugh said. 'An old boy. A master. A friend.'

Like most good public speakers, Waugh was a bit of a ham. He told us to look at the memorial leaflet. He told us to look at the year when Guy Philips was born, and the year when he died. And he said that they were not important. That what mattered most was what came between them. What mattered most was 'the dash'. His life.

He talked about Philips as if he had been

310

a cross between Mother Teresa and Jesus Christ.

I thought of poor dead Piggy. I saw him hurting Natasha at Hugo Buck's funeral. I saw him making his pupils roll in the mud. It seemed to me that he had spent the dash bullying.

But Waugh was a commanding speaker, and I could hear the wet noses and choked throats of emotion behind me. Yet as I looked at the Head Master's stone-hard face I could not decide if Guy Philips had meant everything to Peregrine Waugh.

Or nothing at all.

The Potter's Field College Chapel was packed with what felt like the entire school. Black-robed masters in the first few rows, a great mass of boys in green and purple behind them and, under the stained-glass window, six rows of the choir facing another six rows. More boys and masters lined the perimeter of the chapel, and spilled through the open doorways.

The place was much smaller than I had expected. I had read online that building work had been interrupted during the War of the Roses and had yet to resume, and I had the feeling I always got at Potter's Field — that you could blink your eye and a hundred years would go by.

Captain King walked to the lectern.

'Our revels now are ended,' he read. 'These our actors, as I foretold you, were all spirits and are melted into air, into thin air. And, like the baseless fabric of this vision, the cloud-capped towers, the gorgeous palaces, the solemn temples, the great globe itself — yea, all which it inherit, shall dissolve and, like this insubstantial pageant faded, leave not a rack behind.'

Salman Khan hung his head and wept. Ben King kept his eyes on the shattered face of his brother as Captain King's words filled the ancient chapel.

'We are such stuff as dreams are made on, and our little life is rounded with a sleep.'

Captain King's delivery was matter of fact, yet the words carried real meaning. He was composed and yet replete with emotion. He was good at that. But then he had had a lot of practice.

Captain King returned to the front row, touching Khan once on the shoulder before taking his place next to his brother. Their wives sat behind them — pretty women, sleek and sexy even in their mourning clothes — shepherding well-behaved children with braces on their teeth. The ladies' fat jewels glistened. There was plenty of money and time for their children's bodies, minds and orthodontics.

The King brothers and Khan all had families. And I guessed that they loved those families.

But the real bonds, the unbreakable bonds, the bonds of a lifetime, they were different.

Because they were with each other.

After the memorial service I walked across the playing fields, skirting the rugby pitch where a games lesson was taking place. The boys all wore black armbands for their murdered sports master.

The sounds of flesh crashing into flesh, stud on to bone, cries and laughter faded behind me as I headed towards the stone cottage where Len Zukov lived. I knocked on the door. There was no answer. I walked round the back of the cottage, turning up my collar against the bitter wind. I stopped when I saw the fox.

It lay on top of the compost heap, a ragged sack of fur and bone, waiting for the fire.

Its neck had been neatly broken.

I got back to town at five in the afternoon, the November day already as dark as midnight and London's 180-minute rush hour starting to get mad. I sent Wren a text when

I was on Piccadilly and she was waiting for me outside 27 Savile Row when I arrived. She got into the X5 with a triumphant smile.

'If it wasn't for me,' she said, 'you'd still be dicking about on Google. I'd go through Regent's Park, if I were you. The traffic is always surprisingly light around the park.'

I took the park route and within fifteen minutes we were on the Finchley Road, the traffic heavy but moving steadily; and then it was thinning and the road was rising steeply towards the end of Heath Street as we climbed to the highest point of the city.

I realised that we were close to the meadow where Scout and I had let Stan off his lead and lost him. I had never noticed all the art galleries before. You drive out of Hampstead and they are the last thing you see, a cluster of them, all shapes and sizes, just before you are surrounded by the wild green expanse of the Heath.

As the car crawled higher, I saw that some of these galleries were high end, great lavish spaces with large, expensively lit canvases displayed in the window; other places were far more modest, local artists selling their work to a local clientele. The one we were looking for was little more than a darkened hole in the wall.

'This is it,' Wren said.

NEREUS
Fine Art

I slowed as we drove past and caught a glimpse of a tiny space behind wrought-iron railings glinting under the streetlights. A recycling bin was overturned, its contents spilled over the narrow pavement. Wren was already unclipping her seat belt as I crested the hill. I found a parking space behind Jack Straw's Castle.

But when we walked back to the gallery we found that Nereus Fine Art was closed. Two small landscapes were displayed in the window. A wave of junk mail was washed up inside the glass door. BACK SOON lied a sign.

I stood back. It was a three-storey building: the small gallery had a basement flat below and a flat above. I leaned over the wrought-iron railings, looking down and then up. Both of the flats were in darkness. Broken glass crunched beneath my feet and the recycling bin looked as though it had been rifled through by a fox that had come down from the Heath. He had been out of luck. It was just beer bottles and empty pizza boxes.

315

I looked up and down the street. We were on the edge of Hampstead affluence. Businesses were either booming or going bust. Apart from the galleries, there were a few restaurants and clothes stores, but over half of them had closed down. The buildings all had exactly the same wrought-iron railings as Nereus. The blue and red lights of burglar alarms blinked on even the most modest buildings.

'Let's go,' I said. 'I've got another call to make. Where should I drop you?'

'I'll come with you.'

I looked at her. How old was she? Twenty-five? Younger?

'Don't you have a life to go to?' I said.

'I can't see my boyfriend tonight.' A beat. 'He has to have dinner with his wife.' Another beat. 'It's her birthday.'

She toed the broken beer bottles, then pushed aside an empty pizza box with fossilised cheese on its side.

'A man lives here,' she said.

'How do you know it's a man?'

'Only men live like this. Men and pigs.'

Holloway was a few miles and several light years away from Hampstead.

Wren and I stood before a large dusty shop window where pride of place was given to a showroom dummy dressed as a German soldier from World War Two.

'How'd you know about this place?' Wren said.

'I dicked about on Google,' I said.

Under its coalscuttle helmet the mannequin had the gently pouting features of a young male model. But the clothes he wore were heavy and harsh and made for invading Russia. A thick wool greatcoat was draped over a rough tunic, both far too large for the delicate, snake-hipped dummy, and baggy trousers were tucked into leather boots. It all looked impossibly old and fragile, as if it would disintegrate with one touch.

'Is any of this stuff real?' I wondered.

'Those boots aren't,' Wren said. 'Everything else might be. But the boots — never. The Krauts wore their boots out. On the Eastern Front the Germans used to saw the legs off dead Russian soldiers and defrost them in some lucky peasant's oven, just to get at the boots.'

I stared at her.

'My dad,' she said. 'He liked World War Two. Is that the expression? Liking it? He was interested, let's say. *The World at War* boxed set and all that.'

The rest of the window was full of lovingly presented junk. Buttons. Posters. Faded scraps of metal and cloth and card and leather, all of it displayed like holy relics. SECOND FRONT, it said above the store. COLLECTIBLE MILITARIA.

The lights were going out inside.

I cop-knocked on the door. A long-haired man, not young, stuck his head around the door.

'I'm just closing up,' he said.

'Don't let us stop you.'

He stood to one side at the sight of our warrant cards and we went in.

'DC Wolfe and TDC Wren,' I said.

'Nick Cage,' he said, reluctantly.

I saw rags in glass cases, rusty medals in presentation cases, framed photographs of smiling men who had died screaming a lifetime ago.

'Nice place,' Wren said. 'My old man would love it. Is that a real Luger P08?'

She was indicating a handgun in a dark stained-glass box.

'Replica,' he replied, looking at me. 'It doesn't fire.'

I opened my bag and removed a file. Inside it was a collection of eight-by-ten photographs. I spread them on top of a glass cabinet and felt a pulse of pain freeze my lower back. The photographs were all of a knife that was designed to cut a man's throat. I leaned forward, my palms on the glass case, easing my tailbone and my breath out at the same time. It wasn't a proper dog stretch, but it made me feel better.

'I know you,' Cage said. 'Where was it?' He clicked his fingers. 'The Laughing Policeman film on YouTube.'

'He's dead famous,' Wren said, flicking through a rack of ragged army jackets as if she was in Miss Selfridge. 'He went viral.'

I looked at Cage. 'You don't know me, OK?' I said.

'OK,' he said.

'Do you know what these are?'

He looked at the photos one by one.

'It's a Fairbairn-Sykes commando dagger. They're all Fairbairn-Sykes commando daggers. These are all different generations of the same weapon. I could be more specific if I could see the knives. This one with the green handle is marked PPCLI. That's Canadian — Princess Patricia's Canadian Light Infantry. This one with the French writing — LE COMMANDO INOX, see that? — was used by French Special Forces in Algeria between 1954 and 1962. Laymen think that the Fairbairn-Sykes was only used in World War Two. But Wilkinson's kept producing them after the war and sold them to Special Forces all over the world. This is about Bob the Butcher, isn't it?'

'Did you ever sell one of these knives?'

He shook his head. 'The only place I ever saw one was in a museum.'

'The Imperial War Museum?'

'Yes.'

'What kind of clients do you get in here?'

He was watching Wren browsing the store.

'Collectors,' he said.

The sound of muffled laughter. Wren had put on a gas mask.

'My dad would love this,' she said. 'Christmas is coming.'

'It's six hundred quid,' Cage said. 'You break it, you bought it.'

Wren removed the gas mask. 'Maybe I'll stick to socks and aftershave.'

'What's the appeal?' I said.

Cage looked at me as if he couldn't believe what he was hearing.

'The Second World War was the greatest conflagration in human history,' he said. 'It killed millions of people. It reshaped Europe and the world. We live with its legacy today. We will live with its legacy for ever. The men who come here — and they are all men — think they would have been improved by war. They believe they missed something by being born too late. And they're right. They did miss something. They missed every-thing. They missed the great test of the twentieth century — perhaps of all time.'

'But let me ask you this,' Wren said. 'Why is so much of this stuff about the Nazis? They lost, didn't they? Yet so much of the war memorabilia industry is about them. It's like wanting the replica shirt of the side that lost the cup final.'

'I think the general consensus is that they had the strongest sense of aesthetics.'

'They had the best kit?' Wren smiled.

'Yes.'

'If only it were that simple,' she said, not smiling at him now. 'If only it were that innocent.'

I smoothed the photographs on the glass case.

'Do you recall ever being asked about one of these knives?' I said.

'Well, of course,' Cage said. 'This is one of the great collector's items of World War Two.' A flicker of pleasure in his eyes. 'And the enquiries have been on the rise lately. What with all the publicity.'

'Can you give me a list of people who wanted to buy one?'

'No.'

'Why not?'

'Client confidentiality.'

Wren and I grinned at each other.

'You have to take the Hippocratic oath just to flog a bit of Nazi memorabilia?' I said.

He licked his lips and said nothing.

'Look,' I said. 'I'm not interested in busting you.'

He bridled at that. 'What could you bust me for?'

I didn't know where to start. 'Offensive weapons. Knives. Bayonets. These firearms. Incitement to racial hatred.'

'The idea that all my clients are Nazi fetishists is simply not true!'

'Not all of them. But some of them, I bet. And I bet there's some stuff in the back room or under the counter that you wouldn't necessarily put on display in the shop window. Am I right? Look, I don't want to stop you doing your job —'

'Thanks.'

'Unless you stop me from doing mine.'

I left him my card and a few simple instructions. The shop went dark as Wren and I got into the car across the street. The Wehrmacht dummy stared out into the Holloway night.

'You don't really think that Bob bought a knife here, do you?' Wren said.

'No,' I said. 'But I think he might.'

■ ■ ■ ■

I dropped off Wren at her car in Savile Row and drove south of the river to where two hundred-ton cannons sat in a little green garden. I parked round the back of the museum and rang the buzzer at the service entrance. An elderly security guard who looked as though he had been roused from his slumbers answered the door. Beyond him I could see Carol negotiating her wheelchair down the tight corridor.

'It's all right,' she said. 'He's with me.'

She looked as if she had been expecting me.

22

We went back to Nereus Fine Art the next evening and this time it was open. It did not look so different from when it was closed. But a woman with short fair hair stood stock still in the gallery, staring out at the empty Hampstead street. She had not sold either of the two small landscapes.

'I don't mind you coming in,' I told Wren as I parked behind Jack Straw's Castle.

'Big of you,' she said.

'But let me ask the questions.'

'And what do I do?' she said.

'You tell me if I'm missing something.'

'Mr Duncan doesn't produce much work,' the gallery woman said. She was a slight blonde in black-rimmed glasses, attractive in a brittle sort of way, and with just as much charm as was necessary she was getting rid of me. 'He's a bit of a recluse, I'm afraid. He doesn't exhibit, he doesn't talk to the press. He doesn't need to. All his work is sold to private collectors. Very little of it comes on the market. But if you would like to leave me your card, I'll put your details on file.'

'Because I love his work,' I said, not for the first time.

And it was true. I had never seen anyone paint like that. It was a city that I recognised, if only from dreams.

But she didn't care what I loved.

'Please leave your details,' she said, with the warmth turned down a notch.

Wren was looking at the canvases on the walls. There was a lot of lush green countryside. I guessed there was a big market for that stuff.

'How does he survive?' Wren said.

'Excuse me?'

'How does he make a living? If he doesn't paint much, and if he doesn't sell much, and if he doesn't make much of an effort, how does he pay the rent?'

'Pay the rent?'

The gallery woman stared at Wren. Wren stared right back.

'I understand there's some family money,' the woman said.

'Ah.'

'We have some other interesting contemporary work,' she said to me, handing me her card.

'Do you own the gallery?' Wren said.

'Nereus is owned by my mother.'

Wren thought about it.

'So if your father is an earl, then what does that make your mother? A lady, right?'

The woman had stopped smiling. 'You're not collectors, you're fucking journalists. Get out. Get out now or I'll call the police.'

I was looking at the card.

HON. KRIS HUETLIN
Nereus Fine Art

And I saw what Wren had seen: that the Kris was short for Cressida and the Huetlin came from the German artist she had married at nineteen and divorced five years later. It was the 'Hon.' that she couldn't resist that gave her away.

The Honourable Cressida Sutcliffe, only daughter of the Earl of Broughton, sister of the late James Sutcliffe.

Then I was out on the street, gripping the wrought-iron railings, looking up. Wren had followed me outside and was watching me crouch in the broken glass from the recycling bin. The smashed glass was all from beer bottles.

Peroni. Italian beer.

'We're missing something,' I said, the sound of broken glass beneath our feet. 'Upstairs,' I said. 'A dead man lives there.'

Up a narrow flight of stairs.

The door was unlocked.

Behind me I could hear the Hon. Kris Huetlin arguing with Wren, then falling silent when she produced her warrant card. And then arguing some more.

I went into a room full of canvases, all of them turned to face the wall. I could smell fresh paint. A man was standing in the centre of the small room, next to a canvas on an easel.

The canvas before him was blank.

'Hello, James,' I said.

James Sutcliffe was heavy, bearded, with the weight of the long-term committed drinker. I could see no trace of the delicate boy in dark glasses who would not smile for the camera when he posed in his Combined Cadet Force uniform at Potter's Field. The hair that had been thick and black and slicked back straight off his forehead was now long and grey and thinning. It fell around his shoulders, and over the baggy smock he wore.

'Hello,' he said.

'I'm DC Wolfe,' I said, hearing footsteps on the stairs and then stopping behind me. 'This is TDC Edie Wren. Can we talk?'

'Yes.'

His sister was right behind Wren.

'Even lower than I thought,' she said. 'Not hacks. Pigs.'

I looked at her, remembering her radical past. Then I turned back to her brother.

'I love your paintings,' I said. 'I love the early ones. And I love the later ones, where the city gets darker.'

'Thank you.'

'Do you know why I'm here?'

He looked over my shoulder at his sister.

'Someone's killing your friends,' I said. 'Hugo Buck. Adam Jones. Guy Philips. They're all dead. Did you know that?'

A small shake of his head that could have meant anything.

'I'm going to find the killer,' I said. 'Don't you want to help me catch the bastard who's murdering your friends?'

He focused on me again.

'They're not my friends,' he said.

'You faked your death, didn't you? That summer in Italy. The clothes left on the beach. It was very convincing. But why did you do that, James?'

He closed his eyes and released some

breath that sounded as if it had been trapped for a long time. When he opened his eyes I saw the ancient pain inside the man.

'Starting again?' I said. 'A clean slate? Was that it? And who knew? Your sister here. How many of your friends? All of them?'

'None of them.'

'Hugo Buck knew.'

'No.'

'He had two of your paintings on the wall of his home. One by James Sutcliffe. And another by Edward Duncan.'

He looked shocked.

'I'm not interested in exposing you,' I said. 'Unless you've done something wrong. Unless you've broken the law. Unless you've hurt someone. Is that what you did, James?'

And at last there was panic in his eyes.

'I know how you got away with your disappearing act,' I said. 'They believed you because you were suffering from depression. I saw what you were on. Prozac. Luvox. Lustral. Cipralex. That's quite a cocktail of happy pills, James. But what were you depressed about? What happened at that school?'

He took a deep breath. Let it out.

'When you're young, you try things,' he said. 'You experiment. You're a sponge. You soak it up — all of it, any of it. Dear Mr Waugh — he was more than just a House Master. He was our friend. And he taught us about so many things. Wonderful things. Artists. Writers.' A beat. 'To get beyond the self. "If the doors of perception were cleansed, everything would appear as it is — infinite." Who doesn't want to get beyond their sad, shoddy little self at sixteen? "To be shaken out of the rut of ordinary perception." Sacramental visions. Experimentation.'

'Drugs.'

A short laugh.

'Drugs? My God. Drugs were just the start.'

'Keep talking, James,' I said.

I could see that he remembered it all now, that it was almost a relief to talk about it.

'There was a girl,' he said.

There was silence in the room.

'There was a girl,' I said.

'James?' his sister said. 'I'm going to call Mother. And Mother is going to call Burke. Do you remember Peter Burke? The lawyer, darling. Don't say anything else to these people.'

'It was meant to be . . . not *fun*,' he continued. 'An experiment. Pushing the boundaries of experience.'

He was less certain of himself now.

I glimpsed the pale bracelet of self-harm on his wrists, as wide as a sweatband and as white as a dead fish.

He tugged at his shirtsleeves, knowing what I had seen.

'Who was the girl?' I said. 'What was her name? Where did you find her?'

'How many of you?' Wren added.

'Six of us,' he said. 'No — seven. And she was nice.'

'She was *nice*?' Wren said.

'She was. In another life, you might have loved her. The night is a blur.' He looked at the floor and then at me. 'Did you ever take opium — I'm sorry, I've forgotten your name?'

His sister crossed the room and slapped his face. 'Shut up! Shut up! Shut up! I'm so sick of carrying you. I am so sick of covering up for you. Just shut up when I tell you to shut up!' Then she hit him again.

He ducked away, cowering, taking a step back. Wren stepped between them, and it was enough to restrain the sister.

'Who was in that room?' I said. 'You said seven, right?'

'Six,' he said. 'Seven . . .'

'Seven? Concentrate. You, Hugo Buck, Adam Jones, Salman Khan, Guy Philips,

Ben King, Ned King. Were they all there? Who else was there? What happened to the girl?'

'We were going to let her go,' he said. 'That was the plan.'

'You bastards,' Wren said, to herself.

'We were going to let her go but she hurt someone. Very badly. It got out of hand. All of it.'

'She hurt someone,' I said, and I remembered the morning in the Iain West Forensic Suite, and I recalled what Elsa Olsen had placed in the palm of my hand. 'She hurt someone's eye, didn't she?'

He looked at me with wonder. 'Yes, she hurt someone's eye. Really hurt it, I mean . . .'

'She hurt Hugo Buck, didn't she?'

He looked confused. 'Hugo? Was it Hugo? I don't think —'

'Yes, Hugo Buck. He had a glass eye.'

James Sutcliffe covered his face with his hands. 'I don't remember. It was a long time ago. It was another lifetime.'

'Do you know how I know, James?' I said. 'I held it in my hand. I held the glass eye in my hand when they were cutting Hugo up on the slab.'

Wren said, 'Do you want back-up? I think we should get back-up now. Wolfe?'

'We can handle this,' I said. 'What happened to the girl, James? And what was her name?'

He hung his head. He shook his head. There were no words.

'I think we are going to have to take you in, James,' I said. 'You're part of a murder investigation.'

His sister said, 'You'll kill him!'

But he looked at me, his eyes clear, strangely calm now that he knew for certain it would soon all be over.

'All right,' he said, his voice steady. 'I suppose I'm ready to go.'

He glanced towards the window. Outside the evening was cold and foggy, the street shrouded in the misty lights of winter. It looked like one of his paintings.

'It's a lovely day today,' he said, walking over to the window.

And then he broke into a kind of run, the shambling run of the badly out-of-shape man.

I called out to Wren.

But it was too late.

He went through the closed window with an eruption of glass and fell into thin air. I heard his sister scream and I heard Wren cry out and just a second later we heard a hideous thump as he landed one floor below.

I was already running for the stairs.

The wrought-iron railings had broken his fall, impaling his great bulk, one spike speared into his groin and another through his cheek. A couple more had torn open his guts and buried themselves deep inside.

I heard Wren calling it in at the same awful moment I recoiled backwards as if struck in the face, choking on the sewer stink of a man's spilt intestines.

23

I sat in my car on Prince Albert Road, the lights of the mansion blocks rising up on one side of me and the black vastness of Regent's Park on the other, and I felt the sickness rise in me as Ben King came out of Natasha Buck's block. I grimaced at the smooth Westminster smile as the fawning porter let him out, actually touching his head in salute, as if seeking a forelock to tug.

Even when he was sneaking around his friend's widow after dark, King looked every inch the visiting dignitary.

She must have thought there was time enough to get him off the premises before I arrived. But for some reason there is never much traffic around the park, and I was early.

Natasha was dressed for a date. Candles on the table. Al Green singing about staying together. The smell of roasting red meat.

And the perfumed smell of her as she kissed me on one cheek and then the other and then, finally, on the mouth. A smell to make a man want to start inhaling and never stop.

I was carrying a bottle of wine and she took it with elaborate grace as I thought how wrong, how grotesque, how inappropriate.

A date, I thought. We're on a date.

The rage inside me was directed at myself as well as her.

On the sofa the dog opened its bleary eyes, clocked me and then closed them again, deeply unimpressed, as Natasha brought me a bottle of Asahi Super Dry and a frosted glass that had been sitting in the freezer, waiting for me.

'Scout,' she said. 'She went with her friend? To her playover?'

'Sleepover,' I said. 'Yes, her friend's mother picked them up after school.'

Natasha bit her bottom lip. Laughed. Shook her head.

'Then we can have a sleepover too,' she said, coming in close, holding my arm, looking up at me. 'You must think I'm bad.'

I laughed. Then she wasn't smiling.

'What's wrong?'

I walked towards the sofa but I didn't sit down. I wasn't staying long.

I took a pull on the Japanese beer and said, 'Do you know what it does to a murder case if an investigating officer sleeps with a material witness?'

She took a step back. 'What?'

'Of course you do,' I said. 'Of course you know.'

She had her hands on me and I froze so she stood back, keeping her distance.

'Max,' she said. 'Please.'

Her eyes were shining.

'Spare me the tears,' I said.

She angrily wiped her eyes with the back of her hand. 'All right,' she said. 'I'll spare you the tears if you tell me what's wrong with you. I thought we were going to have a lovely night —'

'Meeting us on the Heath — that wasn't a coincidence, was it?'

She looked away.

'No.'

'You don't walk your dog on the Heath, do you?'

'No.'

'You don't walk your dog at all, do you?'

'*No* — I'm another rich bitch who gets some little Eastern European scrubber to walk her dog.'

'And your husband didn't lose his eye playing rugby, did he?'

'What?'

'Your husband. Old Hugo. That story about how he lost his eye. That was all bullshit, wasn't it?'

She looked genuinely surprised. 'No, that's true.'

'Were you there? Did you see it happen?'

'Of course not.'

'Then you don't know, do you?'

'But I do. I do know.'

Maybe she believed it, I thought. Maybe she really believed in the sports injury lie.

'What was Ben King doing here?'

She laughed with disbelief. 'Is that what this is about? You saw Ben leaving? Don't you think it's a little early to be getting possessive?'

'You fucking him too?'

Her open palm cracked hard against my cheek.

The dog sat up, finally looking impressed.

'I'm not *fucking* anybody. Especially not you. Ben came to collect some of Hugo's personal things.'

'A couple of paintings?'

'I want you to go now.'

'What happened at that school?'

'Please leave.'

'Do you want to know how your husband lost his eye? Do you really want to know?'

She suddenly seemed very tired.

'I don't care,' she said. 'He's dead. It doesn't matter.'

She swallowed hard, and looked around the flat, taking it all in — the candles, the smell of prime beef, Al Green. She ran her hands through her hair. It was all ruined now.

'You're using me, Natasha,' I said. 'You're setting me up. You're telling me lies.'

'You're the liar,' she said, angry at last. 'You wear a wedding ring but you're not married.'

'What happened at that school? What did they do? Who was the girl?'

'I don't know what you're talking about. Where's your wife? What happened to her? You have a ring but no wife? What's all that about, detective? You liar. You fucking liar.'

She was pushing me out of the apartment and I was letting her. And I saw that she was as stupid as me. Another mug.

'You're wrong about everything,' she said, closing the door in my face.

In the morning, just inside the communal front door of our block of flats, half covered with flyers for pizza, there was a package waiting on the mat with my name on it.

As Stan sniffed at the junk mail, I tore the

package open and pulled out a VHS video-tape. It felt cheap, plastic, rickety. Incredibly old-fashioned. I looked at the spine. There was printed felt-tip writing, written very carefully, as if by a bright child.

Our 1st XV v Harrow 1st XV 10-10-88

I searched inside. No note. I looked back at the VHS I was holding, then down at the dog.

'How am I meant to play this?' I said out loud.

'Vice,' Wren told me when I got to work. 'Down on the third floor. Vice has video recorders from back in the day.'

MIR-1 was still deserted. Wren always got in early.

'I've been looking on HOLMES for missing persons,' she said. 'I started with female mispers between the ages of fifteen and thirty within a ten-mile radius of Potter's Field in 1988.'

'Keep looking.'

'I will — but you need to talk to the SIO,' she said. 'You need to talk to Mallory. About what James Sutcliffe said before he died.' A beat. 'About the school.'

'Mallory has the chief super breathing

down his neck. And the chief super is anxious to protect Ben King.'

'You still need to talk to him.'

I looked at the VHS tape in my hand.

'I know,' I said. 'But what did Sutcliffe really tell us? We don't even know who we're talking about, do we? Who was in that room?'

'He told us enough,' Wren said. 'They're not dying because they're rich, are they? They're not dying because they're sons of privilege or symbols of social injustice or any of that Bob the Butcher stuff.'

'No,' I said. 'They're dying because of the past.'

We found a quiet corner of Vice with a couple of dusty video recorders and settled down to watch our videotape.

All around us young men and women were watching writhing bodies on their computer screens, and trying to separate standard filth from criminal obscenity that was likely to corrupt and deprave.

'Is that vulva open?' said one young man.

'I think it's only slightly ajar,' said a young woman.

'Definitely a grey area,' said the young man, making a note.

They were friendly enough but neither

Wren or I knew any of the twenty-something officers in the department.

'They change personnel every six months down here,' Wren whispered. 'In case it does something to their sex drive. One way or the other.'

She posted the VHS into the video recorder and pressed play. The remote had been lost in time.

'Do you want to watch it on fast forward?' she said.

'Just let it roll,' I said.

I recognised the playing fields of Potter's Field. The tree line, the stone cottage, the endless expanse of green churned to mud down the centre of the pitches. Only the haircuts of the boys were different.

It was easy to spot Hugo Buck. Big, proud, confident. A good-looking bully. Calling for the ball. Exhorting his friends. Arguing with the referee. After twenty minutes he scored a try and preened before the camera, his big grin in our faces. I heard the laughter of the cameraman as he said 'Played, Bucko!' and it sounded like Ben King.

Five minutes later it happened.

The ball was kicked deep into the Harrow half. The Potter's Field First XV flew after it, Buck in the vanguard. A Harrow defender caught the ball, fumbled, dropped it, picked it up again. Voices screamed with excitement. The defender made to kick the ball just as Buck reached him.

Buck hurled himself at the Harrow defender.

The Harrow defender lashed wildly at the ball.

Buck beat it down.

And the point of the Harrow defender's right boot speared into Buck's left eye.

He screamed.

The game stopped. Players and pupils and teachers gathered around the boy on the ground.

He was silent now. But the teachers were shouting for an ambulance. The cameraman kept filming. And just before the tape stopped he went on to the pitch and looked over the shoulders of the boys and men gathered around Hugo Buck.

His eye was a ruined pulp.

The footage abruptly ended on that last bloody image.

'So,' Wren said, 'Hugo Buck lost his eye playing rugby.'

'Yes,' I said.

'James Sutcliffe told us he was hurt by a girl, didn't he?'

I paused, considered.

'Is that what he told us? Sutcliffe was doped up to the eyeballs for years. He was doped up when he was at school. He was doped up on the day he died. James Sutcliffe was a poor little rich boy who spent his entire life on medication.'

'Come on, Wolfe. You're the one who said Hugo Buck's wife was lying. You're the one who held Buck's fake eye in your hand. But she wasn't lying, was she?'

I stared at the frozen image on the screen.

We went back up to MIR-1. Suddenly the suite was heaving with people. Swire and Mallory. Cho and Dr Stephen. Gane and Whitestone. Faces were flushed with the fever of a chase that was nearing its end.

'What's happening?' I said.

'We've got Bob,' Gane said.

24

Behind the John Lennon glasses, Mallory's eyes were burning with quiet rage.

'Setting a trap with human bait,' he said quietly, each word chipped from Aberdeen granite, his bald head gleaming under the lights of MIR-1, 'was never the plan.'

'Change of plan,' said Swire.

'I'm not wearing a bullet-proof vest,' Scarlet Bush was telling DI Whitestone. 'Bob was very specific: "Come alone. No tapes I can't see." He might think a bullet-proof vest is a wire. I'm not wearing it.'

'It's not a bullet-proof vest,' Whitestone said patiently, 'it's a Kevlar Stealth. Light-weight, the thinnest we have. Invisible under the clothes you're wearing. I'd wear it if I were you.'

Gane's laptop was open on Bob the Butcher's timeline. Bob had changed his picture again. Instead of Robert Oppenheimer's thoughtful, pipe-smoking skull, there was now a mushroom cloud.

In sleep — in confusion — in the depths
of shame — the good deeds a man has
done before defend him. #killallpigs

'Where's his response?' I said.

'He didn't respond online,' Gane said. 'He
called her.' He laughed. 'On a *telephone. A
landline.*'

Gane grinned, and I saw that Cho and his
techie pals from the PCeU were looking
sour.

'Stick around, boys!' Gane said. 'We might
be able to show you a few tricks!'

'Give DI Gane your phone and he'll fit a
GPS tracking device,' Whitestone told Bush.

'I don't want to carry anything bulky,' the
journalist said.

'It's either a SIM card or some software,'
Gane said, cutting her off. 'You're not going
to notice it. The only people who will know
it's even there are us, OK? But it means we
know where you are. It means we can
pinpoint your movements to within ten metres. If you go beyond a prescribed area, it
sends us an alarm.'

Bush gave Gane her phone.

'The Kevlar Stealth and the tracking
device,' she said. 'Is that it?'

Whitestone nodded. 'That's it. Belt and braces.'

'What did Bob say to you?' I said.

I saw the pride in the journalist's eyes.

'He said he liked my piece,' she said. 'And he said he'd be in touch.'

'How do you know it was him?'

'He told me he would post an Oppenheimer quote in the Bob the Butcher timeline. "In sleep — in confusion — in the depths of shame — the good deeds a man has done before defend him." And then he did.'

There were a dozen copies of her paper scattered across the workstations of MIR-1. In the end she had not goaded Bob the Butcher. There had been no references to sexual preference, childhood trauma or bed-wetting. She had stuck to Dr Stephen's script. Bob was presented as a mixed-up homicidal maniac who was operating by his own rules ('Honour, power and control are clearly motivating factors for this most complex of serial killers') and choosing victims who were something less than totally innocent ('It seems hardly a coincidence that Bob the Butcher selected as his targets a wealthy investment banker, a drug dealer and an inveterate bully'), and also as a slightly volatile folk hero to the dispossessed ('These are horrible crimes, certainly — but they are also a cry of rage in a society where the obscene gap between rich and poor is the new apartheid').

It was more of a press release than journalism. You could see why Bob the Butcher would want to cut it out and stick it in his scrapbook. It made him sound like a psycho Robin Hood.

'He's calling my paper's switchboard some time over the next twenty-four hours,' Bush said.

'We've got call analytics set up on your switchboard,' Gane said. 'The longer you can keep him talking the better. But as soon as he calls we will have the number of whatever disposable or payphone he's using. A landline or a mobile is too much to hope for. But it will give us more than we have right now. And when he gives you the meet you're going to lead us to him.'

Mallory was still not happy.

'I want you to have police protection from this moment on,' he told Scarlet Bush. 'I want two officers to escort you back to your office, and to accompany you to the meeting point, where we'll be waiting.'

'No chance,' she said. 'This is the most important story of my career and I am not going to let you screw it up for me.'

Mallory looked helplessly at Swire, who

shrugged.

'The meet is going to be surrounded with ARVs and SFOs,' the chief super said. 'There's going to be enough Special Firearms Officers to keep her from harm. And I'm all for making sure we don't frighten Bob away.'

'Then I want officers in the room an hour before you arrive at the meet,' Mallory told Bush. 'And I want roadblocks at fifty metres, five hundred metres and a mile. And make sure you're wearing the Kevlar.'

'Bob cuts throats.' Bush laughed, and for the first time I saw the raw courage in her. 'What good is a stab-proof vest going to do me?'

Swire chuckled approvingly.

'And I'll tell you what I want,' Bush added. 'When I get to the meet I want to talk to him before you move in and arrest him.'

'Five minutes,' Mallory said.

'Fuck that!'

Mallory visibly flinched at the profanity.

'I want at least an hour with him.'

'We'll give you five minutes,' Swire said. 'But any sign of aggression and he's coming down.'

Gane returned the reporter's mobile with the tracking device.

'What's in there?' Mallory said.

'In the end I went for the handset-based software,' Gane said. 'It's more accurate than a SIM card with an iPhone.'

Mallory still didn't look happy.

'Let us know as soon as he makes contact,' he said. 'Don't wait for us to pick it up on your switchboard.'

'Of course,' Bush said. She threw her phone into her bag. 'I'll tell you where we're meeting and I'll see you there.'

She left, escorted by the chief super, and for a moment I thought I was going to hear Mallory curse for the first time. Instead he ran his hand over his polished skull and said angrily, 'And I want the lot of you in a Kevlar Stealth!'

In the only quiet corner of MIR-1, Dr Stephen was at his laptop. I walked over to him and saw that he was staring at Bob the Butcher's timeline. The forensic psychologist looked thoughtful. The mushroom cloud was still there.

'Those people in Hiroshima,' Dr Stephen said. 'They had been expecting a massive bombing raid for months. But what they got was the end of all things. What they got was a new world.'

'So what does it mean?' I said. 'The cloud. What's he trying to tell us?'

He shook his head.

'I'd be making a guess,' he said.

'Go ahead.'

'The designated target,' he said. 'It's been chosen.'

The internet café was on the Holloway Road. Wren and I sat on opposite sides of the room while half a dozen weary-looking foreign students checked their mail and Skyped home. It seemed a strange location for Scarlet Bush to meet Bob the Butcher.

And when I heard Gane curse in my earpiece, I knew they never would.

Wren heard it too. She looked over at me and I shook my head.

In the back room was a group of armed officers looking like soldiers from the next century. They wore black rubber goggles, Ballistic Kevlar helmets and shiny boots. They carried Heckler & Koch assault rifles, Taser X26 guns and CS gas spray. Their mouths were thin lines of frustrated adrenalin. Mallory and Whitestone were to one side hunched over Gane and his laptop.

'What's happening?' I asked them.

'We've lost Scarlet,' Mallory said. 'Not the signal from her phone. Just her.'

'She gave our officers the slip at her paper,' Gane said, not looking up from the screen. 'Went out the fire exit, we think. That easy.'

'Wanted some quality time on her own with Bob,' Whitestone said.

'The tracer on her phone told us she was on her way here,' Gane said. 'And now it seems she's not. The signal hasn't moved for ten minutes. Look.'

A red dot pulsed steadily in the map's spider web of streets.

'Where is it?' Mallory said. 'That looks like somewhere near St Paul's.'

'East Poultry Avenue, EC1,' Gane said. 'It's the Barbican.'

'That's not the Barbican,' I said. 'That's the meat market.'

Mallory shook his head.

'That stupid girl,' he said. 'Oh, that stupid girl.'

The hooks hung around the storage room like stainless steel bunting and our breath made steaming clouds in the freezing fog. Huge slabs of bloody meat hung everywhere in the sub-zero air. I could hear Wren and Whitestone calling her name.

'Scarlet! Scarlet! Scarlet!'

Mallory pushed aside a great headless carcass of beef.

'She's not here, is she?' he said.

Gane rubbed a hand over the misty screen of his laptop.

'Well, the phone's here,' he said.

And then I saw the pig's head sitting on a marble slab. The pig's head with its giant, floppy Dumbo ears. Comical and tragic all at once. The albino skin, more white than pink, with just a few delicate smears of blood. The eyes shut as if overwhelmed with exhaustion. And the monstrous snout, squashed flat and rich with blood.

Figures moved in the mist of the cold room, cursing and bumping into each other. Unable to find the thing they sought. They kept calling her name.

My spine throbbed with pain as I reached under the snout and into the pig's mouth and pulled out a phone, its screen smeared with milky blood.

'Sir?' I said.

Mallory took the phone from me. He looked across at Gane, who nodded and closed his laptop.

'He has her,' Mallory said.

My own phone began to vibrate. I took it out. SECOND FRONT CALLING it said, and I saw that the blood of the pig's head was on my hands now, and on my phone, and on my clothes, getting on everything.

'It's Cage from the war memorabilia

shop,' a very distant voice said.

'What happened?' I said.

'I sold a knife.'

25

'This big guy walked into my shop,' Nick Cage said. 'Well, not big — pumped up. Weights. Maybe steroids. A little man but pumped up, you know?'

We had him in an interview room in West End Central. Mallory and Gane and me. Mallory didn't like him.

'I'm trying to help you,' Cage said, looking at me.

'I know,' I said.

'You sell knives,' Mallory said. 'You sell swords. Daggers.'

'Yes.'

'Did you ever see what a knife can do to someone?'

'I sell to collectors.'

'Ever heard of the Offensive Weapons Act?'

Cage's mouth tightened. 'Chapter and verse. This country has the most restrictive knife laws in the world. Not that you'd know it from all the kids in A&E with their stab wounds, their guts hanging out. Look, I don't sell flick knives, sword canes, butterfly knives, throwing stars or gravity knives, OK? I sell to *collectors*. I've got a *licence*. And I want to keep it. That's why I got a photocopy of his ID, all right? Now, do you want to talk about him or me?'

We were running the ID Cage had brought us through the Police National Computer. It was a UK driver's licence for what the PNC database would recognise as an IC1 — a male of white-skinned European appearance. There was a face and a name and a DOB. A young man around thirty with thinning hair. An attempt at a smile that never quite made it past the hint of a sneer. And there was an address. Right at the edge of the city.

'Do you buy this ID?' Gane said to Mallory. 'Bob's up to his neck in security architecture online but he doesn't have a fake photo ID? You know how many sites there are flogging fake photo IDs?'

'Not good ones,' Cage said. 'It's easy to get a bad one. Not so easy to get a good one. That's the real thing. Or better than anything I've ever seen.'

'Did he know his stuff?' I said.

'How do you mean?' Cage said.

'Did he know what he was buying?'

'He was very specific. The men who come in Second Front are collectors. They *all* know their stuff. He wanted a Fairbairn-Sykes commando dagger. Prepared to pay top dollar. I sourced it for him. Found a nice Second Pattern F-S made by Wilkinson.'

'And where did you get it from?' Mallory said.

'I'm not telling you,' Cage said, folding his arms.

Gane made a move towards him as Whitestone appeared in the doorway.

'We've got him,' she said.

The chief super walked into MIR-1, her face tight with tension beneath the helmet of blonde hair. It could have been Mrs Thatcher getting ready to send the Task Force to the South Atlantic, horribly aware that this thing could go either way.

The crowd parted for her and she did not look at any of us until she came to Edie Wren, sitting on her desk at her workstation, a man's face on the screen behind her, like something she had just caught.

'What have we got?' DCS Swire said.

The face on the screen was the same photograph as the one on the driving licence but now it was life-size; now you could see the wary spite in the eyes, the thin scars from ancient acne, the way he had brushed his hair to cover the growing expanse of forehead.

'Ian Peck,' Wren said. 'Multiple convictions. The first one ten years ago for possession of class C drugs — anabolic steroids — and class B — cannabis. Peck was buying in Amsterdam and mailing the stuff to his home address with the name of the previous occupant on the package.'

'That old trick,' somebody said.

Wren dropped into her seat.

'Twelve months suspended,' she said, scrolling down. She shook her head. 'Four — no, five convictions for domestic violence against his girlfriend. She has a restraining order. Peck's a freelance software consultant. After the split with his girlfriend he moved back home with Mum and Dad.'

Wren turned to look at the chief super.

'And that's Bob the Butcher,' she said.

Swire's mouth twisted with triumph. 'Well done, everybody. Start making your preparations. We'll lift him at dawn.'

'A man who beats women?' I said. 'You really think that our perp is a man who beats up women?'

I was looking at Dr Stephen. He had his hands stuffed deep inside his pockets. I believed that he could see it too.

'The perp doesn't attack women,' I said.

Dr Stephen still wasn't looking at me.

'What did you say, Dr Stephen? Honour. Power. Control.' I gestured at the face that stared at us from the screen.

They were all looking at me.

Swire was very calm.

'Did you ever hear of a copper called George Oldfield?' she said.

I nodded. Everybody had heard of Assistant Chief Constable George Oldfield. He was the head of the hunt for the Yorkshire Ripper. Letters and a tape claiming 'I'm Jack' had Oldfield searching the northeast while Peter Sutcliffe was killing women in other parts of the country.

'I'm not going to play the part of George Oldfield here,' Swire said. 'I'm not letting our killer slip through my hands.'

She brushed past me as MIR-1 burst into activity.

But I stayed where I was, looking at the face on the screen.

Honour. Power. Control.

A man who hits women, I thought. Where's the honour in that?

In the first light of the new day we gathered on a suburban street of modest terraced houses and all I could hear was the sound of my blood. It sounds like the sea, a red rushing sound, when it's pumped hard enough. And as we crouched below a little garden wall and fiddled with our kit in those last few seconds — adjusting the straps on Kevlars, the firearms officers checking their safety catches, listening to the subdued murmurs of the Airwave radios — that is what mine sounded like.

It told me what was at stake. A young woman's life. The jobs of all of us who had let her slip away. And something else, something more personal. Because you never know what is on the other side of that door, and what it will do to you.

The officer with the worn red battering ram slung over his shoulder walked briskly down the garden path.

It didn't take long.

Two, three steps and he was at the door, hauling the battering ram from his shoulder and swinging it at the lock in one smooth and brutal motion. The door popped open with the rip and splinter of cheap wood and the officer stood to one side as the rest of us charged into the house, screaming as loud as we could — screaming to pour fear into whoever was on the inside, and screaming to hide the fear in our own hearts.

The two armed officers who went in ahead of me suddenly stopped, still shouting behind their Heckler & Koch assault rifles.

Over the shoulders of their body armour I could see a sickly cat at the end of a suburban hall. It arched its back and hissed, full of cancer and contempt.

A door opened at the end of the hall.

We were screaming again.

An old woman in house slippers slowly shuffled across the hall, ignoring all orders to halt. She did not even look our way.

I saw an old-fashioned hearing aid tucked behind her ear, as huge and pink as a wad of chewed bubblegum. She disappeared through a door on the other side of the hall, the old cat rubbing against her legs as it followed her.

We followed her down the hall and through the door.

In the living room the old woman sat on a sofa with an old man, a biscuit held halfway to his mouth. He elbowed her, and at last she registered our presence. The pair of them stared slack-jawed at the assault rifles that were aimed at their faces. The cat spat at us.

'Mr and Mrs Peck?' I said. 'Where's your son? Where's Ian?'

Still they didn't talk.

There was a small kitchen on the other side of the hall.

'Clear,' said an armed officer, coming out of it.

Boots thundered on the staircase. I could hear them moving around upstairs, screaming as they went through doors, and then the silence of disappointment and relief.

I went into the kitchen. There was a small garden out the back. Beyond the high garden fence I could see more black Kevlar helmets and rubber goggles, mouths tight with tension, the dull gleam of Heckler & Koch assault rifles.

Mallory came out of the garden and into the kitchen. Whitestone and a uniformed officer were with him. When the uniform took off his helmet I saw it was PC Billy Greene, his pale face slick with sweat and fear, but controlling it well. The boxing was doing him some good.

The shouting had stopped.

'Nothing,' I said.

'Did anyone check the basement?' Mallory said.

There was a wooden door just outside the kitchen. No lock, paint flaking. I opened it, reached inside and found the switch for the light.

Somewhere deeper down, a bare electric bulb came on.

I went carefully down a short flight of steps, smelling damp and dust, and then I was under the house itself, the ceiling so low that I had to stoop.

Mallory's voice was right behind me: 'Anything?'

The basement was more than half full with scrap, smashed chunks of concrete and broken bricks, a ragged pile of rubble that almost reached to the ceiling.

'What is all this stuff?' I said.

'Looks like someone dreamed of converting this place into flats,' Mallory said. 'They have to fill the basement. Fire regulations. Then the property bubble burst and the dream got cancelled.' He peered into the darkness. 'Excuse me,' he said, easing past. 'There's something right at the back.'

'Clear,' I heard someone call at the top of the house. Then a brief gale of laughter, like a collective sigh of relief. They seemed very far away.

Mallory moved towards the back wall of the basement. There was a scuttle of something small but living across the rubble and I felt my heart lurch. The tail of a fat rat slithered over the rusted frame of a child's bicycle.

'There's a door,' Mallory said, and he suddenly had his torch in his hand, a sharp white beam in the dull yellow darkness.

PC Greene was now halfway down the steps, staring at Mallory's back. We both followed him.

Mallory was trying the door.

Locked.

Then the lights went out. All of them. The mains. A switch had been thrown. I could hear voices protesting far above us.

Mallory had some sort of blade in his hand and was running it inside the doorjamb. I took his torch and held it on the door as he moved the blade left and right, left and right, lifting the lock tongue from the doorframe socket until he had it.

The door opened with a crack of wood. Beyond it was a metal grille. And from somewhere beyond that came the screams of a woman.

Help me help me help me help me help me.

The rattle of a metal grille in the blackness.

'You hear that?' Mallory said.

'Yes.'

We were talking in whispers now. Mallory was reaching through the grille. It was locked from the inside. But a set of keys jangled on a nail; and then he had them and the grille suddenly slid open.

'You smell it?' Mallory said.

'Yes, sir, I can smell it.'

The stink of shit and petrol.

'Careful in here,' he said, stepping inside.

I followed him and I felt the ground beneath my feet, rough and uneven, and the screaming was louder now and it was recognisably Scarlet Bush, and we moved more quickly because the space suddenly opened up and I was between Mallory and Greene when Mallory seemed to lurch forward and I grabbed a fistful of his jacket and stopped him falling.

There was a ragged hole beneath us, perhaps two metres deep, and Scarlet Bush at the bottom of it, shielding her eyes from the white light of the torch, naked and wet with petrol.

A barbecue pit for cooking human flesh.

A light flared and I saw a man coming round the pit just before it fell — *whoooooosh* — into the pit, and Billy Greene seemed to fall with it as the flames erupted with a sickening pop, and then Greene was in the pit with Scarlet, beating at the flames with his bare hands.

The man was small and powerful, long-haired and simian, and when he punched me in the heart I felt the air go out of me as

I went backwards, falling, smashing my back hard against some sort of work table that collapsed under my full weight.

I felt the pain explode in my back, and then the blow on the back of my skull as my head hit the wall.

I clutched at my heart and felt the rip in my shirt and suddenly I knew that he had not punched me.

He had stabbed me.

I touched the dent in the Kevlar Stealth that had saved my life, felt the sting of the bruise beyond.

I closed my eyes, dizzy and sick from the pain in the back of my head, the rest of it coming in broken fragments.

Screams from the pit. A man's screams now. Greene with his jacket in his hands, beating wildly at the fire. Scarlet Bush scrambling out, her eyes wide with the horror. Light in the room from the fire in the hole. A lot of light, but dancing and uneven, making ghosts of us all.

And the man — Bob the Butcher — punching Mallory in the chest, and in the arm, and in the side of the head. Mallory going down, his John Lennon glasses falling from his face. His face without his glasses no longer as hard as some old Viking, but vulnerable and lost and very easy to hurt.

Then Bob the Butcher gone. Out of the secret space. Past us all. Getting away with it.

And Whitestone waiting for him in the basement.

Bob walking into her forearm smash, the blow turning his head almost 180 degrees, and Whitestone, tiny woman that she was, perched on his back, cuffing him and punctuating his rights by bouncing his face against the ground.

'You are under arrest.' Smash. 'You do not have to say anything.' Smash.

I remembered a line from training days: a formal arrest will always be accompanied by physically taking control. She was doing that all right.

'But it may harm your defence if you do not mention when questioned something you later rely on in court.' Smash. 'Anything you do say may be given in evidence.'

Smash smash smash.

Bob the Butcher finally starting to beg.

And then I heard someone scream Mallory's name as the lights came on and I blacked out.

26

The pain in my back kicked me awake.

It started in the lower ribs and worked its way round to the spine, like some new pain meeting up with the pain that was already there. A bright bar of winter sunshine came through the crack in the curtains, telling me I had not been out for more than a few hours.

I groaned and slowly got out of bed.

They had me in one of those hospital smocks that reveal your behind to the world. I tore it off and found my clothes in the small room's wardrobe. I was sitting on the bed struggling to put my socks on when the nurse came in, a large-bosomed bossy matron — the type that expect to be obeyed. This one was Jamaican.

'How's the boy?' I said, my skin crawling at the thought of PC Greene alone in the pit, trying to put out the fire with nothing but his bare hands and his jacket. The effort of speaking set off a leaden throb at the back of my skull and I touched my head, expecting bandages or blood. There was nothing. Only the thud of pain.

'You're getting back in bed right this minute,' the nurse said.

I couldn't get my socks on. My back would not bend forward far enough. So I tossed them away. Slipped my shoes on. Stood up.

'How's the boy?' I said.

Now I had upset her.

'Do you think I've got all day for this nonsense? You have possible concussion. We're keeping you here for observation. Do you want me to get the doctor? Is that what I have to do?'

I was fully dressed by the time she came back with the doctor. Fully dressed apart from my socks. The doctor was young and Indian. Far too tired and busy to argue with me. Or too experienced. But he clearly thought I was stupid.

'I'm not discharging you,' he said. 'Is that quite clear? You're leaving at your own risk.'

'I get it. Where's the boy?'

'Intensive Care Unit. Top floor. Let me take you.'

PC Greene slept the sleep of the heavily

drugged. Both his hands were wrapped in bandages. There was an IV drip by his side.

That was it. Just his hands. But it was probably enough to end his life as a copper.

'He has second-degree burns on both hands,' the doctor said. 'That means the burns penetrated the deeper skin but as far as we can tell there's no damage to muscle and bone. When he's well enough to be moved, we'll get him down to the Queen Victoria in West Sussex. It's the best burns hospital in the south-east of England.' The doctor turned to leave. 'He's a very brave young man,' he said, almost as an afterthought.

I thought of the day I met Billy Greene, almost unable to stand after a look at his first body, and the raw shame he had felt when they had made him a canteen cowboy. I wondered if he knew how much good stuff there was inside him. And I wondered how he would make a living for the rest of his life.

Then I went to work.

They had Bob the Butcher in an interview room.

In the observation room you could watch through a one-way mirror or on a CCTV feed. There were lots of people I didn't know crowding in front of the mirror. I looked up at the screen.

Whitestone and Gane were sitting across from Bob and his lawyer. She was pretty and prim, dressed in business black.

The lawyers are getting younger, I thought.

Bob had a broken nose and the two black eyes that came with it but none of it had wiped the smirk from his face.

He looked like a cocky little ape.

'Ian Peck,' Whitestone said, and her voice seemed changed as it came through the speaker. 'We are charging you with murder.'

I couldn't believe what I was hearing.

'But it's not him,' I said.

Some of the crowd standing in front of the mirror turned to look at me. But then they looked away.

'This is bullshit,' I said.

There was a big duty sergeant on the door of the interview room.

'You can't go in there,' he said as I came towards him.

I shoved him aside. He didn't fight back.

They all looked up as I came in. White-stone and Gane. Bob and his pretty lawyer. Somebody said my name.

I reached in my pocket and took out the FS commando dagger I had borrowed from

Carol at the Imperial War Museum. It clattered across the table.

'Show me how you did it,' I said.

The duty sergeant was in the room now and, after getting the nod from Whitestone, he put his hands on me. I pushed him away. He was a stronger man than me but he held back.

The lawyer was on her feet, whining about some legal point that I didn't quite catch. The pain was in my spine, and my skull, and directly behind my eyes.

The knife was right in front of Bob.

'Come on, tough guy,' I said. 'Show me how you cut all those throats. You lying bastard, you fucking fantasist, you pathetic little man.'

Gane was shouting at me. They were all shouting at me. Apart from Bob. He looked at me, and at the knife, and back at me, as if weighing something in his mind.

He licked his lips. He stood up.

The room suddenly fell silent.

'Come on,' I said, quietly now, and I smiled to give him encouragement. 'Show me how you did it.'

Bob — Peck, whatever his name was — picked up the knife.

They all started shouting again.

There were hands on me, and my hands

were shoving them away, and Bob was looking at me with the knife in his hand. He essayed a slashing movement in slow motion.

'I cut them.'

I stepped forward.

'You lying piece of shit,' I said.

I took his wrist in one fist and punched his bicep with the other. The knife fell to the table.

'Wolfe,' Whitestone said. 'Max, please listen to me.'

'He didn't kill those men,' I said. 'Hugo Buck. Adam Jones. Guy Philips. I'm telling you, he doesn't know how. It's not him.'

Then I saw the tears in Whitestone's eyes.

'We're arresting him for the murder of DCI Mallory,' she said. 'He bled out on the way to the hospital.'

The duty sergeant was holding me now.

'I'm sorry, Max,' Whitestone said. 'The boss didn't make it.'

MIR-1 was deserted apart from Wren.

She looked up as I walked in.

'You have to see this, Wolfe.'

I walked to the window and stared down at Savile Row.

I thought of Margaret Mallory and how she had told me that Scout and I were a family when it felt like the entire world wanted to tell us something else, that we were not a real family at all, and the tears came then, blurring the traffic on the street far below and twisting my mouth into a rictus of raw, hopeless grief.

They would have told her by now, I thought; she would know that her husband was never coming home again by now; she would be alone in the small house in Pimlico with her dog and her photographs and her memories and her smashed heart. The knowledge choked up my throat and clawed at my insides and made my useless tears feel as though they were without end.

'Max?' Wren said.

I looked out across the rooftops of Savile Row. I wiped my eyes with the palm of my hands. I didn't turn around.

'DCI Mallory died,' I said, and my voice sounded strange to me, as if I was somebody else now. 'Stab wound in the neck. Dead before they could get him to the hospital.'

'I know,' she said. 'He was the kindest man I ever met. And the best copper. But you really need to see this. It's Bob's last post online. Before we went in and got him. Are you listening to me?'

I shook my head. 'No, I'm not listening to you, Edie. I don't care. Whatever it is, I really don't care. I don't want to see it. I don't care what he said.'

'You need to, Max. Because the killer is still out there. Because a world full of vicious little creeps is still out there. Will you please look at me?'

Silence.

Then Wren was suddenly by my side, dragging me to her workstation.

'Look, will you?' she said, not gently.

I looked.

The final message on Bob the Butcher's timeline.

There was no picture of Robert Oppenheimer.

There was no mushroom cloud.

In their place was a small black-and-white photograph. At first sight it looked like nothing — an abstract little squiggle of broken planes. But when I looked closer I saw that it was a city. It was an entire city, destroyed in an instant. My eye flicked across the hashtag, like a command to his one million followers.

#killallpigs

And then I read the message, and I did not understand, so I read it again, the rhythm of the numbers and words so familiar to me that at first I thought they were not on the screen but only in my head.

'Isn't that your home address?' Wren said.

I was gone.

They were coming back from school. Scout and Mrs Murphy and Stan. My daughter and Mrs Murphy looking down at the dog and laughing. Stan trotting happily by their side. Something in his mouth. A scrap of bagel. The smiles vanishing when they saw me.

'What's wrong?' Mrs Murphy said.

'We have to go,' I said. 'I'm sorry.'

I got Scout and Stan into the back of the X5, told Scout to put her seat belt on, and then I drove, pushing down hard, just ahead of the evening rush, Mrs Murphy standing on the street in my rear-view mirror, watching us go.

'But where are we going?' Scout said as we crossed Waterloo Bridge.

'We're going to see your mother,' I said.

She was standing on the lawn of a house on a road in a part of town where you could believe that nothing bad ever happened.

There was a small toddler crawling at her feet and a baby growing inside her.

Not my children. From her new man.

Anne.

It is such an ordinary, old-fashioned English name and I do not think I will ever be able to hear it without it pulling at my heart.

Anne, Anne, Anne.

You might not believe it — I could hardly believe it myself — but there had been a world, not so long ago, when we were as close to each other as we had been to anyone we had ever known in our young lives. When we laughed all the time; when a good life together was before us; when every night we lit a candle in the corner of our bedroom because we were unable to sleep, because it would have meant a kind of parting for a few hours. And now all that was gone; now that is all over, she told me, with one small stroke of the belly that was round with another man's child.

Anne, I thought. And looking at her now on the lawn, happy in this new place without me, I was shocked by something that I could not admit was the remains of our love.

You remember the pain and the anger and the grief of coming apart. You remember the raised voices and worries about money and the tears of a woman who finds that she is living a different life to the one she was expecting. You remember all of that, and you remember the letter that came two days after she said she had to go to stay with her parents to clear her head.

Dear Max, I am sorry but I have to go. I never wanted this to happen. But I love him and I am expecting his baby. He has moved so don't try looking for him . . .

You remember all of that, but you forget the love. It is a shock to be reminded of it, to admit to yourself that it existed at all, and perhaps still does.

I was parked across the road from her house on a beautiful street in a leafy south London suburb. Scout and the dog slept on the back seat.

I did not wake them.

And when another car pulled into the drive, and another man got out, and Anne smiled and kissed him on the mouth, I knew I was not going to.

I watched them go back inside the house, the new man with his arm around Anne's pregnant waist. She looked straight at me as she closed the door. But of course by then it was far too late for anything.

What about Scout? People sometimes ask me how a mother could leave a child. All I can say is, some people get a new home. And some people get a new family. And some people — mostly they are men, but not always — they make a lifetime of excuses for themselves, and they do what my wife did.

They get a new life.

Panic drove me out there. Reality drove me back. But as the night fell black and cold, I still wanted the same thing.

I wanted my daughter to be safe.

And as I drove back to Smithfield I saw that the safest place in the world for Scout would always be with me. Because I would kill for her and I would die for her. I would do anything for Scout because Scout was my everything.

There was a crowd outside our apartment block. Friday night men and women, red faces and white teeth, loud and laughing, bottles and glasses in their hands, making no attempt to move out of the way for a man with a sleeping child in his arms and a dog on a lead beside him.

I barged my way through them, sharp elbows and dipped shoulders, putting my weight into it, daring them to say something, to do something, to reveal themselves. To let me know they were for me, they had come for me, and now was the time. But there was blood in my eyes, murder in my face, and they said nothing. They got out of my way.

Across the street from our loft, the men of the meat market were just going to work as I put Scout to bed without her waking. Stan hopped up beside her, curled against her warmth, and I left them to their rest.

But I watched from the window, waiting for someone wicked to come for us, knowing at last that pure evil was out there, knowing we would meet one day soon, and I saw that the lights of the meat market burned all night long, wiping out the sky and blinding the stars.

DECEMBER
LOST CONTACTS

27

Two weeks later she came to see me.

Anne. My ex-wife.

Surprise visit.

Her old set of keys got her through the communal street-level door but they didn't work on our front door because I had changed the locks when she left me. I heard her key rattling in the lock and I saw her through the spy hole. It took me a while to unbolt the door. Then she was standing there. A knock-out, basically. The same woman but changed by all the time that had gone by, all the time we had not shared.

'Hello, Max.'

'Anne.'

She wore no make-up apart from a light touch of war paint on her lips. The light from the hall caught her shoulder-length hair and there was one single strand of silver running through the dark brown. She was dark-eyed, pale-skinned, and you could see where Scout got the heartbreaking curve of her face. It's hard to purge someone from your heart when you can see a child you love in their features.

Anne didn't bring her new life with her. Apart from the baby inside her, which she reassured and soothed with a hand rolled across her belly. The silence between us terrified me.

'Where's your little boy?' I said.

'Nanny,' she said, and she made it sound like a destination.

I followed her into the loft, fascinated by that single strand of silver in her hair. Not because it confirmed she was getting older — and she would one day be old, something that had never crossed my mind before now — but because I knew she would lose the special shine I had fallen in love with when we were kids. The shine was always going to go, and it wouldn't have made any difference. I would have kept on loving her without the special shine of youth. Maybe I would have truly loved her for the first time. But of course now I would never get the chance.

'Don't look at me like that, Max. It's giving me the creeps.'

'Sorry.'

Scout and Stan came out of her bedroom.

We all stared at our visitor as if she had come from some other planet and not just down the road in London's leafy money-belt. Then Anne was on her knees and all over Scout. That's the trouble with not seeing much of your child. Acting naturally around them becomes impossible. And I felt a flood of resentment that I could taste in my mouth.

Scout should have mattered to you. Scout should have mattered to you more than anything.

Stan mooched towards Anne, tail high and swishing. He sniffed hopefully at her legs and she stood up, one hand at the base of her spine, the other fanning the air, her lovely, ageing face twisted down with distaste.

'I don't do dogs,' she said. 'You never know where their mouth has been.'

I picked Stan up and took him to Scout's bedroom. He gave me a mournful look as I closed the door.

When I got back, Scout was showing Anne the junior boxing gloves I had bought her. In truth Scout had shown zero interest in putting on boxing gloves. She preferred drawing, or hanging out with Stan, or talking to her dolls (Scout insisted she was *not* playing with them — 'just talking'). But I could see that she felt some nameless compulsion to show her mother something new.

So that this time she might stay.

They talked. Mother and daughter. I went into the kitchen and I was in the middle of making coffee when a great wave of grief rolled over me and sucked me down. The feeling gripped my throat and stung my eyes and made me feel that I would never move again.

Then it was gone.

I went back into the main room with a tray. Two coffees and an orange juice.

'I'm not drinking caffeine any more,' Anne said.

I was confused. But she loved her coffee.

'I'll get water,' I said.

'Don't push the boat out on my account,' she said, and that made me laugh. She could always make me laugh.

'Do you want to see my drawings?' Scout said.

'Yes!' Anne's hand rolling over her belly. 'Yes, Scout! Yes!'

Scout went to her room to get her drawings. Anne and I looked at each other. I could see the effort she was making. We turned our faces to the sound of Scout's voice. Stan was making an unsuccessful attempt to escape.

'*No,* Stan,' Scout told him, closing the door behind her as she went into her room.

'Dogs?' Anne said. 'Boxing?'

She made it sound as though I was running a crack den.

Anne moved slowly around the loft, as if checking to see if she had left anything of importance behind, and stepped on a stuffed monkey that gave an outraged squeak.

'There's junk all over the floor,' she said. 'And it's not even Scout's junk.'

It was true. Stan had his own junk. A dog of that age is exactly like a toddler. Stan had junk scattered all over our flat — a squeaky duck, a spiky rubber ball, a bear in a Union Jack bib, assorted bits of chewed bone and gnawed rope.

'And this is really your dog?' she continued, with the amused contempt that I remembered so well. 'You're not looking after it for somebody?'

'Dogs are great,' I said.

Stan was back, having escaped from the bedroom when Scout came out with her drawings, and he shot me a furtive glance.

'Dogs don't care if you're rich or poor,' I said. 'Dogs don't care if you're beautiful or plain, smart or dumb, or what kind of car you drive.'

'That's right,' Anne said. 'Because dogs are stupid. What's that strange smell?'

'Scrambled omelette,' Scout said, placing a stack of drawings before her mother. 'Daddy burned the pan.'

'Scrambled omelette?' Anne said. 'There's no such thing!'

'No, scrambled omelettes are good,' Scout said, and I nearly wept at her loyalty to my simple meals. 'Because you can have what you want in them. Ham. Cheese. And you can eat them with Paul Newman's barbecue sauce.'

Anne touched her hair and laughed. 'Darling, there's omelette and then there's scrambled eggs. There's not scrambled omelette.'

Scout was wide-eyed.

'Lots of great chefs are men,' she said.

Anne shook her head, smiling. She studied the top drawing. 'What's this one?'

'This one's from school,' Scout said. She carefully read the title: 'My Family'.

Anne inhaled. 'But there's only you, Daddy and the dog, darling. Where's Mummy? And your baby brother? Where's Oliver?'

The new man. At least she doesn't call him Uncle Oliver, I thought. At least we are spared that ugly fate.

'I've got more drawings,' Scout said, before Anne could complain any more, and she went back to her bedroom.

'Look,' Anne said to me. 'If you're finding it difficult to adjust . . .'

I stared at her. I didn't know what to say. Adjusting? Is getting on with it the same as adjusting?

A burst of sudden pain throbbed in my lower back.

'What's wrong with you?' she said.

'Daddy's not at work today,' Scout said, her arms full of drawings. 'He hurt his back.'

'How long has your back been bad, Max?'

'I'm fine,' I said.

'Are you sleeping?'

'Like a baby.'

'What — you wake up wet and screaming in the middle of the night?'

We smiled at each other.

'I'm going to be the grumpy sheep,' Scout announced, dumping her drawings on the floor.

'The grumpy sheep?' Anne said. 'What's that?'

'The sheep that didn't want to see Jesus. The story's called *The Grumpy Sheep*. The part I play is the grumpy sheep. It's in the Bible.'

'Scout's Nativity play,' I said. 'At Christmas. I'm not sure the grumpy sheep is in the Bible, angel.'

'Daddy's going to make my costume.'

Anne raised an eyebrow. 'Good luck with that,' she said.

It was time to go. There were promises to see Scout soon. Promises to come again. Promises to have her down, and put her up, and show her a good time. Talk of baby brother and unborn sister that meant nothing to Scout. Promises, promises. If they were kept then everything would be better. Not perfect. Not remade. But better.

And, despite everything that had happened, I knew that Anne loved Scout. But she hadn't made space for her in the new life, with the new man, in the new place. And unless and until she did, Scout would be lost to her, and our beautiful daughter would carry those wounds with her for ever.

'Oh,' Anne said. 'There was a young woman waiting for you downstairs.'

'I get that a lot,' I said.

'I can believe it,' Anne said, walking away from us and back to her new family, her new life. 'They probably like your dog.'

'Hello, Sick Note,' Wren said. 'I thought you were never going to let me in. What's wrong with you now?'

'Torn internal intercostal muscles,' I said.

Wren shook her head. 'You're going to have to give me a clue.'

'The intercostal muscles lift your ribcage when you inhale and exhale.'

'Does it hurt?'

'Only when I breathe.'

'We missed you at Mallory's funeral. It would have been good if you were there, Max. His wife, Margaret, she was asking after you.'

I hung my head and choked something down. 'I can't see her,' I said. 'I wouldn't know what to say.'

'You don't have to say anything, stupid.'

Scout and Stan came out to meet her.

'His hair is the same colour as mine!' Wren told Scout.

All three of them were delighted. Stan began hopping around. Wren offered him the back of her hand to sniff before she started stroking him, and I could tell she was raised around dogs.

'What's your name?' Scout asked.

'Edie,' Wren replied.

'Look at this, Edie,' Scout said. And then to Stan, 'Play dead.'

Stan flopped down on his side, his head lifted from the ground, his eyes wide open and fixed on the Nature's Menu chicken treats gripped in Scout's little fist. He licked his lips. His head quivered with anticipation. In truth, he didn't look very dead. He didn't even look sleepy.

'That . . . is . . . incredible,' Wren said. 'Never seen anything like it. The pair of you should be on TV. Whatever that show's called. Well done.'

Beaming with pride, Scout and Stan went off to her room.

'When are you coming back?' Wren said.

'Tomorrow,' I said. 'Maybe the day after.'

'It doesn't matter. Because this would be off the book.'

There was an A4-sized file in her hand. Small and thin and green. She held it out to me but I made no attempt to take it.

'Mispers,' Wren said.

'What?'

'I was looking for missing persons, remember? Missing girls from twenty years ago.' A glint in her eye. '*You asked me.* Remember?'

I nearly laughed out loud. A spasm of pain shot through my lower back.

'It's over,' I said. 'Case closed. Murders solved. The perp convicted. They got their killer, didn't they?'

Ian Peck, aka Bob the Butcher, was standing up for all the murders. Not just Mallory. Not just the one he actually did, but also the murders of Hugo Buck, Adam Jones and Guy 'Piggy' Philips. Peck was an official serial killer, a superstar of real-life crime. Bob the Butcher's followers were still lighting up the social network sites.

I suddenly felt somewhere beyond exhausted.

'I heard Whitestone made DCI,' I said.

'That's right,' Wren said. 'And she deserves it.'

'And they're giving Mallory a posthumous QPM.'

'And Scarlet Bush has got a book out called *Pigslayer*.'

'A book? Already?'

'*Pigslayer* is an e-book, Grandad.' She flicked her fingers. 'They do 'em fast. Haven't read it myself. The chief super's happy. Looks like everybody in our team is going up at least one pay grade. While you're at home with your busted back feeling sorry for yourself.'

I shook my head. 'It's over,' I repeated.

'No,' Wren said. 'It's only just starting. Because there are still the missing.'

'You know how many people go missing in this country?' I said. 'Every single day of the year?'

'Yes,' Wren said. 'One every three minutes.

Most of them young. Many of them female. Girls running away from care homes. Girls who are being abused by dear old mum's brand-new boyfriend. Girls with drug problems, drink problems and body issues. Self-harmers and addicts of every kind. The waifs and strays. The unlucky ones who fall through the net — who fall through all the nets. Girls who are pregnant. Girls who think they are in love. Girls whose parents are religious fanatics who think they are whores if they listen to pop music.'

'That just about covers it,' I said.

'You know how many girls went missing in the country that year, 1988, the year we're looking at?'

I was silent for a moment.

'I guess it was a lot,' I said.

'You wouldn't believe how many.'

'And you're going to find them all, are you, Edie? Avenge them all? Make it right?'

'Not all of them. Just one. I narrowed it right down. The net — the net you gave me — was much too wide. It turned up too many names. Too many missing girls. So I looked in the immediate vicinity of Potter's Field. During school time. In the spring and summer of 1988.'

'But not all mispers are murder victims, Edie. Some of them — most of them — are just lost contacts. You heard of lost contacts? Did you do lost contacts yet in detective school?'

'Fine.' She began to gather up the contents of her thin little file. 'I'll do it by myself.'

'Mispers are sometimes just lost contacts who got out and moved on and changed their name and were bloody happy to get away from whatever nightmare they were stuck in,' I said.

'That's true,' she conceded. 'But some mispers end up dead in a basement. Or alive — and that's even worse. Alive in some bastard's basement for ten years or more. Chained naked to some fucking wall. And you know that's true too, don't you, Max?'

I was silent for a moment.

'Yes,' I said.

'And you were there. You heard what James Sutcliffe told us. There was a girl, Max. It all starts with a girl! Find the girl and you find the killer and you find the motive for it all. But first you have to find the girl. And we have to find the girl, don't we? We can't just . . . leave her.' She stared at me. 'You really want me to do this thing alone, Max? I can't believe it. I don't think that's who you are.'

'You don't know me.'

'Probably not.'

I walked her to the door.

'You know the worst thing about being on your own with a kid?' I said. 'You care a lot less about the rest of the world. You really wouldn't believe how much less you care. You just do. Your heart gets hardened. Your world narrows down to you and your child. You want to do this thing off the book?'

She nodded.

'But why?' I said. 'The missing will still be missing. Mallory will still be dead. Bob the Butcher will still be getting marriage proposals sent to his cell.'

'We do it because if we don't, they get away with it,' Wren said. 'We do it because if we don't, we're just like the worst of our kind — too scared to do our job. And we do it because it matters. We do it because it's *right*.'

The file slapped hard against my chest.

This time I took it.

'You have a daughter, Max,' Wren said. 'Do it for her.'

When Mrs Murphy arrived I went down to Smiths of Smithfield to look at the file.

There wasn't much in it. Three sheets of paper.

The first featured a passport-sized photograph of a fair-haired girl in her mid teens holding an uncertain smile for the camera, a name, Anya Bauer — German? — and a date of birth: 4 July 1973.

I looked at the photograph and saw that Anya Bauer had teased her hair into some elaborate approximation of some unknown hero. It could have been anything from a pop star to a princess. It could have been Madonna or Princess Diana. No, it was Madonna. Early on, when Madonna's hair was still quite short. Anya Bauer trying to look older, trying to look pretty — trying to do what every teenager in the world tried to do. Anya Bauer was in her mid teens in the late eighties, so she would be on the cusp of middle age by now.

If she had lived.

The second page was a printout from a contemporary missing persons website with the same photograph and a disclaimer:

Note: the child may look significantly different now to these images due to the age and stylistic differences.

The third and final sheet carried the same image of the smiling girl. Page seven of the *Potter's Field Post,* dated 21 August 1988. One sentence: 'Anya Bauer, 15, has been missing from her home for two months and police are anxious to contact her.' And there was a telephone number that had probably been defunct for the best part of two decades.

I looked at Anya Bauer's photograph for a long time, and when I climbed the stairs to my home, just before I opened the door I heard the sound of Stan barking and the untouched joy of Scout's laughter.

28

WELCOME TO POTTER'S FIELD said the ornate wooden sign on the edge of town. FINAL RESTING PLACE OF THE ROYAL DOGS.

Wren snorted. 'They make it sound like the Taj Mahal or Victoria Falls,' she said. 'It's not even all the royal dogs, is it? Just Henry's. They haven't got any of the Queen's corgis in there, have they? And probably not all of Henry's dogs.'

The sign featured the Henry VIII of popular imagination — the portly wife-killer in his middle years, not the athletic young king whose statue adorned the school he had founded five hundred years ago. Some goggle-eyed spaniels frolicked by his silken club-toe shoes. They all looked like Stan's relatives.

It was always a shock to see that there was a town beyond the world of the school. Like a lot of small English towns, Potter's Field hovered somewhere between gentility and poverty. With Wren at the wheel of a pool car, a little unmarked Hyundai, we passed a pretty village green where a group of local youths sat drinking from cans and smoking, their mountain bikes scattered around them.

'DCI Mallory's wife came in,' Wren said. 'After the medal ceremony. Margaret. She was really nice. She wanted to thank everyone. She's a class act, that lady. She was asking after you.' A pause. 'You should go and see her.'

'You want to take the police station or the local newspaper?' I said.

Wren stared at me.

'Did you hear me?'

'I heard you. Police station or the local rag?'

She looked at me for a moment longer, then looked away.

We were on the high street now. There were quaint little teashops among the chain coffee shops and mobile phone stores and supermarkets. I pulled up outside one of the teashops. A life-sized effigy of Henry VIII and his dogs guarded the offer of afternoon cream tea and a taste of English summer.

'I'll take the local rag,' Wren said.

■ ■ ■ ■

They were not expecting me. But my warrant card got me into an interview room with the duty sergeant, Sergeant Lane, a big red-faced copper with the hint of a rural accent. He handed me back my warrant card with a smirking mixture of deference and derision. But he shook my hand and gave me a paper cup of scalding black coffee.

'CID are back?' he said. 'We haven't seen you out here since that unfortunate business with the sports master. But the perpetrator went down, didn't he?'

'This is another matter,' I said. 'A missing person.' I slid the thin file across the table. 'You've always worked in Potter's Field?'

'Born and bred here,' he said. 'The big city never appealed. It's beautiful out here. Very green. You get out in the fields, it's like the last few centuries never happened.'

'Do you remember a missing person called Anya Bauer?'

He was half-heartedly leafing through the file.

'And why would I?' he said. He closed the file and raised his eyebrows. 'Not much of a missing person, was she? More of a lost contact.'

The file slid back towards me.

'So she was reported missing but you never followed it up?' I said.

A slow smile. 'You think we've got plenty of time on our hands? The local yokels.'

I smiled back at him. 'Not at all. You must get busy. All those spoilt rich kids at Potter's Field.'

'Oh, they're no trouble,' he said, bridling. 'We have a good relationship with the school. Always have done. If those kids are smashing up restaurants, then they're doing it in Chelsea and Knightsbridge, not round here.' He gestured at the file. 'Foreign girl, was she?'

I nodded. 'German. From Munich. Would you have tried a bit harder to find her if she'd been a local?'

He laughed. 'Wouldn't have had a choice, would we?' Then his face grew serious. 'Have you got a body? Is that what this is about?'

'We don't have a body. It's more of a hunch.'

I was on my feet, gathering the file with one hand and reaching out to shake his hand with the other. He took it and gripped it for just long enough to demonstrate that despite my age and warrant card and fancy big city ways, he was by far the stronger man.

'Forgive me, but I don't quite understand why you're here,' he said. 'This is an official inquiry, is it?

'Just some old business we're trying to clear up,' I said. 'I appreciate your time.'

'My pleasure,' he said.

Before I was out of the door, he was reaching for the phone.

The offices of the *Potter's Field Post* were located on the high street above an antique shop but Wren had left a text message changing our meet, and directing me to a small thatched cottage on the edge of town where a sprightly woman in her early eighties was tending an immaculate garden.

'She's inside,' she called, 'with my husband. It's not locked!'

An old Golden Retriever lumbered up to me as I went into the cottage. It sniffed my hand sleepily and then trailed after me down the hall as I followed the sound of Wren's excited voice.

She was on her knees in the living room, peering through a magnifying glass at an old contact sheet of photographs. The floor was entirely covered with contact sheets. In an armchair was a white-haired old man

403

with what looked like a large Scotch in his hand. The dog went over to him and collapsed on his tartan slippers.

'Be good, Fanta,' said the old man. And to me, 'Hello, young man. Would you like a wee dram?'

'Single malt,' Wren said. 'Twenty years old. It's very good.' There was a glass on the table but it didn't look as though she had touched it.

The old gentleman started to rise from his chair but I held up my hands, thanking him, but no. Wren pressed the magnifying glass against her eye, and then against the contact sheet in her hand.

'There's nothing at the paper,' she said. 'It's on its last legs. They don't even have proper files. They haven't even digitally converted their old filing system. I found dry rot in their microfiche. Can you believe it?'

'The *Potter's Field Post*?' said the old man. 'They give it away these days! Give it away! A free sheet, they call it!'

'But they directed me to Mr Cooper here,' Wren said.

'Monty!' the old man erupted.

'Monty!' agreed Wren. 'Monty was the staff photographer on the paper for forty years.'

'Man and boy,' he chortled.

I got the impression that Monty mightily enjoyed Wren's company, and was happy to produce his stacks of old contact sheets. He didn't even seem to mind the red felt-tip pen she was waving around for emphasis, and using to circle images of interest.

I sat down beside her.

'Nightmare at the local rag,' she said. 'As far as I can tell, they did nothing on Anya Bauer beyond that one piece when she went missing. They never followed it up.'

'Neither did the law,' I said.

'But look at this,' Wren said, and held out the magnifying glass.

'I photographed this town all my working life,' Monty said, and I could hear an even stronger echo of the old lost countryside that I had heard in Sergeant Lane's voice. 'And once a year, on Potter's Fifth, I photographed the school.'

I was looking at images of boys in military uniform. It was the uniform worn by the seven boys in the Combined Cadet Force of Potter's Field. But here there was an entire army of them, and they marched across the decades.

'Potter's Fifth is the school's big day,' Wren explained.

Monty barked with laughter. Fanta the

Golden Retriever sat up sharply and then slowly curled itself back into sleep.

'On the fifth of May every year the school opens its doors to the great unwashed,' Monty said. 'And the town opens its heart to the school. Or pretends it does. It's the Potter's Field equivalent of the fourth of June at Eton. Of course they've got the river at Eton and we don't have a river.'

'Do you see them?' Wren said.

'No.'

She punched my arm. 'Jesus, Wolfe! Look harder!'

I saw hundreds of boys in uniform. Marching past the statue of the young King Henry. Saluting the raising of the flag. Eyes snapped right as they marched past the camera. And then I concentrated on one central image on the contact sheet that was circled with red and the mist cleared.

They were not as I remembered them — cocky and grinning and unbreakable, as they had been in that first photograph. Now they were serious, upright, stern, in a line of boy soldiers being inspected by Her Majesty the Queen when she and they were twenty years younger.

Seven of them together in a line that stretched beyond the frame of the camera: Guy Philips, Salman Khan, Ben King, Ned

King, James Sutcliffe, Hugo Buck, Adam Jones. And towering by the side of the Queen as Her Majesty frowned at James Sutcliffe, there was Peregrine Waugh, the line of his mouth suggesting that he was about to detonate with pride.

'And this one,' Wren said.

There was another contact sheet she had placed by her side. It too had a red circle around one image.

It was night in the picture. A long shot of some kind of party in a large white tent. Waiters hovered with trays of champagne flutes. Parents and boys and masters and guests stood around grinning and swilling. Another Potter's Fifth had gone well. And on the far side of the party I could see a boy and a girl half turning away from the camera with a smile.

'It's Ben King,' I said.

'It's Ned King,' Wren said. 'Look closer. You can just about see the scars on his face where his brother glassed him over the Coco Pops.'

'And the girl?'

She was young, blonde, pretty. A ponytail bobbing, the shadow of a secret smile as she turned away. She was in T-shirt and jeans, far too casual for an event like the one in the big white tent, far too casual for

Potter's Fifth.

Wren smiled and shook her head. 'I don't know. It could be just a girl. You talked to Ned King, right? You and Mallory.'

I remembered the night out at Brize Norton when Captain King and his regiment were about to get on the Hercules for Afghanistan.

'The killings had only just begun,' I said. 'Ned King was leaving. Mallory was gentle with him. Impressed by him.' I stared through the magnifying glass at the image of the boy and girl at a party long ago. 'We both were.'

'Well, someone has to talk to Captain King again,' Wren said. 'When he gets back.'

'Monty,' I said, 'would that have been your only reason to go to the school? Potter's Fifth?'

He nodded and eased himself out of the chair. 'Apart from pictures we needed for the files,' he said. 'When there was a new Head Master, they would always want a shot of him. And the statue of Henry. The mainstay of our tourist industry.' He was bent over the coffee table, not risking getting down on his knees. 'And the grave, of course. The grave of the royal dogs.' He tapped a ragged cardboard file. 'There you go.'

These were not contact sheets. These were glossy eight-by-ten shots. Some of them were of the Head Masters of Potter's Field, formal portraits. Peregrine Waugh was the most recent but there were also men long retired, long dead. And there were close-up shots of the grave of the royal dogs, taken in all kinds of weather, and all kinds of seasons.

I held one in each hand. One was black and white, the stone slick with rain, the grass around it untrimmed. The other was in colour, the stone reflecting a white bar of summer sunshine, the grass border neat and cut.

But that wasn't the only difference between the two photographs.

'Look at the inscription,' I said. 'Look at the epitaph on the grave.' I held up the black-and-white shot. 'The words are missing on this one.'

On the photograph of the grave taken in summer, the epitaph was there. But on the rain-slick shot, it was missing.

The old photographer smiled, and he didn't need to look at the words to recite them. ' "Brothers and sisters, I bid you beware of giving your heart to a dog to tear." Well, they could hardly put that on the original grave, now could they?'

'Why not?'

'Because the grave is nearly five hundred years old,' he said. 'But those words were written in the early twentieth century by Rudyard Kipling. By my time the grave was literally falling to bits. Collapsing in on itself.'

Wren said, 'Do you have any pictures?'

He looked doubtful but eventually found one image of a small yellow bulldozer parked next to the cracked tomb. You could clearly make out the name of the company on the side: V. J. Khan & Sons.

'The grave was always unmarked,' Monty said. 'Or at least the inscription had worn clean away. I never saw anything on it. It's five hundred years old, remember. But when they restored it, he added the words from Kipling.'

'Who did?' Wren said.

'The Head Master,' he said, sipping his single malt. 'Mr Waugh said he didn't want to leave the grave unmarked.'

29

I left Wren tucking into cheese on toast with
Monty, his wife and their Golden Retriever
and drove the pool car to Potter's Field.
The school seemed shut up and silent
already but the main gates were open and I
left the Hyundai in the staff car park. I
could make out a figure moving around in
the twilight of the playing fields and I was
starting towards him when I heard the
sound of the first shot.

A large-gauge gun, some distance away,
the shot seeming to contain its own echo.
And then there was silence and I started off
again towards the playing fields, the buildings looking so lifeless that you would never
guess they contained one thousand souls.

The old caretaker, Len Zukov, was moving slowly along a rugby pitch with what
looked like a lawnmower. It was only when
I got closer that I saw he was leaving a long
straight white line in his wake as he marked

out a touchline.

I called out a greeting, raising my hand.

'Don't step on that!' he replied. 'Still wet!'

'Remember me? DC Wolfe from West End Central.'

I was reaching for my warrant card. But he couldn't have cared less about my warrant card.

'I remember you.'

'I'm just following up a few details of our ongoing investigation.'

But he wasn't interested. He was already moving off, his machine drowning my words, the straight white line trailing behind him.

'Don't step on my lines,' he shouted over his shoulder, a man accustomed to bawling at generations of boys. 'Got to get this done before dark.'

I walked back across the main courtyard, round the side of the college chapel and into the graveyard. There was a flurry of sound and movement. A squirrel skittered across my path and swiftly up a tree. I reached the grave of Henry's dogs as another shot split the silence. And there was the epitaph.

Brothers and sisters,
I bid you beware

Of giving your heart
To a dog to tear.

Weather and time had etched the words in green moss.

I turned at a shuffling sound behind me and saw Len Zukov coming slowly down the path. Checking up on me.

'What you want?' he said. 'You shouldn't be in here. You should tell someone you're coming. Get permission.'

'Those words on the grave,' I said. 'I never realised until today that they're only a hundred years old. But the grave is five hundred years old. So they had to be put there within the last century.'

His mouth moved as if to say *and so what?*

'I just wondered how I missed it,' I said, talking to myself as much as him, and looking up at the sound of another gunshot. 'Noticing things — it's sort of what I do, Len.'

He didn't take his eyes from me.

'What's that shooting?' I said. 'Twelve-bore?'

'Sounds more like a .410,' he said. 'Better for close range, thick-cover shooting. Vermin.' He rubbed his hands on his overalls. They were locked in permanent fists by his arthritis. He saw me looking at his hands and pushed them deep into his pockets. 'Rats, rabbit and fox,' he added.

'Where you from, Len?'

He frowned at me. 'I told you — I'm from here,' he said.

'Originally, I mean.'

'Russia.'

'Russia? They didn't call you Len over there, I bet.'

'Lev,' he said. 'Near enough.'

'What part of Russia?'

We both looked up at the sound of another gunshot. Closer now. The long, drawn-out, rolling sound of a large-gauge shotgun fired in open countryside. The noise just went on and on.

'Who's shooting?' I said.

He shrugged, like that was another subject he couldn't care less about.

'Farmer,' he suggested.

'So you came over after the Second World War?'

'No,' he said, not quite smiling. 'I came over after the Great Patriotic War.'

I smiled. 'Same war. Different names.'

'No,' he said, unsmiling. 'Very different wars. Very different wars for your people and my people. In Russia there were twenty-five million dead.'

We both stared at the grave. I wondered

what he thought about an English king who built a tomb for his pet spaniels. Not much, probably. Not if he had been in Russia during the war. He had to be somewhere in his seventies, I guessed. That would have made him a boy of eleven or twelve at the end.

'You must have been too young for the war,' I said.

He laughed. 'Nobody in Russia was too young for the war.'

I nodded.

'I'm away now,' I said, and offered him my hand to shake.

It was a mistake. He took his arthritic hands from his overalls and brushed his clenched right fist briefly against my open palm, and we both turned away with our own private shame.

He made no attempt to follow me this time.

Perhaps he figured that I wouldn't be able to poke my nose in where it wasn't wanted. Certainly everywhere seemed locked up, and despite the falling darkness few lights appeared in any of the ancient windows. I looked up at the room where Mallory and I had stared across the playing fields with Peregrine Waugh but I could see no sign of life even there.

But I saw Len Zukov again as I walked

back to the car park. He was in front of his little stone cottage with another man and it took me a moment to recognise Sergeant Tom Monk, the burns on his face a smooth black mask from so far away.

As the old caretaker watched, a cigarette clutched in one balled-up fist, Monk raked a pile of newly mown grass, shovelled it into a wheelbarrow and carried the load round the side of the cottage to where the smoke from a small bonfire was rising. Easing the old man's burden.

I raised my hand in farewell but they did not appear to see me.

Then there was another gunshot as I reached the car, much closer now, coming from somewhere just beyond the tree line. The stuttering shot tore through leaves and took its time to crack the sky. Len was wrong. Whatever they were killing, they were not using a .410 to do it. I know what a twelve-bore shotgun sounds like.

That's big vermin someone's hunting, I thought, happy to get back into the car.

There was something wrong with the silence.

It jolted me from my shallow sleep, and before I was even awake I was sitting by the side of the bed, staring straight into the eye

416

of the madman who sat on my bedside table.

12:05, he told me. Five minutes after midnight?

Outside I could hear the hum and roar of the meat market as it began its night. The clamour of the trolleys, the shouts of the men, still laughing with the long hours of the night ahead of them.

What had woken me?

I pulled on my pants and a pair of light-weight knuckle-dusters that sat in the drawer by the bed. They weighed nothing but would crack open a skull like a boiled egg if you could get close enough. I stepped out of my bedroom, resisting the urge to call Scout's name. Inside his cage, Stan stirred in his sleep.

Our front door was shut. Our windows were unbroken. There was no fresh air coming from somewhere it shouldn't be.

I looked at Stan's cage. It was not a sound that had broken my sleep. It was the absence of a sound.

I knelt beside Stan, felt under him and beneath the blanket that covered his basket and pulled out the alarm clock we had put there to stand in place of his mother's heartbeat. The battery had died some time ago. I smiled at him in the darkness and touched his soft red coat. Then I walked

417

into the kitchen and dropped the old alarm clock into the bin.

Stan didn't need it any more. He was home.

But under the door to my daughter's bedroom, I could see that Scout still slept with all the lights on.

30

Salman Khan opened his front door unshaven and squinting in the pale morning sunlight, a baseball bat in one hand and a cigarette in the other. He held them both loosely, as if either might slip from his hand in a strong wind. He was in a dress shirt, open to his waist, with a black bow tie hanging around his neck like fresh roadkill. He looked like he had been wearing black tie to bed for a week.

'Mr Khan,' Wren said. 'DCI Whitestone received a complaint —'

'Because they're not here any more!' Khan gestured with his baseball bat. 'The officers who were protecting me! The ones who were here after the — what is it? The Osman Warning!'

Wren smiled sympathetically. 'Because the threat to your life is over,' she said, all professional calm. 'The perpetrator has been convicted.'

He laughed viciously.

We just stared at him, letting the laughter fade and then the silence grow.

Khan looked over our shoulders. There was a young Nepalese security guard on the drive. You were starting to see them all across London's money-belt — private policemen hired to watch over just one wealthy street. The rich were getting scared.

But nobody was more scared than Salman Khan.

'Thank you, Padam,' Khan said.

The Gurkha saluted. 'Sir.'

We followed Khan inside his house. A midget motorbike was resting against a double-sided winding staircase. Through glass panels in the marble floor you could see down into the basement area and the impossible blue world of an indoor swimming pool. You could feel its heat, taste the chlorine. Wren looked at me and I knew she felt it too.

These people have so much.

'Your family are away?' I said.

'They can't stay here! It's too dangerous! If anything should happen to them . . .'

This was meant to be routine, one of the last jobs on the Action Book in the winding up of Operation Fat Boy. But Salman Khan could still smell murder in the air.

'What are you afraid of, Mr Khan?' I asked.

'Are you serious? Some of my closest friends have died.'

He stubbed out his cigarette and immediately lit another one.

'Mr Khan,' I said. 'Look at me.'

He looked at me, looked away, and threw his baseball bat aside with a scream. 'Fuck!'

'How's your father's business doing? A building firm, isn't it?'

It took him a moment to recover.

'My father died ten years ago. The company was sold at the time of his death. Why do you ask?'

Wren said, 'Who was Anya Bauer?'

The name seemed to mean nothing to him. He shook his head. 'I don't know what's going on,' he said. 'I don't know what you're talking about. You're supposed to be —'

'What happened at that school?' I said.

'How long are you going to keep asking that question?'

'Until I get the truth.'

'What happened? Nothing. High jinks. Nothing more. I can't deny that we did things. Irresponsible things.'

'Like what?' Wren said.

'God, I don't know! Smashed some glass.

421

Made some noise. Bought some charlie.'

'That's it?' Wren said. 'Petty vandalism and recreational drugs? Come on.'

Khan shot her a wary look. 'But none of it was at our instigation. And all of it was done in a spirit of experimentation and adventure.' He seemed to stop himself, then clenched his teeth. 'We fell under his spell, you see.'

'You mean Peregrine Waugh? He was your House Master twenty years ago, wasn't he?'

Khan shook his head. 'I mean the Master's favourite.' He laughed. 'I mean Peregrine's representative on earth.'

And I suddenly saw who had the most to lose.

'You're talking about Ben King, aren't you? Was he the Master's favourite?'

He couldn't look at me. 'I didn't say that,' he said. 'I didn't give you any names.' He gripped a fistful of his hair. 'You're meant to be here to *help* me!'

'Would you like to make a statement?' I said.

Khan's mouth twisted into a grotesque parody of coquettishness. 'Would you like me to, detective?'

'I think you're ready to talk to us, Mr Khan,' I said. 'I think you know that it's really the only option you have left.' I looked

422

around at all the useless luxury. 'This is no life, is it?'

He sucked hungrily on his cigarette.

'I need to talk to a few people. I need to talk to my wife, my beautiful —' He choked up. Hung his head. Then gathered himself. 'And my lawyer. And my children, God help me. After that, I'll come to your station.' He was starting to compose himself now. 'I believe there's a possibility that I can help you with your enquiries.'

'And when will that be?' Wren asked.

'When I am fucking ready, young lady.'

I shook my head. 'Not good enough, sir,' I said. 'And watch your mouth when you're addressing my colleague. We have reason to believe that a serious crime was committed during the period when you were a student at Potter's Field. I could take you in now if I wanted to.'

He laughed. 'Really? And by this time next year you would be waiting outside in your new security guard's uniform, watching over my children as they unload their mountain bikes from my wife's Porsche Cayenne. Wouldn't you?' He paused, took a breath. 'Tomorrow morning,' he said. 'Afternoon at the latest. I promise. I want it to be over.'

'It will be,' I assured him. 'We can help you. But you have to help us: what happened at that school?'

'What happened? I'll tell you what happened. They break you down and then they build you up. That's what they do at those fine old English schools. That's what your parents are paying them for. They take you apart bit by bit and they put you together again in their image. They take scared little boys and they turn them into captains of industry, leaders of the land, future Prime Ministers.'

He took a long pull on his cigarette.

'The first day I met Peregrine Waugh — I was thirteen years old, he was just an English master — he drew a single chalk mark on the wall just above the blackboard. "That is Shakespeare," he said. And then he drew another chalk mark, at the very top of the blackboard. "That is T. E. Lawrence." And then he got down on his knees — we were all laughing madly, of course — and drew a third chalk mark just above the floorboards. "And that is you." ' Salman Khan smiled a crooked smile as he waved his cigarette. 'And we took it from there.'

It was a busy morning at the Black Museum. A dozen young cadets in uniform were squeezed into Room 101. Sergeant John Caine contemplated them without

424

pleasure or pity.

'Ground rules,' he said. 'You do not touch anything. You do not photograph anything. You do not take a souvenir that you think nobody will miss. Believe me, I will miss it. Everything here is far older and far more valuable than you are.'

A few guffaws. But Sergeant Caine wasn't laughing.

'So show respect,' he continued. 'And keep your sticky paws in your pockets at all times.'

He unlocked the door to the Black Museum.

'Go on. Off you go.'

They set off, excited and laughing, like big kids on a school trip. When the last of them had shuffled into the first room, the one mocked up to look like the original museum in Whitehall, Sergeant Caine turned his attention to me.

'They've come down from Hendon,' he said. 'This spotty shower are coming to the end of their course and sending them to me is an attempt to prepare them for the real world. A new initiative.'

'I'll wait, if that's OK.'

He nodded. 'Best to wait. Join them if you like.'

I followed them through into the Victorian

425

sitting room, nine young men and three young women who were happy to be on a field trip, snickering at the fake fireplace and fake sash window.

They passed under the hangman's noose and reached the table covered with weapons. Shotguns and rifles, replicas and the real thing, walking sticks that were really swords, umbrellas that were really handguns, and a glass case full of automatic weapons. By the time they went through the doorless opening into the museum proper, their laughter had stopped.

They saw the walking stick that turned into a sword that then turned into a knife — the Cop Killer. There was every kind of gun, every kind of knife — some of them dark with prehistoric blood. They paused longest before the display about the officers of the Metropolitan Police who had been killed in the line of duty.

By the end of their visit — and it doesn't take very long to see the Black Museum — they were silent and shaken.

'This place is a learning centre,' Sergeant Caine told them, leaning against his cluttered desk and holding a mug that said BEST DAD IN THE WORLD. 'I hope the lesson that you have learned today is that there are many ways to kill a policeman.'

426

They said nothing.

'Thank you for visiting the Crime Museum at New Scotland Yard,' Caine concluded with a formality I had not heard before. 'Before you graduate from Hendon, I suggest you go to your school's Simpson Hall where you will find the Metropolitan Police Book of Remembrance. Her Majesty the Queen has signed it and, before your studies come to an end, so should you.' He looked at their serious young faces and nodded once. 'Take care of yourself and take care of each other. Thank you, good luck and goodbye.'

When we were alone I opened my kitbag. Inside was a large evidence bag containing the Kevlar Stealth that had been worn by DCI Mallory on the night he died. It was almost new apart from the large stain on the right shoulder from the neck wound that had killed him.

Handling it with great care, I entrusted it to the safe keeping of Sergeant John Caine of the Black Museum, New Scotland Yard.

31

Stan's favourite café in Regent's Park was The Honest Sausage, just off The Broadwalk near London Zoo. We were at an outside table sharing a bacon sandwich, my dog on my lap, when she walked in. Sooner or later, every dog person in central London walks into The Honest Sausage.

'You again,' Natasha said.

She didn't sit down. Susan and Stan did the dog dance, moving in tight, excited circles as they sniffed at each other's rear end. Then the Pekingese-Chihuahua cross had suddenly had enough and turned and yapped in his face. Stan backed off immediately, tail between his legs, edging closer to me for protection.

'Fancy bumping into you,' Natasha said. 'What's the lovely old English saying? Accidentally on purpose. Hello, Stan.'

At least she was pleased to see my dog.

'It's a good saying,' I said. 'I went to your

old apartment block but they said you had moved.'

'Just across the park. Marylebone. I downsized.'

I held out the manila envelope to her. 'Your videotape. I wanted to return it.'

She took it from me without speaking, her mouth tightening. She still hadn't sat down. She wasn't going to now. Not with the videotape of that old rugby match in her hand.

'I also wanted to say that you were right, and I was wrong. About how your late husband lost his eye. I was rough and rude. And I'm sorry, I really am.' I shrugged. 'That's it.'

'And what did you think might happen? Did you think you were going to return my VHS tape and say sorry and then I would take you home with me and have wild sex?'

'Well,' I said, 'it crossed my mind.'

She shook her head. 'We missed our moment,' she said.

I was surprised how sad that made me.

'Did we really?'

'Yes. Men and women have a moment and sometimes they just miss it. Bad timing.'

'Like missing a flight?'

'Exactly like missing a flight.'

My phone was in front of me on the table.

It began to vibrate. WREN CALLING, it said.

Natasha laughed. 'We don't even know each other.'

'I know you,' I said. 'You're one of those party girls with a good heart who wants to settle down but chooses the wrong man and then it all falls to pieces. You can see yourself getting harder and more cynical and you don't like it because you were expecting a better life. Stop me if I'm getting warm.'

My phone was still vibrating.

'Story of my life,' Natasha said. 'But what kind of man are you? Are you one of those men who stop looking at a woman so he can look at his little phone? The world is full of those men. That's not what I want.'

'No,' I said. 'That's not me. I can't stand guys like that. I'm actually thinking of getting rid of this phone.' WREN CALLING. 'But you know what? I do have to take this call.'

'Of course you do.'

Natasha scooped up her Pekingese-Chihuahua cross and walked away on those long legs. Without turning round, she raised one hand in farewell.

I picked up the phone.

'Whitestone heard from Salman Khan's

lawyer,' Wren told me. 'Khan's not coming in.'

'He's not coming in today?'

I could hear her breathing.

'Max, Khan's never coming in.'

Salman Khan's beautiful home had burned for most of the night and the wealthy street stank of smoke and death. A body had been recovered and taken away before I arrived.

Where the house had stood on the leafy St John's Wood avenue there was now a blackened husk, sodden and steaming — a five-million-pound monument to ruin. The great pyre had collapsed in on itself at some point, taking the roof with it, and among the wreckage you could just make out what had once been the subterranean swimming pool, now heaped with collapsed brick, bent steel, burned wood.

Fire Officer Mike Truman stood between two fire engines and watched his men carefully picking their way through the ruin. DI Gane and I were with him, Gane taking notes, while beyond the police tape uniformed officers kept back a small crowd wielding camera phones. They seemed to be mostly hired help walking dogs to the park or children to school. You didn't see the locals walking about round here.

'There's evidence of some kind of accelerant,' Truman said. 'A petroleum distillate like diesel fuel or gasoline. But we also found a small motorbike — a child's motorbike, if you can believe that — at the foot of the staircase, so that could explain the traces of accelerant.'

Gane said, 'That's the fire's point of origin?'

Truman nodded. 'Looks like it.'

'But how did he die?' I said.

'You mean was it the fire or the smoke that killed him?'

Gane was staring at me. 'No. DC Wolfe's asking, did someone cut his throat?'

I had never seen a burned corpse before. I had never seen how death by fire seems to coat a body in a black substance that comes from the very centre of the earth. I had never experienced the double shock of seeing what a fire takes away, and what it leaves behind.

Every inch of living flesh on Salman Khan's body had been replaced by something that resembled a rough black overcoat yet you could clearly see his ribcage, his teeth and the fine bones of his hands, the fingers now long and tapered with all the flesh burned away, like the fingers of a concert pianist.

The fire took away everything but left the shadow of some unimaginable pain. His mouth was open, as if crying out in agony, and his elegant hands were placed over his heart and genitalia, as if protecting himself in the last instant of life.

Whitestone and I were in a viewing room at the Iain West Forensic Suite watching on CCTV as Elsa Olsen examined Khan's charred remains.

'Did you ever see pictures of Pompeii?' Whitestone said, more to herself than to me. 'They look like they're screaming, don't they? They look like they're going to be screaming for ever.'

'He was going to come in,' I said. 'He was going to make a statement.'

Whitestone looked at me and shook her head. 'Mr Khan agreed to be interviewed in the presence of his lawyer,' she said. 'That's all.'

'But how did he die?'

Whitestone gestured angrily at the screen. 'How do you think he died? He died in the fire.'

Then I was through the door and into the mortuary, and Elsa Olsen was looking up from the burned cadaver on the stainless steel slab before her.

'Scrubs and hairnets, Wolfe. You know that.'

'How did he die, Elsa?'

Whitestone was right behind me.

'How did he die, Elsa?' I said again. 'Was it like the rest of them? Did someone cut his throat?'

'DC Wolfe,' Whitestone said calmly, 'get out of here.'

I ignored her.

'Elsa? You have twenty years of experience. You're in a million-pound state-of-the-art mortuary. You *must* know how he died.'

Whitestone gripped my shoulder hard enough to turn me around. How could such a slight woman summon up such reserves of physical strength? There was a rage in Whitestone, and she let me glimpse it now.

'You think someone cut his carotid arteries, don't you, Max?' she said. 'You think someone stuck a commando dagger in his neck and then torched the house. You think our killer is still out there.'

'That's exactly what I think.'

Whitestone gestured at the blackened corpse. 'But why would they bother? I mean, really — look at the state of him. Why would anyone bother cutting the poor bastard's throat?'

'Because he wouldn't commit murder

with fire,' I said. 'Too unpredictable.'

'Why is this murder? I saw TDC Wren's report. I've spoken to Gane and Fire Officer Truman. A rich, chain-smoking drunk drops a cigarette butt near a fuel tank. The next thing you know — smoked Salman. Why exactly does that surprise you?'

'Do you know what oxidation is, Max?' Elsa said gently. 'It's what fire does. It's what fire *is*. Oxidation is what happens when a fuel substance combines with oxygen to produce light and heat. It's what makes fire a living, destructive entity.' She looked at the burned piece of meat on the stainless steel slab. 'There's no evidence that someone cut his throat. Because fire destroys everything.'

At the Cromwell Green entrance to the Palace of Westminster, I showed them my warrant card.

I kept it in my hand as I went through the security turnstiles, Big Ben ringing in the sky high above, then past the armed officers in twos and fours cradling their Heckler & Koch assault rifles and finally through the search point just before you enter the great expanse of Westminster Hall.

Under the hammer-beam roof, the thousand-year-old hall teemed with life —

guides and tourist groups, journalists and lobbyists, MPs and their constituents. I walked quickly past them all and up the stairs at the far end, where a security guard stopped me under the great medieval window that spilled winter light into the hall. I showed him my warrant card too and told him that I was here to see the MP for Hillingdon North.

'And is Mr King expecting you, sir?'

'Probably.'

He hesitated for just a moment.

'Central Lobby, sir.'

I turned left and walked down to the Central Lobby, where great Prime Ministers get full-sized statues and mediocre Prime Ministers get life-sized busts. I spoke to the doorkeeper and he went off to find the MP for Hillingdon North.

He came back with a cool blonde in glasses and a business suit.

'DC Wolfe? I'm Siri Voss, Mr King's PA.' Just the hint of a Scandinavian accent. She was the woman who had called King in when we spoke out on the terrace. We shook hands. 'As you can appreciate, this is not a good day.'

And then I saw him. Coming out of the corridors that led to the House of Commons.

Ben King looked at me, white-faced and shaken.

'Detective Wolfe,' he said. 'I thought it was over.'

'It's just getting started,' I said. 'What did you do twenty years ago?'

He kept walking, trying to shake me off the way he shook off the world. I fell into step beside him. I could feel the light touch of his blonde PA on my arm. People were staring at us. Everyone was staring at us.

'What happened to Anya Bauer?' I said. 'What was Salman Khan going to tell me? What happened at that school?'

He stopped, a powerful man in his prime, accustomed to being in control but suddenly badly rattled by events.

'Can we do this some other time?' he said.

'How about when your brother comes back?'

'My brother? You want to talk to my brother?' His eyes blazed with something I could not read. 'I don't think that will be possible.'

Then he was walking away, and I was suddenly aware of Siri Voss standing right in front of me.

'Please,' she said. 'Oh, please leave him.'

And I saw the two coppers she had brought with her, holding their assault rifles and looking at me with embarrassment more than anything else.

'It's not over!' I shouted at King's back. 'You know that, don't you?'

But there was something in the face of Siri Voss that made me let him go.

I was at home making scrambled omelette for Scout's tea when DCS Swire called.

'You're suspended and under investigation by the police Professional Standards Department pending an IPPC inquiry,' the chief super told me.

'Charges?' I said, stirring the eggs.

'Neglect or failure in duty. Oppressive conduct or harassment. Whatever sticks. There's already more than enough.' A pause. 'Have you seen the news? You haven't even seen it, have you? You don't even *know*.' Swire sighed with disbelief. 'Do yourself a favour, Wolfe, you dumb bastard. Turn on the TV.'

She hung up.

I served up Scout's scrambled omelette then turned on the BBC. It looked like the news looked every night. A bomb in Iraq. A riot in Athens. A meeting in Brussels. A missing child. A flatlining economy. And then came photographs of three soldiers.

'. . . Private Himal Sameer, twenty-two,

Corporal Bibek Prabin, twenty-three, and Captain Ned King, thirty-five, of the Royal Gurkha Rifles —'

'Daddy?'

'Wait, wait. Let me watch this, angel.'

'. . . in Helmand when their armoured vehicle was hit by an improvised explosive device. All three died of their injuries in the hospital at Camp Bastion.'

The two young Gurkhas wore serious expressions in their official portraits, their features rigid with fierce pride and there was Ned King, smiling broadly for the camera, as if he held a secret the world could never share.

32

Peregrine Waugh walked down Potter's Field High Street, his tremendous height raising that gaunt bony head above the crowds and almost brushing the bunting and Union Jacks that fluttered above the streets.

It was just three days since the smiling face of Captain Ned King had appeared on the evening news, and now every boy from the old school was there, gathered in their houses, youngest at the front, but the Head Master said not a word to any of them. He did not need to, for he could make a boy straighten his slovenly tie with just his towering presence; he could kill idle chatter with one fierce look.

Waugh paused when he reached the boy soldiers of the Combined Cadet Force, four lines of them at the end of the high street, self-consciously rigid with military discipline, and for the first time that day he smiled.

The school and the town had turned out for the homecoming of Captain Ned King.

I saw Sergeant Lane, the local copper who had been no help with my enquiry about Anya Bauer's disappearance, taking his duties more seriously today. He patrolled down the empty street, closed to traffic for the day, and greeted the Head Master with something like a cringing bow.

I glimpsed faces I knew in the crowd. On the far side of the high street I saw Mrs Jones, the mother of Adam Jones, the second victim, her face skull-like under her headscarf, almost totally consumed by her cancer now, supported by Rosalita, the Filipina housekeeper, who had a protective arm wrapped around her employer.

A little further down I saw Len Zukov standing with Sergeant Tom Monk, the burned features of the physio from Barrington Court making him look like some exotic foreign guest among the uniformly white faces of the Potter's Field townsfolk. Did I see some of them shiver at the sight of the injured soldier? Did I see fathers and mothers lift their staring small children and carry them away to a less disturbing part of the high street? Tom Monk gave no sign that he had noticed. He stared at the empty road, waiting for the homecoming of another soldier.

And I saw Natasha, standing alone at the end of the street where the crowds thinned out.

Then all heads turned to watch a lone vehicle coming down the empty high street. Murmurs of resentment. It was a sleek black Mercedes saloon and not a hearse.

Sergeant Lane stepped forward, barking commands at the uniformed officers who stood watch over the docile crowds, holding up one hand, commanding the Mercedes to stop. When it did, a uniformed chauffeur sprang from the driver's seat and opened the rear door.

Ben King got out of the car and the crowd let out an audible gasp at the sight of the MP.

He was wearing the jacket his brother had worn on the day he died. A British Army desert camouflage jacket in two colours — swirls of sand and stone — stained with a third colour, a deep bloody red that was already turning brown.

And now I realised that there were cameras for the homecoming. There was TV, press photographers, and journalists. I saw Scarlet Bush stick a sharp elbow in a photographer's eye as the media broke through the loose police cordon and spilled on to the street, swarming around Ben King.

'Dear Ben,' said Peregrine Waugh, suddenly right next to me. 'He always was an exhibitionist.'

'Get them *back*!' Sergeant Lane was shouting at his officers, red-faced with fury.

Ben King walked slowly from the street to the pavement, his face expressionless, his brother's jacket hanging limply on his shoulders and radiating another world of pure horror.

Was he wearing the army jacket over a suit and tie? It was impossible to say. All anyone saw was the jacket.

He stood in front of the Combined Cadet Force. The young soldiers stared straight ahead, trying not to look at him. Cameras capered before them as young police officers tried to restore order.

'Let them see what they have done,' murmured Waugh. 'The words of Jacqueline Kennedy when she refused to change out of the pink Chanel suit that was stained with the blood of her assassinated husband. *Let them see what they have done!* Yes, let them see.'

A scrum was forming on the pavement. Officers had pushed the press back and

King's PA, Siri Voss, was handing out a press release. Two journalists walked behind us, each with one of the A4 sheets in their hands.

'So it's a British Army DPM desert camouflage jacket,' said the first. 'Does it say what DPM is?'

'Yeah, there, look — disruptive pattern material,' said the second. 'There's the front page tomorrow, mate.'

'He should have worn the full kit. Better shot with the full kit.'

'Siri says there was nothing left of the trousers.'

They were silent for a moment.

'God.'

'Yeah.'

There were tears, now. Some emotional dam had broken in the women and the men of the town, and their children took their cue, confused and upset by the unravelling of the adults.

The boys from Potter's Field gritted their teeth, set their jaws and held out for longer.

I looked at Peregrine Waugh. The Head Master was dry-eyed.

'A terrible day for you, sir,' I said.

'Ned was a soldier,' he said. 'I could not wish for a better death for him, only a better war. When did the first British soldier die in that wretched country? 1839? "When you're wounded and left on Afghanistan plains — and the women come out to cut up what remains — just roll to your rifle and blow out your brains — and go to your god like a soldier." '

'Suicide?'

He looked at me with disdain. 'Kipling, actually. But there's no shame in suicide, detective. It's only milksop Christianity that clucks with disapproval. The Romans and the Greeks saw suicide largely as a pragmatic act. A graceful and courageous exit when life has become unendurable. Ah — I think Captain King's coming now.'

A black hearse was moving slowly down the high street. In the back was a coffin wrapped in the Union Jack.

'Suicide didn't seem like a pragmatic act for James Sutcliffe,' I said, watching the first of the flowers being tossed from the pavement. They fell on the windscreen, they fell on the gleaming black hood, and they fell under the slowly turning wheels. 'For him, suicide seemed like an act of despair. Both times.'

Waugh sighed, his eyes never leaving the hearse.

'I'm afraid I have no idea what goes on in the mind of every disturbed adolescent,' he said. 'But I'm with the Romans and the Greeks — every human body is the property of the gods. Good day, detective.'

I thought that the Head Master was going to join Ben King in his bloodstained army jacket. Then I thought he might stand with the stiff fierce lines of the Combined Cadet Force. Instead he disappeared into the crowd, and the next time I saw him he was standing beside a small, snivelling Potter's Field boy. Waugh had placed a large white hand on the shoulder of the boy's green and purple blazer. I saw the Head Master's mouth move.

'There, there,' he seemed to be saying. 'There, there.'

The hearse was passing now, the windscreen wipers swishing once, twice, three times to clear the driver's view of the flowers that threatened to cover the glass. Roses, orchids, lilies — expensive flowers bought and thrown by the people of the town.

The boys of Potter's Field brought no flowers for the homecoming of Captain Ned King.

But later, as I walked through the deserted school grounds, past the chapel and into the small graveyard, I saw that someone had placed a single lily on the tomb of King Henry's dogs.

33

Saturday morning in Smithfield ABC.

I was down on the mat stretching my back. Upward-facing dog — hold it; downward-facing dog — hold it. The pain seemed to release itself. It still hurt but I was not contained in one tight slab. It was looser. It was better. I could feel it.

This was the quiet time in Fred's gym. Otis Redding on the sound system and the sound of fourteen-ounce gloves smacking pads.

There was a young woman banging the heavy bag, an older woman watching the business news as she ran on the treadmill, and, up in the ring, Fred wearing a T-shirt that told you PLAY HARD OR GO HOME as he took some kid in his late teens on the pads. North African, a big toothy grin, either a pro or thinking about it. The kid was fast, slick, hitting the pads very hard without apparently making much of an effort.

'Get that right all the way back to the chin,' Fred was telling him. 'Don't let it fade away. And don't stand there taking photographs. Get out when you've done your work. And throw punches in bunches, punches in bunches.'

When the bell rang Fred would look down at me, the pads still on his hands, and he would name the part of my body that needed to be stretched.

'Hamstring . . . calves . . . abductors . . . Did you do your abductors? Do your abductors.'

I laid the front of my left leg on a bench, placed my right foot on the floor and gently eased my shoulders back, feeling the stretch in the muscles at the top of my leg and the bottom of my spine.

Then Ben King walked in.

The woman on the heavy bag looked at him, then looked again. It had been a week since he was the lead item on the news, since he was on every front page, since he wore his brother's bloodstained camouflage jacket on the rolling news. Satisfied it was really him, the woman looked away and went back to her work on the heavy bag.

He was dressed for a run.

'I wasn't party to anything that happened at Potter's Field,' he said to me. A beat. 'But I know who was.'

I eased myself out of the stretch and sat on the bench.

'You're coming forward with new information?'

'Yes.'

'Why didn't you come forward before now?'

King turned his head as a buzzer sounded in the ring.

'Time!' shouted Fred.

Ben King looked back at me. 'Because I loved my brother.'

'Do you know the identity of the man who killed Hugo Buck?'

'No.'

'Adam Jones? Guy Philips?'

'No.'

'Salman Khan?'

'That was an accident, wasn't it? A fire.'

'What happened to Anya Bauer?'

'Who's Anya Bauer?'

I stood up and took a fistful of his T-shirt near the neck. He didn't flinch.

'Are you wasting my time?' I said.

He shook his head. 'No.'

'Who was Anya Bauer?' I said. 'What happened to her?'

'I don't know that name. I never knew any name. I never even saw the girl you're talking about. But I know that . . . questionable acts were done at that school. I know — to my eternal regret — that my brother Ned was a party to them. And, yes, my friends, too. And I know the name of the adult who instigated those questionable acts. Because he was the same man who sexually abused us for years.'

I still had his T-shirt in my fist. I twisted it until our faces were almost touching.

'Don't lie to me,' I said.

'I'm past lying,' he said. 'People get lost. My brother Ned got lost. When we were boys, I threw a glass at his face across the breakfast table. Why do you think I threw that glass at his face? Because I loved him. Because of the unspeakable things he was doing. Because of what was happening to him. Because of that man.'

'The Head Master,' I said. 'Peregrine Waugh.'

'Oy!' Fred called. He was talking to me. I still had a fistful of Ben King's T-shirt in my hand. 'Take it in the ring or take it outside.'

I let go of King's T-shirt. He was smiling.

'I haven't boxed since school,' he said.

'You boxed at school?' I said.

'Of course! All good schools teach their

450

boys to box. May I borrow these?'

He was pointing at a pair of yellow fourteen-ounce Cleto Reyes gloves.

I shook my head. 'I don't think that's a good idea,' I said.

His mouth twisted with amusement. 'I'm sure you're right.'

I stared at him for a moment.

'Find a headguard,' I said.

He was a boxer not a fighter. He kept his distance, up on the balls of his feet, dancing sideways as I advanced, and for a moment I thought he had lost his nerve and did not want to fight.

Then I stuck out a left jab that fell short and he came back with a stiff counter that went straight through my guard and smacked hard against my nose. By the time I had angrily swung back, he had skipped away.

We repeated our little dance. He would wait for me to strike, then slip, block or move out of range, and come back with a fast, straight counter.

The sweat was pouring under my headguard. I had not sparred for weeks and I could feel my ring rust, that tiny loss of pace you get when you haven't boxed for a while. I was one second too slow in everything I did, and nothing is more draining than being hit without having the chance to hit back.

A buzzer sounded. One minute gone and his confidence was growing. And that was good because I jabbed, he countered with a jab, and stayed close to smack me with a right cross. It caught me high on the head-guard but not hard enough to stop me slipping inside and burying a left hook into his bottom rib.

King went down on one knee, one glove pressed against his ribs, and his face contorted with pain. A body shot sticks around in a way a head shot never does, and when he got to his feet he was less cocky, keeping his distance, happy to get in the odd counter, happy to stay away from another dig in the ribs.

The buzzer counted down from ten and it was over. We had sparred for three minutes and were both totally spent.

'Christ,' he said. 'That's harder than squash.'

Fred was smiling at us.

'Nice spar,' he said. And to Ben King, 'Keep those elbows tucked in. Going to do another couple of rounds?'

'Perhaps some other time,' King said, still breathing hard.

Fred laughed and went off to collect the

towels that were strewn around the gym. King and I sat there saying nothing, drenched in sweat, locked in the strange intimacy of two men who have just shared a boxing ring.

'What do you want, Max?' he said.

'I want justice,' I said. 'And I want the truth. And I want it to be over.'

He fixed me with his politician's look — that look that suddenly saw you, the look that endlessly flattered you, the look that saw you in your true light for the first time.

'And I want what you want,' he said.

'The abuse started as soon as we arrived,' King said. 'Mental abuse before the sexual abuse. "Shakespeare is here, T. E. Lawrence is here, and you are here because you are nothing, you are specks of dirt on my shoes". And then the building up — feeling you were special, almost acolytes — by this God-like and punitive father figure who knew everything there was to know about history, art, literature, war and the ways of the flesh. We were thirteen years old! There was, shall we say, a disparity of power. We wanted to please him. My God — we wanted that more than anything in the world.'

The grey ribbon of motorway hummed

and unfurled ahead of me, eating up the miles. I let him talk.

'And he gave us all what we were looking for. The insecure — Adam, Salman — were made to feel as if they belonged, as if they were part of a family, a country, a secret world. The strong — Hugo, Ned, Guy — were made to feel they were clever. The exceptional — James, of course — were made to feel that they were touched by God. And he told us we were special, and he taught us to sneer at the rest of the world, and he talked of beauty and truth as he put us in his mouth.'

He was silent for miles.

'I bailed out,' King said eventually. 'I don't know why it was possible for me and not the others. Some basic survival instinct I had and they lacked. They were all exceptional boys, in their own way. James — James was brilliant, truly gifted. Adam was a child prodigy. Hugo was the school's athlete. Guy — Piggy — was a force of nature. And Salman — Salman was so touching, trying so hard to fit in, so determined, so much more English than the rest of us. And everyone loved Ned. Ned was *good*.'

'Why did you throw the glass at his face?'

'They were getting older. It was no longer

enough to perform sexual acts on the Head Master in his study and then sit down for a chapter of *The Seven Pillars of Wisdom.* They were curious, they were growing boys. Hugo and Guy had been caught in town with a couple of local girls. Women — grown women — went wild at the sight of James.' He laughed. 'And Piggy was masturbating himself into a coma every night.' He chewed his bottom lip. 'It was a world without women. So he told them that he would find them one. A woman. A girl. And let them see how little they were missing.'

'What did your brother tell you about the girl?'

'He told me she was being given as a special treat.' A pause. 'Which was the exact moment I threw the glass at Ned's face. And after that, he told me nothing.'

I turned off the motorway. In the distance, across the empty fields, you could already see the black towers of Potter's Field.

The boy was small for his age and he wore a Potter's Field school blazer over his fencing whites. He sat on the steps of the main building, pushing back his mop of dark hair as he stared at the paperback in his hands.

'Any good?' Ben King said.

The boy looked up, startled. 'Sir?'

'Book any good?'

King held out his hand and the boy passed him the paperback, standing up as he did so, self-consciously smoothing his green and purple blazer.

'*The Seven Pillars of Wisdom* by T. E. Lawrence,' King said. He opened it up and read, as if to himself. ' "But at last Dahoum drew me: 'Come and smell the very sweetest scent of all,' and we went into the main lodging, to the gaping window sockets of its eastern face, and there drank with open mouths of the effortless, empty, eddyless wind of the desert, throbbing past." I read this one when I was your age. How you getting on with it?'

'Just started it, sir. Pretty good stuff, sir.'

King nodded at him. 'Waiting to see the Master?'

'Sir.'

'Private lesson today?'

A red flush flooded the boy's pale face. 'Yes, sir. Every Saturday morning this half. Immediately after fencing club.'

King handed the boy his book. 'Lesson's cancelled.'

'Sir?'

'Go back to your house. Practise your lunge and parry. Do your prep. Write to your mother.'

The boy looked doubtful.

King clapped his hands once. 'Go on then!'

The boy went, and we climbed the stairs to the Head Master's rooms.

Peregrine Waugh answered the door in a plain white kimono. His bliss-heavy eyes took a moment to focus. A smile leapt to his face at the sight of Ben King and died when he saw me.

'Ah,' he said.

We followed him inside. Heavy brocade curtains, pulled shut at noon. A thick fug of smoke from whatever had been in the water pipe that sat unlit on an oak desk. Piles of books everywhere.

'To what do I owe —'

'Actually we've come here for the truth, Perry,' King told him. 'Finally.'

I couldn't breathe in this place. I pulled back the curtains, opened the windows as wide as they would go. On the playing fields, there was the First XV playing rugby against another school watched by a scattering of pupils and two sports masters, and more boys in bright training bibs carrying cones and five-a-side nets to the football pitch. Their shouts and laughter drifted up to me.

'The truth? You wouldn't dare! Think of your career, Benjamin. The Right Honour-

457

able Member for . . . what's the name of that dreary little suburb you represent? It's slipped my mind.'

'Hillingdon North,' King said.

Waugh dropped backwards on to a red velvet sofa, pulling primly at his kimono as one hairy leg with the dimensions of a small tree popped into view. And then, again, the savagery of the despot who has no experience of being challenged: 'You would not dare.'

'The world is changing, Perry,' King said calmly.

'Really?' Waugh said. 'How unfortunate.'

'It is for you, Perry. Because we're finally learning not to despise the victims of abuse.' He let it sink in. 'You broke a bond of trust. You abused the children in your care.'

'Genius makes its own rules.'

King shook his head. 'If you have a genius, Perry, then it is for destroying the lives of children. How many would you say? Over the years.'

'Ratting me out, are you, Benjamin? You little snitch. You little shit. You *grass.* Is that the correct term? Everybody hates a tell-tale, King.'

'Hundreds?'

'Oh, more. Thousands. An *MP.*' Waugh laughed. 'A *politician.* And I wanted greatness for you! Remember?' Measuring the air with a languid hand. 'The good old days. "Shakespeare is here. T. E. Lawrence is here. And you boys are here."'

'Oh, Perry,' King said. 'Then where does that leave you?'

I picked up the pipe and breathed in, inhaling something that stank like a curry made of gasoline and flowers. A heavy, musky, strangely beautiful smell. I had never smelled it before. I had only heard tales.

'Opium?' I said.

Waugh sniffed. 'The honey of the gods,' he said, smiling to reveal a jumble of crumbling teeth, like the mouth of an elderly weasel. 'The keys of paradise. The gardens of gold. "Boy — as you love me — I charge you to fold — pipe over pipe into gardens of gold". Did you ever read Aleister Crowley, detective? No? Not your *thing*?'

I crossed the room.

'What happened to the girl?' I said.

The Head Master looked genuinely perplexed. 'I thought we were talking about *the boys.* I thought that's what you were going to arrest me for. *The boys.* I thought that's why I was being thrown to the baying mob. The thousands of *boys.* What bloody girl?'

The open palm of my hand cracked against his cheek.

'Ouch,' he said, recoiling as if I had hurt feelings more than flesh. 'That was very painful.'

'Anya Bauer,' I said. 'German. Blonde. Pretty. Around fifteen years old when she passed through your hands some twenty years ago.'

'Oh,' he said. '*That* girl.' His eyes darted across the floor. Then he closed them. 'She rests. She sleeps. Perchance to dream.'

'Where?' I said.

He was looking at Ben King.

'What do you expect me to *do,* Benjamin? Beg for forgiveness? Seek counselling? Repent my sins?'

'What would the Romans have recommended, Perry?' King said. 'Or the Greeks? Or T. E. Lawrence?'

'I don't know. A cup of tea and a nice lie down?'

I slapped him again. Harder this time, leaving my red mark livid on his skull-like head.

'Where?' I said.

'With the *dogs,*' he said. 'With the bloody *dogs.*'

'The dogs?'

'You've hurt me now,' he said, edging away from me, gathering his kimono in his long bony fingers. 'Truly. I'm very upset.

460

Police brutality.' And then he began to snivel with self-pity. He turned to King, pleading. 'May I change? Before we leave? Ben?'

'Look at me,' I said quietly.

Waugh looked at me.

'What did you do to her?' I said.

He gathered the neck of his kimono. 'I never touched the little tart!' he said. 'Not until it was time to put her down. Nobody else had the stomach for it.'

King was looking at me, struggling to breathe.

'My God,' he said, white-faced with shock. 'My God.'

'Your keys,' I said to Waugh. 'I need all the keys to this place. Move!'

He moved stiffly across to his desk, rummaged for a while in a drawer then gave me two sets of keys. One was a little domestic set for Waugh's front door and car. The other could have been a gaoler's keys from a fairy tale, perhaps two dozen of every shape and age on a rust-flecked metal hoop — apparently the means of access to every door in Potter's Field.

When I had double-locked them inside Waugh's rooms I stuffed both sets of keys in my pockets and went quickly down to the chapel and round the back to the old graveyard.

I saw now, and for the first time, that there were many gravestones so old that time and weather had erased every word of their epitaphs. Their blank faces stared back at me. My pace slowed and faltered when I saw what someone had done to the tomb of Henry's dogs.

I could see it through the ancient trees and the rusting iron railings that guarded the grander tombs; I could see it quite clearly waiting for me on the far side of the leaning headstones and the forest of crosses and the cracked grey vaults. Watched by the sightless eyes of stone angels, I walked towards a great splash of red and black.

Poppies.

Someone had completely covered the tomb of King Henry VIII's dogs with poppies.

There were poppies in the shape of a cross, and poppies in round wreaths of every size, the wreaths of old soldiers and young children, all of them coming apart after spending long winter weeks out in the elements resting against monuments to the glorious dead.

And there were single poppies that had come astray from the wreaths, or perhaps been worn for that week of remembrance in November and then discarded.

Where had they all come from? Some must have been collected from the war memorial at Potter's Field, but others must have come from war memorials in the town itself, and in surrounding towns.

My vision filled with the red and black of the poppies, and even as my mind raced to understand, their message was clear.

You are never forgotten.

Fighting back an overwhelming urge to turn and run away, I pulled out my phone and called Elsa Olsen, reaching her voice-mail.

'Elsa,' I said. 'It's me, Wolfe. Sorry — Saturday, and all that.' I knelt by the tomb, touched the stone beneath the poppies, so suddenly and unexpectedly cold that it made my blood shiver. 'And I'll clear this with Whitestone and Swire as soon as I hang up, but I wanted you to be the first to know.' I picked up a single poppy and held it in my hand. 'I need an exhumation certificate.'

There was a red Lexus parked outside the main building. King's PA, Siri Voss, sat in the driver's seat tapping away on a phone. She got out when she saw me, wearing jeans and leather jacket, off duty now, her quick smile changing to a frown of concern.

'You all right?'

'Sorry,' I said, confused. 'What are you doing here?'

'I'm Mr King's ride back into town,' she said. 'He called me. He doesn't want to waste your time, or police resources.' Her hand was on my arm. 'Can I get you anything?'

'I have to go,' I said. 'Upstairs.'

'Of course.' She hesitated. 'When you have a chance — when things are better — when this ghastly business is over — I would love to talk to you. Mr King wants to start a charity in the name of your late colleague, DCI Mallory. A fund for the families of policemen killed in the line of duty. Is that something you would be interested in?'

Her hand was on my arm again. It was a strange touch. It stayed there a little too long, yet somehow not long enough.

'How's Mrs Mallory coping?' she tried. 'How's Margaret?'

'I don't know,' I said, and felt a stab of real shame.

She smiled and fell in behind me as I climbed the stairs and made my way to the Head Master's rooms. Ben King was sitting at Waugh's desk, his head in his hands, and when he looked up I saw the tears on his face.

'I knew that boy,' he said. 'The boy out-

464

side. I knew that boy. Because he was me. And he was Ned. And he was all of us.'

Siri flew to his side.

'Where is he?' I said, but King was good for nothing now, the pretty PA rocking him like a child as he wept.

I moved quickly through the rooms, a feeling of dread rising in my stomach.

And then I saw the water coming from under the bathroom door.

It was locked from inside so I slammed my shoulder into it — nothing. And again. Nothing.

The water was through my shoes and soaking my feet. I felt an icy calm descend on me as I remembered how to open a locked door quickly. I took a step back to give myself room and kicked the lock as hard as I could. The door flew open with a crack of metal and wood and I saw one of Waugh's long white arms hanging over the side of the bath, fresh blood pouring from the open veins on his wrists, staining the side of the bathtub and the white tiles of the floor with long crimson streaks.

There were soft white towels on heated rails and in little piles stacked neatly under the sink. I snatched them up and, sliding on the sopping floor, pressed them against his open wrists, and tied them tight around his limp white arms, and then threw them aside and started all over again when, in what seemed like seconds, his blood soaked through.

I was screaming and cursing and calling for help as I pressed the towels against the open veins of Peregrine Waugh. It was only when I ran out of towels that I saw the lifeblood had drained from his body, that his eyes were staring at the ceiling without seeing. I stood there with no breath and no strength to move until I finally remembered to turn off the hot and cold running water.

In the sudden silence the only sound was the boys down on the playing fields and, from the room behind me, the subdued sobbing of a grown man.

'Open it up,' DCI Whitestone said.

By now the December night was cold and black but the lamps of the SOCOs encircled the tomb and drenched it in blazing light. A bitter wind whipped through the graveyard, rustling dead leaves and the poppies that someone had swept from the grave.

A forklift truck was slightly tilted on the slope of the old graveyard, and it seemed to rock dangerously as its long metal fork eased beneath the grey stone of Henry's tomb.

The Murder Investigation Team from West End Central stood just behind the SOCOs, their mufti evidence of their interrupted weekends. Whitestone was in a parka thrown over jeans and T-shirt, as if she had come straight from home. Gane was in a tracksuit, as if he had come straight from the gym. And Edie Wren was in a short dress and killer heels and complicated hair, as if she had come straight from seeing her married man, or maybe trying to forget about him.

I saw the chief super exchanging words with Sergeant Lane of Potter's Field, their faces ghost-like in the fierce artificial light.

And then I looked back at the tomb as the wheels of the bulldozer fought for purchase in the soft soil. All at once the great slab of stone came away with the crack of torn granite. It rose in the air, clumps of dirt and cement falling away, and the grave was suddenly open.

A dozen officers in protective clothing moved quickly forward, and there were shouts and groans and protests as they heaved the lid of the tomb on its side and eased it up against an ancient oak. The white-suited SOCOs and the uniformed officers edged forward, but the grave was pitch black, buried in the darkness.

Somebody adjusted a light.

And there in the earth were the small bones of perhaps a dozen spaniels, their legs as thin as fish bones, their skulls the size of tennis balls, locked for eternity in the embrace of what were unmistakably human remains.

34

Natasha came down The Broadwalk in Regent's Park, her perfect face impassive behind dark glasses, long of hair and arms and legs, the little Pekingese-Chihuahua cross trotting by her side with a stick in its mouth, and she looked like the one for me.

It was sixty hours since we'd found the lonely bones of Anya Bauer. I had not slept and I had not eaten since we'd opened the grave, but after taking Scout to school on the third morning I knew that I desperately needed to do both. You can go without food and sleep for three nights and then you begin to fall apart. A single parent can't afford to fall apart.

Then I saw Natasha coming towards me as I was finishing my second bacon sandwich at a table outside The Honest Sausage, and I saw that I needed her even more.

'My stalker,' she said.

'The merry widow,' I said. 'Sorry.'

'No daughter? No dog?'

I looked under the table. 'I knew I'd forgotten something.'

'Too bad,' she said. 'I like your dog and daughter.'

Susan had abandoned her stick and was snuffling at my hand.

'They like you,' I said, wondering if it was too much. 'My daughter and my dog.'

'I can't think why.'

'Me neither.'

She indicated the little Pekingese-Chihuahua cross who was eating out of my empty hand.

'I didn't know Susan cared for you.'

'Nothing to do with me. Everything to do with my bacon sandwich.'

Natasha took off her dark glasses. She seemed younger than I remembered, and not quite as tough as she wanted to be.

'Listen,' she said.

Later, as we lay side by side, and I knew her for the first time, my hands moved across those long limbs and skin that was as white and unbroken as snow. And I remembered that I had seen her naked body once before, long ago, the first time we met.

She kissed my mouth and read my thoughts, and the traffic down on Marylebone High Street seemed to be coming from some other world. She held my hands and made me feel her, made me know her properly, made me understand what had changed.

The bruises were gone.

'I healed,' Natasha said.

We loved and slept the day away.

I had not slept by someone's side for a long time. It was a delicious feeling, a private world of warmth and safety and longing. But then, too soon, it was time for me to go.

I slipped out of the sheets, and the dog at the foot of the bed stirred with annoyance and then went back to sleep.

Natasha was half awake, and I sat by her side and smoothed her hair and very softly ran my hands over the smooth warmth of her skin and all of that seemed to make her more sleepy and smiley.

'Oh, come back to bed,' she said. 'Don't make me call the cops.'

I kissed her arm.

'I have to pick up my daughter.'

'Then come back tonight. Both of you. I'm not a cook but there are some great restaurants round here. What does Scout like?'

'We have to do something tonight. Family stuff.'

She hugged me.

'OK,' she said, waking up a bit now, the real world creeping into this secret room. 'I know you're a father. I know a dad has to do what a dad has to do, right?'

I kissed her cheek, her neck, her mouth.

'Right,' I said.

'But we'll work it out,' she said, and I believed her.

I parked the X5 outside a terraced house on a quiet street in Pimlico.

Scout was in the passenger seat, holding Stan and a bouquet of white flowers that was almost as big as her — lilies and roses and flowers that neither of us knew the name of.

Bringing flowers always felt like an imposition to me. A vase had to be found. Stems cut, water added, topped up at regular intervals, and one week later the dead flowers had to be thrown out, the stinking green water poured away, the vase washed clean.

It felt like you were asking a lot of someone when you gave them flowers.

Then Scout grinned at me as we got out of the car — a new smile, a gappy smile, because she had lost two teeth at the bottom, the first of her milk teeth to go — and I knew the flowers didn't matter a damn. What mattered was her, and us, and knowing that coming here was the right thing to do.

Scout rang the bell. Stan barked once, then again, his feathery tail revolving with excitement. From beyond the door's frosted glass I heard the excited yap of a West Highland Terrier.

Then I saw the shape of Mrs Margaret Mallory coming down the hall, and the outline of her face through the frosted glass, and the start of her smile.

35

Soho was our canteen.

It meant that odd, unexpected couples were sometimes seen sharing a meal together in the backstreet restaurants.

PC Billy Greene and Dr Stephen were in a corner table of the Siam Café on Frith Street. Greene's hands were no longer bandaged. He was in uniform. I was about to join them when I realised that this was not a chance encounter. This was therapy.

'Please,' Dr Stephen said. 'Our fifty minutes are just about up. So you're no longer suspended, Max?'

I shook my head. 'One day you're the cock of the walk and the next you're a feather duster,' I said. 'Or is it the other way round?'

I joined them.

'You found the missing girl,' Dr Stephen said.

I nodded. 'We just got the results of the forensic autopsy from Elsa Olsen. Identified her body from dental records sent over from Germany. Cause of death was a broken neck. Peregrine Waugh snapped Anya Bauer's neck like she was some kind of wounded animal.'

'And twenty years later,' Greene said, 'he opens up his veins.'

'And gets off too lightly,' I said. 'I wanted to see him in court. I wanted to see him in a cell.'

We were silent until I nodded at Greene's hands.

'How are you doing, Billy?'

'Doing good,' he said. 'The pain is easing off. The physio is coming along. My fingers are working better, although the right hand is still a bit stiff. The more exercises I do, the better I feel.'

The waitress brought a plate of fruit. I saw that Greene's hands were stained black with burns, and that he held a fork with difficulty.

'Stick with it, Billy,' I said. 'Stick with all of it.'

But he didn't want my pity.

When a piece of mango slipped from his fork and slid across the table, he stabbed at it repeatedly until he finally speared it. He popped the mango in his mouth and laughed.

'Lunch takes a bit longer,' he said.

Dr Stephen stared at his plate and then back at Greene.

'Funny thing is, they gave me sick leave,' Greene said. 'After the night we got Bob. And I went to Vegas — because I always fancied Vegas. So I flew to Vegas.' He paused dramatically. 'But they wouldn't let me in!'

Dr Stephen had obviously heard the anecdote before. I had the impression that Greene had told the story many times, and that his fellow uniformed policemen had enjoyed the punchline. It was the kind of punchline that coppers would find amusing. 'They wouldn't let you in?' I said. 'You mean, into the country? When you landed?'

He nodded, still looking cheery, still seeing the funny side and assuming that I would see it too.

'The Americans fingerprint everyone when they pass through immigration — part of the tightened security after 9/11, right?'

I shrugged. 'OK.'

Greene held up his hands like it was a conjuring trick. 'And guess who doesn't have fingerprints any more! They put me on the first flight home!'

I stared at Billy Greene's blackened hands and I kept on staring until he placed them on his lap, below the table, where I could no longer see them.

'Harry Jackson,' said Sergeant John Caine. 'People tend to walk right past old Harry Jackson.'

It was true.

The Black Museum was so full of gory artefacts, from the endless variety of firearms and blades that had claimed policemen's lives to the pots and pans in which serial killers had cooked the flesh of their victims, that it was easy to walk past the small, unassuming display devoted to Harry Jackson.

There wasn't much. A glass frame containing a short newspaper clipping, yellow with age. Two typewritten paragraphs of explanation.

And the whorls of a dead man's thumbprint.

'Harry Jackson was the first man to be convicted in England because of fingerprint evidence,' Sergeant Caine said. 'Harry was a burglar. In the summer of 1902 he climbed through a window in Denmark Hill, stole some billiard balls and left his thumbprint in wet paint on the windowsill.' Sergeant Caine chuckled. 'Silly bugger. He got seven years.'

I peered closer at the newspaper clipping.

It was a letter to *The Times,* signed by someone calling himself A Disgusted Magistrate.

> Sir, Scotland Yard, once known as the world's finest police organisation, will be the laughing stock of Europe if it insists on trying to trace criminals by the odd ridges on their skins.

'Eight years later, the rest of the world was catching up,' said Caine. 'Thomas Jennings of Chicago became the first person in America to be convicted by fingerprint evidence.'

'Another burglar?'

'No — Jennings was a murderer. And soon the French were at it, nicking a reprobate by the name of Vincenzo Perugia — doesn't sound very French, does he? — on the basis of a left thumbprint.'

'What had he done?'

'He stole the Mona Lisa from the Louvre. Took the Frogs two years to find him because they only had his right thumbprint on file. I hear you solved your case. DCI Mallory would be very happy.'

I nodded, staring at Harry Jackson's thumbprint.

'Twenty years ago, a girl called Anya

Bauer was the victim of a gang rape at Potter's Field,' I said. 'The Head Master, Peregrine Waugh, killed her to stop her talking. Bob the Butcher — Ian Peck — cut the throats of the men who had been the boys who attacked Anya. We got two murderers. We got their motives. The pieces all fit. The trouble is, John, when you look at them, those pieces don't make much sense.'

'Why not?'

'Peck is going to get life for Mallory's murder,' I said. 'And his prints were everywhere in his parents' house.'

'I heard.'

'But they were not at the murder scenes of Hugo Buck, Adam Jones and Guy Philips, the other murders he confessed to. No prints there. Not even a partial. Not even a glove print.'

'Yes,' said Sergeant Caine. 'I heard that, too.'

'But why would he lie?' I said. 'Why would Ian Peck confess to murders that he didn't commit?'

'Because he's nobody,' said the keeper of the Black Museum. 'And he wants to be somebody. They're all the same. Serial killers — you think they're criminal masterminds? They're not Hannibal Lecter, Max! They're all just grubby little men. They're all psychopathic losers. Who are they? Albert DeSalvo, Peter Sutcliffe and Ian Peck. They're germs, they're insects. But their crimes make them the Boston Strangler, the Yorkshire Ripper and Bob the Butcher. It wouldn't surprise me if Bob the Butcher is standing up for murders that he didn't do. It's what Albert DeSalvo did. He wasn't even in jail for killing those thirteen women in Boston. He was in jail for rape. That's the kind of vicious little woman-hating creep we're talking about. But then he becomes the Boston Strangler and suddenly you've got Tony Curtis playing you in a movie.'

I was still staring at Harry Jackson's thumbprint.

'No prints,' I said. 'Who has no prints, John?'

Sergeant John Caine of the Black Museum reached out and straightened the frame on his neglected Harry Jackson display.

'Only a man with no hands, Max,' he said.

36

Midnight on the school playing fields, the black silhouette of Potter's Field behind me, a jumble of towers and spires and architecture from the last five centuries.

Blink your eye and a hundred years go by.

It felt like the world was dead.

I checked my phone one last time — no new calls, although I had left urgent messages for Whitestone, Gane and Wren on my drive out here — and then began across the playing fields.

The wind whistled through the trees in the distant woods and I shuddered, as if the eyes of Anya Bauer were watching me. Soon you will be at rest, I thought. Soon you will be at peace at last.

There were no lights on in the little stone cottage as I felt in my pocket for the Head Master's keys, the large set that looked like they were from a fairy tale, holding the key to every lock in every door in Potter's Field.

There were two locks on the front door of the cottage. A standard Yale lock and a flush bolt. Nothing complicated. But I still had to try a dozen keys before the door swung silently open and I stepped inside.

I stood there listening for a moment, my eyes adjusting to the light, slowing my breath, and then I quietly eased the door shut.

On the table there was an empty teacup, a copy of the local newspaper and a .410 shotgun.

It was a small cottage. A servant's quarters given a quick coat of rural comfort. To the left was the bedroom and the bathroom, both doors shut. To the right the small living area ran into an L-shaped kitchen only large enough for one person at a time.

I stood there, seeing in the darkness now, but not knowing what I was looking for until I glimpsed it under the sink.

I moved quickly to the little kitchen, crouched down and pulled the door all the way open. An ancient leather bag was sitting with the bleach and disinfectant and insecticide. Its dark brown cowhide was worn and cracked, the brass hardware and locks blackened with rust.

But somehow you knew it was still being used.

As something very small scuttled away in the skirting board, I reached in and took out the worn-leather Gladstone bag.

A Murder Bag.

I turned to carry the bag back to the living space and there he was, old Len Zukov, sitting at the table with the .410 shotgun in his arthritic hands.

I held up the bag for his inspection, as if he had asked me to retrieve it.

'Your bag, Len?'

He sniffed. 'Of course.'

I set it on the table, saying nothing.

'You don't believe me,' he said, the accent forever caught somewhere between rural England and his Russian homeland. 'You never believe a word I say, do you?'

I watched his hands on the .410. Despite his condition the shotgun rested easily in his strong arms and those locked, arthritic fists. He was more comfortable than I had ever seen him. And I looked towards the door, wondering if the .410 was even loaded, and how much mobility he needed in his fingers to pull the trigger.

Not much, I thought. The .410 is the lightest shotgun, often used for teaching children how to shoot.

'Sit down now,' he said, interrupting my calculations.

'My colleagues will be here soon,' I said, hearing the doubt in my voice.

He liked that. 'Perhaps not soon enough,' he said. 'I told you to sit down.'

I remained standing.

'You didn't come forward to claim the body,' I said. 'Anya's body, Len. Anya Bauer. We know it was her remains in the grave with the dogs. No doubt about it. We obtained dental records from Germany. What stopped you coming forward and claiming the body? What were you afraid of? You knew her, Len.'

'Did you ever see what a shotgun does to a man's face?' he said.

I joined him at the table. There were only two chairs. He wasn't one for doing a lot of socialising.

'Poking around in the night,' he said, shaking his head. 'What you looking for?' He indicated the Gladstone bag that I had placed on the table. 'That old thing?'

'Not you,' I said. 'I'm not looking for you, Len.'

'Maybe you should be,' he said, and he shifted the shotgun in his paralysed hands.

'Why don't you put the gun down, Len. Then we can talk.'

He gripped the .410 tighter.

'You asked me how I came here,' he said.

'I came with the soldiers. I rode on the back of a T-34. Do you know the T-34?'

'It was a tank in the war. The Second World War. The Great Patriotic War, you call it. The T-34 was a Russian tank.'

'No,' he said. '*The* Russian tank. The T-34 was *the* Russian tank. The tank that bought your freedom. The tank that paid for your democracy. Britain, America. You said once that I was too young for the war. You were right. I was eleven years old, too young for a war of annihilation. The Germans were coming and I was in the fields and I ran away. Then the Red Army took our town and I returned. But the town was not there any more. Because we were sub-humans. To them. You understand? My mother. My father. My grandmother. My sisters. Sub-humans. I never cried so much as at that time. The last days of my childhood passed in this way.'

He was silent, lost in memory, or listening to the night.

'I went west with our soldiers,' he said. 'West, west, west. The First Belorussian. The *frontoviki* — frontline troops. Through a world in ruins. Do you know why they kept me? Because I had almost the same name as their leader. General Georgy Zhukov. What do you call it?'

'A mascot,' I said.

'A mascot. I wanted to live. I wanted to stay alive. But I wanted to see Germany destroyed. I closed my heart to pity.' He shook his head with wonder. 'They had so much! The Germans were so rich! The farms, the animals — why did they come to us when they already had so much?'

'They wanted more, Len,' I said soothingly. 'They wanted the world. It was madness.'

But he wasn't listening to me now.

'Our soldiers wanted women,' he said. ' *"Frau, frau, frau!"* I wanted something else. For my dead family. For my grandparents. For my sisters. For my parents. For my gone family. Our *frontoviki* placed me inside a cellar. One by one, a dozen Waffen-SS men who had destroyed their papers and ripped off their badges were sent inside. I could hear them screaming on the other side of the door. *"Nix SS! Nix SS!"* Our soldiers had showed me what to do. You know? The knife through the neck, then pull, then kick the Nazi down the stairs. A dozen of them. So, you see an old man. But you're looking at a killer.'

We stared at each other.

'I think it's been a while since you killed anyone,' I said quietly. 'I think it's been a lifetime.'

He pointed the .410 at my face.

'You hate the Germans,' I said. 'But Anya Bauer was German, wasn't she? And you didn't hate Anya, did you? You loved her.'

'Anya's father was German,' he said. 'But her mother was Russian. My daughter.'

'And Anya came to stay with you when she was fifteen years old. Your granddaughter came to stay with you at Potter's Field. What was that? A summer holiday? Trouble at home? A bit of both? I bet there was some kind of trouble at home, wasn't there?'

'Stop talking about her,' he said.

His voice flat and hard, levelling the .410 at my chest, giving himself a bigger target.

'And then one day Anya was gone,' I said. 'Somewhere between a missing person and a lost contact. And you didn't know what happened — or maybe you suspected, but you were never sure until you saw what was in Henry's grave. When it was collapsing. When it was falling to bits. You saw her bones, didn't you? Human bones in there with the bones of Henry's dogs. Or maybe you saw them later, when the grave was being renovated. But at some point you saw inside the grave and you knew it had to be Anya.'

'Shut up now,' he said, the shotgun moving between my face and my chest.

'And you put it all together,' I continued. 'Anya coming to stay. The boys who were sniffing around. Hugo Buck and his little gang. And then Anya gone — for a night, and then a year, and then for ever. Were there rumours, Len? Did you hear anything about what Peregrine Waugh's followers had done to some girl? Were they afraid of the truth coming out? There must have been talk after James Sutcliffe killed himself — or pretended to. Somehow you suddenly knew what had happened to her — what they had done. And you drew up a list of the boys who must have been in that room when Waugh broke her neck and they treated your beautiful girl like something to be thrown away. And you wanted revenge. Is that what happened?'

The .410 seemed to seek out my heart, and stay there, steady at last in his paralysed hands.

'What matters,' he said, 'what matters is that I avenged her. Do you believe me at last?'

'I believe all of it, Len,' I said. 'I truly do. Except the last part. I don't believe that you've killed anyone since you were a boy.'

The door opened and Tom Monk came in, an old army jacket slung over jeans, carrying a twelve-bore shotgun and a lifeless brace of rabbits. Behind the terrible burns on his ruined face I saw his eyes widen and grow cold.

'Ah,' he said. 'I was wondering when you might turn up.'

'A young policeman I know burned his hands when we collared Bob the Butcher,' I said. 'A brave young lad called Billy Greene. He was going to spend his sick leave in Las Vegas. Champagne cocktails by the pool in Caesar's, chorus girls, all that.'

'Very nice,' Monk said.

'But guess what? They wouldn't let him in. Sent Billy straight back to Gatwick. Because the Americans fingerprint everyone at the border now. And they couldn't get any prints off him.'

Monk held up his hands, a mocking gesture of surrender. And for the first time I saw that the reason we could never find any prints at the crime scenes was because the flesh on his hands was as destroyed as the flesh on his face.

'Remind me to steer clear of Las Vegas,' he said.

'So what was in it for you, Tom?' I said. 'Keeping your hand in? Spot of vigilante work? Never kicked the killing habit?'

He stopped smiling.

'Justice,' he said.

I tried to smile but my mouth merely twisted, and my heart began to hammer in my chest as I realised what was going to happen to me tonight.

'You're right,' he said. 'It's a joke. How can there be justice in a land where they let the bravest and the best sleep on the streets until they work up the nerve to top themselves?'

'So you cut the throats of Hugo Buck and Adam Jones,' I said. 'Botched it with Piggy Philips, didn't you?'

'Oh, I don't know,' he said. 'I don't think he's going to be taking double games for a while, do you?'

'But you missed out on Captain King, didn't you? The Taliban beat you to it.'

Monk's mask-like face clenched with sudden fury. 'You're just another stupid policeman. Captain King was a brave man. A warrior. One more lion led by yet more donkeys. Same story in this country for a hundred years.' He leaned against the door and shook his head. 'Captain Ned King was never on my list.'

'What about Salman Khan?' I said. 'Was he still alive when that big house went up in flames? Or did you break in there, open up his throat and then torch the place?'

'One of his kids had a motorbike,' Monk said. 'Have you ever heard of such a thing? A child with his own little motorbike? I served my country for ten years and all I've got is a second-hand bicycle.'

'What outfit were you with in Afghanistan, Tom?'

'I told you. The Royal Green Jackets.'

'I don't think so. You're too handy with a knife. Too good at creeping around, un-armed combat and covering your tracks. I reckon you were with the Special Forces Support Group. Or maybe the SAS? Or the SBS?'

'You calling me a liar?'

I nodded.

'You going to cut my throat, Tom?' I said, knowing that was exactly what he was going to do.

'Should have done it when I had the chance the first time.'

I looked at the old man opposite me. 'You should have gone to the police, Len. If you wanted justice for your granddaughter. You should have come to us. Not waited for Rambo here to turn up.'

Monk laughed. 'Who was going to get justice for Anya? Or for Len here? The police? The courts? You? You with your soft judges and weak laws and tricky lawyers selling rich man's justice? You with your bad back!'

'Enough,' Len said.

And I turned my head just in time to see the old man shoot me in the chest.

The roar of the .410 split the air.

I was blown backwards and over and flat on my back with my head in the open fireplace, the deafening sound of the .410 fired in a tiny space still ringing somewhere deep inside my eardrums, and I was calling for Jesus and God to help me as my fingers scrabbled at my heart.

The excruciating pain of two cracked ribs beneath massive bruising told me that I was not yet dead.

The .410 shell had ripped a hole in my leather jacket and my T-shirt but had not passed through the lightweight CV1 body armour.

I kept calling for Jesus and God.

'You're better off shooting him in the head,' Monk said. 'I need to go home now.'

'Yes,' Len said. 'Go to them now. Go to your family. It is time. Your work here is done. Thank you, my beloved friend. Thank you, my brother.'

I struggled to sit up but the pain in the top half of my body held me down. I could not move.

Oh God . . . oh Jesus . . .

I realised that the chair I had been sitting on was underneath me, smashed to pieces.

I saw Zukov kiss Tom Monk hard on the mouth and I saw Monk leave the cottage without looking back.

Len shuffled off to his bedroom, and when he came back he had a box of shells with him. I saw him break the .410, laboriously push in a three-inch red shell, then snap it shut.

Oh God . . . oh Jesus . . .

He shuffled across to where I was lying and pointed the shotgun at my face.

Oh God . . . oh Jesus . . .

'No!'

Edie Wren was in the doorway.

Len Zukov swung the shotgun at her and paused.

'Please,' she said. 'What do you want? Talk to me. Please talk to me, sir.'

He looked at her face for a moment and then, as if in answer, he placed the shotgun on the floor and, half crouching, set the barrel under his chin.

I heard Edie scream and I heard the shotgun roar but then the darkness overwhelmed me and the night was black.

37

We drove back to the city. DCI Whitestone at the wheel of my X5. DI Gane beside her in the passenger seat. Edie Wren and me in the back. Every time I was drifting off, thinking I might steal some sleep, the road rushing under our wheels and the white-hot pain in my cracked ribs shoved me awake.

'Sergeant Tom Monk came back from Afghanistan and he never went home,' Whitestone said, her eyes not leaving the road ahead. 'I spoke to the people at Barrington Court. Monk returned from Helmand with a Conspicuous Gallantry Cross and third-degree burns on his face and hands. He spent a few months in an ICU and then went to Barrington Court for his final rehab. Treatment for his burns. Extensive physio. Therapy sessions with a psychoanalyst. The usual routine for a veteran with his injuries. When he had recovered, he stayed on helping out at Barrington Court.

And they were glad for an extra pair of hands. Nobody seems to know what happened. But just before he was due to leave Barrington Court, Monk put on his dress uniform and had his photo taken at a small studio in Potter's Field High Street. Then he mailed the photo to his fiancée back in Stratford.'

Whitestone fell silent. I thought of the face that had been burned beyond recognition, and I thought of his girl back home, seeing a posed photograph of the damage for the first time.

The road kept slipping past, lit by nothing but the high winter moon.

'Nobody knows if she ever wrote back. Or sent him a text, email or message on Facebook. Monk never talked about it. Maybe she told him that it was over. Maybe she never contacted him again and that told him all he needed to know. Who knows? But Monk never left Barrington Court. He stayed on — unpaid, unofficial, helping out with the rehab of other badly injured veterans. Taking the men to Potter's Field for exercise.'

'Where he met another old soldier,' I said. 'Len Zukov. The start of a beautiful friendship.'

'I understand why Len Zukov wanted payback for what they did to his granddaughter,' Wren said. 'And I get why his friend would want to help him. But — did Monk want to kill evil bastards? Or did he just want to kill somebody?'

Whitestone glanced at me in the rear-view mirror. I had no answers. All I knew was that the state had trained Monk to be a killer and in the end that was all he had left, and all he could do, all he could offer, even when the state wanted him to stop.

'Edie,' Whitestone said. 'Some stuff we never get to know.'

You could see the piercing blue lights of our cars cutting up the night from a mile away. They illuminated the sleek, futuristic buildings of the Olympic Park and the urban wasteland that surrounded them.

'Now Monk's returned to the place you go when you've run out of places to go,' Whitestone said. 'He's finally come home.'

In the shadow of Olympic Park, a dozen armed response vehicles surrounded a shabby block of flats that managed to be both modern and derelict. They were out of place in a neighbourhood where the buildings were either neat little flats and small houses that promised a nice life in the new East End, or they had been wiped from the face of the Earth. It looked like the surface of the moon after a few years of serious gentrification.

We lowered the windows of the X5 and dug out our warrant cards. Beyond the police tape you could hear the digital cackle of the Airwave radios, the occasional bark from one of the police dogs, and the shouts of officers who were pulled tight by nerves.

Armed officers waited between the ARVs, their Heckler & Koch assault rifles held at their favourite forty-five-degree angle, butt high and business end pointing down, sweating hard in all that kit despite the chill of the December night. They looked like the future.

Tom Monk was standing alone on a scrappy patch of grass outside the block of flats, looking up, his gaze unswerving. And I saw now that there were half a dozen Glock 17 pistols pointing at the back of his head.

They had evacuated most of the residents from the flats. In almost every window the only signs of life were the fairy lights of Christmas, twinkling, white and red and green.

A young woman appeared briefly in one window, a toddler under her arm, and then she was gone. But Monk kept looking up at her window, even after the light in the room had gone out.

'That's her,' said Edie Wren, and the tears on her face shone bright in the riot of flashing blue lights. 'That's Monk's family. That poor girl. That poor man.'

'No,' DCI Whitestone said. 'That's our killer. Let's nick the bastard.'

The armed officers stood aside as the K9 unit came forward with their German Shepherds. The handlers knelt by the flanks of their dogs, fingers scratching the back of those noble heads, whispering their final words of encouragement.

Monk turned at the sound of the dogs. His old army coat swung open and I saw his weapon sticking out of the lining, stuffed inside what looked like one of those big secret pockets that shoplifters use — the 12-bore shotgun that he had carried all the way from Potter's Field.

Then voices were shouting all around and someone screamed 'I have the shot!' and Whitestone said 'Take the shot!' and the crack of gunfire tore the night, ripped it wide open, shockingly loud, one single shot that was so stretched-out and jagged it made your heart leap, and Tom Monk was falling backwards, his head twisting sideways as if suddenly and savagely punched, the top of it flying away in a clump of blood and hair and skin and bone and brain, and then he was lying very still on the scrappy piece of grass looking like what he was now — a fallen British soldier.

I moved towards the lifeless body, any hatred I had felt for him suddenly turned to a sour kind of sadness; but I felt Whitestone's hand on my arm, making me wait, taking no more chances.

'Enough for one night, Max,' she said. 'It's almost Christmas.'

She gave the command and they let loose the dogs.

38

Sunday morning.

Scout sat at the window, waiting for her mother. Across the street the great meat market of Smithfield was closed for the weekend, the crowds all gone, and the white dome of St Paul's Cathedral rose above a scene of perfect stillness.

On TV, the MP for Hillingdon North was entering 10 Downing Street, Siri Voss one pace behind, cradling a thick file of papers. Ben King smiled shyly at the journalists who called out to him.

'Congratulations on the promotion! A few words, Minister?'

'The youngest Parliamentary Secretary to the Treasury in history — how does that feel?'

'What kind of Chief Whip are you going to be, Mr King? Are you going to put it about a bit? Are you going to give them some stick?'

There was a policeman on the door. King murmured good morning to him. The policeman touched his helmet in salute. Ben King and Siri Voss disappeared inside as a spasm of pain racked my lower back.

Stan was sleeping at Scout's feet. But as I flinched the dog stirred and stretched — downward-facing dog, then upward-facing dog — all the while watching me with those massive round eyes, as if to say *you must do the stretching every day of your life, don't you even know that?*

Or maybe he just wanted some food.

In the pocket of my jeans, my phone began to vibrate. Then it was still. And then it began to vibrate again. I took it out and read the message from Anne, and I thought, there is no greater stranger than someone we used to love.

'Angel,' I said to Scout, with a lightness that I did not feel. 'Your mother's not coming today. Something came up. I'm sorry.'

Scout watched me with impassive eyes.

'She's very busy,' my daughter said.

I nodded, and I could not tear my eyes from her as she went to the table and took out her box of pens and opened her drawing book. I walked over to her and watched her work for a bit. She was drawing Stan's head, and she had captured him very well.

The bulging beauty of the eyes, the extravagant ears flowing like the hair of a girl in an old-fashioned painting, the nose like a squashed prune, the feathered glory of his tail.

I touched her hand and her eyes met mine.

'Scout,' I said, 'it's just you and me now. But we're all right, aren't we?'

She looked at her drawing and then back at me.

'Yes,' she said. 'We're all right.'

I breathed again.

'Scout?'

'What?'

'I'm very, very proud that you're my daughter.'

She got up and gave me an awkward embrace, her arm around my waist as I kissed her on top of her head. Then she broke off and went off to her bedroom, Stan trailing behind her, his tail up like a periscope.

I turned to the TV as Ben King came out of Number Ten and began walking towards the camera. Siri Voss was beside him, hugging her papers, but as they reached the camera she stepped aside with a smile, waiting for him just out of shot.

Ben King smiled. Then he cocked his head at the camera, and looked into it the way he had so often looked at me — a penetrating, lopsided look, disarmed and disarming, as if he saw something in you the rest of the world had yet to see.

Something glinted for a moment but I couldn't tell if the fragment of light was on the TV screen or just inside my head.

And then I realised that Ben King had a glass eye.

And I saw that what James Sutcliffe had claimed was true. Someone had lost an eye in that room twenty years ago — a small forfeit for a young girl's life. But it wasn't Hugo Buck.

How had I missed it?

You, I thought, as Ben King smiled for the cameras in Downing Street. *You.*

And I saw a vision of two boys at a breakfast table, twin brothers, arguing with a fury that neither of them had known before, identical in every way apart from their hearts, and one of the brothers threw a glass with full force at the other's face. And I knew it wasn't Ned who was in that basement room the night they stole Anya Bauer's life.

It was his brother, Ben.

'Daddy?' Scout said.

She was holding the junior boxing gloves I had bought her — one of those unsuccessful presents that parents so often buy for their children, when they still hold on to the vain hope that their mutual interests might possibly coincide; one of those presents that are admired for the sake of politeness and then tossed into a drawer, never to be seen again.

'I want to know how,' she said. 'Show me.'

I helped her to put on the gloves. They were the smallest size available and they were still comically enormous on her. But we did not smile. I held up my palms.

'When you throw a punch,' I said, 'it should be like catching a fly. You ever catch a fly?'

She shivered. 'I saw Stan catch a wasp once.'

'Well, think of that. The hand should snap back as fast as it snaps forward.'

I demonstrated, and then held up my palms again.

'You try.'

Scout frowned.

'I can't hit very hard,' she said.

I touched her shoulder.

'Angel,' I said. 'It's got nothing to do with how hard you can hit.'

Scout started punching.

Then suddenly there were just a few days to

Christmas and there was the promise of snow in the grey city skies.

I sat in a dark school hall and I watched angels in bed sheets with sellotaped paper wings, five-year-old wise men with wonky cotton-wool beards, stuffed toys standing in for the animals in the manger in Bethlehem and, at the centre of it all, a grumpy sheep waving her small fist at the heavens.

'It's all right for the angels!' the grumpy sheep said bitterly. 'The angels can *fly* to the manger! But I must *walk*!'

The grumpy sheep — Scout under an old white rug superglued to an even older rucksack, her nose blackened with make-up — narrowed her eyes at the heavens.

'Why must I walk to the manger? It means nothing to me! I don't even want to see this baby they call Jesus.'

She regretted it in the end. On her knees in the centre of the stage, shaking her head as the wise men and angels milled around in the background.

'Oh *why* was I so grumpy! Why did I complain? I see clearly now! At last, I see it all.' She raised her head and stared out into the darkness. 'This is a special child!'

Mrs Mallory — Margaret — was sitting next to me and she reached across and squeezed my hand as I sat there in the darkness with all the other parents, choking down wild laughter, and the hot tears streaming down my face.

AUTHOR'S NOTE

The first grown-up piece of journalism I ever wrote — the first article that did not involve staying up all night with rock stars — was out of 27 Savile Row, London W1 — West End Central.

The young men and women I met there were among the finest people I have ever met. They are real, but this book, which roams freely about their place of work, is a work of fiction.

I have taken the liberty of using real life to give *The Murder Man* some grit — for example, the Black Museum really is at Room 101, New Scotland Yard, and the 'From Hell' letter by someone claiming to be Jack the Ripper is quoted accurately from contemporary photographs.

The letter itself is said to be lost, and its location in this book is a product of the author's imagination.

Tony Parsons
September 2013